Joan Barfoot is an internationally acclaimed novelist. Her novel, *Gaining Ground* (The Women's Press, 1980), won the Books in Canada award as the best first novel of the year when it was published under the title *Abra*. Her other novels are *Dancing in the Dark* (The Women's Press, 1982), made into the award-winning film of the same name; *Duet for Three* (The Women's Press, 1986) and *Family News* (The Women's Press, 1990), both Feminist Book Fortnight Selected Twenty Titles; *Plain Jane* (The Women's Press, 1992); *Charlotte and Claudia Keeping in Touch* (The Women's Press, 1994); and *Some Things About Flying* (The Women's Press, 1997). Joan Barfoot lives in London, Ontario, where she is also a newspaper columnist.

Also by Joan Barfoot from The Women's Press:

Gaining Ground (1980)
Dancing in the Dark (1982)
Duet for Three (1986)
Family News (1990)
Plain Jane (1992)
Charlotte and Claudia Keeping in Touch (1994)
Some Things About Flying (1997)

joan barfoot
getting over edgar

Published in Great Britain by The Women's Press Ltd, 1999
A member of the Namara Group
34 Great Sutton Street, London EC1V 0LQ

First published in Canada by Key Porter Books Ltd, 1999

Copyright © Joan Barfoot 1999

The right of Joan Barfoot to be identified as the author of this work
has been asserted by her in accordance with the Copyright, Designs
and Patents Act 1988.

British Library Cataloguing-in-Publication Data
A catalogue record for this book is available from the British Library.

This book is sold subject to the condition that it shall not, by way of
trade or otherwise, be lent, re-sold, hired out, or otherwise
circulated without the Publisher's prior consent in any form of
binding or cover other than that in which it is published and without
a similar condition including this condition being imposed on the
subsequent purchaser.

ISBN 0 7043 4626 5

Printed and bound in Finland by WSOY

o n e

wen can't take her eyes off Edgar being dead. As if seeing has much to do with believing.

It doesn't matter to her, she is scarcely aware, that this is not a private activity; that there are people behind her in this large room, although wisely, given her somewhat unpredictable mood, they aren't coming too close.

What does matter is her last opportunity to scrutinize Edgar; who, being dead, is necessarily silent and still, flying hands at rest finally. Neatly folded, too, in an over-the-belly clasp that would not, in life, have come naturally.

Amazing, what a good undertaker can do when he sets his mind and her—Edgar's—money to the task.

Regarding Edgar, her head tilted slightly, contemplatively, Gwen is considering among other things last moments, and the not-unhappy side effects, such as money, that death may create. Not, of course, for Edgar. There would have been nothing positive for him about straddling the railway track in his little red car, watching the huge single headlight of the 8:20 eastbound get bigger and bigger until it filled up his vision—Edgar finally seeing the light.

She imagines the sound would be something else, too; not just the shriek of the warning whistle, but the thundering of the train cars, the vibrating track. A disruptive surprise for all involved.

The newspaper said buses came to take passengers to their destinations, which must have made them hours and hours late and thrown all their appointments and plans, small or momentous, out of whack. As for the poor crew, they would have been even worse off than Edgar. If it was hard on him to see the train bearing down, at least the experience would be brief. Think, though, of the enduring horror of the train driver, standing on the brakes, eyes wide with shock, screeching helplessly into Edgar and his tinkertoy.

Men and their machines: a fatal attraction. Apparently Edgar could have leaped clear, there was time. But he may have been paralysed, by terror or even indecision; he was not a man who often rose to a crisis with appropriate speed. Still, he could have lived. Instead, he died in his racing gloves, silly leather things without proper fingers; he went down with his red convertible ship—top up or down? No one said, and Gwen neglected to ask.

That's where too-fervent attachment gets you. Edgar's devotion to his new car, his new racing stripes and new racing gloves, his all-new, taking-another-run-at-it life got him dead. Gwen should take care not to smile. These are odd and awkward social situations, without established etiquette, but she is aware that being Edgar's widow, at his funeral, makes her at least theoretically responsible for setting a certain tone.

Her cherry-red suit comes close to the shade of Edgar's sporty red car, which is the reason she's wearing it, but she hadn't entirely taken into account how much it would stand out in this sombre crowd. It also stretches more tightly than it did a couple of months ago, and now, in this funereal light, doesn't quite give the impression of real silk she was hoping for.

She thought she looked fine, reflected in the full-length bedroom mirror an hour ago (just an hour! How peculiar time has been, recently), although it's clear that in recent weeks she has let a few matters slide, such as her hips, and there are some new lines at the sides of her mouth. Her best features, though, her narrow nose with the small, interesting bump on its bridge, her wide lips which today she should really try to keep shut, and the dimple in her chin which seems to make people imagine she's someone optimistic and cute—all have been, as far as she can tell, unaltered by catastrophe. More important, her eyes are clear again, her vision sharper than, she thinks, it's ever been.

Not sharp enough to see through Edgar, however. She still can't tell what she should be seeing when she looks at him. She is also very angry that now she never will know. That right to the end, he has kept his enormous, stupid, shattering secrets.

Although obviously he is far more shattered than Gwen. Look at him!

What a farce, the two of them: Edgar out there with his dull, dim-witted adventure; Gwen home in her kitchen soothing mortally wounded feelings with starch and chocolate, mounds of pasta and potatoes, boxes of candy, blocks of cake—she smooths her hands over her hips. How firmly she exists; how entirely Edgar does not.

Indeed, he is the very picture of absence.

Apparently she doesn't know whether, as Edgar's mother Grace would have said, to laugh or to cry. Her aim, one aim, is to get through this day without doing either.

Last time Gwen saw Edgar, alive at any rate and in one piece, was ten days ago, when he rolled into the driveway without even phoning ahead, as if he had no manners, and no idea he could no longer do that. Gwen was startled, which made her briefly angry. Then she laughed, which made him angry.

What did he expect, though, with his tan leather gloves with all the fingers missing, and little holes for air to get through if he happened to find himself driving quite fast? And ping-pinging as it cooled, that convertible, tiny and red, racing-striped and transparent. And the new wire-rimmed specs circling his nervous blue eyes, and the old unalterable wrinkles around them, which would get worse now that he'd have to drive squinting not only against light but against rushing air.

Last touch: brown cap, close-fitted, peaked and tweedy. Edgar never before wore anything on his head, including, recently, much of his formerly abundant hair. With the cap, there was no telling how far back his forehead extended, or how grey the remains of his golden locks were becoming.

Now look at him. Wouldn't he be embarrassed!

Definitely, he used to say, he didn't want an open casket when, as he put it, he "went." He was cross about what happened when Grace died, upset that she looked, he said, "like a hooker, rouge and lipstick and that hair—she never wore it like that, twirled all over the place. God forbid." Edgar revered Grace, which Gwen, until the past couple of months, took as a good sign. She thought a man who admired his mother must be basically well disposed towards other women as well. Towards, specifically, his wife.

The past seven weeks (and three days) since Edgar walked, full of bravado and hope, out the door have given Gwen plenty of time to reconsider many ideas. She was on the brink of getting bored by her own interminable train of thought when this thing with a real train came along.

Since she is, despite these domestic dislocations, his widow, she naturally got to arrange the details of his funeral. So: let everyone see him more or less as he was. No tweedy cloth cap, no racing gloves, no casually open-throated, devil-may-care shirt; instead, an old blue suit, glaringly white shirt and too-bright red tie, something else to match his car. Even the plated cufflinks are leftovers from their early, struggling days. The undertaker has tightened his lips and given him a slightly failed and seedy expression, with a tinge of pink for colour.

Edgar's appearance, however pathetic, is a tribute both to the considerable skill of Austin Webster, the funeral director she picked from the phone book, and to Gwen's own insistence, no matter how many pieces Edgar was in. As it turns out, he's in three main pieces, with the odd bit still missing. Fortunately the parts that are visible were salvageable, and the rest is camouflaged by clothes and some strategic padding.

"Really, Mrs. Stone," urged Austin Webster, "in cases like this, it's simply not done. In the event of an accident of such severity. When there has been—damage."

"Really, Mr. Webster," she answered briskly (irritable anyway that right to the end Edgar imposed on her, interrupted her, impeded her progress; maybe even, twenty years late, that he'd ever entered her life in the first place), "I assumed you'd appreciate a chance to challenge your skills. As a professional." Shifting gears, casting her eyes downwards, she sighed. "It's what he would have wanted."

Well then, said the rather attractive, lean Webster, no guarantees, but he and his staff would assess the situation with a view to making the attempt. He quite saw Mrs. Stone's point. And certainly every effort was always made to honour the wishes of the deceased, not to mention those of loved ones. Only, there were sometimes circumstances in which even the deepest wishes must be overturned by events.

Gwen could not have agreed more. There are indeed such circumstances.

Edgar would just die if he could see himself now.

"I only wish," she said to Austin Webster, "that we could have buried him in his car. He did love that car." Webster's head twitched slightly and his professionally sorrowful gaze got suddenly sharp; but heavens, he must be used to mourners saying odd things, disoriented by grief. "He'd just recently bought it, you know. He spoke of what a thrill it was, driving it."

What Edgar actually said on that occasion ten days ago, after she'd stopped laughing, was this: "I've had more thrills in a few weeks with that car under me than I've had for years with you under me." And he sometimes accused her of a nasty tongue!

"How charming, Edgar. How gallant." She couldn't say she wasn't wounded, though. She couldn't say she wasn't hurt right through the heart.

They saved, it seemed, their most cruel weapons until weeks after the end was clear. Or the end they assumed, neither of them dreaming of today's true, ungovernable one; although there were moments, it's true, when in her shock she had wished him dead. Edgar was less gentle, or less frightened, ten days ago than on the day he left, and she was certainly more coherent, not to mention far, far colder. They were both pale: him, cap off, with his receding hair and light blue eyes and slightly sagging cheeks and chin; her, with her tangled, still-red-tinged hair and darker eyes and the small beginnings of puckerings at her throat. She knows she was trembling slightly; was he?

Anything can be said after the end, no holds are barred, all bets are off. What a surprise, really, abruptly to learn that much has been going on, unspoken and even mainly unfelt, under a fairly unrippled surface. And then once there's no hope, there is apparently also no need for camouflage, and very little restraint. Foul stuff spills all over the place, a sewer that finally, after years of tiny unheeded troubles, backs up, flowing unnaturally into basements and bathtubs.

"Ed," he complained. "People call me Ed. But of course you never would."

Not an illegitimate grievance, she would admit, although not to him. She shrugged. "Blame your sainted mother, then. Blame Grace, she's the one who named you Edgar, Edgar." After an uncle from whom Grace had hoped, correctly, for an inheritance. And when her turn came, she was able to pass on much of that inheritance to Edgar; who did quite well with it, and with his own financial efforts, and now look who ends up with it!

Clever Grace. Kindly, generous, long-dead Uncle Edgar. Carefree great-nephew Edgar, who didn't think to change his will first thing after he walked out Gwen's door. Foolish for a lawyer, but there you are, it's probably typical. Edgar, having been reborn at the age of forty-four, must have figured he had a lifetime ahead for tidying up dreary details affecting his dreary wife.

Gwen could use another snack, and then a nap. This isn't getting her anywhere; there are no answers in his sealed-up features.

She's getting bored staring at him.

Time to say goodbye. Goodbye, Edgar.

"Call me Ed," she could order chiselled on his gravestone; although funerals are expensive enough without fancy carving, especially when you have to pay a premium for sticking a body back together and making a terrified, broken face presentable.

She could just mark his grave with a little chrome bumper, then. Or an enormous train headlight. Or a rising cement penis, to mark his second coming.

Impatient people are starting to give up on waiting. She can feel them over her shoulder, coming closer, gathering around. Who are they? A few faces from the neighbourhood, that's very kind. And it looks as if the places where she has volunteered her energies and expanses of time, the heart people and the cancer and the food bank people, are represented as well. That's also very kind. Those sorts of organizations designate people to attend funerals. She wonders if the neighbours did that, too. Even if they did, it's a civilized effort. They are also civilized enough, or cautious enough, or know her just well enough, to hang back farther than the others.

There are of course men and women Edgar worked with, colleagues she doesn't know very well. A few he played with, too, whom she knows even less well. How many of them understand that this is, if not quite a hoax, not quite on the level, either? Probably all of them. Edgar's been celebrating his departure, his new life, for almost two months, and who knows how many knew what he was going to do long before Gwen did? She may be viewed as something worse than a grieving widow: a rejected one. Pity may be getting its sticky fingers all over her bright red suit.

Let it. Their pity has nothing to do with her.

Her own is another matter; there was quite a lot of pity for herself seven weeks and three days ago when grief, along with much else, nearly stopped her heart. Breakage itself did not seem out of the question. She recalls, to her shame, standing across the dining-room table from him, staring into his shifting, uneasy, entirely unfamiliar eyes, and asking over and over, "But why?" Not that it was an unreasonable question, but it became clear enough that he had no clear enough answer, and there was no point going on about it.

It took a while to grasp that he didn't have the words to explain what he was doing. In his place, Gwen would have had them precisely prepared. Perhaps he did, too, but muddled them when the time came.

"It seems to me, Edgar," she said, surprisingly cool (or in shock), "that you must have thought about this in a lot of ways for a long time. That's why I'm amazed you can't say why. It shouldn't be such a hard question."

"Change," he answered. "Need." He flung his arms wide. "My life!" he cried, spreading his hands.

"And mine?"

Well, she'd only had a few moments, and the dining room with which she was so perfectly familiar still looked very dim and far away and foreign. Once she got her wits about her and the weeks began to nip by, each day bringing something new in the way of what Edgar might call "change" and "need" and "my life!" she regretted asking. It was obviously one of those far-too-late questions, a waste of time and breath.

And yet it's true, she still longs to know. And here he is, in an eternal state of refusal.

Maybe he sat in his little car a few seconds too long because he felt a bit of dangerous doubt; because his new life wasn't what he'd cracked it up to be; because, longing to go either backwards or forwards, he didn't know how to do either.

Too bad.

"Mrs. Stone." A man's voice, low and respectful. "Gwen. I can't tell you how sorry we all are. As head of the firm, I want you to know if there's anything we can do to help you through this, you have only to ask. We're all here for you."

Is that true? Lawrence Parker is not a man who gives things away. He is a man who, unlike herself, really is wearing silk, grey and perfectly tailored, and he gets to have that suit, and a matching grey Porsche, and a very fine, almost indiscernible hairpiece, because he is not a man who gives things away. What can he mean?

A gesture to the widow of a useful colleague who worked very hard. Edgar liked to say he despised Lawrence Parker, but it sounded to Gwen mainly a loathing not of chemistry, or even of principle, but of something smaller and mean: mere envy.

"Thank you, Larry." She tries out her new tremulous widow's smile. "You're very kind. Shall we say Tuesday?"

His face flattens, goes blank. "For what?"

"Oh, for two or three hours, I should think. I don't imagine straightening out Edgar's affairs will take much longer than that, do you? At least getting the basics in place. How's early afternoon?"

"Unhh. Possibly. How be I have my secretary call you tomorrow, see what you think you need? It may be our services aren't best suited to you, but we could certainly steer you in the right direction."

It is one of Gwen's firmer conclusions, after seven weeks and three days of serious thinking, that people should take care to mean what they say. Previously, perhaps like Lawrence, she wasn't averse to the courteous lie, the polite evasion, the generous but quite unmeant gesture. But life, and Edgar is right here for proof, is too short.

If Edgar hadn't lied, evaded and gestured, they might both have gotten on with things much more briskly and usefully. As it is, she's forty-two and has little time to waste.

Oh, she sounds bitter. She hopes this will pass. She would not care for permanent bitterness.

A certain tartness, however, is useful. "She can call to set a time if you like, but Tuesday's best for me. I'd like to get everything in order as soon as possible. It's the details of death, you see, they make the situation so much more difficult. So I feel easier, Larry, knowing you'll help me." It's amusing to see him give in, with a little pursing of lips. No match for Gwen, not these days.

Perhaps she, instead of Edgar, should have been the lawyer. Poor Edgar was said to be quite good, but in such a large firm, a man confined to commercial interests was unlikely to become a star. Certainly not one like Lawrence, with Lawrence's public face.

"You don't have lawsuits in mind, do you?" he asks warily. "Against the railway, that sort of thing?"

"Heavens no. It was obviously Edgar's fault entirely, the whole thing, start to finish. Well, you know yourself, Larry, he was terribly thorough, very professional, and useful, I expect, to the firm, but it did take him quite a while to reach a conclusion. I suppose he sat there on the track thinking, and it took him just a fraction of a second too long to figure out what he could do."

A tiny flicker of shock appears briefly at one corner of Larry's mouth. He has an interesting mouth—how would it feel to kiss lips that barely exist? He must keep the largest part of them tucked inside, against his teeth; in order to maintain inscrutability, to keep from giving too much away.

Gwen has noticed this before about the lips of powerful men: they get thinner and thinner over time until they've nearly vanished. Lawrence must be, what, in his early fifties? And powerful beyond the courtroom, apparently. Edgar called him a "bagman" for his political party—some sort of money person, one of the movers and shakers, a member of the out-of-view group that causes events to occur. He's smooth, smooth, standing here in his silk suit, with his full head of distinguished, silvering, fake hair and his artfully camouflaged little belly and his pearly manicured fingertips.

"But I mustn't monopolize you, Gwen, with so many people here to pay their respects. It must be comforting to know how many people cared for Ed. And of course we all care a great deal for you." He begins edging away, but Gwen touches his arm.

"Thank you, Larry, that's very kind. We'll aim for Tuesday, then." His mouth starts to open, then closes, and he nods slightly and smiles his thin smile, and she releases him.

That was almost fun.

Now, who's this clump of strangers?

Must be people from Edgar's new life, the one he tried to describe to her ten days ago before bogging down, stumped for words. Edgar's incapacity for spontaneous speech and thinking on his feet helped keep him hunched over law books and contracts, well away from the courtroom, Gwen imagines. Edgar said it was mainly his own inclination, but he was hardly a man who would shrug and admit, "That's just not something I'm good at."

He preferred to emphasize the positive. As in: "I'm the best corporate contract guy in the place. There's nobody can touch me."

Maybe. Could be.

In the course of changing his life, did he plan to alter his work, as well? Whatever the law's equivalent of a little red convertible might be, was that what he was going to try next? If so, considering how quickly he got into the swing of consumption (and very conspicuous consumption, at that), it obviously did not involve sacrifice. So there would have been no storefront legal aid clinic in Edgar's future, no running off to help some developing country just learning the ropes of corporate contracts.

And if he didn't do that, use what expertise he had, what could he do but keep trudging? Edgar was almost as spectacularly untrained for making his way in the world as Gwen is herself. He only knew one way to make a living, which, while one more than she has these days, wasn't much.

His goals still sounded a bit vague as he tried to explain his sense of new life, flinging his arms for emphasis, or coherence.

"I want to be *happy*. I've always done what I was supposed to do, and now I'm doing whatever I *want* to do." As if being happy and doing what he wanted would naturally turn out to be the same thing. Or as if he had even "always" done what he should.

"What a fool you are, Edgar. I'm embarrassed, you know, to have been married to a fool. For so long."

"No, Gwen. No." Whatever that meant. "I couldn't let the past hold me back. A person only has so many years."

Or, as it turned out, so many days.

She was not inclined towards mercy; nor is she yet. "You may not be able to do *everything* you want, Edgar. Don't imagine I won't have my share."

"I hope you've got a good lawyer, then." He, of course, would.

How determined he was, and how certain. But determined to what, and certain of what?

The details of separation would, she imagines, have become far more onerous than those to do merely with death. But what a good thing she hadn't yet got round to finding her own sharp counsel. Now she has everything, with no difficulty whatever. Except for Edgar's difficulty, of course.

A shame their last words to each other were angry and greedy and harsh. Too bad that after twenty years they didn't have better things to say to each other. Still, as he said himself, "Life changes, Gwen. You can't look back, or feel bad, all you can do is go on and do better."

So true. Thank you, Edgar.

How badly it appears she is behaving. Perhaps distractedness can look like grief, though, and brittleness like sorrow.

Much worse than how she looks is how she feels.

The man facing her, leading his small posse of strangers, male and female, grabs at Gwen's hand. "I'm Al Benedict. I guess you're Ed's wife."

"Gwen Stone, yes. And you knew him how?"

"I'm—we're," and he gestures towards the three companions behind him, "from Ed's building." He shakes his head. "The

Ed-guy, eh? We're sure going to miss him, real life of the party. Good guy." He frowns, still shaking his head. "Bad way to go."

Ed-guy? And what party? Still, he did turn out to be a man of surprises, to Gwen at least.

And what building? Obviously when a man moves from one place he must move into another, but how did he find it, and when? How long before he walked out the door—this is a question that has haunted for weeks—was he planning, preparing? What a good secret-keeper the Ed-guy turned out to be, toddling obediently home, eating her meals, sleeping soundly beside her, signing leases in his spare moments.

She supposes she now owns whatever possessions he bought for himself, whatever optimistic, middle-aged men look for when they're beginning again. Leather sofas come to mind. Glass-topped coffee tables. Perhaps an enormous, hopeful, satin-sheeted bed. In Edgar's case, probably much greenery, also.

How tiresome, having to deal with all that, as well as all this. One of the downsides of widowhood. "Tell me, do any of you know someone in your building who might buy Edgar's furnishings? It would save me the trouble of unloading it if there were somebody handy."

"Gee." Al turns for help to his group. "I don't know. We could ask around, maybe. Anyone?"

They shake their heads mutely, watching Gwen carefully. What do they know about her? What might the Ed-guy have told his new friends? He wouldn't have truthfully been able to complain she is cold, or suffers from grave hardening of the heart, because those are mainly recent achievements, unfamiliar to him. Very likely he merely implied he'd changed and she hadn't. "It's for the best," he might have told them, as he also told her. "In the end," he said, standing in the dining room seven weeks ago, cautiously gauging her shock, "you'll be glad. You'll have the chance for something new, too, before it's too late."

Brave words, under the circumstances. For all he knew, she might have gone for his throat right about then.

Lucky for him she was stunned rigid.

But think: if dogged, head-down Edgar could remake himself into Ed-guy, life of the high-rise party, surely an essentially benign if sharp-tongued Gwen could transform herself without much strain into ice queen. Severe unsentimentalist. Chilly revisionist of love.

She finds it interesting how much she's been underestimated, even by herself.

Perhaps that's the sort of thing Edgar also was learning about himself.

The two women in this small group aren't quite what she'd pictured, imagining Edgar's vision of seductive freedom. They must be in their fifties, a decade or so older than Gwen, one bottle-blonde, the other bottle-blue. Nice-looking, though. Anxiously sympathetic, concerned. "I'm Annette. And this is Frieda." They fold Gwen's hands into theirs.

"And you all knew Edgar. How nice. He'd be happy to know he made such an impression in so short a time." They seem puzzled—that she calls him Edgar? Perhaps he never confessed.

"And I'm Frank." The second man steps forward, frowning and shaking his head just the way Al did. "It's tragic, what happened. Tragic."

"Yes," Gwen agrees briskly, freeing her hands from Annette and Frieda. "And unnecessary, as well."

All four look confused, until Frank's expression clears. Gwen has an urge to reach out and tug his brown thatch of hair to see if it's real, which it surely cannot be, a mean, mischievous impulse. "I guess it always feels unnecessary," he says, "or something like that, when somebody goes before their time. When they're young. Worse, in a way."

Several people have said things like that. Gwen frowns. "Well, Edgar wasn't what you'd call young, he was middle-aged. And I don't expect death is often welcome or especially timely, whenever it happens. At any rate, necessary or not, Edgar's time certainly came, and with quite a bang, wouldn't you say?"

What's the matter with her? Words pop out without warning, firecrackers exploding before she's aware their fuses are even lit. Still, they make her smile; no small trick today, and no small relief.

"Uh," says Al.

Annette and Frieda are both wearing black, in nice contrast to Gwen. Frieda's the blonde, Annette the bluish tint, which must have been a mistake. Maybe they dye their own hair, or each other's, saving money but risking unhappy results. Gwen's own hair is undyed and not yet much different from the dark red, short, curly style of her youth. She hasn't made a decision about how to approach her own aging, occupied and bemused as she has recently been by how Edgar chose to approach his. She might, though, have previously said she would take, within reason, what comes: lines, sags, grey hair, whatever. Now, it's all up for grabs. If she wants, she can be dyed, lifted, tightened, massaged and pummelled into perpetual, if grotesque, middle age.

"They did a nice job of Ed, didn't they?" Annette says rather desperately, looking down at him dubiously. "He does look different, though, doesn't he?"

"Well, he would, I suppose," Gwen replies, too dryly. Oh dear. "I mean, you must have known the new Edgar, whereas this is the old one I lived with." Of course they don't know what she's talking about.

"I'm surprised," Annette forges on, "you were able to have an open casket. I guess I thought that wouldn't be possible."

"It nearly wasn't. The undertaker was against it, but I insisted, and really, in the end he did a very nice job. Considering what he had to work with. More a jigsaw puzzle than a regular body, from his point of view."

"If you'll excuse us," Al says abruptly, taking Frieda's elbow. "We've taken too much of your time." He looks offended, almost angry. Perhaps he's thinking not only of the Ed-guy but of some domestic disaster of his own. Perhaps he's picturing sharp words at his own funeral. Or perhaps he's just taken a fast, strong dislike to Gwen. Hardly surprising.

In the past, she has liked to be liked; but then, most people do, don't they? She used to try to say the proper, kind word, perform the appropriately inoffensive action. She is not now exactly aiming for the unkind word or the action that gives offence, but the discipline of liking to be liked seems to have given way.

She also seems to have a desire to punish someone, for something.

Not Beth-Ann and Joe, though, now approaching, the only couple among the shifting neighbours on Gwen's street who've lived there longer than Edgar and Gwen. Beth-Ann brought a casserole the day they moved in, and dropped by the other night with a chocolate cake, which Gwen has already demolished. In the years between, Beth-Ann and Joe, Gwen and Edgar, came closest of anyone on the block to being actual friends, moving casually between each other's houses for dinners and barbecues and conversations and coffees. Gwen has been fond of them, Beth-Ann especially, but there have to be limits. Beth-Ann and Joe have their own troubles; mainly that Joe enjoys women who are not Beth-Ann a little too much, and if Gwen would not confide Edgar's most grievous failings, she also did not want to hear a great deal about Joe's.

In a neighbourhood, it's wise to sustain some divisions and proprieties, in her view. Otherwise how would people look each other in the eye day after day, year after year?

Now Beth-Ann takes Gwen's hand. "Are you okay? See you tomorrow, maybe, when all this is over?" Gwen nods.

Joe slings an arm around her shoulders. "Hang in," he says. This is the first time he's touched Gwen in years; since he put his hand on her ass late one night in Gwen and Edgar's back-yard and leaned close and said, "It could be good, you know. I'd like to try it, would you?"

Beth-Ann and Edgar weren't far away. Gwen didn't suppose Joe was especially serious. She didn't want to draw attention or make a scene. She drew away and made her mouth thin and stared at him, and Joe, who is neither insistent nor stupid, backed off.

Gwen never thought he meant much harm, but he has nevertheless done harm to Beth-Ann. That's what Gwen means, though, about keeping some distance, having a little discretion. As long as they maintained certain privacies, everything could go on as usual.

Now she's a widow, and nothing goes on as usual.

Beth-Ann and Joe each squeeze her hands one more time and move off. Gwen looks down once more at Edgar.

Twenty years! She could feel some grief for what seeped away from them, separately and together. Certainly they began better than they ended. Better intentioned, better affectioned. Better people, each of them, than they became.

Speaking for herself, if not for Edgar, she was also once much stupider. More naive. Far more gentle and elastic. Even seven weeks and three days ago, moments before Edgar stood across the table from her in their dining room and began his brief, stumbling farewell speech, she was stupider, more naive and gentle, and far more elastic.

Now what may become of her, if all that has sustained her likability in the world is her small capacity for looking stupidly and stubbornly on the bright side? Whatever will happen to Gwen if that's the case?

A question for another day. Because this one surely is Edgar's, his big moment, his very last chance to have Gwen's, or anyone else's, fairly complete attention. All eyes are finally on him, even if they are generally horrified eyes. Would he have enjoyed being so much the centre of attention?

Probably. What else could the red convertible have been for? And surely any human yearns, even just once or twice a lifetime, to be the focus of some form of human theatre; although preferably a happier one than this.

Gwen's big day, when it came to human theatre, was twenty years ago. That's what people say, isn't it: the wedding day belongs to the bride? And she was so *pretty*. She was so *pink* and *white*. She was so *hopeful*, and so heart-poundingly *panicked*.

Such a nice girl.

Pausing at the church entrance, clutching her father's arm, she watched Edgar watching her from the other end of that long aisle lined with mellow faces turned towards her. And with a sudden, sharp pain she was struck breathless, practically knocked back out the doors by the absolute certainty that she hadn't properly understood this would be real, and that as reality it was an awful mistake.

That the awful mistake was already made, since it was far too late to turn back, or undo. Pure inevitability freaked her out (as some people still said in those days). She felt the high ceiling descending, the ornate dark wooden walls closing in. The ruby blood tones of stained glass spoke of unforeseeable, unpredictable wounds. "My dear girl," her father said tenderly. "Always remember today. This will always be your moment."

Her hand holding his arm jerked and almost pulled free.

Gwen's two best high school friends, Marcia and Elspeth—where are they now?—stood opposite Edgar, dressed in plum with little veiled matching hats perched on stiff, sculpted hair, keen on their roles as her bridesmaids, as if they, too, were under the impression that this wasn't real life.

But then, it wasn't their real life, was it?

They were matched with Edgar's twin younger brothers, Max and Sam, who were at distant universities then, so Gwen barely knew them. Edgar's parents, Grace and Max Senior, were in the front row on Edgar's side, Max stern and straight, Grace a bit quavery, trembly. Her dear oldest boy.

It was not clear to Gwen, however, how people who cared about their children could stick them with such awful names. Edgar! Sam! Max! It made her uneasy; made her feel as if some far more sinister emotion than love must be in invisible play among them.

Gwen's own name, while scarcely beautiful, was at least honest, straightforward. Old-fashioned, but not actually ugly. She had been named, without expectation of profit or benefit, for the favourite aunt of her father, a woman she never, herself, met.

Gwen's big, buoyant mother, Florence, "Call me Flo," stood out vividly across the aisle in a tight, bright yellow dress as bold as she supposed herself to be. There was no talking Flo out of anything she set her mind on, and she thought, apparently, that she looked spectacular. Which in a way she did; just not in a mother-of-the-bride way. What was her view, turning to look back up the aisle at her daughter, her husband? What did she see? Did she think tender thoughts of Gwen as an infant, a child? Did she feel any sentiment?

One thing: if she had seriously believed Gwen was making a serious error, Gwen has no doubt Flo would have stood up on the spot and made her views known.

Until her last months, when cancer diminished her, shrank her, made her finally (her worst punishment) helpless in the hands of others, Flo was, to Gwen, a woman who desired her own way and saw no reason not to have it. She dedicated evenings to going out with her friends. She wanted to take courses, ridiculous things like accounting, art history, astronomy, and simply enrolled. She wanted to see islands off Greece, and went ahead and booked flights, only then asking if Gwen's father would care to go too. If not, naturally, she could find somebody else; one of the harsh-voiced, strenuous women she was attached to.

Gwen, growing up warily, alert to the withering effects of Flo's boldness, understood that Flo was, among other things, an example of selfishness and unconcern Gwen should take care to avoid. Only in her dying did Flo become vulnerable: looking out at her world, not so much with fear, Gwen gives her that, but with bewilderment.

At no longer being indomitable?

Then, finally, Gwen nearly was touched. Sometimes she patted her mother's gaunt hand, as if she could almost understand Flo's loss, and as if she herself no longer minded a mother who lacked the soft, spongy give of other, more comfortable mothers.

None of this was Gwen's father's view. "She was such *fun*," he mourned at Flo's funeral. "She kept me going." And evidently she had, because in less than a year he too was dead, of a heart attack.

Gwen was oddly upset to find herself orphaned. She wondered if it should have caused such a hole in her heart, a woman then well into her thirties.

She wasn't alone, of course, she still had Edgar; or believed that she did.

All that was only eight, nine years ago; long after Gwen's big day when she stood beside her father, staring down the aisle, petrified by what she was doing; that father who had tears in his eyes, whose arm slightly trembled, whose legs she feared might buckle, since in general she considered him a buckling sort. Not a strong man, no match for Flo.

She stood there with him and thought the whole bunch of them were a mistake, from Marcia and Elspeth, to Max and Sam, to Grace and Max Senior, to her own parents, to the entire congregation of friends and relations of one side or the other, and likely the minister, also. She wanted to cut loose from them all, with their complications and confidences and memories and trusts and quarrels and demands, the dainty minuets they danced, and the boilings of their various chemistries. She was sick of being implicated in so many lives: how they all got on, went on.

Such a nasty girl.

Such a young and unrealistic, ungrateful and panicky one. Flailing and, for those moments, furious with fear.

But then the music changed, became "The Wedding March," and like good soldiers, off they stepped together, she and her sentimental dad. He had tears in his eyes, but Gwen knows that any moment of high emotion, even high drama, can bring a tear to the eye, and it's only an overflow, a welling up, a spill.

Edgar's golden hair looked as polished as the pews. He had the most tender smile, waiting for her. Neither she nor her father buckled. When she reached Edgar finally, he touched his fingertips to hers. She shivered, his fingertips a sign and a symbol. Up close she saw she adored him, and inevitability became, as it sometimes does, reassuring.

It was the bride's day, all right.

Naturally, she herself was costumed in white, lacy and inappropriately virginal. She carried a small bouquet of white, mauve and yellow crocuses—it was an early-spring wedding. Her feet were in satin, her head sheltered within a veil of white netting.

There is altogether too much gauziness, too much *material*, swaddling a typical bride, that's what she thinks now. A bride might better be outfitted plainly and starkly; more like Edgar today. Then impacts couldn't be cushioned so readily, or realities dodged.

But what her damp-eyed father said was exactly true: that day was her moment. The trouble with being her kind of bride was that, after the moment, she was on a downhill trajectory. Brides like her peaked too early.

No, that's unfair.

Still, who dreams of picking out, one day twenty years off, a reasonably inexpensive casket (because there's no point in a lavish one) to contain the shattered husband of a shattered marriage? Who dreams specifically of all the troubled, tragic, joyous days between?

That's what Gwen thinks at the moment, anyway; but her ideas have recently been, to put it mildly, in flux.

Sometimes at a funeral, the immediate family has its own separate room for its own private outpourings of grief. This is not the case at Edgar's. All their parents, his and Gwen's, are dead, the last to go Edgar's father, incoherent and memoryless, by the end a husk of a creature curled into his own bones. The twins, Max and Sam, are not only far apart but also far away. Max is in Mexico working, Edgar considered foolishly, with some poor group of Indians; Sam is in Saudi Arabia working in some financial way, Edgar considered enviably, with some unimaginably rich group of rulers. Such extremes of outcome! Edgar was until very recently their sturdy, dependable, probably dull and faint-hearted big brother, and now he's no kind of big brother at all. But perhaps they're long past needing one, or even remembering one. They have each sent a telegram and regrets, letters to follow.

So Edgar's immediate family here is only Gwen, and if he hadn't died, she too would have continued her spin into far spaces, becoming less than immediate. And vice versa, of course.

She could almost weep. Death is, after all, a more momentous event than departure.

Also, she wasn't finished with him.

She is a one-woman reception line, and is surprised to find herself missing her mother. There was no one like Flo for uplifting various sentiments or, alternatively, squashing them flat. Either would be handy right now. "You think I'm behaving badly?" Gwen could ask these people. "You should have met my mother. You couldn't stop her tongue for any occasion on earth if she had something she thought needed saying. If she were here, I could be nicer. She'd take care of everything." Including, for that matter, comfort. Flo's flamboyance was also, on occasion, embracing.

Or, a child at each shoulder could also have comforted.

Gwen can almost feel a tall, strong, protective young man on her left, a tall, strong, protective young woman on her right. She doesn't know why they're both tall and strong in her mind, she certainly isn't, and, for a man, Edgar wasn't either. But imaginary offspring might just as well have sturdy genes, there's no need for a phantom son who shows signs of balding simply because that's what happened to his father. Or, to be fair, no need for a daughter who's lemon-bitter just because tartness has taken to flourishing in her mother. As figments, they can be anything she'd like.

She would name them Sarah and John. Loyal, dependable names. Names for people who would keep other people away today, out of concern for her; or concern, perhaps, for their father's dignity.

The hand of Austin Webster cups her elbow, urges her towards her front-row, solitary seat. "The service, Mrs. Stone. It's time."

It's really difficult to predict the turnout at a funeral. "I have no idea," Gwen told him when they were discussing the arrangements. "Although I don't believe you could exactly call Edgar a *popular* man."

They settled on one of the smaller rooms, although at the time it looked unnervingly large. But rows of folding chairs make quite a difference, and of course the casket itself eats up, weighs down, a lot of space.

There are a few empty seats, but Edgar wouldn't have to be embarrassed by low attendance. Like Gwen, he liked to be liked; and probably he was liked well enough, if not passionately, by these colleagues and acquaintances.

She sits very still. If these people could see deep inside Edgar's casket, they would face torn flesh and brokenness. If they could see inside Gwen's head, they would face much the same thing, metaphorically speaking.

Who dreams, on her big day, of sitting alone at a funeral home twenty years down the road with no sturdy John, no strong Sarah, not even a Flo, beside her? Who dreams of saying goodbye twenty years down the road to whatever has become of the tenderly smiling, fingertip-touching, young, promising fellow at the end of the aisle?

Let's get this thing moving. It's beginning to verge on the sad.

Goodbye, Edgar, for heaven's sake.

The minister, a tame one enlisted by the funeral home, never met Edgar. "Perhaps you can suggest some music he especially liked?" he asked her yesterday, as they sat on the green faux-leather sofa of a small, set-aside mourning room. "A hymn, or some song that would recall his spirit?"

"Little Deuce Coupe," sprang to mind. "Let the Good Times Roll."

Or maybe the one that starts, "I hear the train a-comin'.'"

"Not really," she told him. "He wasn't especially musical. He liked very old rock, Beach Boys kind of stuff, but I don't suppose surf songs would be very suitable."

He looked at her doubtfully. "Then perhaps the usual tape? "Old Rugged Cross," "Amazing Grace," that sort of music? Would that be all right?"

She shrugged. "Good enough." She imagined funereal Muzak, which turns out to be exactly what it is: an organ solo of mournful, solemn, hummable music, playing and replaying itself.

"Can you help me," he asked then, "find words to express your late husband's life? His hopes and goals and achievements?"

That's the kind of question that makes the mind go either blank or doleful. "He worked hard," she heard herself saying. "He enjoyed gardening."

There were a couple of ways she could think about that, both of them dismal. One was that, when it came to the point, she had no real idea what Edgar was like, or what his passions might have become. The other was that she knew some aspects of him very well, and was sharply aware of them, but that these should hardly be spoken aloud at his funeral.

"How about an anecdote?" he encouraged. "An illuminating moment or two?" She didn't like to disappoint him so gravely. He was young, perhaps innocent, certainly trying to do his job as well as he could. He leaned towards her, clerical elbows resting on clerical knees, clerical hands clasping each other.

"How about," she might have said, "when squirrels and skunks dug up his bulbs and he put out poison? You could say he was a man who preferred dead animals to dead plants, do you see what I mean?"

Or, alternatively, "How about when we drove to the east coast and got up really early one morning and stood at the very edge of the continent, watching the sun rise, and he put his arms around me and said in the strangest voice, 'Oh Gwen, imagine. All the world we can't see, but it's out there.'"

Perhaps he meant by that more than he said. Or more than she heard. She had put her arms around him, too, said simply, "Yes." She'd thought they meant the same enormous thing: an awe for which there weren't proper words.

Would that be an anecdote about him, or an illuminating moment?

How about the illuminating moment when she was finally pregnant (with John? With Sarah?) and started to bleed and called him, and he said, "Oh God, Gwen, I'm just meeting a client, have you talked to the doctor?"

"Yes."

"What did he say?"

"I should lie down with my feet up."

"Then why don't you do that?" The effort of patience was clear in his voice.

"I am. I'm lying down right now. Only I'm scared, Edgar. I'm really scared."

She thought he must just not have understood, and that naturally, when he did, it would be clear to him what was necessary: for them to be frightened together.

"I'll be right by the phone," he said. "If you need anything, call. The doctor knows his stuff, though, just do what he said and don't worry. You'll be fine."

And so she was. The fetus, however, was not.

Later, by evening, when it had bled itself away, Edgar hurled himself, raging, around the house. "The son of a bitch should have *known*," he cried, slamming his fist into a wall. "For Christ's sake, he's supposed to *know* when there's trouble and what you should do—we should sue his ass off."

Gwen was silent. She had no words for this man, her absent husband, father of a clot of bloody flesh.

An illuminating moment? For her it certainly was, but again, scarcely right for a eulogy.

There is no service for lost children, no particular words to speak over something that never quite existed. There ought to be ceremonies. People said, "It's likely a blessing, there must have been something wrong with it," and, "Never mind, dear, you can try again, there's plenty of time."

If words like that can be said when a child fails to materialize, why can't they be spoken when a grown man vanishes? Imagine the minister saying here, today, "It was likely a blessing, there must have been something wrong with Edgar Stone." Or these mourning acquaintances telling her, "Never mind, dear, you can try again, there's plenty of time. Say, I have a cousin you'd probably like, how about I set something up?"

Edgar was not a particularly sensitive man. Gwen does not mean by sensitive someone who can be dazzled by a sunset, or stopped in his tracks by a rose, but someone who actually feels the existence of another human. Edgar was no slouch at sunsets and flowers, but he was unnerved by sorrow and equally unnerved by joy. Gwen's, at any rate.

He'd have been entirely flummoxed today.

One does not, Gwen thinks, recover from so profound a falling short. Things get fractured in a matter of hours.

"What's wrong with you?" he demanded, pulling abruptly out of her one night not long after that first loss. Perhaps she'd forgotten to move, or to touch.

A similar question, asked in a different tone, at another moment, might have indicated a willingness to hear. Just willingness, even without ability, would have meant something. Asked the way he asked it, however, and in that circumstance, it struck her as unanswerable and bound to end in tears. So she got out of their bed, pulled on her robe and went to the living room, where she sat on the sofa for the rest of the night. "For Christ's sake, Gwen," he called after her, "I'm sorry."

She had two more flawed pregnancies, and for those losses, he took care to be present. Children were their mutual, mostly unspoken, regret. Otherwise she'd supposed the marriage was mainly like life, with ups and downs and compromises, a rhythmic uneventfulness; only what was to be expected, if not necessarily what one had hoped for. Hardly thrilling but mainly fond and not, she imagined, out of the ordinary.

Until, of course, Edgar set off in search of the extraordinary.

Was a train extraordinary enough for him?

Come to think of it, though—come to think of it, it might not be too late. She sits up straighter. What a thought! She's only forty-two, and the problem might have been mutated sperm, who knows? Other women get pregnant at her age, it's not out of the question. There really could be a chance of a whole new life, just as Edgar insisted.

When he left, with visions of a new life dancing like sugar-plums in his head, could he have been thinking, "If I got close enough to healthier ovaries, fallopians, uterus, I could still have all the children I want"? Even better if all that apparatus were attached to a firmer body than Gwen's, and to a more malleable, unbetrayed heart.

Imagine Edgar's enthusiasm!

Naturally she pictured another woman. He denied it, and might have been telling the truth. At least it rang true, if incoherent, when he said, "It's not that. Not that simple." Once again, he flung wide his arms. "It's me, Gwen. Or us. Nobody else. That's not it."

What the hell is that minister going on about, what's taking so long?

The minister himself looks potent enough. And clergy are now famous for their odd enthusiasms. He might enjoy disrobing with someone a good ten years older, who would ask so little of him. He might even call it therapy for a lost, bereft widow. "I helped her get her feet on the ground," he might be able to say.

And Gwen would be able to say, "I helped him get his feet off the ground."

She is babbling inside her own head. Getting foolish.

"Let us bow our heads," the minister's saying, "and observe a moment of remembrance for our husband, our colleague, our friend." Or in his case, she thinks, our complete stranger. "Let us pray for the soul of Edgar Stone."

So.

Good luck, then, Edgar, Gwen thinks in the silence. Too bad about those last moments of yours. I'd sure like to know what came clear to you then, although I'm even more curious about what came clear to you long before that. Too bad about the car, as well. I can't imagine how much it meant to you. Really. I can't, and you were no help. Also, thank you for going while I still had some time. And for all the money. I guess it doesn't matter wherever you are, but as you know, it does here. So what can I say, except thank you? I hope you're happy I'm finally saying thank you, since as I understood it, that's more or less what you thought I should say when you left. And you know, I am sorry, really, that things turned out badly. I wonder if we could have done better? I wonder how?

"Amen," says the minister, and there are rustlings of relief throughout the room. Is it over?

Somebody had better make a move.

Apparently it's supposed to be Gwen; the minister is looking her way, eyebrows raised expectantly. For heaven's sake, does she have to do everything?

She stands. Now that the final, final moment has come, it is a bit strange. Stepping forward, she reaches out to touch the shining wood, looks down one last time on Edgar's battered, shuttered face. The eyes behind those closed lids have looked at her with every expression imaginable, from adoration to tenderness to passion to dislike to anger to terrible unconcern. The narrow lips tightened over his broken teeth have pressed themselves to all parts of her, from the top of her head, to her fingers, to her toes, to the insides of her thighs. The clasped, shattered hands, likewise.

In his absence, the house is unrelievedly empty and silent.

And already has been for seven weeks and three days.

So, "For the last time, Edgar, goodbye," Gwen says in a clear, impatient, exasperated voice. She gives the casket an encouraging pat, straightens and marches briskly out of the room, past everyone gaping, through one set of doors and down a hallway to a heavy set of wooden doors, out into the parking lot and sunshine.

She's had enough. More than enough. She spreads her arms and lets loose a whoop into the shining, hot sky.

two

Gwen has not previously been a woman who makes exuberant noises in public. Nor has she been a reckless driver, but now she peels out of the parking lot with an eye to the rear-view mirror instead of ahead. Other mourners emerge more sedately. The hearse idles in the entranceway, behind it the black sedan in whose back seat she was intended to sit, weeping or thinking sad, kindly thoughts, following Edgar all the way to the grave.

Funeral processions aren't what they used to be. Cars don't pull over, pedestrians don't pause on sidewalks, and today it appears widows aren't necessarily much interested, either.

Where will this unsentimentality end?

Without unsentimentality, Gwen might burst through her skin. Parts of her are already in fragments. There is not much holding her together right now.

She has no idea where she is going, except not home. Pulling into the driveway, facing that two-storey sprawl, the unmowed lawns, untrimmed shrubs, unweeded, rampant gardens, would be insupportable. The sound of the front door closing behind her, the view of the hallway opening into empty space after empty space—all this, while not new, today could cause her to drop to her knees, bent low with grief for, not Edgar exactly, but at least for twenty years.

What she needs right now, this minute, is something untouched by any history of hers, or Edgar's, or theirs as they used to be, together. "Gully's," says the sign swinging over a door off to the right, and in smaller black letters below, "A Good Place to Drink."

Can't say better or plainer than that.

Nevertheless, once she's in the parking lot, switching off the ignition, she does have a moment of wondering what she thinks she is doing. The building itself is plain and square, two-storey, built entirely, it appears, of whitewashed cement blocks, with tinted, reinforced windows and out front a single, dark-brown metal door smack in the centre. Not, on the face of it, the place for a solitary, middle-aged woman in a bright red suit that's a shade too tight.

She feels nearly removed from herself; as if it isn't Gwen Stone who is stepping out of her car, walking to that metal door and entering darkness, pausing then, blinking till her eyes adjust. Apparently she has changed in recent days, and weeks, from someone of whom it could be said she was not previously this or that sort of woman into one who now, perhaps, is.

There's not another female in the place. On the other hand, there aren't many men, either, and those there are look gloomy, even desolate, certainly beyond interest, benevolent or malignant, in her.

Seven weeks ago, or six, or five—then Gwen, too, was aimless, often enough staring dumbly at nothing, like the top of the kitchen table, or a section of living-room wall; not unlike these guys hunched over round, veneered tables, making circles of damp with their glasses. Maybe they, too, are having trouble absorbing the shock of the irrevocable and unredeemable.

By four weeks ago, she was pulling herself together, at least coping as long as she didn't look too closely, was even starting to look for a bright side these men appear unaware of. Or perhaps this is their conclusion: their bright side.

The two cops at the door four nights ago threw her badly off course. Or their purpose did. "Mrs. Stone? I'm afraid we have some bad news." Then, "Can we call someone to be with you?"

No, they could not. The most familiar, closest person in whom to confide, with whom to share new knowledge, still, as it turned out, was Edgar. A very old, deep habit: she almost said, "Please call my husband."

His funeral was at one o'clock; by now, he's being lowered into the ground, the first loads of dirt are being tossed down on top of him. Are there still people gathered around? Are they murmuring with happy horror about Gwen and her appalling absence?

It's a long way to the bar, a long walk past these scatterings of men who know nothing about her. Isn't that nice. And how enticing, the scents of beer and tobacco and men and closed windows and darkness mixed together deliciously. Edgar wouldn't dream of coming to a place like this. Put that another way: he wouldn't have dreamed of coming to a place like this with Gwen. For all she knows, he hid out in bars just like this for years, or has been exploring like crazy in recent weeks on his own.

Silly of her, and thoughtless, to have gone so few places without him. She reads of the surgeries that separate Siamese twins. This business with Edgar has involved a process just as difficult and delicate, a snip here, a suture there; although the final slice was still a shock.

"Rye and ginger," she tells the skinny young bartender, and from some old movie hears herself add, "Make it a double." That should hit like a hammer, she hasn't had a rye for years, for that matter doesn't usually drink ginger ale. The bartender squints as if he'd like to say something, but shrugs instead. "Coming up. You sitting here or a table?" Better here at the bar, perhaps, until she gets her bearings. She hoists herself onto a stool.

Hey, this must be like driving a truck, sitting up in the cab overlooking the traffic. She turns and turns, swinging her feet, to see what she can see.

In the old days, in her old life, a couple of months ago, she and Edgar went out together every week or two. At restaurants, bars and at home, he drank Scotch in the winter, beer or gin in the summer; Gwen drank white wine or red wine or nothing, all the year round. They spoke, although with many silences, about events, other people, and their own thoughts and ideas about events and other people. She supposes those conversations, those outings, constituted a social life, along with the odd neighbourhood barbecue or company gathering.

Where do people alone go? What do they do? Who do they talk to, and listen to? How do they speak?

"Ma'am?" asks the bartender cautiously, placing her drink on a coaster—how genteel, how courteous!—"I don't mean to be rude or anything, but are you sure you want to be here?"

"Why not?" What harm is likely from this limp, grizzled collection of men? The bartender's the only one who doesn't look limp and grizzled, and he's just a boy. He could almost be her son, except if he were, she'd have taken care that he not grow up scrawny and pinched-looking. If prosperous, powerful men grow thin-lipped, so, it seems, may their opposites.

"No reason. I just thought you maybe made a mistake." Oh. He means she doesn't belong, and may be here for the wrong reasons. Tourism, for instance; not the out-of-town, but the stare-at-the-human-zoo kind. "Thank you. I don't want to cause any problems, but I'm perfectly comfortable.

"You see," she leans towards him, spreading her elbows on the bar—and she's not even drunk yet—"I just came from my husband's funeral, he got hit by a train, and I decided to skip the burial and get underway with my future, and then I was driving by and the future suddenly called for a drink. So mainly I'm here instead of at a cemetery. Although this seems just about as dead as that would have been." She grins as if she expects he will share her joke.

His face screws up with concern. "Geez, that's too bad. You okay? No wonder you wanted a drink, geez." He shakes his head. "A train, eh? Man." Not exactly eloquent, but sympathetic. Well-intentioned.

"Yes. But he'd already left me almost two months ago, so it could have been worse, I could have still cared. What's your name?"

"David. Dave."

The rye is warming, it's toasty and cosy. "You worked here long?" Stupid question; anyway, he's too young to have worked anywhere long.

"All my life, sort of. My dad owns the place and I do a few shifts." He pauses, regards her more closely. "But I'm mainly a student. It's not," he glances out over the room, "like it's a tough job, at least not usually for another couple of hours. Then things can start flying. But this time of day, it's pretty much old retired guys, or a few that's out of work maybe. It's just a draft beer crowd."

"What kind of student are you?"

"A good one." He grins. "No, seriously, university. Law."

So much for assumptions. Presumptions. She has much to learn. "Edgar was a lawyer. That's my husband. That *was* my husband. Can I have another rye?" She shot that one back awfully fast. She is already tippy on the stool. Her tongue feels loose and flappy. "I'm usually a wine drinker. That's the tipple of a respectable lawyer's wife. Or a lawyer's respectable wife." She waves her hand. "Whatever. So tell me David, Dave, has your family always owned this place?" Not that she cares. But it's nice to hear stories, good to have empty air filled.

"My grandfather bought it just before my dad and mum got married. We lived upstairs, so when I was a little kid, I'd sneak down here at night to watch the action. Sometimes they'd stand me up on a table and I'd do a couple of little-kid songs, until my mum or dad scooped me back upstairs. It was fun." His eyes are smiling. The longer Gwen looks at him, the less scrawny and thin-lipped he seems. She guesses any acquaintanceship will round out a picture. She guesses you just can't ever tell.

"But," he, too, leans closer, "you sound like you've had a bad time. Aren't you real sad?"

What kind of question is that? And what business of his? Still. "Sort of. Although sad's not quite the word. Anyway, as I say, he already walked out on me seven weeks and three days ago. Poor Edgar, what a snippet of time he ended up having. How old are you?"

"Twenty-three. How about you?"

For a moment, she's startled. It's not a question that's asked, ordinarily, by a young man of a much older woman. "Forty-two."

"Heck, that's not old."

"Exactly." She beams. How perceptive he is, how well he sees into her. A glow is forming around him, something rosy and golden. He rather resembles, in her blurring vision, Christ in a Sunday school portrait. She giggles. Gosh, she hasn't giggled for years, what a sound, so girlish, so young.

"You're going into law, then, not taking over the bar?"

He throws up his hands. "No way. My mum would have killed me. She used to say, 'David, we work this hard so you can have more than we did. You're smart, and you can have every opportunity in the world if you work hard enough, too.' And my dad," he smiles, and his lips no longer seem narrow, but generous and disarming, "he doesn't talk much, but he means the same thing."

Gwen should have paid such respectful attention to Flo. "Do you like Edgar?" Gwen asked her twenty years ago.

"Well enough, I suppose." No ringing endorsement. "I'm not sure he's one for the long haul, though, I'm not sure he has the depth for that." What would Flo know about depth, that's what Gwen thought. Now she wonders if what she saw as Flo's insistent restlessness wasn't something far more serious: a true, gaping, open-mouthed, unspeakable yearning.

"I bet your mother's proud of you now," she says to David.

His expression goes soft—how could she have considered him pinched? "I think she would've been. She died when I was just finishing high school, but she already knew I'd been accepted at university, and that made her happy."

"I'm sorry." And Gwen is sorry. The death of that dedicated and determined woman, the bartender's mother, a stranger, feels more acute, immediate and touching than the far more recent, messy death of her own husband. Probably, she thinks muzzily, that's peculiar.

"It's okay. It was a while ago. Like I said, I know she'd be proud. I am, too, for that matter, and so's my dad." What a close, loving family. Gwen could weep, this is such a nice story, nice people, nice young man.

"If you go into law, what will happen to Gully's?" She wants to keep words moving between them, between her and silence.

"My dad wants to sell someday and retire, so it'll probably end up torn down for offices or apartments or something."

"What will your father do then?"

Edgar and Gwen used to speak occasionally, vaguely, of the time years down the road when they'd be free to do what they wanted. They had no particularly firm or fervent ideas, but Gwen wonders if Edgar's heart sank just a little, as hers undeniably did, at the notion of the two of them meandering together, rootless and underoccupied, through their days. She'd supposed vaguely that they might develop some compelling mutual interest that would keep them going. Good thing she didn't put much effort into wondering what that might be. In fact, putting things off seems to have turned out fairly well for her, by and large.

"He's got property on a lake up north. He goes every year to fish and plan the cottage he's going to build when he gets out of here." David laughs—what a jolly young man. "It gets bigger and more complicated every year. I think what he's got now is like the plans for an inn, or a lodge, something like that. Excuse me a minute."

He's been keeping an eye on the room. Stooping slightly, he fills three draft jugs from a tap and ducks around the end of the bar. Gwen, swinging around on the barstool, watches him slap them down on two of the tables, collect money and empties, give change, take a cloth from a pocket and swipe at a couple of other tables. She is, frankly, admiring his grace, the shift of his hips as he slips between tables, the bones of his spine prominent under his shirt, the worn jeans and slim hips—she decides he is beautiful. She wonders what was wrong with her when she first came in and failed to recognize this.

By now Edgar is deep in the darkness, weighted by earth, all alone. It's the alone part that feels worst, the eternity of dark, heavy solitude he faces. Poor man, poor pathetic, sad man. Oh dear, that's a tear. And another one. She appears to be crying, tears rolling down helplessly. She can't seem to make herself stop.

Edgar was beautiful once, too, that's what's so pitiful. He was once twenty-three, and in law school, and seemed loving and kind, and had no idea his life was more than half over.

"Oh, hey." David has come up beside her. "Hey there." His voice is uncomfortable, and so is the hand he puts on her shoulder. "You must feel really bad. Sorry for going on, I was just trying to take your mind off things, but I probably shouldn't have. Don't cry. Or I guess cry if you want to. Want me to leave you alone? What can I do?"

He's sweet, and anxious, and funny—there's a little grinding of gears in her throat as the tears switch to laughter, but it's also breathtaking, and just as helpless.

"Shit!" That's not quite under his breath and, like a slap, straightens her right up. She doesn't want to be a worry to this nice young man who could be her son, but happily is not.

"Sorry." She's slightly winded. "I'm okay now." She inhales as deeply as she can inside the tight suit jacket. "It's been quite a day."

"Yeah, I guess." He returns to his side of the long bar, watching her closely. She is very fond of brown eyes, which look to her deeper and wiser than blue ones like Edgar's. "You should maybe think about going home, though. The place starts filling up around four, and I really don't think you want to be here then. Are you driving?"

She nods.

"You live far?"

In a subdivision six or eight kilometres, and a universe, away from here, is her and Edgar's second and final home; the one they bought, leaving their first small apartment, soon after he joined Lawrence's firm, when he was twenty-six and she was twenty-four and they still believed that all its rooms would be filled, and the huge, treed backyard and little-travelled street would be excellent playgrounds, and the neighbours would be suitable, the parks close by, the shopping handy, the community unpolluted by need or particular drama.

In time, Edgar came to use the yard for his mysteriously complex arrangements of flowers and shrubs. The rooms took on unpredicted purposes, like his home office. It was naturally foolish of them to have mistaken unremarkable exteriors for an absence of neediness or spectacular drama. Some frolicking infants grew up to steal cars, break into houses and worse; or became reliable baby-sitters, university students, with intentions to become social workers or doctors. Wives, including Gwen, found themselves weeping late at night, on living-room sofas or at kitchen tables, but got up smiling in the morning. Husbands went mad, vanished, lashed out, and embraced their children, their lawns, their eavestroughs, their wives. On summer weekends people laughed and waved and nodded and talked, and sometimes formed friendships, like Edgar and Gwen, Beth-Ann and Joe, and held parties and barbecues.

This is what a normal neighbourhood turns out to be, a normal life. Gwen will have to be leaving it soon.

It's funny, isn't it, that instead of a twenty-year movie unreeling on a mental screen smoothly and sensibly, what she is mainly left with is a handful of snapshots?

"I'm sort of going that way, I could give you a lift when my shift's up." David checks his watch. "Another fifteen minutes, that okay?" What a sweetheart! "You can come back for your car tomorrow, it'll be fine. Nobody messes with our parking lot. Sound good?"

Sounds perfect. Splendid, even, although that's not a word Gwen can get her tongue around at the moment. "Thank you. That's kind of you. I'm going to the washroom, be right back." Her words are slow and, she thinks, precise. She slips off the stool, and her left knee almost lets her down. Her steps feel as slow and precise as her words. Oh, peeing is lovely! But all that lost, wasted rye.

Returning, she manages on her second try to hoist herself back onto the stool. Good to know she can still do difficult things. Except hold on to Edgar. So she must have wanted up on the barstool more than she wanted up on Edgar. She hears a guffaw and slaps a hand over her mouth.

"You know," nice young David says solemnly, "you probably should take it easy. It must be a weird kind of day, but you're a really pretty woman, and you don't want to get yourself all wrecked up. You want to take care of yourself. You got kids?"

"John and Sarah." That's out of her mouth before she can stop herself. "But they're—not anywhere. Not actually available." If there's an afterlife, will Edgar have to explain himself to them? Just that tiny, tiny part of his life he spent with a client while one or the other, John or Sarah, bled their way out of existence?

She would like to rest her head, just briefly, on the narrow shoulder of this unexpectedly generous, perceptive and thoughtful young man. She hasn't looked properly, or improperly, at another man for years. She didn't think it was relevant, she supposes. Now it's also a matter of whether anyone can ever be believed or trusted.

Or a matter of deciding whether belief or trust are of consequence any longer.

She watches David distribute more rounds of draft. She sees him greet an older man coming through the door—odd to glimpse sunshine, that there's still daylight out there. She dreads dark thoughts lurking ahead in the night. Nights are the worst.

"I'm off then, Dad," she hears David tell him. So this is his father, the hard-working, taciturn man whose wife is dead and who draws plans of an elaborate cabin for his retirement. "I'm just going to give this lady a ride home. Her car's out in the lot, she'll be back for it tomorrow."

The man frowns. "Why don't you call her a cab?"

"No problem. It's not out of my way, no point doing that."

His back is towards Gwen; she can't see what unspoken signals he might be making, but his father watches him closely, still frowning, finally shrugs, throwing his hands slightly upwards.

And suddenly, with David's hand on her elbow, she's across the dark floor, at the door, out in the heat of the sun, and it's still only a couple of hours since the service for Edgar.

In strong light, does she look very old to this young man holding her arm?

He tucks her into a tiny green car of the sort it's easier to get into than out of. "You okay?"

She nods. All days should be so full of this and that. The rye was nice. David is nice. Edgar was not nice, and Gwen may yet be nice, or not. The universe at any rate is a really interesting thing—thing? place?—and interesting is also really nice. She is, for instance, quite interested in the muscle structure of David's narrow arms as he steers, the tendons of his sleek hands shifting under his skin, performing turns of the wheel.

He doesn't seem to mind her staring.

She lets her head fall back on the seat, more at peace in the careful or careless control of this stranger than she has felt for many weeks. Isn't that odd. Perhaps it's only a matter of events, for that matter her actual life, being beyond her own responsibility for these few moments. Very relaxing.

Although she wouldn't want to end up like Edgar.

"Left here," she tells David. "Right at the next corner. Third house on your left."

Oh Christ, this house: with its secrets as sealed against her as Edgar's dead face. Pulling into the driveway sobers her right up. Terrifying. Her head snaps forward. She cannot do this.

"Would you come in?" She doesn't want to sound pleading or desperate, but her voice shakes a little. "I'd like to thank you for the lift. Let me offer you a drink."

It's a long moment—insultingly long?—before he nods, says finally, "Okay. I can't drink when I'm driving, but sure, I could use something cold."

Now, with a witness, an audience, she can manage to walk briskly to the little porch, turn her key in the lock, march into the hallway. She gestures David to the right, into the living room, while she heads to the kitchen.

Returning, she is halted in the doorway, startled by simultaneous visions: that he is standing on one leg, like a stork, uneasy, awkward, out of place; and that her carefully cultivated beige-blue-brown living room is appalling, a room so unedged and dull that words, deeds and emotions must all be absorbed and smothered within it.

Is this what Edgar saw, coming home?

Well, not David, she doesn't mean that. He certainly never saw David standing stork-like in his living room.

"I never realized," she says softly, "what a godawful room this is. The whole house, I guess."

David turns slightly, both feet now on the floor, eyebrows raised over his deep, knowing, fluid brown eyes. "You think so? I like it. Like, it's peaceful, you know? This is the kind of place I used to envy when I was a kid. It wasn't always great living over a bar. Sometimes I used to want something, I don't know, *normal*, I guess."

Light. He stands in the late-afternoon light of the window, talking on about rooms, and himself, and histories, ambitions and hopes, and Gwen barely hears. She is watching his hands: narrow, bony, hard-looking, hairless and pale. One hangs by his side, the other by a thumb from his jeans; no flinging, no fidgeting. Their stillness and their seriousness of purpose, their newness (how many places could they have been, how many things could they have done, in just twenty-three years?), their toughness—oh my.

She is setting down the two icy glasses. She's stepping towards him. She's undoing her suit jacket, shrugging it off; unhooking her bra, shrugging it off. She is taking his hands, lifting them, placing one on each of her breasts. These breasts have been in the world almost twice as long as his hands.

What is she doing? She is not herself. Or, she is remote from herself. But very close to him. She can see his eyes widen, and his nostrils, as he takes in sudden breath.

When he says finally, "Your neighbours," his voice sounds as if he's been running. How thoughtful, pointing out in the midst of his own upheaval what might be troublesome for her. It's hard to read his desires, but her own are shockingly, hypnotically clear.

When, one hand on each of her breasts in the full, bright view of the living-room window, he mentions the neighbours, she draws him to the floor, below the level of the sill.

They land with a clumsy thud. She can feel the intimate scratching of deep beige wall-to-wall on her back. Her spine discerns individual fibres, possibly even bits of thoroughly deep-hidden lint and other tiny debris. They do not speak. She is listening to the changing, deepening tones of his breathing, as he is also, possibly, to hers. She doesn't want this pure sound of desire broken by an actual voice or definite words. Silence seems to her literally golden: gilded particles flickering around their connected, intimate bodies.

Her hands reach down to free him, undoing, unzipping his fly as if she were accustomed to lust. Playful as a boy, he pulls her on top of him, rolls them over and over like puppies to the foot of the stairs. She feels the plushness of her own flesh, and the unyielding sharpness of his bones.

They stand, and climb the stairs fast, eyes aiming at the top. On the landing he says, "Shower? Wait for me?" and runs a finger along the line of her jaw. She listens to the water, picturing it splashing down his lean limbs. How hungry she is!

She also thinks that pausing in the pursuit of desire is not necessarily a good idea. That she is thinking anything at all seems to prove that. Still, her heart, or some part of her, leaps to see him emerge, clouded in steam. He smells of her soap. He looks at her anxiously, as if he has perhaps taken liberties. How winning.

Leading him by the hand to the bedroom doorway, she is momentarily stopped by the sight of her and Edgar's marital, her own post-marital, bed. Not from reverence, or particular sentiment, although it's true only one man has ever been in it, and he was buried today; but because the sheets haven't been changed for more than a week. Will David discern the scents of late-night threshings, or the depths of unconsciousness she has several times fallen into?

It's difficult, learning to fill up a whole bed. Edgar took a good deal of space, although, while bulkier than David certainly, he wasn't a large man. He merely spread himself out.

Gwen sets her fingers to dancing on David's ribs, and elsewhere. He is more hesitant. Or more generous. "Tell me what you enjoy," he whispers. "Tell me what you like best."

She doesn't know. Everything; anything, maybe. Someone new; something different.

His fingers seek out parts of her, his mouth other parts, his penis roams, nudges and intrudes. Comparisons, since there's only been Edgar before, are inevitable, but not very important. This is clumsier than with Edgar, but that must mainly be unfamiliarity. It's also far more exciting; which may equally be due to unfamiliarity.

David's brown eyes and her blue ones are locked so that they watch each other's shifts of response. Pleasure. She feels slightly awkward, unsure, and imagines he does, also. But ravenous. To both of them, each other's bodies must be broadly known but individually strange.

She likes David's compassion, as well as his passion. He is, it seems, as wondering and amazed as she by this turn of events.

Very soon, though, his eyes lose focus, his jaw tightens, his arms turn rigid and his head flings upward. She grows humid and hot as a greenhouse. "Unnnh unnh," he cries. Edgar used to shout actual words, such as "Jesus!" and "Christ!"

They fall apart, breathless and steamy. Did she enjoy that? Oh yes.

He has a mole on his hip, resembling the one on her thigh, and another near the top of his ribs. His eyes are closed, one arm flung over them, and a tiny smile turns up the corner of his mouth. She could count his ribs, and his hipbones are jutting and sharp.

Edgar's body used to be lean, although never this lean. Over the years he gained, not fat exactly, but heft. Substance. His belly slightly preceded him, his arms thickened, his thighs turned less than taut. He never became unattractive, though, viewed dispassionately. Which is how, for the most part, she did come to view him.

Which came first, her dispassionate view of him, or his of her?

At the moment, for the first time in a couple of months— well, for the first time in much, much longer, really—she has an urge for Edgar's body. Would like to revel and nuzzle and roll in it. Most familiar Edgar; complete and unknown stranger Edgar. Both.

"Well," she thinks as if he, too, were here in the bed. "Well Edgar, how about that? Surprises all around, for everyone."

Not least for David, apparently. Next thing she knows, she's waking in darkness from a sound, dreamless sleep to a weird thumping noise. Rolling swiftly, she flicks on a lamp, and sees David hopping around, pants partly on, looking dishevelled and again somewhat stork-like. Startled, he almost falls over.

"Goddamn, you scared me." She doesn't even try to hide the irritation of relief.

He looks stricken. "Oh gosh, I'm sorry. I was trying not to wake you up. I'm really sorry."

How young he is. How unlikely, raw, barely formed. "What time is it?"

"Almost eight. I hate to do this, but I've got to go. I'm going to be late."

"For what?" Although this isn't her business, and she doesn't especially care. Actually, she rather wishes she'd slept through his departure, awakening to a memory instead of to a slight headache and this clumsy moment.

Now he has managed to get both legs into his pants, and is casting about for his shirt. Gwen knows right where it is—beside her, on the floor by the bed. She has a vivid picture and sensation of gripping it, drawing it off his bony body, she can see her arm flinging it over and down, a white flag, out of the way.

"I gotta go!" he is muttering frantically. "I gotta get out of here." Well, in that case. Reaching down, she picks up the shirt, hands it towards him.

"Was it so dreadful?"

David stops his desperate movements and stares at her. "Oh. Gosh, no. It was great. You're terrific, you really are." Perhaps he is accustomed to women desiring reassurance, or pledges of affection, or warranties of their skill. "I didn't mean to sound like I want to leave, because for sure I don't. It's just, I have to. My, uh, my study group, we meet Tuesday nights and I have to turn in a paper or I'm in really big trouble. That's all, but I want to stay, I wish I could." He is so earnest and skinny, an unpadded young body, with little in the way of protection.

Men fill out eventually, and it gets hard to see, much less reach through to, their bones.

"Tomorrow, when you pick up your car, could I see you? Please? You could come into the bar and then we could go someplace."

Oh dear, there's always debris left behind; in this case her abandoned car and a few leftover emotions. There's always sweeping up to be done. Seven weeks and three days ago, Gwen could have hurled glasses or lamps or chairs and even large sofas at Edgar, but then she'd have been the one to clean up the mess, of course, picking through broadloom, hunting down tiny sparklings of glass.

David has managed to get himself into his shirt, and to get it buttoned and tucked into his pants. He's on his way, it appears.

"I'm on the bar again at noon tomorrow." He runs a finger along her thigh, and she learns she is not a woman who necessarily enjoys afterward the gestures that gave pleasure before.

"Don't you have a girlfriend?"

He flinches, his face shutting the way Edgar's sometimes used to. "Well, yeah. But I don't see what that has to do with you and me."

Well, yeah, Gwen can't either. Isn't it odd, though, that people who feel free with intimate acts are uneasy with intimate information? That inquiring about a girlfriend was simply too personal?

"Why are you laughing?" he asks, more puzzled than offended.

"What the fuck are you laughing at," Edgar demanded ten days ago, thoroughly offended, too steamed to be puzzled.

"I'm sorry," she says. "I'm not laughing, I'm really pleased we ran into each other." Which is true. He's only a boy, still fragile and easily damaged. "Perhaps we'll see each other again. But we both have lives to get on with, don't we?" Was this how Edgar felt, trying to explain with his fumbling words and flinging arms?

And is this situation not rather peculiar? Well, obviously; but what she means is, here is this not-unattractive young man, with ambitious, loving parents, one dead, one alive, and a promising future, a fully occupied present, and even a girlfriend, it seems. And here is Gwen, a not-unattractive but two-decades-older woman, who lives in this dreadful bland house, who has put on a few hip-and-thigh pounds recently, and who, most to the point, buried (or failed to show up to bury) her gruesomely deceased husband just a few hours ago. Does this not strike David as odd? Does he not wonder whether she's even sane to have lain here in the dark with a young stranger on such a day?

Doesn't any of this make him nervous?

She could be his mother. Although she still thinks that if she had been, she'd have nourished him better. It wouldn't be so easy to count the ribs and spiny knobs of any son of Gwen's. "We'll see." This is, she understands, what mothers often say when they really mean no.

Like children everywhere, he takes this as hopeful and positive, nods happily, leans down to give her a quick, light kiss. "I really gotta go. See you, okay?"

One last touch of her fingers to his thin, narrow chest. "Do you mind letting yourself out? Just push the button on the doorknob and it'll lock itself behind you." Without lights, he stumbles briefly on the stairs, but then she hears the door shutting behind him and, moments later, his old car coughing.

What will the neighbours think?

Probably it's all safely beyond their imaginings.

Gwen lies back, hands folded behind her head. She can feel small bruises making themselves known on the insides of her thighs, where his hipbones ground into her. She stretches her heels down, her toes up, feels a tightening ripple along her body.

That's two men she's said goodbye to today. This may be some kind of record.

What on earth is happening to her?

But imagine if all her impulses turn out to have such charming results. Imagine if she had behaved properly, had dutifully climbed into the black sedan behind the hearse, had stood, head bowed, at the graveside, and had finally had to come home, alone, to desolate silence. Imagine if her eye hadn't had a chance to be caught by the Gully's sign, with its promise of being a good place to drink.

Imagine, then, all the events and small turns she has missed because of not seeing, because of averting, because of a habit of resisting. And now, already, she is forty-two! Oh Edgar, is this what you suddenly felt? Did knowing you'd missed so many invisible possibilities make your legs kick up, your hands fling about in the air? Was your aim not cruelty or resentment or anger, did it have only to do with longing for the impulsive, mysterious act?

If so, Gwen can see how invisible she would have become. She would have been a speck in the corner of his vision, to be dealt with swiftly and surgically, in the sole interest of achieving clarity. "Even so, Edgar, it was unkind and cowardly, not to put more effort into explaining," she says aloud. "Not nice at all, leaving me to start over from scratch with no warning." She thinks he might have helped, or been instructive. Might even have given some honour to their twenty years. But perhaps he felt he had no time to spare.

As indeed, it turned out, he didn't.

This mattress with its careless sheets is soft from years of their bodies. They've embraced, lain apart, argued bitterly, slept deeply. They've snored and touched hands in the night and crawled out, eagerly or grumpily, for years of early mornings. And now a young, total stranger to them both has shaken it up. This *must* be similar to Edgar's experience. What a shame he didn't feel able to tell her about it.

What a bastard.

After twenty years, it may just be too difficult to broach new subjects.

If he supposed their marriage was oppressive and difficult to escape, he had no idea, did he? Because now, while she stretches herself across their soft mattress, with all her soft, delighted flesh alive, there he is boxed up in the hardest of woods, with only a small satin pillow for comfort, and all around him hard-packed earth settling and muffling and weighing him down. Now, that's oppression. That's something truly difficult to escape.

Oh, poor Edgar. She finds she is weeping again, quietly and helplessly, like this afternoon, not with the terrible heaving of a few weeks ago. Poor Edgar, no longer alive, like Gwen, or young, like David; no longer hopeful, with all his dreams ahead; no longer burning with visions and desires (although she doesn't believe he ever actually burned). No longer tender, even, or especially kind. No longer anything.

So much lost.

Something of David continues to hover: something alive, that alters the air, displacing staleness with a slight freshness that has little, actually, to do with David himself. Gwen sits up, tosses her legs over her side of the bed as she has done hundreds and thousands of times. Oh. She forgot she was naked.

With darkness has come a small chill. She walks, toes alert to beige broadloom, to the walk-in closet across the room. Hanging from two hooks on the back of its door used to be two robes: Edgar's a blue-and-green tartan, Gwen's a peachy cotton. These little changes can still leap out and startle her.

She goes downstairs, moving easily through the darkness, her body familiar with every depth and angle of the place. In the kitchen, she flicks on lights and puts on the kettle for tea. Even as a child, she drank tea after dinner with Flo and her father. Every family has rituals. Her and Edgar's family would have had rituals, too, although she can't quite picture what they might have been.

The least she can do for him tonight, after such an eventful day and long acquaintance, is sit up with him and drink her tea. She can at least keep watch one last time: over him in his silent, heavy darkness; over herself in her bright, warm kitchen.

Her whole bright, warm house. After a while, she gets up and wanders from room to room, upstairs and down, turning on every light in the place. Music, too: Beach Boys, why not? She still owes Edgar, however he failed, and he did certainly fail, some kind of tribute. Some full, proper attention to another human, if not a good, exceptional or especially worthy one.

It's hard to tell if all this light and sound make the place feel more empty or less.

Edgar may have made his various departures with insufficient grace, but if Gwen also falls short it's not, at the moment, intentional; nor is it bitter. This may be David's gift.

David himself was a gift: an unexpected, temporary passion, a nod to the mysterious impulse in which Edgar, too, must have discovered some faith. "Is this what you meant, Edgar?" she asks. "Is that what you were trying to tell me?"

If so, she has much to discover, a good deal to learn. Much, also, to discard. What are all these framed prints on the walls, the sofa, the chairs, the dining-room table, the candles, the carpets, what is this whole ridiculous house?

This ridiculous house is warm at any rate. And bright, and fairly safe. This is a good deal more than can be said for Edgar's situation. Not what either of them would have chosen. "But there you are, I guess. Poor you, Edgar, but as you would say yourself, that's life, that's that."

three

eaving Gwen after all that bedside chatter-chatter, making his way down the stairs in the dark, letting himself out the door, remembering to push the button to lock it behind him, getting into his old green clunker and driving away, David feels—what? Frenzied, really, and in a confused, wholly new way: ecstatic with surprised, stupendous pleasure, terrified he's going to be late, and very worried that he may have made another mistake. At least that he may be responsible for another occasion of his father's grief, not to mention his own.

It doesn't feel like a mistake—quite the opposite—but that's no gauge or guide. David's difficulty, as he has recently been encouraged to realize, is seeing *beforehand* how much trouble some action might result in. It's easy enough afterwards, although not always immediately afterwards, but his father can talk and talk, and so can Fink the shrink, and right then, maybe he gets it, but in the moment, at the sweet silky touch of temptation, the beckoning gesture of desire, he tends to forget.

What just happened with Gwen, that tipsy, delicious, middle-aged, enticing new widow, doesn't fall into any of his previously known, troublesome categories, however, so driving away, he can't judge its potential. He doesn't even know if he should discuss it with Fink, if it's one of those things—"issues," as Fink calls them—that require analysis. Sometimes Fink fixes on some little detail that David wouldn't dream was important and worries away at it like a terrier with a pant leg in its teeth.

And sometimes David arrives with some piece of information, a remembered picture, some portion of his history, that he could swear should be significant, and drops it like a bone on Fink's desk, and it's practically ignored. Dismissed with a little wave of inconsequence.

No wonder David still has some trouble judging his actions, much less controlling them. He can never feel there's more than a thin surface of solid ground under his feet.

David is not on his way to a study group. He has no paper to turn in. He is not a law student, or a student of anything else. His grandfather did buy Gully's when David's mother and father got married, and it is true that his mother is dead, and that he grew up over the bar. For that matter, it's true that he used to sneak downstairs and make himself small bits of change piping childish songs to the customers.

The other true thing he told Gwen is that he is twenty-three. He did not mention that, until this amazing situation arose today, in which her fucked-upness and his own encountered each other and meshed, he was a virgin. Never slept with a woman, made love. Never been close.

That was such a totally weird thing, and such a secret, such a darkness not to be admitted, ever, to anyone under any circumstance no matter what—and now, thank God, it's over. And so incredibly easily, without effort or intention on his part; something that came about as magically and unaccountably as other but far more dire and unpleasant events have also occurred.

What a relief! What joy, the small achiness of certain muscles, the unaccustomed slight soreness of his dick bringing back sensations and pictures, keeping him warm and indulged and also shivering with luxurious remembrance.

He doubts Gwen could tell. He thinks, in fact, that he did quite well. He could talk to her, beforehand at least, about his imagined hopes and ambitions nearly as smoothly as he speaks truer matters within his own head but can almost never say out loud. Maybe that's because beforehand, she seemed old to him, and impossible. And he's proud he considered the neighbours, and then got himself and Gwen off that scratchy broadloom and upstairs fairly gracefully; that he took time for a quick shower; that he troubled to inquire about her preferences. These would all be signs of an experienced lover, he assumes, no overeager, overhasty man-child.

He can scarcely believe how easy it was: that she only had to make one unmistakable gesture, and he was so startled that his terrors just flew out that great, sunny living-room window.

He does wonder why her unmistakable gesture should have had so different an outcome from his own not dissimilar gestures. Because she's a woman and can get away with it? Because she took his hands and made him touch, while he has never performed, never considered, such a bold act?

He hopes his other small, impulsive crime—surely small—doesn't undo her pleasure. Or trigger worse results he failed to consider at the time and now cannot predict.

Where he's going now is not to a law school study group, but to his appointment with Dr. Fink, who has office hours Tuesday evenings so he can take Wednesdays off. David doesn't know a lot about the doctor's other patients, but he imagines Fink's job is not unlike working the bar: you listen and listen and sometimes, like today, it gets really interesting, and other times you can hardly stand another word and wish people would just shut up and get on with things.

By and large, he expects Fink earns his Wednesdays off. Still, these Tuesday night sessions are inconvenient. Tonight's is much more, it's nearly enraging. David would have loved, loved, to have stayed with Gwen, watching her sleeping with the face of a child, stroking and touching her awake, seeing if one success would lead to another. Instead he drifted off and woke in the dark in a panic, very scared he'd screwed up and was late.

Is Gwen's skin smellable on his? Dr. Fink affects a pipe, fitting David's and evidently his own image of an important shrink, but if he can still detect some hovering sexual scent, he'll be all over David. He'll want to know every detail and movement; not for salacious reasons, probably, or out of voyeurism, but to discern any aspect of the event that could cause a problem. David, with his apparently deteriorating ability to assess his own acts, doesn't feel like being surprised by some awful outcome Fink might, nodding and chewing his pipe stem, take it upon himself to predict.

It feels far too strenuous, an hour of dodging and fencing with Fink. What David would deeply prefer, if he can't be with Gwen, would be a retreat to the darkness of his own room, alone above Gully's, where he could replay and replay the wondrous events of a miraculous day. Even for someone who has spent many hours dreaming of it, growing more and more paralysed by fear and desire, the reality was astonishing. The difference between jerking off and stroking and nestling inside the humid warmth of a woman—who knew? And yet, however startled he was by this extraordinary, unfamiliar pleasure, he held back, held off, restrained himself as long and carefully as he possibly could.

He's proud of that, and expects Gwen appreciated it.

If he described that restraint, and the pleasure it resulted in, and his pride, would Fink be pleased? Would he lean forward, little crinkles around his unreadable eyes, and say, "Well done, David. Now let's work with that, shall we?"

He doesn't give praise very often, but he's often looking for something to work with. Although his interests can be offbeat, not always obvious.

David might also then confess to stealing the bedside photograph of Gwen's dead husband, and how could he possibly explain that? An actual crime, however small, and a new kind he has never committed before. What does he want with it, now staring up from the seat beside him? First, flushed and satisfied, he watched Gwen fall asleep, then his eyes began to explore. And what was that small golden frame doing tipped on its face on the table beside him? Reaching out, he carefully, silently set it upright and saw a man staring back, middle-aged, not bad-looking, blue-eyed, not smiling. So unremarkable he struck David as entirely inscrutable, a source of mystery and puzzlement. A man who could only be Gwen's crushed husband, whose fate led, in semi-direct fashion, to David's own: lying beside this man's sleeping wife. Widow.

David leaned carefully over the side of the bed to push the small portrait into his left sneaker.

Did Gwen notice, when he was leaving, that he was carrying his shoes, not yet wearing them? Will she notice that the portrait is gone? Why would she have kept it there, but turned face down? Perhaps she won't see that it's missing until many more people have been in and out of the house, and none of this will be traceable to David.

What got into him? He has not stolen before. Still, glancing down, he finds the portrait retains its mysterious, overwhelming appeal.

Are not mysterious, overwhelming appeals the cause of David's troubles, though?

David and Dr. Fink have these unmissable Tuesday night appointments because they're a condition of David's probation. They've been going on once a week for six months and will run for another six. David is almost getting used to the way Fink will sneak up on him, circle around him, dart at him from unexpected directions, but sometimes he still feels doomed by the suspense. When will Fink finally go for the throat, clamp down with those protruding incisors?

The probation officer, Keith Miller, with whom David checks in once a month, goes directly to the bone, perhaps because their contacts are brief and, comparatively, far more impersonal. "So Dave," he likes to ask, "you keeping 'er zipped okay? No problems with drafts in your pants?" One day, David's going to haul off and smash Keith Miller, just for that jocularity, for treating him lightly. At least Fink appears to take him seriously, which at least makes him feel as if Fink considers him *worth* treating seriously.

Only none of them, not Fink or Keith Miller, or David's father, or the police, or the several lawyers and judges involved so far, nor David himself, can put their finger on how to fix whatever it is about David that needs fixing.

He cannot properly explain, even to himself, what it is that happens when he sees somebody, a woman, and there's something about her, about how she's moving or the way her hair shifts, or how her legs look or her arms swing or her hips sway—some damn thing—that tweaks some deep part of his attention, so that suddenly his fingers are operating all on their own, working away at his pants, pulling his dick out, and boom, somebody gets upset.

This first happened when he was seventeen, and it came out of the blue. It no longer exactly startles David; he is more familiar now with the pleasure, and also with some of the unhappy outcomes.

The pleasure is in the soft exposure to the air, the gentle contact between his tender, yearning dick and a little breeze, some warmth, a small outing that would be perfectly quiet and unobtrusive and harmless, left to itself.

Often enough, it is left to itself. Women walk past, looking away. Sometimes they gasp, or stare at him hard. The trouble is when they get really upset. One started to cry, which made him feel bad, but some of the others have turned ugly. Nobody seems to understand that he means no harm, no harm whatever. He wouldn't hurt a soul, truly, but nevertheless, unlike some seriously dangerous people, he's been arrested three times. Last time it was when two really nice-looking girls, well, women, about his own age, stopped dead in front of him, and one said, "You little fucker," and the two of them grabbed him, and it turned out they were stronger and far nastier than they looked. He tried to run, but they hung on, and then a cop came along, and that was it for him.

"What? What?" David cried, looking innocently from one face to another. He couldn't any longer imagine what it was about either of these women that caused that ping that starts in his brain before travelling lower, a sweet current of desire; certainly he didn't feel it now. "I don't know what they're talking about. I was just walking past, minding my own business. I think they must be crazy." Of course once the cops checked him out, he was screwed.

He isn't like Gwen, he doesn't insist that they touch, he doesn't go sticking himself right in their faces, he doesn't pull their hands onto him. He doesn't even want that; has never dreamed of it; wouldn't, he thinks, have cared at all to be so close. Although that's something he might now reconsider.

What is he thinking? He mustn't let an idea, a picture like that even begin to leak and seep into his head. He has enough trouble with leaking ideas, seeping pictures. He knows perfectly well, even if he doesn't always quite comprehend, that all the warnings he's heard must be true.

His other trouble, which is possibly even more serious, or difficult to cure, is his capacity, his desire, his *urgency* for lies, even random, unnecessary ones. Like, he probably didn't need to tell Gwen he was a law student, she seemed content enough thinking he tended bar, although it's also true she looked at him differently after he told her. A lucky choice, in a way, what with her dead husband being a lawyer.

A train! Man, that must have been an awful way to go. Unless she was making up a dramatic tale to get David's attention, compassion, whatever struck her as desirable at the moment. He's done that sort of thing himself, becoming some more coherent, interesting, dramatic person for just a few minutes. It works, too, although not, before, with women. Would Gwen, for instance, have asked him into her house, or bared her breasts and then the rest of her, if she didn't think he was on his way to some big deal career?

For a while today, he almost persuaded himself that he is driven to the practice of law; that his great ambition is to serve the poor, the downtrodden, the helpless—"like," as he said to

Gwen in her living room, "the guys who come into my dad's bar, that get into these nickel-dime problems that turn into big ones just because there's nobody'll help them before it gets out of hand. The people who get screwed altogether, that's why I'm going to law school, for them." He felt, momentarily, like a hero of the class wars: a revolutionary, or a saint. He felt *big*, and really liked the intent, approving way he felt her looking at him. He thought she would be bound to compare him to her husband and find him, David, far more noble.

He wouldn't mind being a lawyer, actually, although it would be difficult, given his history. Besides the criminal record, he didn't quite finish high school, although he doesn't think, himself, that should matter so much since he learns a lot on his own. He's good with a story, and, until circumstances arise that reveal his deceptions, feels fairly persuasive. Of course sometimes, like with cops, it doesn't work so well, and people like Fink actively lean towards being unpersuadable, and his father any more is sceptical at best.

One great thing about David's mum was her willingness to believe. Her faith was unalterably in his innocence, and also in the vast possibilities of having something you did misunderstood, mistaken for telling a lie or doing a bad thing. He thinks, trusts, hopes that when she died, she still believed.

She died after the first time he was arrested but before the trial, and at the time, even though she was rail-thin and weak, she raised herself up in bed, on fire with indignation and cancer, and cried, "That evil, evil girl. How could she do such a thing? Doesn't she know the trouble she's causing? Doesn't she care? My poor boy!"

If she'd been well, none of it would have happened. Not that he wouldn't most likely still have had those unaccountable urges, and he never feels at the time that he has much choice about acting on them; but she would have rescued him. She always rescued him, when it was within her means, from more minor, childish difficulties, like schoolyard fights or unsympathetic teachers. Her purity of faith would have freed him from this, too.

His dad is loyal, but his loyalty takes a different form, which doesn't end in David being exactly rescued. It ends with a lot of money to the lawyer, and humiliating moments in courtrooms, and dangerous ones in jail, and frustrating Tuesday evenings pissed away with Fink. The worst thing David's dad ever said to him was, "Thank God your mother is gone. All this would have killed her."

That was during a recess in David's first trial, actually his only real trial since that time he refused to plead guilty, not believing he truly was, in some way. Maybe this small event had occurred, this moment of releasing, unleashing his dick, but it was never going to *cause* anything. It astonished him how the woman talked about him when she testified; she was shaking and her voice trembled, she was so angry. There was nothing about her now that he could see that stirred any impulses, but maybe it wasn't just a matter of her mood, but that in the courtroom she wasn't walking towards him. It must have been something about the way she moved before, out on the street; it generally seems to be.

Her attitude was also far different from how it was when it happened. Then, she'd screamed. David couldn't believe that, either. He thinks his mouth must have fallen open, he was so startled. She was scared, and she screamed! And of course since a scream gets attention, it was the first time he got caught.

Something happened between then and the courtroom that got her mad, he guessed. "I thought it was *disgusting*," she testified, which David felt a flash of anger about, because his dick was not disgusting, for God's sake, but then she was going on, "that it's not even possible to walk down a street in broad daylight without some punk exposing himself."

Punk! But David's lawyer said her anger was good; that it would have been worse if she'd cried, because that would have made the judge want to punish David more for getting her so upset. "But a judge doesn't like an angry woman any more than anybody else does." His lawyer grinned. That wouldn't get David off, though. His lawyer didn't believe in David's innocence at all. "All we can do is point out every mitigating circumstance we can think of, and hope for the best." He patted David's father's shoulder, but not David's.

What he told the judge was that, at the time of the "offence," David's mother had been dying, and now she was dead. "My client," he said, "was seriously troubled by these tragic circumstances, and briefly behaved out of character."

David spent three long days, and two much longer nights, in jail that time, and the lawyer said he got off easy. David's dad seemed to agree. "Jesus," he said to the lawyer, "thank you." Later, when David was home again, his dad grabbed his shoulders and shook him and said, "Do not ever, ever do such a thing again. If there's any more trouble, you'll be on your own, I will not lift a finger for you."

He did, of course. David's dad would never abandon him. The next time, though, he got something worse than angry, which was sad. He even got tears in his eyes, and his shoulders slumped, and he hardly spoke, just shook his head. But then right away he called the lawyer.

"Why do you do this?" his dad asked. "Tell me what it is."

But what words could define a certain movement, a shape, the smallest of gestures, that couldn't be predicted but happened randomly, a kind of magic? Weeks might go by, and David could see hundreds of women and feel nothing. Well, not necessarily nothing; like any guy he might note to himself, "pretty," or "great legs," but nothing impelling any irresistible action.

And where for that matter were words to define irresistibility? That his dick wanted air, demanded exposure, insisted on making its own, independent response; that it briefly, and after all only occasionally, commanded its own release and there was no stopping it. Really, none at all. "Hey there," it insisted. "Hello. Here I am. Look at me."

No one, not his father, the lawyer, the court, the shrink—no one would comprehend that, or be persuaded.

Gwen didn't think his dick was repulsive. She even reached for it herself. Gwen didn't see him as a punk. She demonstrated a pure kind of belief, taking him straight to her bed. What could be more trusting, more faithful?

But now he has stolen from her. Again, he glances down at her husband's portrait. Why did he do that?

The second time he got arrested, the lawyer said, "You better plead guilty. We got no hooks this time." He meant, no recently dead mother. "And this time you have a record. There's no way in the world to get lucky again." As if he had been lucky before.

The third time, the lawyer sighed and said, "Well, all we got going for us now is that you're not escalating, you're not doing anything worse than you've already done." David got two months, which turned out, the way the system works, to be one, and one year on probation after that, and a requirement that he see a shrink for the term of the probation. Which is why he's stuck with Fink, and vice versa, for another six months.

Until tonight, he has seen no reason why irresistibility won't overwhelm him again, at any moment, and then it's the luck of the draw whether the woman is somebody who walks on or somebody who makes a big fuss, and either he stays free or goes back for what his lawyer said would be "a big one, next time."

But maybe what happened today changes things?

What if, say, Gwen doesn't notice anything missing? What if she thinks about him a lot, and when she returns tomorrow to pick up her car she picks David up, too, and back they go to her house. Again and again, until whatever the trouble is gets worn, through diversion or exhaustion, right out of his system? What if he's out on a street and sees a woman slip-sliding towards him with whatever that sway is, or that toss of the hair, or swing of the arms, and nothing whatever goes off inside him, or ever gets triggered again? What if his dick is content to stay right where it ought to be?

Would that mean he's cured, or that he has toppled into something more dangerous; worse in the long run?

Also, how would he keep her believing he's a student of law, just like her husband was once? Until now, his lies haven't needed sustaining for long. He began with his mother and practised on her, but naturally didn't try to fool her about the basic facts of his life, which she already knew, probably better than he did. He lied about lost report cards, dogs that chased him, stomach aches so bad she took him to a doctor, who would find nothing wrong, but would urge bed rest in case— but honestly, it felt like performing his own plays: he tried out his entertainments and she fell happily into every word. As a mother and as an audience, she was a dream.

He told something like that to Fink in one of their early sessions, but it turned out to be one of the things Fink didn't seem to find significant. This surprised David. He thought psychiatrists were supposed to be keen for connections between childhood behaviours, parental relations and adult outcomes. That's why he brought it up. Not that he wanted his mother dragged into this, but on the other hand, he thought Fink would be gratified. "Mmhmm," Fink said.

"Certainly," he told David at the start of their sessions, "we need to identify possible sources of your difficulties, but we'll also want to assess your strengths and come up with some ideas of how you can develop them to your best advantage. Instead of focussing on deficits, or things you don't have."

Not so easy. Not all that promising, being a self-educated, twenty-three-year-old part-time bartender employed by his father, with what David views as a minor criminal record, but a criminal record just the same. His strengths, or at any rate the parts of him that feel strongest, are that overwhelming impulse, which so far has had unfortunate outcomes and he really doubts even Fink could come up with a positive use for it; and his small skill with homemade dramas that liven things up without, for the most part, doing much harm.

Might that have an undiscerned purpose? Acting, perhaps? Could he take that "personal deficit," which is the category into which Fink puts his lying, and transform it into an extraordinary, enhancing gift? Imagine spinning stories, not to individual humans, like Gwen, or Fink, or his dad or the cops, but up on a stage, or in front of cameras, all eyes admiring, never sorrowful or contemptuous. "He captures," he might read about himself, "the essence and vitality of every character and tale to which he lends his considerable talents."

Men would admire him, women adore him.

Great liars, great actors, possess electric appeals. So he would become irresistible himself, not merely have irresistible impulses.

Pulling into the parking lot behind Fink's office building, David is tremendously excited by these pictures in his head. Could that outrageously delicious release of himself inside a place that's so warm and protective and soft have released so much else, too? Ideas, their spermy tails wriggling, are struggling and swimming upstream in his head. Skipping the elevator, he leaps to the third floor by the staircase, double-stepping all the way up.

He's not a virgin! His body, his whole life, have been changed! In the space of a day!

By the time he reaches Fink's office door, which is a heavy dark wood, with a brass nameplate, and scars and dents where maybe patients tormented beyond reason by Fink's circling, tail-twitching-in-the-high-grass hunt for their psyches have tried to cause some retaliatory damage, by the time he's pulling down on the brass-plated handle and pushing the door open, David has decided to keep his news, all his news, to himself. Because it's fresh and might spoil in the telling; and because, once launched on a confessional, a set of revelations and dreams, where could he stop?

When a client sits down in the waiting room, which David does because the red light is on over the door of Fink's private office, which means somebody's in there, there's a pastel-patterned loveseat, and a side table with magazines, and a dark table kind of thing across the way that Fink calls a credenza, with spikes of dried flowers sticking up in an unsettling sort of arrangement on top of it. The room's supposed to be relaxing, Fink told David and his father at David's first appointment, when his father came with him, probably to make sure he showed up, and also in case Fink wanted him to answer any questions, which apparently he did not.

For the first time since he's been coming here, David feels something attractive about this little room, familiar and nice. But of course: it resembles Gwen's living room, with its soft colours, soft furniture. Soft flesh, as it turned out.

He can imagine comfortably passing his evenings in a big, plushy space like her living room, watching TV or looking out the window into the darkness or sitting on the sofa with his feet on the coffee table, reading or eating popcorn or jerking off. No, not jerking off. Turning to the woman beside him. Who is no longer impossible. Now that he can be touched, and touch.

"Happy thoughts, David?" Shit, Fink's other patient must have left and Fink, peering into the waiting room, has caught him smiling. "Did something good happen today? Come on in and tell me about it."

Fink's patients don't run into each other because there's a back way down, which goes out into the parking lot. David hasn't decided how much he cares if people know he's seeing a shrink. He figures maybe if they didn't know why, it'd make him seem sensitive, or intriguing. Great people and geniuses see shrinks for their various torments, it's not only fuck-ups and geeks. Some anguish is normal, and great anguish can sometimes be put to grand uses.

Maybe medium anguish made Fink what he is. His name, David thinks, could hardly be more difficult to live with. What torments and taunts he must have endured—although psychiatry might have been a bad move, Fink the shrink coming so lightly to the tongue.

It's hard to know if he's generally any good at his job, but David thinks that in his own case, Fink misses the boat. "The key to adult relationships," he has told David with regard, mainly, to David's blunderings, "is a mutual level of regard and respect. Obviously this is impossible if one person sees the other as an object, or as someone who doesn't exist independently. Or also if one person feels as if that's how he or she is seen."

He tends to speak to David slowly, as if David's a bit slow, or hard of hearing, or very young. David wants to tell him how clear this makes it that Fink regards him as an object, and lacks respect and regard for him; and that he is not alone in that. It's probation officers, too—"Look, you little asshole," said Keith Miller, making some point about the risks of exposure, or the rights of women to walk the streets, as if David denies that— and lawyers who talk over your head, as if you're not there, or as if you're too contemptible to bother with, and parents who want this, insist on that, deny permission for the other thing, and say both cruel and loving words.

Power makes all the difference: Keith Miller gets to call David an asshole, and Fink gets to talk to him in little words and simple concepts like a child, because they have power over him. Even his father can say or do to him what he wants, and all David can do is trust that his intentions aren't malevolent, which they aren't.

All those people see David as an object, whether of discipline, or improvement, or love. And feel free to yammer on at him and insult him.

Fink's patients sit in a maroon leather chair, with solid arms and little brass tacks hammered all around the seat and back, in front of Fink's desk. Fink himself sits in a rolling swivel chair behind his desk, sometimes leaning back, sometimes forward, sometimes swinging from side to side slowly and rhythmically, like he's trying hypnosis.

Tonight David also sees Gwen, swinging on the bar stool, looking brightly around a dark Gully's.

Did she see him as an object? He knows she looked at him one way when he was a bartender, somewhat differently when he told her he was a law student, and a new way altogether when she placed his hands on her breasts. He isn't sure how he sees her, either, but is fairly certain that if he described their relationship, which he is not going to do, Fink would not call it equal, healthy, adult.

It's something, though.

"So, David," Fink asks, leaning back, smiling invitingly, seductively. "Did something make you happy today? You're a good-looking young man when you smile, you know that?"

Is he? Has he grown into features that have always seemed to him sharp, peaky and narrow? What is "happy"?

He shrugs. "Not really."

"Then what were you smiling at?"

Nobody would call Fink good-looking; although he must be married, there's a framed picture of dad-mum-two-kids-a-dog behind him on his bookshelves, turned sideways so patients can't see their faces, just figures. Is the ordinariness of dad-mum-two-kids-a-dog relaxing after listening all day to hard luck and bad feelings, or maddening? Is it heartening after a day (or a Tuesday evening) in this office to retreat to embraces and barks and cries of "Oh good, Daddy's here"? Or does he go home to more of the same: tormented hearts displayed in bouts of weeping, hurled dishes, slammed and dented doors?

Actually it's unfair to say Fink is not good-looking; like the family photograph, he keeps himself somewhat hidden, with large black-rimmed glasses, for one thing, and a grey-black mask of moustache and beard that leaves only a little flesh open to air and light. The real shapes of important features—chin and lips, for instance—are impossible to discern behind all that.

"David? What did you do today?"

"Worked the bar. Drove around." Still, there's fifty minutes to kill. David brightens. "But I had a real narrow escape, driving. Almost got killed. I guess that's why I was smiling, because I didn't. But man, it was close."

Fink's eyes lose some of their lively interest, which anyway David assumes was false, and stops shifting in his chair. He folds his hands in his lap, says quietly, neutrally, "Yes?"

"Yeah. I was running around for my dad, picking up stuff for the bar before my afternoon shift, and, you know, I guess I kind of had the radio turned up and the sun's shining and I'm kind of boogying because it's a nice day and I feel pretty good, and then boom!"

He pauses, so Fink has to ask, "Boom?"

"Yeah, all of a sudden the car coughs out on me and drifts into a stall, and I'm sitting there turning the key and turning the key and there's nothing, not a thing." David is talking faster now, and louder, and moving his hands with enthusiasm, excitement. "So I hear cars honking, and I figure people are mad because I'm blocking the road, but then I finally look around, and shit!" He pauses again.

"Yes?" Dr. Fink sounds too dispassionate; this is exactly the sort of thing that's so irritating about him, and must have caused other patients to kick at his door.

"I see I'm on a railway track, and the car's stopped right across it. And besides the radio" (wait, if all the power was gone, would it still be playing? Too late, the words have been said) "and the car horns, I hear this one huge sound off to my right and Jesus, I look over and it's a train! A big freight, not right close but not very far away, either.

"So for a couple of seconds I'm just kind of frozen, I can't get myself moving, and then I think, for Christ's sake get out of here, but I'm fucked because now I can't deal with the seatbelt, my hands are sweating and they're slipping on the catch, but then I'm finally out the door and man, the train's really close, there's no way it's going to stop, and that horn's just howling and people are screaming."

"My goodness."

Asshole.

The thing is, David *feels* the terror, the urgency and horror. His blood *does* alternately freeze and boil at the desperate movements, the panicking sounds, the potential end of it all. He feels the sweat on his palms, on his back, between his thighs and toes.

He is making this true, and "My goodness" is all this asshole can say?

"But you know? Sometimes people are really brave and good." It's necessary to say this, since Fink probably doesn't see a lot of human virtue. "I'm out of the car, and I almost trip on the track, I almost fall down, but the car, it's in my mind I have to save it, too, it's all I've got, and I'm racing to the back and I start to push and I don't know what I'm thinking except the car is gonna be wrecked if I can't get it out of there, and all of a sudden there's two big guys beside me, helping push. Which makes it easy, it's across and on the other side in a couple of seconds.

"Just in time because the train screams past, its brakes are slammed on but it can't get stopped till it's gone way beyond us. The three of us are standing there wiping off sweat and, well, you can imagine."

"Yes, indeed," Fink says, but it seems impossible that he can imagine much of anything. Has he, from listening to grief and pain after grief and pain, day after day, year after year, simply shut himself off, made himself somehow immune?

Does he have any faith whatever in cures any more? Did he ever?

"It took ages before I stopped shaking." David shakes his head now, still astonished by the experience. "I could have been dead, you know? I'm alive by a whisker. It makes you think, it really does. So I'd have to say, it's been a pretty good day."

"It certainly sounds like it. And your car?"

"What?"

"Why did it stall, did you find out what was wrong with it?"

David squints slightly at Fink; a meeting of suspicious, narrowed eyes.

"The garage said some wire fell loose all of a sudden. I'm getting a real tune-up while they're fixing it. I never want to go through something like that again."

"How did you get it to a garage?"

"Towed. Been busing it since."

Shit. The car's in the parking lot, three floors below where they're sitting. Does Fink have ways of knowing that? What if he's already seen it? What if he walked his last patient out to the parking lot; not something he's ever done with David, but you never know, people do one thing with one person, something entirely different with someone else. David's usually a lot sharper than this. Getting laid, making love, whatever, has fogged up his head, maybe.

"So you can see why I'd be smiling." He finds himself looking at Fink almost pleadingly; but the thing is, the story nearly is true. Something like that must be what happened to Gwen's husband, although as she told it (if it wasn't a story), it was at night, and the train was a passenger not a freight, and whatever caused his car to be stopped on the tracks, he didn't get out of it in time. What a freaky few minutes.

David almost knows how frightful they must have been, because he almost just endured them himself.

Now there are two vital sensations Gwen's husband experienced in his life that David's experienced, too.

Fink is leaning back in his chair again, rocking slightly, holding a yellow pencil to his lips, looking at David as if he's trying to decide something. David looks steadily back. Unwavering looks are essential to the telling of stories.

"Why do you do that, David?" Fink's tone is gentle, calm, and strikes David therefore as ominous.

"What?"

"Why do you think you have to tell people—me—things that aren't true?"

Fuck.

Why does David tell stories? Lots of reasons. To add, to be generous, to make something where nothing existed. Some people make buildings, some people make cars. They fill up empty spaces. He could say any of that but, "Why do you wear a beard?" he asks instead.

"I beg your pardon?" Bushy dark eyebrows, like some old Russian premier's, lift daintily.

"Why all that hair on your face?"

"I don't know what you mean. That has nothing to do with my question."

"It might, though."

Creases appear in Fink's bulky forehead. "You're behaving very strangely tonight, David."

He's behaving more boldly, anyway, can feel a kind of courage he might not have had, say, yesterday. "I'm in the right place then, aren't I? For being strange?" Previously, David has been mute, sulky or co-operative. He has told lies, exaggerations and several times truths, as best he can. Although Fink has occasionally tossed words his way like grenades, he hasn't tossed any back. Now he stares Fink straight in the eye. What can Fink do?

What can Fink do? He can declare David hopeless, make him vulnerable to Keith Miller, lawyers, the courts, the whole hassle. That's his power. It's why David couldn't for a moment consider staying with Gwen tonight. David's eyes drop. He hears Fink exhale softly but in a big way, as if he's been holding his breath.

"Let's go back: what do you think makes you want to tell people lies?"

"What makes you think they're lies? Why can't you believe me?"

Fink rocks back and forth, considering. "Fair question. That train story, you told it pretty convincingly, and I can't say quite what gave it away; maybe it just sounded too unlikely?"

Jesus, a car stalling on railway tracks sounds "unlikely" to a guy who hears truly weird shit from cons far more ferocious than David? This is a guy who makes house calls to prisons, for Christ's sake.

"It's not unlikely, it's true," David says. Fink gives a tiny shake of his head. "It *is* true, except the ending. I met somebody today and that exact thing happened to her husband. Except he got killed. He didn't make it out of his car. So I don't know why you think I made it up, or it couldn't happen, because it did."

"But not to you. Why did you pretend? Are you pretending when you tell things like that?"

"I'm ... imagining." This is hard. "It's a way of feeling, do you know what I mean?" That's odd. It's the truth. Where did it come from—not the truth, but saying it? He got cocky, and now he's given Fink a hook, an edge. He regards Fink anxiously. Did he notice? Of course he did, he isn't stupid.

"That's really interesting, David." He sounds cautious. "The idea of imagining as a way of feeling. Does it work?"

A strange question. It's David's turn to be puzzled. "It's what you do, isn't it? Imagine how other people feel? I mean, imagine *hard*? Don't you have to do that?" As if it's a gift and a professional requisite, not a bad habit.

Fink nods judiciously. "Within limits, yes. Part of my work is certainly concentrating on motivations, trying to understand how other people see what they do. Not necessarily to feel it myself, though. That might be going too far."

"Why?"

"Well, David," he sounds surprised, "because for one thing, what other people feel may not be very healthy or desirable. But also, you know, we each have to be aware of our essential core. Our own being. We can't go around looking through other people's eyes, we have to find our own visions. Those are the ones we have to learn to see clearly."

"Can't you do both?"

"Wouldn't that be confusing?"

Well, yeah. Obviously. Maybe Fink isn't as smart as David's given him credit for. He doesn't see you can be inside and outside yourself at the same time? He doesn't know about having one life all the time, but with ideas and pictures of other lives running like films or TV shows, only more gripping and real, in your head?

Like, just sitting here David's almost been in a train wreck, has almost touched the very last experience of somebody he's almost close to. He feels attached to Gwen's husband now, as if they, too, have been intimate. It's more than a photograph down there in the car. These are amazing circles, not mere lies as Fink seems to think.

"What we should be aiming for here, David, is for you to fit into yourself better. To feel more familiar and comfortable with yourself. Then you'll be able to stop feeling such a need to, oh, adopt other events as your own. I don't mean it's easy, but what you've been saying about feeling and imagining gives us a very good jumping-off place, and we can go on to deal with, maybe, how you can learn to feel that strongly and intelligently about your own events instead of other people's, or ones you make up. What do you think?"

What David thinks is several things. One is that for a moment they were almost talking like two interested adults, but Fink put a quick end to that. Another is that if Fink got his way, David's pictures and plots would shrink down to nothing better or bigger than anyone else's: all those people who only see out of their own eyes.

"Do you ever think about flies?"

"I beg your pardon?"

"Flies. Any insect that sees in all directions at once? Wouldn't it be wild, all that stuff coming at you that your brain'd have to be putting together all the time? Like for flies, it's mainly so they can spot food or enemies, whatever, but if we could do that, it'd be a way bigger deal, a lot harder for our brains to keep figuring out, all the time we're awake, right?"

"I suppose." Fink looks lost. "What are you getting at?"

"Or, like, how come you're a psychiatrist? What did you want in the first place?" David himself is somewhat confused, but excited.

"I think, David, that you're trying to avoid having us deal with your issues. I understand curiosity about me, a client naturally has a desire to know who he's discussing intimate matters with. But however normal, it's not what we're here for. Perhaps I should have made it clearer that you need to think of me as a blank paper or an empty movie screen. I can guide your direction when we seem to be wandering off the track—that's what I'm doing now, as a matter of fact—and I can make suggestions if I think that's useful, so in that sense I'm not a piece of paper or an empty screen. But for the most part, I'm just a tool that can be useful in helping you achieve your authentic self and have a healthy and productive life. Who I am should not be your concern. You are your concern, and mine. All right?"

"Does it make you nervous?"

Fink sighs. "Does what make me nervous?"

"If I'm interested in how come you're a shrink, does it scare you? I mean," David feels close to an indefinable victory, "you back off when it's personal about you, so does that mean you're afraid to be—what do you call it?—authentic?"

"David." Fink's voice is sharp. "Stop it. This isn't a night school welding class, you're a young man with some serious problems and our job is to get you free of them so you can get on with a life that'll be more successful than it has been. Period. That is hard work, and we're not here to play around in the corners of it. Because if you don't get down to business, and that's your decision, I can't force you, you should know you're going to encounter a great many misfortunes, and someday you'll look back and see how many of them could have been avoided if you'd been willing to do the work now."

Wow. Strict. Like a vice-principal. Fink's piggy eyes are snapping.

"I don't see many young men like you, David. You've been given an opportunity most people don't get. I usually see men who are older, and who are in far deeper trouble and have far more terrible experiences to contend with, and that means not just actions they've taken, but also actions that have been taken against them. I don't mean it's too late, but at that point their work is much harder than yours could be. So I'm saying, do it now. It's a struggle, probably the hardest you've had, but save yourself a lot of grief. Save other people a lot of grief while you're at it."

Oh yeah? Fink and what army? But David does feel scolded and chastened.

"Now then," Fink continues, sounding strangely angry, or closer to an edge—is he really, or is this a technique, or a lie?— "if you're interested in imagining your way into the feelings of other people, try those women who are out shopping, or going for lunch, or to work, whatever they're doing, just going about their lives and suddenly there you are exposing yourself. Can't you find better ways to be noticed? Do you think you have some right to frighten them? Intrude on them? Harass them? Just because you have what you seem to think is only an urge or a whim? Does that make some kind of sense to you, that you can do that to women, that they don't have more rights than that? Imagine what you'd think of somebody who did that to your mother, for instance. You seem to want to imagine, David, but you're not very interested in knowing."

Jesus. David's nearly as startled, and even scared, as he was when that first woman screamed. And using his mother as a weapon against him—but even shrinks must come unstuck, their minds must go around and around from knowing so much about minds that there's no end, no unmuddled understanding. He takes a deep breath and says, conversationally, "I had a hamster when I was a kid."

"David!" Fink cries, but David plows on.

"It was in a cage and it had a ball to play with, and a wheel. And me, when I was home, but mostly it just went around and around in its wheel. When I was eight or nine, I was on my way out one day and I looked at poor old Hammy inside his cage, racing and racing and never getting anywhere, and I thought how mean it was, keeping him cooped up in that little space with nowhere to go. So I took him out to a bunch of trees at the edge of the parking lot behind the bar and set him free. I was sad, but I thought I was doing a good thing.

"Turned out I wasn't. My parents set me straight when they found out. They said he couldn't live outside his cage, and what I'd done would kill him one way or another. I went right back to the parking lot and the trees, and I called him and looked and looked, but by then he was gone. My mum said, 'Sometimes what looks cruel on the surface is really a kindness.' And you know, when I was older I figured out it's true the other way round, too. I still feel bad about Hammy, though. He must have been so scared. I kept imagining him hunched up and twitching and sniffing for enemies, or food, or some safe place to hide. Wanting to be back upstairs in my room, in his cage, running around in his wheel.

"But then I also thought, even if it was only for a little while, maybe he had a good run, and got somewhere before it ended and figured it was worthwhile. You know?"

Nothing, no response except a slight shake of Fink's head.

"I thought about Hammy when I was wondering why you don't let your brain be free. Because it's too scary?" This is so outrageously daring and brave, given Fink's uncertain temper tonight, that David feels winded. What does he think he is doing, what fates is he tempting?

David's parents didn't scold him for setting his hamster free at the edge of the parking lot. He didn't set it free. He didn't have a hamster. His parents agreed with each other that a small apartment over a bar was no place for a pet.

Why did they think it was okay for a little boy?

Instead of answering, Fink asks his own question. "So you felt guilty about freeing your little animal?"

David snorts. "Think I might mean my dick instead of my hamster?"

Fink's shoulders rise, then fall wearily. "All right, then, why don't we get into that again? What can you tell me about your feelings when you expose yourself?"

"What do you mean, my feelings, exactly? And shouldn't you say exposing my penis? Or do you think my self is the same as my penis? I mean, you're the expert, but that doesn't sound so healthy to me."

Is he nuts? As with Gwen, his words are remarkably coherent. He is a brave, defiant man tonight. A sexual man. A man, large and full-grown with power. Who knew a woman could have this effect? Touching the skin of a woman, he means, being inside one; not a woman herself.

Fink glances briefly over David's shoulder; David knows what he's doing: checking the clock behind David's back, over the doorway. They both have a keen sense of time, for one reason and another. "This new attitude of yours," Fink says. "It's not very productive, is it?"

David shrugs. "I'm just asking. You grab onto words you think are important, or clues to something, so naturally I want to know what exactly you mean."

"You've just wasted our hour together, David. It's another one gone, and I can't stress too strongly how disastrous it's likely to be for you, if you won't put more effort into this. You don't have to like me, but I wish that you'd trust me." Why, that almost sounded heartfelt. Nearly sad.

The faint, delicate, two-toned chime goes off inside Fink's desk drawer—must be a clock he sets and keeps there—signalling the end of their time. "Next week, then, David. Please think about what I've been saying. It's past time for getting down to real work."

David nods, meaning nothing in particular, and leaves through Fink's rear office door and down, down the three flights of back stairs. Strange, all that; not that everything about seeing a shrink probably isn't, but this was an unusual session.

Like he was somebody different from who he's ever been.

And for a few moments there, so was Fink. For a few moments, he seemed to be actually talking to David.

He's pulling out of the parking lot when he wonders if Fink's looking out the window, by any chance, observing David and David's car, working just fine. Well, but it hardly matters, does it? Fink knew right away the train was a story.

But not to the man whose face, framed in gilt, looks up from the seat beside him. What secrets lie behind those blank, speechless eyes? Any foreknowledge of doom rushing down? And what images of Gwen are locked behind them, in the memory cells of the invisible brain, flattened onto shiny paper and tucked under glass?

Gwen's eyes were mysterious too. They looked fixed on David, all full of signals and passion, but they must also have had a whole long past running behind them. David lost his virginity today, an unspeakably enormous event, but her day included the funeral of her train-crushed husband (if her story was true), getting pissed in a bad bar and making love with a stranger, and a much younger stranger at that. A hell of a day, in entirely different ways from his.

And now what? Is she okay? Is she regretting, weeping, pacing the living room she despises, pounding the pillows on her bed out of unbearable grief? Guilt? Or is she smiling, recalling the pleasures of David himself? Or something else altogether that David can't picture?

If he could see her, what would he see?

He could find out.

Twenty minutes later, after a little confusion with twisting suburban streets, he turns the last corner and sees her house. It's totally lit, top to bottom, the only house alive on the block. That's weird. He had to creep down the stairs in the dark, could have tripped and killed himself, but after he's gone she turns the place into a Christmas tree? It looks strange, and maybe wrong.

He parks down the street, watching, pondering, wary of going too close, or being spotted. He gets into enough unpredictable trouble without getting caught up in some extraneous strangeness. He knows almost nothing about her, after all. A day like this, it might have driven her over an edge, even into suicidal despair.

That would be something to tell Fink—"I made love, slept with a woman for the very first time, and I thought it was great, it changed my head around, but she wound up slashing her wrists. I found her that way."

Fink would assume he was making it up. Another story, requiring further sharp words.

"I don't see how I can ever go to bed with a woman again," David might say. Or, more to the point, he might actually believe. "First time out and the woman kills herself? It's pretty tough to get it up after that."

"I can see that it might be. Let's work on that, shall we?"

It's creepy out here. Miles away, on David's own turf, there are lights and voices, permanent, perpetual movement. That's what he's used to. These suburban byways are a foreign country, and a menacing one. But he has to know. Quietly he lets himself out of the car, not quite closing the door. He pauses at the end of Gwen's driveway. He could still bolt; she is not necessarily his business, or his burden. But he sees that red suit jacket being shrugged off. He feels her hands taking his, and placing them on her breasts. Not a forgettable moment. Then the rest of it.

Okay. He's going to advance up the driveway, onto the front walk, and the two steps up to the little porch and the wide front door. No, wait. He's going to take a look into a couple of the lighted windows on the main floor before he goes ringing any doorbell.

What if somebody spots him and calls the police? He's already been warned by practically everyone, "You cannot afford any more trouble. You really have to watch your step."

No one imagined him stepping through darkness around a suburban home far from his own. No one pictured him peeking through windows. But what if she's dead?

What if she's sitting by the window looking out into the darkness? What if she screams?

Gosh, she's pretty. She's old, but still so pretty; not like women at Gully's. She's graceful, too, as she drifts through the living room, picking up a little animal carving, putting it down, pausing to examine a picture, gliding around the big dark-wood table back in the dining room, resting a hand on a silver candlestick—it's almost like an old-fashioned slow dance she's doing all by herself, disappearing into the hallway and now reappearing into the living room, right in front of his eyes. He can't hear music, but maybe she's playing it quietly. There's some rhythm she's following anyway, in the air or her head.

Her hair sticks up here and there. There are little lines around her eyes, but her mouth has a slight, sweet smile. His lips were right there a few hours ago; hard to believe. Her peach-coloured robe reaches the floor, except for flaring up slightly when she moves around a chair or the sofa. He can't tell a thing from her expression. Maybe she's crazy, or only restless. Or maybe she's happy. At least she's not dead.

She falls into an easy chair, beige, the no-colour she said she despises. Perhaps it was her husband's chair; she looks small in it. Also loose-limbed and sprawled, legs and arms stretched out and apart. Not very feminine; but then, she doesn't know her lover is watching. David himself sits differently, and composes his features and expressions differently, when he's in public than when he's alone. That's only natural.

Watching Gwen, he can see a lifetime for himself: of days spent working at some unspecified but satisfactory job, and evenings spent with some unspecified but satisfactory companion, in a room just like this, and going to movies and for long walks hand in hand (he would never be tempted, there would be no unhappy impulses), watching TV, or reading, and late at night making love before sleeping, and waking up to go through much the same quiet, peaceful, perfect routine all over again.

Where is the woman who would be that companion?

Not the one in this brightly lit room, smiling with her eyes closed. This is the woman who makes all that possible, though, a real vision, no impossible joke on himself.

Is it greedy to wonder what more he could learn from her?

It's eerie out here. David sniffs. Something unfamiliar in the air, he thinks. There are all sorts of smells David is used to but can hardly bear: greasy ones like sweat, dirty hair and French fries; which aren't to be confused with the ones he loves, like exhaust fumes and fresh asphalt, flesh and perfumes and the leather of shoes combining into the delicious, tempting scent of his walks that sometimes get him in trouble.

If he could define his senses better, break them down, he might figure out just where that trouble lurks. But it's certainly not out here in these dark streets, where the main smell feels like, yes, the colour of green: fresh-cut grass, heavy, lowering trees, and money.

Perhaps he hasn't met his right companion not because of fear, but because his desires form such a complex and precise combination of scents, of tastes. Better than the idea that he has a switch in his head, or elsewhere, that operates randomly and without warning, but to disastrous (for him), distressing (to others) effect. Or that he's crazy.

Gwen liked his dick well enough. She seemed to appreciate what it can do. He stares at her fondly. She's too old, but she took him into her body. He would like very much to be there again.

He could stand here in the darkness, and he could (his fingers twitch) take out his dick and jerk off to the day's memories and the vision of Gwen. He'd like to do that, to feel the cool, dark, silent green air on the most vibrant and yearning part of him; but it would also be exactly the wrong thing to do. It would wreck something to do with Gwen that he needs to think about: a hope she contains, the possibility she has already given.

He still watches for a while, though, before he leaves. Because there is something about her, that she has, that he wants.

four

Something about death, or maybe sex, or maybe an igniting combination of the two, must recharge the batteries, rev the engines. At any rate, Gwen is buzzing about tidying this, clarifying and cleaning out that, in a frenzy of sorts, quite the opposite of the complicated inertia that followed Edgar's mere departure.

Well, it wasn't "mere" at the time; it has just paled, naturally, in posthumous retrospect.

Is it possible that when he left she imagined he might still come back? That he would show up at the door looking sheepish and pleading, full of regrets and apologies? Surely not. Would she have let him return? Who knows—what was she ever thinking, what did she ever suppose she was doing?

She'd thought she was having an ordinary kind of life doing ordinary good works, filling her time in ordinary ways among ordinary people, keeping an ordinary home, enduring more or less ordinary sorrows, sleeping beside an ordinary husband with whom she had her ordinary ups and downs. What a surprise!

Now there are lots more surprises. The house is booby-trapped with Edgar memories and mysteries, so that she keeps being ambushed by one explosive thing and another.

Young David gave her a boost, of course; or rather, being desired gave her a boost. So, "Thank you, David." And of course, "How about that, Edgar?" She's become quite chatty with Edgar.

Although one-sided, she now finds their conversations entertaining, even sometimes informative, and certainly there is much to discuss. Not that he has turned into a pal, a buddy, a friend—rather the opposite, in fact—but she does feel he is the only person who could possibly know what she's talking about.

Perhaps it's something to be said for a marriage that even after twenty years it has its surprises, and still stirs curiosity. Is Edgar surprised and curious, too? Wherever he is, whatever he's doing?

What she is most frenziedly doing is clearing out the house, preparing it to be sold, although where she's going is still unnervingly vague. Sometimes she wakens in the middle of the night startled, even now, to find herself not only alone but also terrified, nearly panicked. She feels in those brief dark moments as if she's driving full-tilt towards a blank and unforgiving wall.

Still, that's better than having an unforgiving train bear down full-tilt.

Oh, cruelty also keeps her going. Bitterness is a fuel.

Except when some small thing, one of those marital booby-traps, stops her dead in her tracks.

There she stands, cleaning out the kitchen drawers, a trash bag in one hand, a rusting, misshapen corkscrew—and why ever would they have kept such a thing?—in the other, and suddenly she is seeing a picnic, a sunny day by a lake, a bottle of white wine chilled in the cold shore water until a struggling Edgar wrestles it open with this very instrument, gnarling it beyond hope in the process.

For some reason they must have toted it home and replaced it in the kitchen cutlery drawer, where over the past five or ten years, since whenever that picnic occurred, it worked its way to the back. She recalls from the day of the picnic mainly small touches of hands, and the vast stillness of an isolated place remote from city noise. She remembers the quiet procession and recession of waves washing sand; the sharpness of cold wine from plastic glasses; the cosy taste of warm cream-cheese-and-tomato sandwiches, dark rye bread gone damp and pliant.

She recalls a gentle day. What she cannot bring to mind is why they undertook that picnic in the first place. Was it a kindly, benevolent impulse, or carefully planned to some lost purpose? Did they make sandwiches, pack up corkscrew, glasses and wine out of boredom, affection, quest for event, celebration, desire to patch over some hostility? Somewhere in her head, in brain cells here and brain cells there, must be an infinite series of moments that constitute her life so far, her sense of what those moments were and what they may have meant; but right now they are lost to her.

Likely just as well.

Of course the corkscrew goes into the garbage. But what's she supposed to do with Grace's china, its eight gold-rimmed, violet-centred place settings? When his mother died, Edgar made a place for it in their china cabinet. A few months later, Gwen took it out, washed and wiped it and set it out for a dinner party of Edgar's law firm colleagues. She thought it would please him to eat from plates recalling Grace. She remembers her intentions clearly, and they were not ambiguous.

"What the hell are those doing out?" he demanded. "I don't want them used, ever. We have our own dishes, we don't need my mother's."

Oh. Well. Very sorry.

There are a few things, including Grace's eight place settings, that Gwen ends up selling to an antique shop, although they are not, she is told, of any great value. Gwen and Edgar's own good china, their wedding gift from her parents, stark white with stark black rims, the plain fashion of the time, she will send, along with much else, to a second-hand dealer. Furniture, silver— the whole shebang. "What do you think, Edgar? But I forgot, you'd already said goodbye to it all, so what do you care?"

He didn't take all his own possessions along when he walked out the door. She finds, for instance, finally tackling his bedroom bureau drawers, two pairs of his pyjamas, as demure and pin-striped as his suits, although paler and far softer.

When did he begin wearing pyjamas? She can see him years ago, roaming about naked; and she can see him a few months ago coming out of the bathroom wearing these things. But when was the change? And why did it happen: did he abruptly turn modest, or shy? Did he suddenly, somewhere along the line, feel the need for some material substance, however flimsy, between them?

"Evidently," she says, "you didn't want them in your new life, anyway. Even so, Edgar, you might have been kind enough to throw them out, instead of leaving them to me. What did you think I'd do with your old pyjamas? Really, how rude and thoughtless you were, in every possible way."

Actually they do come in handy. She tears them into worn, soft cloths for dusting and polishing furniture. And then throws them out.

The shiny tables, gleaming chairs, beige sofa and mahogany bureau and bed—gradually, room by room, they're all being hauled off by the happy furniture dealer. Everything, out!

The absence of some things, like old plates, is unremarkable. When whole roomfuls of furnishings vanish, though, it is a shock; looks shocking, until she adjusts to new views, echoey qualities in the air, blank spaces where there used to be things surrounding her. Adjusting takes a few days, a week. Then she can go on, creating more absences, adapting to them.

She eats sitting on cushions. She sleeps on the old mattress, left behind on the floor. She is paring down, to no particular purpose: not just possessions that accumulated over a couple of decades, but also the hips and thighs that compounded during her original bereavement, when Edgar was only gone and not yet dead. She is not very hungry these days, and both thinking and cleaning consume a good many calories. Is she wrong, peering into the mirror over the bathroom sink, to think she is looking much younger?

She certainly looks younger, although she is five or six years older, than the sleek real estate agent she picks from an advertisement, a blonde woman named Gloria Wright, featured and pictured as her company's top-earning salesperson of the month. Just the person for Gwen.

"You shouldn't necessarily be clearing the place out," Gloria tells her, gazing across the beige broadloom expanses. "It's an easier sell if people can see how it looks furnished."

Gwen shrugs. "Too late, really. And I don't especially care."

"Yes, I see," although she hardly could. "Still, it's a good neighbourhood. We do well in this area. It's just that it's better if a place looks lived in. Homey." Homey! "And if there's art on the walls so there aren't those faded spots. See where you can tell where the sofa and chairs were, from the shade of the broadloom? That's the kind of thing makes selling that little bit harder."

"I expect it does."

Do real estate agents ever reject potential clients? Gloria sighs, looks peeved, but nevertheless her little sign goes up on Gwen's lawn, and her lockbox over Gwen's door.

Gwen bundles old magazines for recycling. Beth-Ann and Joe take their favourite sketches, landscapes and houseplants, before other neighbours pick over what's left. "Are you sure you're not moving too fast?" Joe asks. "Shouldn't you take things a bit slower?"

Beth-Ann sits at Gwen's kitchen table and sighs. "I wish things didn't change. I don't like it, that everything can't stay the same."

Gwen, on the other hand, now sees the danger in hoping that a life can be ordinary, much less unaltered. "I suppose," she says, "but then again, I'd rather have everything change than be fooled." Gwen knows what she means, but Beth-Ann looks puzzled. They have fallen swiftly apart; sometimes Gwen doesn't answer the door. It's hard to remember the relaxed, easy place they all used to have in each other's lives. Gwen's years in this house have flattened, grown distant, losing even whatever muted, minor colours they might have had.

That, she imagines, works both ways. Other neighbours, too, express some concern and even regrets. "Where are you going?

What are your plans?" they ask. "Do keep in touch, we'll miss you around here," which is kind and well-intended, but doubtful. People soon forget the existence of those, once perfectly familiar, who are no longer visible. Like water, communities of any kind ripple briefly, then close over.

"I don't know exactly. I'll miss you, too." Because whatever else, however false, it has felt safe for the most part here on this mainly quiet street. Gwen supposes it's why she could nod off like Sleeping Beauty for a few years; although her awakening has been considerably less romantic than a kiss from a lissome prince.

Unless she were to count David as a lissome prince; which actually she does not. She doesn't quite know how to think of him, except as a useful and pleasing experience she has not for a moment regretted, nor intended repeating. It's her belief that anything more would only lead to further knowledge and possibly even some slight, unlikely affection. A perfect stranger is best, "Right, Edgar?" She assumes he'd agree. "Still," she sighs, "he was very nice. So young, you know, and keen, and sweet."

Clearing out and exploring her home, remembering and failing to remember, an old theory from bad movies and books about parallel universes functioning invisibly alongside the known one begins to make sense. More and more it seems to her that parallel, untapped lives went on here that were not visible. "What a shame," she tells Edgar, not for the first time, "how we let things slide, don't you think?" For this, she holds herself equally accountable; for the results, she does not. "But for you to assume I had nothing to say—that pisses me off, Edgar. That really ticks me."

Anger helps her haul the fridge away from the wall, so she can scrub the floor under it.

She has delayed entering the office Edgar kept at home, a room facing the backyard that would, in one of their more successful parallel universes, have been a bedroom for Sarah, or John. She's leery of this room and the Edgar memorabilia it contains, given how badly she can be jolted by an old corkscrew and pyjamas.

Nevertheless, these things must finally be done. Gloria turns up with people now and then, and eventually she will manage to sell the place. Gwen wants to be ready to leave on a moment's notice. So: Edgar's office.

A big executive leather chair and a large desk, both brought home used from his real office, is all it contains. That and some dying plants in the window. The desk has four deep drawers, two on each side, with a small narrow one across the top.

The narrow one is where Gwen discovers, not even hidden or locked away, Edgar's plans. Literally, these are plans: carefully folded and refolded, thin-papered blueprints. For what?

She flattens the light, fragile paper, surprisingly large, on his desk. Hand-drawn, blue-inked lines curve through a fine, narrow grid imprinted onto the paper. Some lines are dots, others solid, like maps showing varying qualities of highways and roads. And here are little circles, there, larger, fuzzier ones. It has the look of a project both hazy and precise. It's the longest time, as she moves around the desk for different, unrevealing perspectives, peering up close, then moving back for the long view, before she understands she is looking at the dream of a garden.

Their garden? His? She looks out the window and down at the drawing, back and forth—are there connections? Hard for a garden to be as contained and exact as lines on a grid, but if she stares hard enough, she can, yes, see patterns. Much, although not all, is in the ground and spreading, or growing tall and full-leafed, full-flowered, if not yet as lush as it could be.

When did he do this: hours, days, weeks of planning, designing, making changes and new shapes—this blueprint is so perfectly tidy it could only be the outcome of a long, intricate, messier process. Years, given how long it takes plants to flourish as some of his have.

In other desk drawers she finds earlier, more muddled, erased and scribbled-on drafts. "Only a garden," she tells herself. Just flowers and greenery. Why the shock?

Why the secrecy?

Of course Gwen knew Edgar enjoyed his garden; or the act of gardening; or both. That was hardly a secret, he spent hours out there. But this—this intensity of purpose, this hidden universe, is as breathtaking as if she'd wandered one day into their bedroom and found him embracing another woman. Or a man, for that matter, since not much she thought she knew has proven especially solid.

The point is, was this not an infidelity? A secret longing that stole time and attention, and one so vivid and vital he held it entirely to himself?

He must have peered for hours out this window, alone in his private room, considering and measuring out these lines. Then, in the actual yard, he occupied himself transforming lines into reality; a very special pleasure, no doubt. At the end of a day he must have sat back in his chair, looking out over his work delighted, contented, feeling benign towards himself and his plans and his progress.

Going downstairs, he would join Gwen for dinner, an evening of TV, not speaking a word about this huge matter close to his heart. How could he do that?

He spent hours planting, weeding, squatting, touching, peering and adding. It was beautiful, of course, increasingly dense and intricately coloured. Closer and closer towards the house it came as he dug new plots, devised new pathways and designs, discovered more obscure and dazzling plants. Gwen came to dislike it all slightly, felt uneasy. So yes, she must have understood something about it. But not that it was this sort of unspoken, true passion.

Tiny names are etched in dark ink onto the blueprint, strange and foreign names of plants, and some common and familiar: lupin, Philadelphus, bridal wreath spirea, astilbe, columbine and hosta; Sweet Cecily and Sweet William, whoever they might be; lilac, iris, hydrangea—all those names becoming literal, forming shapes and colours below, reaching up, looping down, trailing over each other.

"Edgar. How could you do this?" This is as close as she's recently come to despair, although that sounds ridiculous. The man's dead, for heaven's sake, and in any case was only planting a garden.

He plotted narrow trails of brick and stone and chip so nothing growing would be stepped on. "Careful!" he'd cry when Gwen did venture into it. How stupid she must have been; more dense than the shrubbery.

Other widows, other wives, have made much more shocking discoveries, tripping over ugly pornography, or illicit love letters. Gwen knows that. But a blow to the heart is a blow to the heart. It's the vast, daily conspiracy of the lies and the secrets that counts, more than their literal content.

"Did I do something so dreadful and big, Edgar, to cause a betrayal like this?" Honest to God, she can't think of anything large; so maybe only an accumulation of small things? "But you did small things, too, and a few large ones as well, and I never dreamed of deserting you."

Only a failure of imagination, perhaps.

She hadn't even had a huge secret he might have discovered, and been offended by. Now she does, but that was then.

It also strikes her as bitter that he could have his garden, but she could not have her children.

And then, after all this, or still in the midst of it, he left? Packed up, moved out? What, then, was the enormous desire that overrode this one, luring him sirenish away? Not a whim for a sporty new car; something much grander and more compelling than that. Standing over his desk, regarding the blueprints, Gwen feels her body sag and get small. There have not been many moments recently when she has entirely lost strength, but this is one.

A couple of days after the funeral, she and Larry Parker zipped through Edgar's will, setting in motion a swift settlement on her of his assets. As she'd expected, it was an excellent outcome, leaving her, as Larry said, nicely set for the rest of her days. "Let's leave the rest," Larry also said, "until you're more ready to deal with it. The apartment looks to be paid up for a while. And there'll be his office, I guess, although we're in the middle of transferring his work files."

Now she again calls Larry Parker, the man with the keys, the man taking care of things, not very willingly. "He can't today, Mrs. Stone," says his secretary. "Let me give him a message about what you need, and one of us will get back to you."

"Today," Gwen says firmly. "He should get back to me today."

Larry calls later, from home, sounding weary. "I'm sorry," she tells him, her own patience stretched like a wire, "that Edgar's death causes you so much inconvenience." Unfair; she is upset with Edgar, not Larry Parker. "I'm sorry," she says again, in a different tone.

"Having a tough time?" Now he sounds cautious.

"Today's been a bit odder than some, yes." He is not required, after all, to deal with her. It's kind of him to call, and kinder to agree to meet her at Edgar's apartment tomorrow. She sleeps uneasily, dreams of voracious flowers and menacing darknesses and of Edgar appearing here, vanishing there, in grimacing, jack-in-the-box forms that cause her to waken sweating and shaken.

Doing is better than waiting; knowing has to be better than not. She arrives slightly early at the high, white, many-balconied apartment building on a mapled street nearly downtown. Larry's a few minutes late, looking harried but still, emerging long legs first from a taxi, rather handsome, in a settled, buttoned-down way.

Gwen decides she prefers rougher edges, some surprises; like, perhaps, David.

What would Larry Parker do if she reached for him, drew down the fly of his elegant trousers, drew him down onto whatever form Edgar's bachelor bed takes?

Why, she wonders, surprised again by herself, would she do such a thing?

Curiosity. Sensation. An impulse, also, to turn her head on Edgar's own private pillow and say to him, "See? I know you never liked Larry Parker, but what do you think of me at the moment?"

A bit late to undertake to teach Edgar lessons. She laughs aloud in the elevator, and Larry looks at her sharply.

So this is the building Edgar escaped to. This is the elevator in which he went to and from work, to and from the parties of which he was said to be the life. His feet followed the path of this rose-coloured corridor, his key, now in Larry's hand, went in and out of this very lock on this same grey-painted door. He, too, might have been aware of the muffling of sound, the closed-in air, the stifling atmosphere noticeable in apartment buildings to people accustomed to houses. All this makes his move even more remarkable.

But where's the lavish leather furniture, the glass-topped chrome tables, the enormous bed with its seductive satin sheets? Where, for that matter, are the overflowing plants, the lush greenery? Another surprise: Edgar's final weeks were lived in spartan fakery: pseudo-wood coffee table and end table and bedside table, matching the pseudo-wood double bed with its plain, white cotton sheets, cheap, plastic-shaded floor lamps and the same sort of beigey-tweedy sofa and easy chair he and Gwen had in their own living room, except poorer in quality. It's all new, but would have quickly become aged and shabby. Didn't he know that when he bought it?

There's a TV set on a rolling metal stand. She pictures him leaning over to wheel it from room to room. That strikes her as the saddest thing.

Everything about the place feels insubstantial, temporary, bleak as tundra. For this, Edgar gave up his dream garden? Not to mention Gwen? "Well," Larry says heartily, "this doesn't look as if it'll be so hard to deal with." Is he surprised, too?

There aren't even good hiding places. None of the clues or revelations she counted on, not on closet shelves, or in the pockets of his suits and shirts, or tucked into the bureau with his underwear. No pieces of paper explaining himself. It could have been any man living here: someone dull, entirely lacking in interests, much less passions.

She stands finally in the living room, empty-handed, feeling—what? At least she'd been able to suppose that if Edgar left for a dream, it had to be a large dream, or a glossy one; some big picture, however stupid, in his head. This, though—this is exhausting. This makes her furious again.

Larry looks at his watch. "I have to get back to court. You okay here on your own? I'll leave you the key. Let my secretary know if you have any problems." She actually touches his sleeve, weakened and grateful and reluctant to see him leave. She could use an embrace; on the other hand, she's had more than enough of men in a hurry to leave her. "There's still his desk at the office. We can take care of that and send anything personal on to you, if you'd like. There was nothing personal in his computer, or in his files. We haven't touched the desk, though. We haven't needed to take over his office yet."

She takes a deep breath. Last call, surely, his office. "If you don't mind, I'll come in and go through it with you."

"Tomorrow then, late morning? It shouldn't take long." No doubt. He must want to be rid of her. And then he's gone, and Gwen is alone in Edgar's apartment, with her trash bags and amazement and rage.

All his new clothes—his jeans and sweater-vests and open-throated shirts, his smooth and hand-tooled loafers, his array of tweedy caps, and two pairs of driving gloves besides the ones he was wearing the night he spent those few seconds too long on the tracks—she shovels them all into bags to chuck in a charity bin on the way home. (But what use have the needy for caps and fingerless racing gloves? Never mind.)

Another charity can pick up the furniture. There's nothing to keep, and nothing significant to the altered life he seemed so excited about but failed to describe; except for a package of condoms, unopened, in the drawer of the bedside table. What does unopened mean? That he hadn't got lucky yet, or was tearing through women so fast he bought box after box of the things?

The condoms take her aback; not because of Edgar, but because of David, who was inside her body, if only once, utterly carefree and naked. "Oh gosh, Edgar, I didn't even think. I know nothing about him." Nor he about her. How dim, knowing things but not, at a critical moment, considering the information relevant to herself. David has a girlfriend, and beyond that could have been anywhere, done anything, for all Gwen knows. But she can almost see Edgar shrugging, nearly hear him saying, "What's done is done. No point fussing when there's life to get on with." Right again, Edgar.

But this was his idea of life? This featureless space with a TV that rolls from one room to another? "I can't see it, Edgar," she says from the doorway. "You caused all that upheaval for this? Surely not."

Now only his office desk remains, and how much that was private would he likely have kept there?

Well. A fair amount, as it happens. Right off the bat the next day she and Larry stumble over a little grenade. Or not so little, depending on what Edgar intended it for, and how they handle it now.

She has arrived hesitantly, as always feeling strange in the place Edgar worked: this large, quietly hurried, gently decorated space inhabited by intent and elegant people with whom Edgar spent his long working days. She used to come in now and then to meet him for drinks, or for one of those law firm parties that rolled around a few times a year. Elsewhere she might have a life, she might be fund-raiser, organizer of events for cancer, heart disease, hungry children, trained if unpractised nurse, kind if generally uninvolved neighbour, hearth-keeper, all that; but here she was wife. Spouse of. Merely someone related to the real person with whom these mysterious people had real conversations, real plots, real involvements.

"Hi there, Gwen," he used to say, looking up from whatever paperwork was absorbing him, "come on in, make yourself at home, I'll be a few more minutes."

Make herself at home? "What did that mean to you, Edgar? What bells did the word 'home' ring for you?"

Now she and Larry are behind the desk where Edgar used to sit. They are standing close, sorting through dull detritus: paper clips, pens, electric razor, piling up, throwing out. Gwen is losing hope.

"Private" says the brown envelope inside a file inside the locked bottom drawer, the word penned several times, front and back, in Edgar's meticulous script. "Oh shit," Larry breathes, dumping the contents over the desk. "What's all this?"

First, records of two personal bank accounts Gwen knows nothing about, each with about thirty thousand dollars, and with figures showing unaccountable but increasing incomes, and unspecified expenditures going back a couple of years. "Christ," says Larry, "I hope he wasn't dicking around." Naturally he is concerned that these lines of numbers involve matters that, unravelled, might reflect badly on the firm.

Also there are telephone numbers, identified by initials, a dozen listed on lined paper. "What the hell's this?" Larry asks; as if Gwen would know. And a separate, fat, disorganized envelope of what look like bills and receipts. Larry riffles through a few. "We're going to have to check all this out. I'm sorry, Gwen, but I'm a little worried now, what he was up to."

Gwen sees, sadly, that everyone, at home and at work, took Edgar for granted; assumed, as people do with familiarity, that what they could see was what there was.

"Do you want to know about these phone numbers? If they're personal, by any chance?" Larry asks. He means, of course, that they might belong to a dozen women not herself. "We can let you know when we've traced them, if you like." He is trying to be kind; although she wonders also if he doesn't consider his offer a betrayal of sorts, of a man who was not only a dutiful colleague, hard-working partner, but also a man, like himself.

She frowns. "I'd like to know. Yes."

So maybe after all Edgar was interesting. In his ways. Gardening was one of his ways, evidently, and these pieces of paper imply something else intriguing, if unlikely at this point to be much more painful than anything else. If the phone numbers belong to an assortment of women, that will be only another secret. If that's the case, she might ring them up. Have a party. Compare individual aspects of Edgar each might know and which might add up to a complete, comprehensible man.

She laughs, and once again Larry looks at her.

Turns out she and Larry are both sort of right. Edgar wasn't doing much wrong on a large scale, but equally those phone numbers and bank accounts are tainted, to put it mildly, by both infidelity and corruption. When, a couple of days later, Larry calls to report, she's in the kitchen and, hearing his voice, sits on the floor with a thump, listening with her head down, hand over her eyes. She is trying, again, to see inside Edgar.

The trouble, she thinks, turns out to be Edgar's capacity for thinking askew and very, very secretively, but always too small: a backyard suburban garden, a pathetically barren apartment, a silly new car and ridiculous death. And now also, according to Larry, two women "friends," as well as, more serious from his perspective, money in those private accounts from little kickbacks for, apparently, certain small, tucked-away clauses in certain large, complex contracts. Besides the two "friends," the phone numbers belong to Edgar's contacts in the companies involved. Gwen doesn't fully understand what business he was up to, but then again, she doesn't try particularly hard. It's the facts of all this that matter, not the details.

"We've figured out where it was coming from," Larry says. "What he spent wasn't so much. The car was the only big thing. Otherwise a few clothes, meals, booze, the furniture, nothing interesting, I think. And I'm not inclined," sounding very serious, "to take it any further. I think we'd all be better off forgetting it happened." He is talking, of course, only about the money; the women, he takes care to imply with his silence, are her problem to deal with as she chooses.

"Okay. So the money," just to be clear, "comes to me, then?"

"It'll have to, you're his beneficiary. In a way it should go to the firm, but I'm sure as hell not risking the rest of the partnership for the sake of the odd sixty thousand he's left." Nor is he about to unleash the infinite upheaval that would result from trying to return the money to those from whom it had come.

"You devil," she tells Edgar. "You dickens."

She imagines him smiling, tickled by illicit successes, and she's angry again, and her fist slams down on the kitchen counter. "You son of a bitch. You thief. Did you laugh at how you could fool me? And then you robbed me, you prick." He stole years from her with his lies. How could she have made any reasonable choices at all, when he withheld all this information?

If she were attending his funeral today, she would be looking down at him with somewhat different, wider eyes. He is rounder now than she had supposed, fuller and more complete than she'd imagined, and also much smaller; fairly pathetic in his desires.

"But you had no business making me pathetic too, you bastard."

What do other people, women, do in these not-uncommon circumstances? She imagines they call up friends for consolation. She could do that, she could call, say, Beth-Ann, who knows a good deal about these matters, but consolation is not exactly what Gwen's looking for. She wants information, interpretation, some fresh, true knowledge. Who better than the women at the mystery numbers? It's even possible her small joke about hosting a party will be no joke at all.

"You have reached the home of Stuart and Angela Edwards," says a firm, recorded male voice. "Please leave a message and your call will be returned as soon as possible." A couple, then, Angela Edwards a wife herself. Although, at this point, not out of the question for the person concerned to be Stuart.

"This is Gwen Stone." She is back on the kitchen floor. "Widow of Edgar. Regarding a private matter. Whichever of you understands what it is, call me by eleven tonight." She likes the idea of pressure, force, setting a deadline. Getting this shit over with.

The second call wins her a live human, a soft, female "Hello?"

"This is Gwen Stone. Widow of Edgar. To whom am I speaking?"

A gasp, a small cry, a click. Gwen dials again. It rings, she counts, thirteen times before the voice, harder this time, says, "All right. What do you want?"

"I want to know everything you know about Edgar." Gwen could have said "my husband," but at the last second, that seemed too accusing.

"What do you mean?"

"How you knew him. What sort of person he was, as you understood him." And oh, what the hell—"What you look like, who you are, what you do, what you did with him, and when, and for how long. That sort of thing. The usual, I expect."

"I see." Long pause. "All right. But you have to promise you won't ever call me again."

This woman thinks she can set rules? Or that Gwen is at the moment inclined to obey rules? Never mind. "Don't worry," she says.

"Okay." There's another long pause. "Okay, I met him almost two years ago in a bar. The Downstairs, you know it?" Yes, Gwen does, as a matter of fact; she and Edgar went there several times, a bar in the basement of a hotel in whose dining room they sometimes had dinner. A private, dim sort of place, plush booths, tiny fake oil lanterns on every table, and false Tiffany lamps casting faint coloured light from the ceiling.

"He was there after work and so was I. I'm a stockbroker."
Oh. Gwen is sitting in her damn kitchen talking to some clever
professional woman—no wonder she loses a little heart. "We
got talking, and I guess we hit it off. We split from the people
we were with and went for a walk. And then, I don't know, we
just went on from there. For a while."

"Went on? For a while?"

"Three or four months, I guess. I met somebody else anyway. So
you see. I'm sorry. I just liked him. He was nice. Fun to hang out
with. I read what happened, and I was sorry. He didn't deserve that."

How strange, Gwen thinks, that people suppose death has
something to do with deserving. "How was he nice, in what
ways was he fun? What did he talk about?"

"Not you," the woman says in a rush, as if this is important;
and maybe it is. "He never talked about you. Just about his work,
and mine, too, and people we both knew. We laughed. I don't
know how to say how he was fun, just that we laughed a lot."

Actually, that stings. Gwen hadn't expected to hear about
laughter. "And of course you slept together?"

"I'm afraid so. I'm sorry."

"Did he talk about his home? His interests? His garden, for
instance?"

"His garden?" She sounds puzzled. "No, he never mentioned
anything like that. I'm serious, he didn't talk about anything
personal. I mean, personal to do with just him."

"Was he good in bed?"

"Oh," a little cry, "do we have to talk about that?"

"Yes."

"I don't know what to say. This is too weird. But okay, I guess
I thought he was considerate. Kind. Tender, you know?" As if they
might, having opened the subject, go on to exchange girlish
anecdotal comparisons. As Gwen recalls, it's true, though, there
were times Edgar was tender. "He said he'd never done anything
like that before. Had an affair, I mean. He told me he wasn't sure
what he was doing. What he wanted, you know?"

Now, Gwen knows. She didn't then.

"Then what happened?"

"Oh, there wasn't enough to go on with, I guess. It wasn't worth it, even though we liked a lot of the same things. The same kinds of movies, stuff like that." They went to movies? That hurts, too; because, Gwen supposes, this woman and Edgar had a semblance of an actual normal life for a while. Another parallel universe. "But he had too many other things to do. And anyway, like I said, I met somebody else. But I'm sorry what happened to him. How did you find out about me?"

"He kept your phone number. When you say he was funny, what do you mean?"

"I don't know. Witty, I guess. He didn't tell jokes, exactly, just said things in funny ways."

He certainly did.

"I don't think I was very important to him. I mean, it was pretty clear he wasn't going to make any big moves. He was just kind of confused, I think. Kind of looking for something."

So it seems.

"I don't know what to say to you. He was nice, I liked him. I wouldn't want you to think he was a bad guy or that he loved me or anything like that, I mean, he never even said the word. Actually, I don't think he talked much about feelings at all."

Probably not.

"And honestly, that's all there was to it. Oh, I can't do this. I have to go now. I'm sorry. Goodbye." And she's gone.

Sorry that it happened, or that this was "all"? It's quite enough for Gwen, who is staring at the phone but rapidly rolling back memories to see if there were differences in Edgar two years ago, any unaccountable changes, or for that matter events that, in this new light, are now recognizably lies.

Well, obviously, he lied about where he was spending his time. Movies! Walks! A strange woman's bed! Gwen gently hangs up her own phone.

Two years ago—what? For three or four months. Was it around then that Edgar complained of weariness, overwork, a slight, enduring illness that put him to sleep at the drop of a hat? "Just a touch of flu, probably," he said, although it was nothing Gwen caught. She can see his head tilting back as he nodded off in his chair, mouth falling open. She remembers being irritated, wishing he'd just go to bed, and waking him up to send him there.

"No wonder you were tired, Edgar. All worn out from tenderness. The effort of being nice, and kind, and amusing. Not to mention the energy screwing must have drained out of you. Sounds to me as if you took up with an amateur, though—imagine packing it in after just three or four months! Not a woman, I guess, with much patience. Not like me, I guess. Were you hurt when she ended it, were you wounded at all, you cocksucker, you prick?"

She'd have done better to have found these words to hurl at him long ago. Better late than never, though, as he himself must have decided, about many matters.

She forgot to get the woman's name, or find out what she looks like; but what difference would a name make, or an appearance? Might as well think it's important to know exactly which plant, with which-coloured flowers, would go where in Edgar's garden design. Hardly the point.

Just after nine o'clock the phone rings. "Please," a woman's voice whispers, "please leave me alone."

"Mrs. Edwards? Angela?"

"Yes. I'm sorry." Well, isn't everyone? "But I can't talk to you. I have a good husband, we have a good marriage." And what would one of those be? "It was nothing, it didn't mean anything, please don't let it mean something to you."

Gwen makes her voice hard. "No, really, you can't suppose I'd leave it at that after going to the trouble of finding you. If you're worried I'll discuss this with your husband, you should know I have no interest in that, as long as you tell me a few things about mine."

"Oh, what?" It's a rare whisper, surely, that also manages to be a kind of wail.

"About what you'd expect. When, where, why, that sort of thing."

A deep, weary sigh, more furtive, anguished whispering. "Please! It was six months ago! And only for a couple of weeks. I was a temp in his office, we got along, I was having some troubles and he was—sympathetic. I fell apart, but truly, it was just a couple of times. It was a mistake, that's all. I'm so sorry."

Poor Edgar. No one important. Just a mistake. His kindness and sympathy wasted.

And poor Angela Edwards. Her terror vibrates through the phone. This is not, after all, entertaining. "Oh look, forget it. Thank you for calling." Gwen's hand, hanging up, trembles. Sometimes it's very hard to be civilized.

What a complicated life Angela Edwards must have briefly led. And Edgar, for a good deal longer. Only Gwen got to have, quite mistakenly, a simple one. Lucky her.

"Way to go, Edgar. What did you suppose you were doing, did you have any idea that wanting something doesn't necessarily mean you should have it? Did you have any idea that other people might want a few things, too? I'm very disappointed in you, Edgar, very disappointed indeed. You're not the man I thought you were."

Well, she does have to laugh. That's how one might speak to a child who has not measured up. At what point did Edgar become a child? When did his interests turn to immediate pleasures, when did he stop thinking ahead?

Gardens, kickbacks, lovers—whatever next?

It's not funny, though, that her own judgments were so bad. She has, with better luck than Edgar's, a lot of years to live. She may not, thanks to Edgar, need to earn a living, but she obviously has to do something, and how is she supposed to decide what that is with such an awful track record? If she misgauged the person sitting, eating, sleeping right next to her, what can she possibly know about anything?

Long, long ago she trained as a nurse, but never worked as one. She married Edgar, who said he saw no need, and preferred her not to, and anyway, they had their family to anticipate. She was absolutely agreeable. It even made her feel bolder, in a way, than other women, her working acquaintances, although of course it would have been different if nursing had been a true desire. She liked the uniforms—their tidiness, the crisp way they fit—but never blood. It was not her calling anyway, but her father's, who suggested when Gwen was in high school with no honed ambitions that it would be "something you can always fall back on."

Flo, typically, had no advice beyond "Do something you want." At the time, that sounded lackadaisical, as if Flo couldn't trouble herself to come up with something concrete. Now Gwen hears her differently. Now she'd like to know what Flo meant about a number of matters. Not least Edgar.

And her father's "something to fall back on"—what did he mean by that? A career like a mattress, something giving and soft? He could have known nothing about nursing, although in Flo's later months, and his own, he certainly learned a good deal.

Now, even if she wanted to, there's no way Gwen could be a nurse. Too much has changed, she lacks far too much know-ledge. And she still does not want responsibility for life, or pain, or even the relief of pain. Now it isn't even "something to fall back on," it's just another brief and useless piece of history.

Waiting for Sarah, or John, finally giving up waiting, she did of course occupy herself, "although not, Edgar, in ways as interesting as the ones you obviously found." Because of Flo, out of some retroactive, backhanded desire to have cared enough, she took up with the cancer society, raising money, sitting on committees. Then, because of her father, she did the same in the cause of heart disease. Hungry children living, hideously unfairly it seemed to her maternal heart, in awful and unnecessary states of want, touched her enough that she spent three hours a week at a food bank. But that's as close as she let herself get. Other people's actual in-the-flesh children, needy or not, would have caused too much grief.

Really? Does she mean that? A different slant on things, then. "Did you know that about me, Edgar, does it sound true that I didn't want to get so close it would hurt? That I drew lines?"

Good works aside, the sense of time filled and well used, what she truly enjoyed about cancer, heart disease, the food bank was not the meetings, the committees, particular organizational chores, although she was efficient enough at those, but the chore that hardly anyone else leapt to: knocking on doors seeking donations. She liked catching glimpses over householders' shoulders of other circumstances and tastes, and hearing strangers' voices calling out, laughing, shouting or playing in the background, and seeing the art people put on their walls, and what shapes and patterns of upholstery they chose for their sofas. She did this not in her own neighbourhood but in less-familiar parts of the city, a harmless spy into other lives.

"Too bad I didn't do more spying close to home, right, Edgar?" Poor Edgar, doomed, or graced, to be her mute and captive audience. He must be wild! Sometimes she feels him simply dying to speak up.

While emptying the house, she is busy also emptying her life. "Oh dear," says the cancer society's director of volunteers, "I'm so sorry you're leaving us. Although of course I do understand." Well no, she doesn't, how would she? The oddest, most unpredictable things bring tears to Gwen's eyes now. A remark like that, hardly ever the obvious things.

With the obvious, such as selling the house, she is stone-hearted. Her voice, speaking to Edgar, sounds increasingly hollow here. Almost every noise is only her own, and some of the noises that aren't can feel creepy. Mainly, though, if a false Edgar lived here, it seems a false Gwen might have also, and that's an idea that's very hard to stay here and bear. The place feels as fabricated as the set of an old Western, all front and no substance.

She understands more now about how people come to punch their fists right through walls.

Wouldn't that upset Gloria on her determined appearances with possible buyers! Bad enough the house has so few contents remaining, without obvious signs of violence leaping to the eye as well.

Gwen has sorted, donated, sold and discarded. She has dusted, vacuumed, polished and cleaned. And still she is explosive, volcanic, cannot settle down. Did Edgar consume that much of her energy, then? She wouldn't have thought so, but she sure has a lot to spare now that he's so thoroughly gone.

She begins going out every day, trying to burn the excess in long drives and long walks, roaming alone (although sometimes taking off she sees Beth-Ann looking hopeful, or concerned, or confused) and randomly, except for taking care to avoid the neighbourhood of Gully's. She has no interest in repeating a whim, however successful; although imagine how many possibilities she has missed because it never used to occur to her just to go for a drive. Like swinging into Gully's, that Good Place to Drink. Something that simple.

One thing about walking: she gets an up-close view of the varieties of men in the world. Appearances, as she found out with David (and for that matter with Edgar), do not necessarily have a great deal to do with sensation, and it's sort of thrilling to consider what unknowns this man or that might be shielding. Or, if invited to, offering. Thin, fat, tall, short, balding, hairy or burly—it's like looking up into the night sky at the stars, trying to discern familiar and unfamiliar constellations.

Who are these creatures? The same species as she is? Was Edgar typical, if there is such a thing? Why wouldn't she wonder what any of these others, his fellows, might do for her in the way, not of mysteries and disasters, but of great, abundant pleasures? "Or maybe, Edgar, I'm just horny."

She could act on that, she could approach someone who appeals, saunter up invitingly. It worked with David. Not everyone's like Edgar, some men would appreciate, and enjoy, not run away.

It seems that David occurred at a particular moment and mood, however, and weeks later she is not in quite that mood. "I wouldn't want you to imagine you've put me off, though, Edgar. Not at all. Men look quite tantalizing, actually, some of them."

Driving has other virtues. Look, just look at the regular lives going on all over the city and deep inside neighbourhoods: people walking dogs, playing with children, watering lawns, pushing shopping carts; for that matter turning tricks and dealing drugs in the dark recesses of alleyways. A universe of activity. She wonders what police officers see, driving these streets. Where she may see innocence, they may well discern layers of activity not apparent to her. She would like to have the keen sort of vision that sees beneath surfaces.

What she finds, instead, is an immediate future.

She is tooling aimlessly around the outskirts of town when her eye is oddly caught, off to the left, by a long, high, cream-coloured vehicle, under a big red and green banner that says "Franklin's Recreational Vehicles and Equipment." This is something. She slows, turns around, drives back to see just what sort of something it is.

She pulls onto the Franklin lot, stares for a moment and gets out of her car. Walks around the thing, runs her fingers over its flanks much as she ran them over David's (and, long ago, Edgar's).

It's cool, it's smooth, it smells metallic and glassy and rubbery. She leans against its front and stands on tiptoe, peering in.

"Pretty, isn't she?" The man who approaches turns out to be Ralph Franklin himself. Just like Edgar, introducing her to his new car: "Isn't she a beauty?" This, though, this inelegant structure strikes Gwen as a superior beauty. "Want to see inside?"

Ralph Franklin unlocks the narrow metal door, mounts the three metal steps that automatically unfold, and she follows him blindly up and in.

"Look, just look at this." He begins happily opening tiny triangular cupboards, unfolding beds that become tables and seats and vice versa, demonstrating the narrow tube-space behind the shower curtain, and the operations of the little toilet, compact bronze fridge, miniature two-burner bronze stove with built-in bronze oven above. "Amazing, isn't it? Nothing wasted, everything perfectly comfortable, and it's as easy to drive as any big car. Easier, really, since you sit so high up. You can see everything."

True: she sits in the driver's seat, behind the fat oversized wheel, and imagines freeway perspectives and country-road visions.

She finds she is in a mood for new views.

And in this thing, you'd see a train coming for miles.

"Lots of room, too," he says, although with him aboard that isn't quite true. He's a big fellow; they can't easily get past each other in the centre aisle. "The other thing about it is, when the time comes the kids are grown, or you decide you've done enough travelling, it won't have lost a lot of its value. You just bring it back and we'll get you a good price. Assuming it's still in good shape." An excellent salesperson, this Ralph Franklin: speaking as if it's a done deal.

Gwen herself is entranced by the miniatureness of it all. She thinks a person could live in this space in a tiny and quite focussed way. Nothing wasted, nothing extraneous. No space for anything like deception.

"Let's take it up the highway a piece." Friendly Ralph, this man in green pants riding low on a tuberous belly. Nervous Ralph, too, a very tense passenger, feet moving as if he's reaching for the brake, or the accelerator.

It is fairly easy to drive; Gwen is surprised. She's never been behind the wheel of something so massive before. "Relax," she tells him, "we're fine." And, when she's turned around, driven back, pulled back into the lot, "I'll take it." Just like that.

Outrageous. Ridiculous.

There are a couple of hurdles, a few things to get through Ralph's head: that her husband will not be co-signing for the loan, that indeed there will be no loan. This confuses and worries him for some reason. "I don't know." He keeps frowning. "It's unusual. Cash, on your own, I don't know."

"I'll want you," she says firmly, "to keep it here till I'm ready, and I'm not sure how soon that will be. Also I want a TV and microwave installed in the price, and it should be gassed and tuned up and ready to roll the minute I want it." Roll where? She has no idea. Something to do with moving away, moving towards. It turns out she's not entirely happy with the symbolic, the merely figurative; now that she's seen it, she discovers an urge for the literal.

"What the hell was that about, Edgar?" she asks, driving back to the house. "What have I done, how'd that happen? A fair use for that dodgy cash of yours, though, don't you think? Found money for a found home."

"I guess," she continues later, lying awake in the night, "I'm not ever going to know about you, am I? I guess I just have to get used to that. Understand never knowing. That's maddening. Monstrous, really, but I can do it. I expect I can get used to just about anything now. And if I can't, at least I'll be able to do what you did: just drive away."

In the morning she heads out with a purpose, and returns with an armload of maps. She also finds Gloria and a couple named Greene, with a child, on the front lawn.

Gloria isn't that pleased to see Gwen but smiles anyway. "Don Greene, Tessa, and this little cutie is Isabel." They've already toured the house and are now taking a close look at the outside.

"That tree in the backyard would be perfect," says Don, "for a swing for Isabel. It's an awfully complicated garden, though.

Looks like too much work for us to keep up. Would you mind very much that we probably couldn't?"

"Fine with me."

"And the neighbours are friendly?" Tessa asks.

"Oh yes. You'll like them."

If they buy the place, Don, Tessa and Isabel will go to the communal barbecues, and sit on the neighbourhood porches on summer evenings, and maybe sometimes, for a while, Gwen and Edgar will be discussed. Edgar died dramatically and badly, and Gwen turned peculiar quite fast—that'll be the drift of the street talk, she expects, until in a short time they're mainly forgotten, even by Beth-Ann and Joe.

"Where will you be moving?" Tessa asks.

"Into a smaller place." Indeed.

"Looks like you've kept it up pretty well." Don says, "I like that it's so light and bright." Evidently they are heartened by beige. "And a good basement for a workshop." He tells Gwen he enjoys refinishing furniture and creating small wooden artifacts, such as candleholders, in his spare time.

"But why are you selling?" Tessa Greene asks. This is naturally important information: could be plugged drains, dry rot, shaky rafters.

"My husband was killed. Run down by a train. So I need to get on with my life." This is generally, Gwen has found, a real conversation-stopper.

"Oh dear. I'm so sorry."

They all go back inside and lean against kitchen cupboards and walls. While Gwen makes coffee, little Isabel, who's four, kicks rhythmically at a cupboard. "Are we going to live here now?" she asks.

"Would you like to?" Of the two parents, Don seems the gentler, more attentive one, although this might be just another false front.

Apparently they'd all like to live here, because late in the day Gloria returns with an offer, and although it's not quite the price Gwen was asking, she scarcely cares. They want to move in as soon as it can be managed. They have, Gloria says, high hopes for themselves in Gwen and Edgar's house. As they should, Gwen thinks. They're young, and ought to be hopeful.

Gwen just wants out. Then she'll only have to figure out which direction to drive that thing.

Lying flat on the floor of the living room, now empty so that she's already experiencing a kind of camping out, maps unfolded in front of her, Gwen feels as if her skin must be glittering. She traces with fingers and eyes alluring place names, highways that reach across the country or the continent, and roads that just peter out.

This may be how Edgar, upstairs at his desk, regarded the blueprints of his garden.

"All this in only a couple of months, Edgar. Isn't that strange—it seems like a few minutes and also forever since those cops came to the door, and so quickly everything's different. Still, you were keen on changes yourself. You likely don't care a bit about the house, either. The new owners remind me a little of us when we moved in, except they have a little girl. Or I guess I mean they remind me of the life we said we expected. I hope it works out for them.

"Too bad about your garden—child, swing-set, they speak of getting a dog—well, it can hardly survive all that, can it? Careless young feet. The parents aren't as interested in gardening, either, as you might have liked a new owner to be, but then again, why should you mind? Another thing you'd already abandoned anyway."

Her voice reverberates in empty rooms. "Remember when we came, Edgar? The house was so new it still smelled of paint and fresh wood, remember that?" He probably does. "Remember what we imagined?"

Everything they little by little collected—the dining-room set with its six chairs and china cabinet and the table over which, towards the end, she and Edgar faced each other with radically mixed emotions, the sprawling bedroom suite with, besides its bed for their presumably mutual pleasures, the double dresser, the ornate dressing table—every stick is gone.

How did it end this way?

She has only a little time left here. She isn't sorry to leave, but should she not be sad?

What she feels instead is that she's worn out her welcome in the heart of the place, as it has worn out its welcome in hers.

It has also become increasingly strange. As it's emptied, she has heard more and more peculiar sounds she's never noticed before, and outside there are often odd noises. Probably it's only that, in Edgar's absence, local wildlife is learning to kick up its heels: no more capital punishment for digging up bulbs, chewing at a few leaves and blossoms. So go for it squirrels, raccoons, skunks, eat your hearts out; if it is indeed you out there, rustling about?

five

Squirrels, skunks, raccoons might well have made merry in Gwen's yard, gnawing and chewing, uprooting and tearing at Edgar's vulnerable garden remains. But David, rummaging about in the light and the dark, seeking shelter, hunkering down, no doubt caused some inadvertent damage as well.

David misses Gwen. Her absence is almost a presence inside him: a black weight (a cannonball? A bowling ball?) hanging heavily in a region he locates just below his heart. One of the worst moments he can remember was watching her drive away for the last time.

There is no reasonable accounting for why this ranks among awful moments that also include arrests, courtrooms, jails and a dead mother; but unreasonableness makes no difference. The level of his mourning floors him. It leaves him, and likely just as well, without energy for his long pacings through the city's temptations; and so he isn't even sure what temptations the city still contains for him.

Knowing something is going to happen doesn't make it feel better when it does. Like, knowing his mother was dying didn't mean he wasn't stunned when she did die; or knowing he was going to jail didn't mean he wasn't shocked by the words of a judge or the grim closing of metal doors behind him. Just so, knowing Gwen intended to abandon that house didn't mean his own insides didn't feel they were being dragged behind as she drove away for what was clearly the last time.

She had filled him with purpose and hope and desire, and then she emptied him out. He didn't wave. She didn't know he was there, waving or not waving.

He still can hardly believe that soft-fleshed, warm-hearted woman could do this to him. "What did she do to you?" he has inquired of her husband's photograph, now on his own bedside table in the apartment over Gully's.

Gwen never returned to Gully's, except evidently to pick up her car when David wasn't around; nor did she call him. They did not meet or speak after that single, precious encounter, but until she actually drove away from her empty, desolate house, David did not feel they were ever much out of touch.

All those weeks and weeks during which she carried household contents to her car and took off, returning without them, or when the "For Sale" and then the "Sold" signs went up on her lawn, or when she vanished for hours a day, returning in the evenings to sit drinking her tea or wine, talking to herself, packing, a few times weeping, sometimes smiling—all those weeks, he observed, absorbed, deduced, wondered. Trying to see whatever it was he should see, needed to learn; what Gwen had to offer him.

That first night he watched her move around her lighted rooms just a couple of hours after he'd left her—their—bed, he went away, finally, unnerved by the private nature of what she'd been doing and why she might have been doing it. He felt endangered by one thing and another: not just alert neighbours, police, but the streets themselves, and Gwen's own mysteries, strange and foreign to him; unreadable, illegible.

He woke before dawn the next morning, though, with a considerably different view. The venture of observing seemed less hazardous, for one thing—what could be so dangerous about distant, curving streets of similar homes, with their grey and pinky brickiness, their two-car automatic-doored garages, their stunted front yard trees and hedges, their tiny, two-chair porches, their black-paved double driveways, their tidy, weedless lawns and, mainly, their astounding silence? In daylight that neighbourhood, menacingly exotic the night before, would surely feel almost safe; as it probably did to its own people, who must live there for its peace, for its secure distance from the lights and alleys and bloody noses, dislocated jaws, of David's own familiar turf. Funny that he would hardly hesitate to pick his way in darkness through an alley of dumpsters and fire stairs, of broken glass and ominously broken hearts, but be freaked by a silent residential street and a black sky speckled bright with stars.

From his bed, he again examined the photograph of Gwen's husband. This man had crossed the same carpeting as David, had walked and run up and down the same stairs, washed himself in the same shower and lain in the same bed, with the same woman. This man had been exactly the same places as David: inside Gwen, and with hands and lips elsewhere. There are no hands in the photograph, but these lips—they, too, fixed themselves around her nipples. This man asked about her wishes and desires, or simply came to know them. He, too, had exploded into her body; but had he ever been, like David, rearranged in the explosion? He must have fallen asleep in her plump white arms, across her plump white thighs.

And one day he left all that. How could he?

David also left; wakened to stumble in the darkness down the stairs and out the door, racing towards the useless Fink instead of staying where he might have gained something of grave importance. What sense did that make?

Did her husband ever go back? Was he tempted to witness how Gwen went on? To see what her feelings were, and how she survived? To try to glimpse messages that might be vital to him?

Vital. David was up and on the road and back at her house so fast and early he was in time to see Gwen going downstairs in her rumply peach robe, with her rumply reddish hair sticking up in curls here and there. For the longest time, she just stood in the kitchen sipping coffee and looking around the room as if its contents were surprising and had nothing to do with her.

By then David was sheltering in the backyard: a very good place, he discovered, filled with dark spaces and huge flowering plants and lush shrubbery—all sorts of unfamiliar verdant this and that. Some parts smelled too heavy and sweet, like the funeral home at the service for his mother, and from such places in Gwen's garden, as usefully dense as they might be, he cautiously removed himself.

From different vantage points he could see clearly into different rooms. He could even, looking up, see her regarding herself in the mirror over the bathroom sink, again just standing there, staring, for quite a long time. When the window steamed up, he figured she was taking a shower. Then he could make out her shape through the steam, towelling herself briskly. He could even see that her bath towel was a deep, royal blue. Then she was in the bedroom, appearing at the window buttoning a black and yellow blouse. He couldn't tell if, below the level of the window sill, she wore a skirt or slacks.

He had touched that body, unreachable on the second floor. Now her posture, her figure at the window, appeared to him to warrant, nearly, reverence. Something about the bodies and movements of women—some touching the impulse that made him flourish his dick, but this one touching a quite different desire, to know something that would change what he saw, heard and hoped for: that kind of profound transformation.

This lay not in words—he has many times since, through open windows, heard her voice speaking on the telephone, and he has heard her out on the street speaking briefly with neighbours and with a woman who turned out to be a real estate agent, that sort of thing—but her words were not for him. It was her body, her movements, her routines and intimate gestures that would contain their connection, his and Gwen's, and its promise: the prospect of a grave alteration which, if he could look carefully and closely enough, would eventually become clear, and would save him.

From what?

He came to think they had a silent agreement that those few hours they'd spent, those touches of skin, those tremendous soarings and expansions of the spirit and of his very horizons, were so entirely, hopefully pure that they should remain suspended right where they were, in memory and time. This seemed to be what she'd decided, and although maybe at first he'd entertained other pictures, he finally saw for himself that further shifts and jostlings between them would be bound to create a small impurity; like a tiny slip in cutting a perfect diamond.

How wise she was. He supposed it was because of her age and experience. But then, how could she simply drive off? She was wrong to take that step from exquisite stillness to abandonment.

That she could simply discard, to history and new owners, their beige, momentous rooms! If David could have bought the house himself, he would have, if only for the sake of sprawling in that living room, curling up in that bedroom. Of embracing those spaces; cherishing them, like a shrine. Yet there was Gwen, leaving, and with, by and large, a light-heartedness that was really wounding. How would her husband have felt about the easy way she trashed possessions, then locked the door behind her?

Still, it was David's presence there, not her husband's, that counted.

Edgar was his name. Her husband's. Poor guy, is that what people called him? It's the sort of name, anyway, that makes David glad to be David.

David looked the whole event up in the library. He likes libraries: sources of random information, the wandering sort of knowledge that comes of uncharted reading, picking up this book and that one for no other reason, necessarily, than its title, or its cover, or whichever section of the library he has more or less aimlessly steered himself into. This is the haphazard form his real education takes. Also, libraries are places where it is not odd to be alone. Not like movie theatres or bars, or school for that matter, where being alone looks pretty pathetic.

Libraries are sources of desired, specific information, too, and so of course it was easy to find there the newspaper accounts of Gwen's husband's final adventure (along with a copy of the same photograph David keeps on his bedside table). He couldn't on his own remember the name—did Gwen mention it?—but anyway, of course the man died in a spectacular enough way to be in the papers. David's own story, the one he told Fink, was a lot livelier than what got written up, but the facts were there, with a few colourful adjectives. And the name, Edgar Stone, to go with the face in the frame.

When he's not home, David leaves the picture face down at his bedside, same as Gwen did. David thinks he can trust his father to respect closed doors, but who really knows, and what would his father think if he happened to poke his head into David's room when he wasn't there? "Who the hell's that?" he might well wonder. "What the hell is that stranger to my son? Is this some new trouble?"

It's not a large picture, and although David has stared and stared, it remains unrevealing. Who was this man with the slightly wavy light hair, the unremarkable chin, the pale blue eyes and narrow nose (although not as narrow as David's own), the cheeks beginning to get jowly, but with their bones still perceptible?

There is no forewarning here of a dramatic end.

David wishes that instead of a formal portrait Gwen had framed a picture of Edgar (they must exist?) that showed him alive, smiling, frowning, blowing out birthday candles, reading, talking, mowing the lawn, having a beer—something. They have so much in common, Edgar and David. Edgar must have information to share, if David could only discern it.

Nothing like the way Gwen had information to share, though, if David could only have discerned it in time. There are moments when he could throw back his head and let loose a howl. He wonders, if he did that, what might pour out besides his voice. All sorts of unpleasantnesses, maybe.

All those weeks, between watching Gwen, peering at Edgar, working at Gully's and keeping his various appointments, he was far too occupied to get into trouble; unless Gwen, and Edgar, were the trouble themselves. He *needed*, however risky it was, to watch her. This was the woman who had touched him, allowed him to touch her, and that had to mean far more than skin. This came to seem perfectly obvious to David; and, he imagined, it would be obvious to Gwen, also, although she gave no sign of knowing.

Three times (but only three), he saw her cry. She'd just be standing someplace, like the kitchen, and look at something and start to bawl. David hasn't cried, himself, since his mother took her last, worst turn. That was when she came home from another treatment in the hospital, blinking in the abrupt dimness of Gully's doorway, thin and thin-haired, trembling on his father's arm. David whipped around the corner of the bar and carried her upstairs, and she was as light as his mythical hamster. "Be careful," his father warned at the turn at the top; as if David wouldn't be.

David set her down, terrifyingly easily, in her living-room chair, soft from years of her former, larger body relaxing in it. She was the one who had trouble catching her breath. Her skin was so translucent, her bones so prominent he thought she already looked the way someone might look after a long time being dead. "David," she said, "I have to tell you something very hard." He wept and wept, but he didn't feel any better, and she still died, didn't she?

He didn't cry at her funeral, when people who were practically strangers, or at any rate only customers, wept. He couldn't see that crying got a person anywhere, or changed anything.

When David's father has cried—when David's mother was ill, when she died, a few times David has overheard since—it's sounded choked and gulping, as if, like David, he's inexperienced and unfamiliar with the process. One sure thing is, nobody looks good when they cry. When he did it, David's own face puffed and pinkened in some spots, turned narrower and paler in others. Gwen got sort of bloaty-looking and blotchy. Sometimes in books, David has read of men being tenderized by women's tears, leaning forward to stroke or kiss them away with light, loving, sentimental touches of fingers or lips. Not David, who didn't want to see Gwen ugly, and turned away.

That might have been his mistake; that might have been when a message was being passed, while he was turned away.

Otherwise, as much as he could, he kept watch, for two whole months, right up till the end, as if any movement of her hand, any step, any motion of her head or of the tiny muscles around her mouth or eyes, any shift in her expression, might contain an illumination for him.

What did he want from her?

If he knew that, exactly, it might have been almost the same as getting what he wanted. She was a woman who had lived, she'd more or less told him, an unnoticeable, unremarkable life for quite a long time. She had lived, her own strangenesses camouflaged, in beige rooms until startled out of them. And she had touched him. So maybe what it came to was, if he was receptive and alert, she would transmit the gift of ordinariness, or the appearance of ordinary feelings and desires and capabilities, to him. That would change everything.

And then she drove off with nothing transmitted. Or maybe he is a man for whom there are no messages, and now no hope of any. Or, there was a message, and he missed it, due to turning away at a critical moment, or to the demands of what passes for his own life. He still had to turn up for his Gully's shifts, and for appointments with Keith Miller and with Fink the shrink. He had to spend some reassuring time with his father. "Where've you been?" his dad has had occasion to ask. "You may think it's none of my business, but you must understand that I worry. After all." Kind of him not to specify after all what, exactly. Other young men might get away with saying, offhandedly, "Oh, I just went for a walk," but that would hardly soothe David's father.

Of course David, skulking around Gwen's house, knew this would not appear, to his father or Keith Miller or Fink or anyone else, an improvement over his previous offences. He did see that however he felt about it, or whatever he hoped for, he would be in big trouble if he were caught. It was even likely that this was an activity that would be defined, by police, his lawyer, the courts, as an "escalation" of his previous troubles—the only advantage, his lawyer pointed out last time, he still had.

As with those irresistible moments of drawing his dick out into the sunshine, one side of his brain could very well know this was perilous (unless for once he was lucky and the woman in question for once smiled, nodded and just understood), while the other side of his brain went right ahead with instructions to act.

Fink's job, and apparently David's in the long run, is to stimulate the cautious, foreseeing side to triumph over the impulsive side. They will meet six more times. Keith Miller's job is to intimidate David and his brain into the same result. They have just two more meetings to go, including today. Intimidation must be judged faster and more immediate, and possibly also more effective, given that David meets with Fink weekly, with Keith Miller only monthly. At any rate it's supposed to amount to a one-two punch of behavioural alteration, and neither man knows that, really, it's Gwen who's the key to the difference.

If there is really a difference. If, with her gone, he doesn't slide back into disaster.

He knows Gwen was nearly twice as old as him, and too old to be beautiful. He also knows there was something weird about her, that day at least. He knows she had some long, other life before him, but having seen her throw out so much of it, he doesn't know exactly what she kept, or might have regretted.

She saw him, she touched him, she even invited and welcomed him. A miracle, the enormous blessing of an end to his virginity; which surely makes Gwen herself a miracle, too.

He tried jerking off to her memory, but that was awful. The motions, the very idea, threatened to contaminate her, to turn her oily and sludgy in his heart. So it's no good: if he's going to be thinking of Gwen, he must keep his hands off himself. He can still jerk off, but it can only be a relationship with his own skin.

It was simpler, watching at night. Late, after ending his shift at the bar or, on Tuesday nights, leaving Fink's office, David could circle the whole house in the darkness instead of huddling out back in the garden. He sure used a lot of gas with all that driving back and forth. His father seemed happier, though, to think of David out in the car instead of walking the streets.

After the street's unofficial, inflexible bedtime, when only Gwen's house might still be showing its lights, he felt easier about ambling around her yard and even onto her porch, looking into the living room, the dining room, the kitchen, another smaller room that seemed to be for sitting, or thinking, or studying—some inert purpose, anyway. He came to see why Gwen hadn't been at home there. He could see it wasn't a reflection of her, however comforting and appealing he found it himself, which made it more remarkable that she had managed it for so long. The place was subdued, not like how David saw her, which was large-spirited and bold, or else how could she have behaved as she had? The placid one must have been her husband, which was borne out by the closed-in, shut-down unremarkability of his photograph. Although something about him must have been overwhelming to have imposed so flat an effect on all the rooms.

The eerily lush garden, it seemed to David, reflected Gwen much better than the house.

Imagine just two people inhabiting so much space! They might easily roam about and almost never see each other, far different from David, his mother and his father tripping over, edging past each other in the small rooms and narrow hallways of their apartment over Gully's. That was friendly and companionable, by and large, but hardly private. In Gwen's house, it seemed to David, almost anything could be unknown, almost any life could be conducted, no questions asked, no notice necessarily taken.

David could hear his parents going to the bathroom, clattering dishes, trying to hold low-voiced conversations, or perform low-volume acts. That was in the night and the morning, the hours Gully's was closed; when it was open there was that racket floating up the stairs, through the floors, all one big place then, upstairs and down, filled one way and another with people, just corners for David himself. In his childhood, the place hummed and shouted, his mum and dad serving out drafts, hustling and running, speaking lightly and cheerfully to downhearted customers, making them welcome, bringing them back day after day, night after night.

Later he heard not only ordinary family sounds and Gully's noise, but also his mother moaning, throwing up, his father's sad, murmuring voice, her cries.

Many larger groups of people live for long periods, even their whole lives, he knows, in much tinier spaces, generations of far-flung relatedness piled atop each other in mud-walled huts or single rooms. The apartment, with its low ceilings and six small rooms (including kitchen, including bathroom), but also its expanse of street-facing windows and bright, flowery, pastelly slipcovers and curtains and cushions, all chosen or sewn by David's bright, flowery, pastelly mother, is a breeze, compared.

David would like to be as brave, determined, hopeful and stubborn as either of his parents. These qualities must not be genetic. No chromosome or DNA containing hope, or courage, or determined will can have transferred to his body from theirs.

After all, lucky David, to have been warm, sheltered and loved. "Tell me the first thing that comes to mind about childhood," the increasingly insistent (or desperate) Fink asked last time. "An event. Or a feeling. Whatever comes to you."

"It was great. Just fine. Really good." Honestly, David wasn't trying to torment Fink; that honestly was what came to his mind.

How does Fink, sitting in that rocking, swivelling chair behind his expanse of dark desk, scrutinizing David in his narrow-eyed way—how does he expect David to put years of brief, tenuous moments of colours, tones, impressions and expressions, fears, events and remote memories of events, into words, into play in the air between them, making them visible, real and coherent? So coherent and patterned and true, in fact, that Fink can reach up and pluck meaning and import, cause and effect, symptom, diagnosis and cure right out of that very same air? Is any patient, any doctor, so skilled that such things can happen?

Or so trustworthy?

Not David. And not, he thinks, Dr. Fink. If David were to speak every word he knows, and every memory he can drag up, he's pretty sure neither he nor Fink would be closer to knowing why his dick has felt the need to come out for air on the street. And even if such a eureka moment did occur, what then? What difference would it make, knowing why?

Gwen made some kind of difference, but where did she go?

The only time he was almost caught there, as far as he knows, was when people went to look at the place—the two-parents-one-kid family who eventually bought it and by now must have made it their own, repainting and tearing up carpets, putting new oddments and bits of their history all over it, obliterating Gwen's long presence there, and David's much briefer one.

He was late waking up, late heading out, and worrisomely late arriving at Gwen's. At this time of day, people might actually be about, although they rarely seemed to be; or Gwen herself could be busying herself with something that might cause her to glance out and spot him.

Parking where it had become his habit, at a strip mall at the edge of the subdivision, he set off on the three-block walk to Gwen's house, blue-and-brown-checked shirt hanging outside beige pants. He mainly prefers loose clothes: shirts that drape off the shoulders and cover his ass, pants that hang bulkily around his thighs, making it harder to discern the bones that lurk close to the surface of his flesh. His clothes hide the worst of his body: its insubstantiality, its lack, in his view, of heft and a vital sort of reality. There is, he thinks, a difference between people, women, most women, who look through a guy, and a woman like Gwen, who looks into him. To most women, when he was out, say, on one of his walks, he was transparent, it seemed; at best opaque. Apparently they saw nothing to him (unless he demanded their attention in his peaceful, not ill-intentioned but criminal way). Gwen was the first woman whose eyes went to his bones and locked on them, and whose hands skipped up and down them as if they were a delight. What was that but a miracle?

It was, as it turned out, a good thing he ran late that morning. If he'd been earlier, he could well have been in the backyard, huddled in one of the garden's dim, cool spaces, when the family, plus the real estate agent, went rampaging through. If no one else did, the little girl would surely have gone tripping into, over, him. Children, like animals, sniff things out.

David could do that himself, years ago: ease himself downstairs, for instance, into the bar, and comprehend instantly the degree, if not the cause, of joviality or tension among its various patrons on any given night. This must be a kind of discernment that fades, so that by the time they're adults, people practically have to be hit over the head before they notice certain events or emotions. Like maybe the women who've encountered David on some of his walks, who would never have seen him if he hadn't drawn himself so obviously to their attention.

He saw, as he turned the corner down the street from Gwen's, people getting out of their cars, the little family from a little compact, the sleek agent from something larger, darker and more elegant. He saw various gesturings and words being spoken, before they all headed together up the walk, onto the little porch where he himself had hung around the night before. The agent got out a key and helped herself to Gwen's house. Could she just do that? Where was Gwen?

The people were inside for quite a while. David dawdled on the sidewalk uncomfortably, fairly sure he should leave before anyone looking out started to wonder, or had his image impressed on their memory. He'd known the house was for sale, had already been badly jolted one night by the unexpected sign on the lawn. But he hadn't got around to supposing someone might actually buy it.

He really did not believe that would happen, but right then, he wanted to be sure these people hated the house, were cross because it wasn't at all what they were looking for. He wanted to see them leave smartly and crisply, the woman and child piling into the car while the man impatiently twisted the ignition key. So from a distance down the block, he watched.

They went outside. The man stared upward, hands on hips, at the roof, or the eavestroughs. They walked around the side, towards the garden, pointing at various windows. They disappeared from view for a while, then finally returned to the front. The woman and the man made earnest comments to the agent, and she nodded and smiled and said something back.

Gwen's car pulled in. The agent frowned briefly, but then they all started talking and gesturing, Gwen and the agent and the family. The little girl tugged on her mother's hand. The mother spoke to her smiling but with a look that said, "Just wait. Be good." They all went inside again. David, not a complete fool, didn't go close enough to see, but imagined them in the kitchen, Gwen putting on the kettle to make tea, or filling the filter for coffee.

Finally it was too dangerous to stay. He wondered, though, if later, when he returned, he could knock on Gwen's door and say hello, how are you, and ask her, please, not to sell the house to those people, or to anyone, just to stay there, and let him watch her and wait for messages. Because otherwise he didn't know what might happen to his life.

He still doesn't, and she's been gone, it feels, forever, although it's barely a couple of weeks. He can still try to see her in his mind's eye, packing things up and discarding them, undressing and dressing and driving away, regarding objects in her hands and on her walls and in her mirrors, curled up reading and watching TV, putting casseroles in the oven and plants and paintings into the hands of her neighbours. But for how long will he be able to make out the bones of her wrists and the tiny lines at the base of her throat? He sees her shaving her legs and running creamy hands over them, and the small frown as she peered, lying on the living-room floor, tracing lines on a map with her fingers. A tapping finger would catch his attention; a sudden tilt of her head or turn of her ankle.

Except for that one time, as far as he's aware, he was never close to being caught. On the other hand, how would he know? Some small, furtive movement in the garden might have almost caught Gwen's attention as she stood in her kitchen, or an unfamiliar misalignment between the colours of his clothes and her flowers might have vaguely struck her as wrong and mysterious. At night, his bumpings about in the dark might have scared her, or alerted her neighbours. She might have sat frozen, waiting for another small sound, or an identifiable one, while at the same moment he stood still and frozen outside, trying hard not to make another small or identifiable sound.

The sad thing is, it doesn't matter now how narrowly he might have escaped. It didn't matter much then compared to the urgency of being near Gwen, but it doesn't matter one little bit any more, and he has no idea what does. He supposes he could break down and tell that to Fink. If it was Fink he was going to see, the way he's feeling he might even do that. Instead, he's running a bit late for his second-last appointment with Keith Miller, and he had better get his chin up, and his courage, or at least his defences.

He used to arrive right on time, but now gives himself leeway. Keith Miller's tiny cubicle is in the probation office on the seventh floor of a tall, dark-windowed government building downtown. He always has to wait at least half an hour, sometimes much longer, in a large room which for a number of reasons is not very comfortable. The chairs are hard plastic, and the company is kind of unnerving.

Today when David arrives, half a dozen other guys are in the waiting room, mainly young, but a couple of them middle-aged, Gwen's age, maybe. It's not smart to talk to anybody, but that's no big deal, he's pretty used to staying inside his own head, although it can get sort of steamy and pressured in there. Like today, it feels as if his eyes could pop out, or his nose start to bleed, from everything getting so hot and jammed up.

These other guys are also waiting to see Keith Miller or one of the other probation officers. David expects many crimes are represented in this room at this moment. Especially whatever the older guys have done—hardly anybody starts doing crimes after thirty, or forty, so by middle age the worst has likely already been done. David cannot imagine that his own misdeeds come anywhere near the severity of anyone else's here. Can they tell? He always tries to look as fierce and disinterested as the next man.

Mainly, everybody picks a position and holds it: legs stretched out, hands loosely, alertly, folded in laps; or bodies leaned forward, elbows on knees, attention on the grey-tiled floor. One guy spreads himself wide, arms across the backs of two empty, neighbouring chairs, defiantly taking up space. Eyes are unfocussed, but not necessarily contemplative. It's not a good idea to meet them, any more than it's a good idea to try talking. These guys could be killers (although evidently free or rehabilitated ones).

But what if they're all like David? He doesn't believe it, but what if they're all prone merely to irresistible but minor offences? A little smash-and-grab here, shoplifting there? Criminal, okay, and maybe even bad, but nothing actually scary. But here they all are, silent and shifty-eyed, looking tough, or greasy, or tattooed, or wiry, or just plain desperate, carefully avoiding any movement, word or glance that might trigger dangerous, even homicidal impulses in each other. How dumb would that be?

David hates this waiting time. He's too harmless, too smart to be here, although, it seems, not shrewd enough to avoid being here.

Keith Miller doesn't agree. At David's first appointment, he briefly assumed Keith's contempt was for the tininess, the insignificance, of David's offences. That Keith had bigger fish to fry, as Fink must, too, in grander criminality—those robbers, rapists, murderers who are surely also consumers of his time—and must be irritated by the waste of energy that David represented.

But David was wrong. "So," and Keith Miller looked up from David's file. He's only five or six years older than David, but with pale, remote blue eyes (like Edgar's, come to think of it) and blond hair worn just long enough to pull back in a wisp of ponytail. "So you're the kind of asshole can't keep himself zipped around women."

David's own eyes, which he personally thinks are his best feature, perhaps his only really good one, all warm and brown, velvety and defenceless, like a calf's eyes, or a fawn's—those eyes widened, and his jaw dropped. "What?"

"Shut up, fuckhead. Listen to me." Keith Miller leaned forward, stared silently at David for a moment. "This is easy, what I'm saying here. Don't do it again. Don't think about it, don't dream about it. Do it again, I'll take your hand off. Or your cock. I don't much care which. You probably do. So don't fuck up. That's all. Get out of here. Be back whenever you're supposed to be back." He slapped David's file shut, reached for another, opened it, began reading.

Why did Keith Miller care so much? David almost asked, even drew breath for the question, but stopped himself, and silently left.

Since then, Keith Miller's contempt has mainly been more dismissive: that cursory, "So David, you still keeping 'er zipped?" and a brief notation on one of the many forms bulking up David's file, presumably saying he has shown up on the right day at more or less the right time, and that he has been successfully "keeping 'er zipped." David will be glad when he never has to see Keith Miller again. He is also aware of a tiny, premature grief, or worry, about losing more of the precarious structure of his days.

The place is running behind today even more than it usually does. A problem with some probationer who has fallen off the tracks? Derailments and spills must occur fairly often, and this must be one of the main places they get corrected and cleaned up. The other's supposed to be jail. Like school, only a whole lot more dangerous.

In jail, as elsewhere, David turned out to lack stature. His crime looked minuscule but risible to other men, insignificant but nasty, bad but not even close to wicked. All this made him vulnerable to superior whims. As well, he discovered a peculiar strain of gallantry among men who might do many awful things but did not care for those who randomly upset women.

"Some guy did that to my chick," growled one large man still memorable because he loomed over David on the very first day of his very first sentence and scared him half to death, "he'd never see his prick again. I tell you that for sure."

He did sound sure. David was convinced.

"You like flashing your prick so much? How about hauling it out for me? Or maybe you want to see mine? I don't get mine out for nothing, though, I'm not an asshole like you. I get out my prick, I got a reason for that." His hand clasped his crotch. "Means I want something done with it. Know what I mean, asshole? You take out yours, I'll tell you where to stick it, you bet. I take out mine, you better stick it where I tell you." He was a big man, with a big beard, big legs, big head, little eyes. David could imagine him riding a Harley. He could also imagine him riding David himself. Oh Christ. David looked around, desperate. They were in the rec hall with plenty of people around, it wasn't like they were in a cell, just the two of them, where anything could silently, forcibly happen. Others were watching, including a couple of guards. They looked amused, or detached. Christ!

The guy's enormous hand reached back and began to swing, ponderously, towards David's head. David flinched; his eyes blinked shut. The fingers touched his cheek, very lightly. "Don't shit yourself. We don't like it when assholes shit themselves. We don't find it—attractive." He tapped David's cheek a shade more sharply and, tipping his head back, laughed a great roaring belly laugh. Others laughed too, even the guards.

David, who had previously thought he might get through his three days playing table tennis or cards in that rec room, and reading magazines or a book or two, huddled after that, as much as he was allowed to, in his cell, and otherwise skirted prisoners and guards both with great caution. He knew terror entertained them. He imagined that, like school, people picked on people so they wouldn't be picked on themselves. It was one of those situations, like school, though, where understanding why things happened didn't help how they felt, and didn't prevent them, either. Understanding, in many, many situations, is completely useless, it seems to David.

Also he didn't learn jail's intended lesson. Maybe the vagueness of memory when it's confronted by immediate, in-the-flesh desire just isn't strong enough; so even knowing the dangers of jail, its possible informal punishments, didn't help the next time, out on the street, when his dick sought warm air again.

"David." This is Keith Miller paging him, finally, from the doorway that leads to a corridor of cubicles. Imagine spending whole days here! It's uncomfortable and barren enough in Keith Miller's tiny space, with its straight, fake-leather Keith-chair, its fake-wood desk, its orange-plastic client seat that's hard either to perch on or to settle into—it's unappealing enough for just a few minutes, never mind for a whole career. No wonder Keith Miller is curt and unfriendly, with his remote eyes and skimpy ponytail, his cheap blue shirt and tan pants, and his dark blue blazer on a hanger on a coatrack in the corner. His desk is bare, except for a pen and a tidy heap of files. Also a box of tissues. Do men weep here? David supposes it's possible.

At the end of the day, when he packs up those files and tosses his jacket over his arm, does Keith Miller kick up his heels? Do his eyes warm up, does his skin get flushed, his step become jaunty as he heads away from a day of bad stories towards pleasures in which he can be a whole different human? If so, what might those pleasures be?

For all David knows, Keith Miller dedicates his evenings to the battered and oppressed, patting hands and heads, offering solace and advice. That would help account for his lack of sympathy for people like David, who admittedly do not exactly make the world a lighter, brighter place but who can't claim to be among the battered and oppressed.

Or, alternatively, Keith Miller trots home to a tiny, adoring wife, a couple of tiny, adoring children and a mortgage on a little bungalow they are struggling to pay off. In this picture, all the humans in Keith Miller's household are tiny because they must be able to look up at him adoringly. Keith isn't particularly large, but David does see him as a man desiring admiration.

Most likely, David figures Keith Miller for a smoother, more successful version of David himself: a man who wants to be visible, but who has less startling ways than David of going about it. So maybe at the end of his work day, Keith Miller slings his jacket over his arm and heads off to a bar where there are other office men and women who labour drearily or doggedly by day and then go looking in big, dark, noisy, clever rooms for a little fun and companionship, also carrying in their most secret hearts a huge, invisible hope for love. The women's purses match their shoes, and their stockings go all the way up and do not have runs. The men's hair is styled, their ties are loosened artfully. Night after night, eyes are alert, wary, optimistic.

"Right," Keith Miller begins, opening a file, leafing through briefly. "You'll soon be done with all this, won't you?" He looks up sharply—what does a woman see in those eyes? Any possibility of affection at all? "Any problems?"

David assumes the question has very small boundaries and shakes his head.

"You're still working?"

David nods.

"No more troubles between babes and your cock?" David's hands clench. "Speak. Any more troubles, or not?"

"Not."

"You're seeing the shrink when you're supposed to, I see." Does Fink report to him? Are David's symptoms, Fink's diagnoses, written down for Keith Miller's instruction, and his entertainment? Keith looks up. He must see something. The surprising thing to David is that he's *capable* of seeing something. "Don't worry, it's just a record of appointments, nothing private. Whatever you say is between you and him." He leans forward, elbows on the desk, looking earnest. "Because the deal is, at the end of all this you should be able to stay clean. If nothing else, you're too old for that kind of shit, Dave—that's kindergarten stuff, waving your cock around. Right?"

Not exactly a trick question, but also not exactly an answerable one. David shrugs.

"You figure the shrink's done you some good?"

Again, David shrugs. He wouldn't want to commit himself, or Fink, to anything. "Maybe."

"Even having somebody to talk to, that's something, isn't it?

Helps get things off your chest. Puts them out where you can take a look at them, see what you can do about them. Right?"

This is remarkably chatty. "Yeah," David concedes, "I guess."

"See," Keith Miller leans even farther forward, confidingly, keeping his eyes locked on David's and inching his elbows ahead, "it's not all about punishment. I mean, you fuck up and you get punished, all right, that's the law, and it should be. But a guy like you, you're not out robbing banks or selling heroin and crack or killing people, you're just doing something really dumb. Or you were." That comes close, although not quite close enough, to David's own view that he's committed impulses, not necessarily crimes, except technically.

"But people have to be able to get along together somehow, so part of the deal is not crossing over into somebody else's rights. You don't get to have some whim to fling your cock around when it scares somebody, or upsets them. Do what you want when you're alone, but you can't go against other people's right not to be scared or upset."

"What about mine?" David hears himself blurt. What on earth did he mean, and did he sound as anguished to Keith Miller as he did to his own ears? He shakes his head, looks down.

"Your what? Your rights? Jesus Christ." Keith Miller sits back, flinging himself farther from David, reminding David, in a way, of how some women react to him. Is he so repulsive? Disgusting? Stupid? Out of whack with the world?

"If you still don't get it, Dave, take it up with the shrink. I'm not here to hold your hand, just to make sure you're not fucking up." Shouldn't it be part of his job, though, to explain why some matters are importantly right, and others importantly wrong?

"You know," and David again surprises himself—what does he suppose he'll accomplish, besides pissing Keith Miller off even more?—"you might be better at your job if you didn't treat people like shit. I'm not shit. You shouldn't talk to me like I am." He is dismayed to hear his voice rising, as if he might be about to burst into tears. He takes a deep breath. "You should treat people right, that's all." Why, when in his head he often thinks in coherent and even complicated sentences, do his words come out muddled? Another reason, he guesses, to keep silent. Either he doesn't say what he means, or other people can't hear it.

Keith Miller's head tilts up sharply. "I'll be goddamned, you've got a voice after all. Good for you." That still sounds mocking, but he begins rubbing his forehead as if he too has an ache there that needs easing. "You're right. I apologize."

He heard something. David exists to him for the moment, and they are two youngish men sitting across a cheap desk from each other, however unwillingly. Maybe they could go for a beer. Maybe David could say, "Hey, why don't you come by my dad's bar? I'll buy you a round."

That particular possibility doesn't suit any of David's pictures of Keith Miller's life; although he can imagine that, say, twenty years down a road of diminishing, discouraging prospects, Gully's could become a natural hangout for a Keith Miller kind of guy.

At which time David might still be there to greet him, still tending the bar.

See how they could be, though, he and Keith Miller? So similar in so many unexplored, undiscovered ways, they could come to hear each other's unsaid words? Because now Keith says, "You figure you'll go on doing what you're doing? I mean," he adds quickly, "working in bars?"

"I don't know." David shrugs. "I like it okay. It's good." He means bartending is just as good as being a minister or a therapist or a social worker. Sure as hell as good as a probation officer, or shrink. Because moving around the bar, handing out beer, David offers portions of himself, as well: his ears, for instance, a hand, a shoulder. If an old wispy-haired woman with terrible veins roping her legs, wearing her scuffled old sneakers with white ankle socks, grabs his arm for a few minutes to confide her various pains, does she not leave better, happier, than when she arrived? Do unshaven, red-eyed, shambling men with stories of domestic disasters, rock-hearted women and awful addictions to fate and other substances not benefit from David nodding at the bar?

David feels these people in his bones. They are the people who, as he told Gwen, scooped him up when he was a child and set him on tables to sing. They are not losers, not defeated by any means. They just endure, doing their best and their worst, neither of which is likely to be of public significance. They try not to suffer too much, but suffer anyway, often enough at their own hands, and still have enough guts to get up the next day. David even rather likes the idea that lives don't have to be especially meaningful. This doesn't strike him as despairing at all. It strikes him as just about the most determined of outlooks, to not expect a day to bring joy, or satisfaction, or even some glowing moment when, just for a second, everything's golden and fine— to not expect any of that, but to be awfully pleased on the off chance it happens, and in any case to go on getting up.

Even in just a couple of hours, it was clear that Gwen, too, suited Gully's. She might have dressed differently, or had better-kept hair, but when she turned up, except for being a stranger, she was in the very right place for the woman she was right then: aimless, a bit lost, but doing things anyway, taking some steps, taking a drink or two, going right on. He recognized the rusty edges of her voice, the kind of thing intended to protect soft places, the spots that really can be hurt.

Keith says, "You with me here, fella? The bar? You planning to stick with it? Got any interest in retraining in some other field?"

Sometimes completely inoffensive sentences come at David out of the blue, so that he looks down and sees his feet poised at the edge of exactly nothing. This happens now.

He can see his dad, nearly confident that David's on the right track, is fixed, cured, has learned his lesson, whatever, selling the bar and heading north finally, blessedly free of the burden of his errant son. Maybe he'll meet a plump, frowzy woman he'll introduce one day as David's stepmom, and they'll slide into a woodsy old age, with fireplaces and cottagey furniture. Very nice and well-deserved for him, but what about David? Gully's will become a hole in the ground, and David will fall into it. He will be buried under new developments. He even spoke of this to Gwen. Only like much else, apparently, it hasn't been real. He stares bleakly, or perhaps wildly, at Keith. "Retrain?"

Keith shrugs. "Well, sure. Says here," tapping the file, "you've only ever worked in a bar, and that's fine if it's what you want. But you're what, twenty-three? And working your way out of trouble? And getting some help? So this might be your chance to try some other stuff as well, get a good grounding for the rest of your life. You know, turn everything around while you're at it?"

Acting: David remembers suddenly that admirable vision, the night of the day he met Gwen, when he saw adoring faces, heard adoring applause. Now he shivers: all those people staring! And words having to come out of his mouth, in the right order, in the appropriate tones to make people feel certain ways—what was he dreaming? That he could be another kind of human entirely than the one he is? Can people do that?

He doesn't like people looking at him; or at any rate at his face, into his eyes. Acting requires beauty of one sort or another, and David has no beauty.

"You could," Keith Miller continues, "take some aptitude tests. It can help, finding out your skills and interests and the different places they could lead you. Sometimes fields you'd never think of on your own, ones you've maybe never heard of."

It's funny, or terrible, the things a person can know and not know, all at the same time. "I really like what I'm doing," David blurts, because that's absolutely true; and he means, specifically, Gully's.

"Forever?" asks Keith Miller.

"Do you want to do this forever?" David gestures around Keith Miller's cubicle. "What's forever?" But in fact he can see dying in Gully's one day, pumping a last jug of draft. That'd be okay with him.

"Anyway." Keith Miller closes David's file, sits back. "Keep it in mind, think it over. See you next month." He's fed up, evidently. People do get fed up, although it isn't David's intention to weary or annoy. Only, there's something about getting along he doesn't have the hang of, some secret nobody's told him.

"Okay." He stands, and for a second has that impulse again to invite Keith Miller to Gully's. He doesn't even say goodbye, though; one more word might make him cry.

Isn't that strange.

His chest is tight, feels filled to overflowing with some sour substance. He is sick of himself. He is sick to death of the state he's in.

He heads down the hallway, through the doors into the big room where other men still wait for their appointments, out to the elevators and down to the ground. On the street, people and cars and signs and buildings look fantastic: all sharp, bright colours and two dimensions, cartoonish props in the movie running behind his eyes. Is he moving while the street is still, or is he still while it goes on with all its busy varieties of lives? He stands, shaking his head to clear it, or to rattle something free.

Three young women in blouses and skirts, with confident legs and gesturing hands, turn the corner, heads turned towards each other, laughing, hair flying, purses bouncing off their hips. They are people who know things. David's fingertips touch the cool metal of his zipper. There is that quivering, electric desire: not for the young women, exactly, but for what they carry through the world with them, likely without even noticing. He pauses, wondering just exactly what that is, what the word for it might be, and then they're swinging past him and are gone, and his hand drops, loose and empty, to his side.

Momentarily, he is bewildered, feels bereft of something mysterious but critical. He is left with nothing to grip, nothing, not even his dick in the air, to hold onto.

Once again, he could nearly weep. He has to get to work, he's late, his father worries. He longs to know what Gwen took away with her that could have been his. He longs for skin again, and to be folded warmly inside another human body. His ribs desire the play of fingers up and down them, and his hipbones cry out for matching flesh to sink into. He would like to feel a small female hand on his head, or his shoulder. He would like, just, a touch. A simple human touch. Which is not for him, it seems, ever going to be simple at all.

six

"I wish," Edgar once sighed, memorably, "you enjoyed yourself more." In bed, he meant; words that reverberated and echoed, although Gwen took them as inept, not malicious. She also assumed he was wrong. She felt warmth, if not always heat, and certainly in their early days there was delirium, a fever of exploration and fresh sensation. But surely it's natural for a settling to follow exploration, and by definition, repeated sensation is no longer fresh.

Also his timing was sometimes off, and off-putting, going back to those moments he reached for her, say, while she was frightened, having lost Sarah, or John, of bringing more grief on herself.

"Tell me what I can do," he asked, "to loosen you up."

These memories of him flicker back inopportunely. Nevertheless Gwen says, although speaking silently these days, "I guess you were right again, Edgar, I really could have enjoyed myself more. Is this as loose as you'd have liked me, could I get looser, do you think?"

It's funny to realize that everyone she meets now will forever be a stranger to Edgar. This makes it more complicated to keep him on top of events; much the way Jack is on top of her at the moment, relaxed but continuing to embrace.

How *exuberant* he is. Perhaps what she and Edgar needed was not more skill but simply more enthusiasm. Jack's gusto, or David's notable concentration, are factors in her new appreciation of pleasure, along, perhaps, with her own previously unplumbed willingness.

And, she suspects, impermanence. That they have no future weighing them down.

Jack tells her he's a poet. She's not exactly up on poets (except, recently, in the most literal way) and hasn't yet seen any of his work. "A good bookstore in a proper city," he promised, "may carry it." She watched him this morning, hunched outside in one of her plastic lawn chairs, writing words on a pad of lined paper. He didn't show her what he was doing. "It's too early," he said, and certainly she noticed him frowning, erasing, giving up and starting again.

"I don't expect I'd understand anyway." Her knowledge of poetry is sparse and involuntary, limited mainly to school days. She hasn't thought before of poetry having much to do with life, or for that matter of poets being particularly lifelike.

Jack has arms like a welder, legs like a wrestler, a head that rears back and roars. What she sees in him is not a life story, although, since he's fifty, he obviously has a substantial one. Nor does wide accomplishment especially interest her. She sees kindness; bulky gentleness; clever hands; generous, attentive body and heart.

"I'd like to make you happy," Jack tells her, a goal larger than he knows, and probably a good deal more than he intends, but then, the contexts in which these words get said are temporary and specifically horizontal. "If you're happy, I can be, too."

Now she can hear his breathing shifting into darker rhythms. He is large and she is small, but even falling into sleep he does something with his weight so she doesn't feel crushed. For the time being, she thinks she could lie this way forever.

She might be wrong, they've only been together five days, counting the stormy one they met, and so far, what they've done together is rescue each other, drive, explore and inhabit this small space. Moving through daylight, they talk and sing, sometimes even harmonizing; his voice has a way of dipping around hers that's quite pleasing, to their ears at least. His one-person tent is rolled tightly into a drawer beneath one of the beds, his green, grimy knapsack in an overhead cupboard. His few clothes have joined her few clothes in the narrow closet and in several cleverly tucked away drawers. They have already, as he has remarked, seen each other at their worst, and in a sort of crisis. "Some people, it takes years, and then what a shock it can be!"

Gwen would hardly disagree with that.

If she is wrong about him, if he is not what she thinks, it won't matter in any horrific or life-altering way (unless of course, as cautious Edgar reminds, she is badly, dangerously wrong). She and Jack have a conclusion and a destination not that far ahead and are not profoundly attached. Except right at this moment.

They have told each other their own stories, or at least the brief parts that leap out in their lives for being crises of various kinds. Gwen's own most interesting tale appears to be Edgar's—and what does that say about her? Never mind; her stories grow by leaps and bounds, thanks to people like David, and Jack. Eventfulness overtakes uneventfulness even with Edgar still looming large.

But not as large as Jack, enclosing her bear-like, breathing regularly above and around her.

That meticulous beige house of hers feels a million miles and a million years away; someone else's life, in another time. This has happened so quickly, in a matter of days, really, that it's horrifying in a way. Although actually driving away was not so easy. Well, what kind of human wouldn't feel a tug, a pang, in such a circumstance? It was rather like looking down at Edgar at his funeral; or being touched by the sort of emotions veterans may feel, saluting a cenotaph: an acknowledgment, if nothing else, of a history experienced.

She'd phoned Beth-Ann to say goodbye, but by then Beth-Ann's voice was remote. Insulted, maybe. Or hurt.

She'd taken a last wander through Edgar's garden, but really, she still couldn't see what it must have meant to him; only that she was left out of whatever it was.

Of course, if he wandered into her new rolling home, he wouldn't be able to see what it meant, either, but here she is anyway, barrelling away from those twenty years and getting better and better at driving the thing, although it does take some getting used to. Having so much behind, and so little in front, and sitting so high, was unnerving at first and is still sometimes disorienting: figuring out corners and turns, simply getting it stopped. It's been relaxing, the past few days, to share the driving with Jack. And also to share some of the other burdens Ralph Franklin pointed out in a last-minute, more precise tour of her vehicle. He seemed fretful about her abilities with the propane for the fridge and stove, and keeping various batteries charged. The chemical toilet, he explained, was a scientific balancing act all its own. Apparently he had earlier failed to point out, and she had failed to think through, the many ways even a rolling home remains attached to the earth.

"Now, you got to be careful," Ralph warned. "It's all safe as houses, but you got to do these things right. Propane's nothing to fool with, believe me." There are manuals, however, and she only has to follow the steps exactly. She has a long history of taking care which finally, it seems to her, has some useful purpose.

It was one thing to drive away fast from the house, not looking back. It was another, a couple of hours later, to leave Ralph Franklin's lot and get on with an actual future. She sat for a moment, frozen and scared, at the edge of the highway. What was she doing, what had she done? People didn't do this: impulsively change their whole lives, their whole ways of being.

But of course that wasn't true, some people, Edgar for one, did exactly that. But surely people like Gwen did not just head out on some completely undefined, unconsidered adventure.

Well then, why didn't they? What stopped them? Responsibilities, maybe. Loyalties and affections. Lassitude, moreover; a kind of inertia.

And layers and layers of lies. Tiny, tiny falsehoods that build up, one atop and around another, over years, until they form a sort of geological formation. Separately they might not amount to much, but in time they are rock; in time they are as large as the mountain range far ahead that she is driving towards.

She shifted gears and headed out, aiming westward mainly because, from her starting point, there was more west than east on the map before she would topple into an ocean. Then there could be thousands of miles south, or, however unlikely, a huge expanse north.

For the time being, she snuggles deeper beneath Jack. He smells, oh, kind of like Gully's: dark, beery, smoky. A tang to him.

Highways are a world of their own, a shifting community in perpetual transit. Other motorhome drivers often make signalling waves from their windows, flashing headlights, not because there's anything wrong, but in greeting. Soon after launching herself onto the highway, Gwen began waving back, and flicking her own lights.

Edgar used to signal that way when he'd just passed a speed cop, in a brotherhood of highway warning.

On the road, pots rattle in their space beneath the little stove. Plates tinkle lightly overhead. All cupboards and hooks and containers are so precisely and miniaturely built that there is little room for crashes or breakages. Those small sounds behind her have become rhythmic and comforting. Domestic sounds, she supposes, and therefore familiar. A musical percussionist bridge between one life and another.

Jack, now rolling slightly away from her, is starting to snore: a comforting sound, at least for the moment. Since between them there's no endurance involved, she is free to look on the bright side, even of snoring. As a daylight companion, he is also admirable, happy with silence, or telling stories in his north-England lilt. He sings, with or without her, and without any need for the radio.

Musically speaking, driving with Edgar was a real pain. He could never hit on a song or a conversation he wanted to hear all the way through, kept turning radio dials through a jumble of rock-blues-talk-sermon-ballad confusion. "Sorry," he sometimes remembered to say, but still he drove on, one hand on the wheel, the other one fiddling.

Remembering, she sounds even to herself such a lump, but it's not that she was scared to speak up, it's that it wasn't worth bothering. Which, as it turned out, might have been their entire, mutual problem.

Those were the days, heading off on a holiday road trip, or to Edgar's distant home town, where their sole surviving parent of the four they began with, his father, lived in a nursing home and had to be visited, although he no longer knew his son, or for that matter his own name—those were the days when Gwen sank into the passenger seat and immediately commenced to feel swampy: damp and soggy in the head. She didn't do any driving because Edgar said he wasn't happy being a passenger. "You can navigate," he said, although what navigating there was to be done on a trip taken a hundred identical times she couldn't imagine. Likely he didn't feel safe in her hands. He must not have trusted her judgment.

Another thing about driving with Edgar: he hated stopping to let her go to the bathroom, unless it happened that he also needed to. "Just hold on," he'd say, "There's a service centre in half an hour. If we get off the highway now, we'll lose fifteen minutes." It seemed that he didn't empathize with any bladder but his own.

On that issue, naturally, she did make a fuss. "Okay, but you'll lose a lot more than fifteen minutes cleaning the upholstery when I wet myself. Not to mention the medical bills there'll be in a few years from holding it in."

Sometimes, as in that circumstance, Edgar might say, "Your cleverness, Gwen, can make you sound very nasty." No doubt.

What were his good qualities, then, the pleasing aspects that held her to him in that house all those years?

Oh, who cares? Or, she could care too much. She doesn't want to think about what might have appealed about Edgar.

She spent her first night on the road at one of those service centres he seemed so attached to. She parked at the end of a row of transports, some silent, some apparently empty but running. Across a concrete barrier was the world of tired families taking breaks and stretching legs; Gwen herself now belonged on the side of professional, real, living-on-the-road drivers.

There are terrible stories; awful fates, especially for women alone. These things happen. It's not reasonable to believe they can't happen to anyone randomly. Nevertheless, she stepped heedlessly to the ground and locked the door behind her, went inside to use the too-bright, busy washroom. She saw in the merciless mirror her hair sticking up here and there as if she'd been running her fingers through it, although she couldn't recall taking her tense hands off the wheel.

Still, she saw something in her face that looked fresh as a flower.

Not a flower; too Edgary. Fresh as a baby? Not right either; too innocent, too new. Too much desired.

She got herself ready for bed: a brief business of cleaning teeth, scrubbing face, leaving herself pink and slightly roughened. This was formerly a more detailed process involving make-up removers and creams, and fingers massaging in specific, uplifting directions. She also used to have softening lotions for her legs, and others for her hands. All that got chucked, just like Edgar's garden blueprints, just like old useless corkscrews.

She was a stripped-down queen of the road now, a highway honey, a motorhome mama. She grinned, and winked at herself in the mirror, saw a teenager watching and winked at her, too. What the hell.

Exhausted and ravenous, she picked up a steak on a bun, a side order of fries. Across the barriers in the carpark, a couple of worn-out kids yelled at each other, and a baby was crying.

She stopped for a moment to listen to that.

Four truckers hunkered over a small folding table in a sheltered space between two transports, playing cards, their harsh voices in the dark a pleasing, rough, masculine sound. Inside her motorhome, the door locked behind her, the narrow white slatted shades closed, the two roof vents opened for air, she tucked herself under a sheet and settled in with her meal. "Goddamn! Shit!" rolled across the parking lot, followed by men's laughter.

She was alone in a relatively flimsy vehicle, but felt far braver than in the old days—a few months ago—on one of those nights Edgar worked late, or whatever, when she could keep herself wide-eyed swearing she heard a cracking at the front door, whisperings in the hall, furtive steps on the carpeting, coming upstairs, approaching closer and closer to her, lying helpless in bed. In her imaginings, the person climbing the stairs carried an axe.

She didn't actually believe that. She enjoyed the thrill, that's all, and sometimes felt deflated, hearing Edgar's key in the door finally, his late-night approach as stealthy as any murderous robber. After he left, those entertainments were no longer amusing. She could no longer afford to manufacture night-terrors; especially when unidentifiable night sounds truly would have disturbed her, if she'd allowed them to.

It's relaxing, though, to lie here with Jack, even with his snoring. She'll admit she's been a bit scared on her own a few times, including during that godawful storm when they met.

She didn't stay on expressways long, only until she felt beyond reach of that city, and that house, and as much of her history as would most easily fall away with the miles. Then, since she wasn't hurrying towards anything in particular, she turned to slower, more interesting roads. These were ones she might have traced with her finger on maps as she lay on her living-room floor, and here they were, come to life with their grassy ditches and pocked surfaces and little signs, their stunted trees, and wildflowers, and weeds.

Was this how Edgar saw his garden, glancing from blueprints to flowers? From barren plan to lush reality?

She pulled in, weary, a few days later at a small, primitive campground, its only amenities washrooms and a few shrivelled scrub pines, some failed farmer's idea for making a little money from rocky land. In the evening, the sky grew suddenly, drastically dark. Sheets of rain smashed down, along with outbreaks of ear-cracking thunder and heart-stopping lightning. Crouched in her metallic home, Gwen was petrified by the possibility that she was unprotected from that flaring, random electricity.

Surely, though, motorhomes were not allowed to go roaming through the countryside vulnerable to violent weather? On the other hand, in hurricanes and tornadoes, they were always first to smash up and fly off. As if God looks unkindly at the mobile, or the unrooted.

The storm went on through the night, and into the next day, easing briefly, then surging back. One roof vent, stuck slightly open, let trickles of water slip through to splat onto her table. She had towels out to absorb it, but they couldn't keep up. She was getting desperate by the time she decided, in a lull, to haul herself outside and onto the roof to try to fix the damn thing.

She was reduced, drenched, swearing and nearly despairing, to hitting it with her fist, when a drenched, swearing Jack—he does not seem to have an aptitude for despair—appeared through the muck. "Fucking tent," he was saying. "Fucking weather. Fucking country." But when he looked up and saw her, he began to laugh, the first time she heard that full-bellied sound. "A glorious sight you are, lady," he called up to her. "Pink as the dawn and magnificent as the goddess of endurance. Whoever she may be. If you're not too inclined to be stubborn, I could offer a hand." It turns out this is how he really talks sometimes; it's grown on her, although it struck her as affected at first. Now it seems merely a charming, exaggerated effort to hold on to something he brought with him to this country.

"Although I should warn, my hand's none too handy. You wouldn't know about fixing a tent that's developed more holes than a colander, would you?" He looked down sadly at his armful of canvas, then swept his arms wide, letting it fall to the ground, where he gave it a kick. "My cause is hopeless, but maybe yours isn't." He'd climbed the metal ladder fixed to the back of her motorhome and was halfway over the roof before she could wonder if his weight might plunge them through, tangling their limbs and her life in further disaster. Bang! went his closed fist, and down, perhaps irrevocably, went the vent, now dented inward. "Sorry," he said.

Edgar used to say the first scratch on a new car was the hardest to bear, and Gwen took his word for it; she herself drove used cars. Jack made the first wound in the first vehicle she'd ever bought for herself, and she shrugged. "If you made it stop raining inside, I'm happy." So she was. "Can I offer you a drink in return?"

"That and a brief shelter from the storm would be a great blessing. I'd be most grateful."

He seemed to take up a good deal of space, once they were inside. But when, after a couple of hours, during which she told him more or less the story of her recent life, he kissed her hair and touched her breasts and drew her to the narrow bed, he became a comfortable size in her eyes, bulky but extremely flexible.

Did she hesitate? Sure. For a moment. But really, the only reason to hold back was custom. A habit of restraint over decades; automatic denial. Or, truthfully, that nothing like this had ever occurred to her while she knew Edgar, and since Edgar, only once. Heavens, what if Edgar was her chastity belt, and unpadlocked at last she starts flinging herself, or sinking, into any open arms at all?

Well, so far, so good.

Jack's attitude towards his own domestic history is—what?—at least more mellow than hers. His destination, his reason for being on the road, is to attend his ex-wife's wedding, and in the process visit with his two children and a grandchild. "I'm quite looking forward to it," he told her their second day out, when they'd reached a small, appealing, blessedly uncrowded campground still further kilometres north and west, through rock and bush, from the drenching place they'd met. They were sitting outside, content under a pale, early-evening sun, sharing a drink and waiting for steaks to char on the tiny barbecue they'd picked up at a roadside junk shop.

Jack is excellent at roadside whims; quite unlike Edgar.

"Is that not very sophisticated?" Gwen asked. "I can't imagine Edgar inviting me to his second wedding, if he'd managed to get around to one. Or that I'd have gone if he had. Or asked him to mine."

"Why ever not?" Jack's dense eyebrows lifted. There are occasions when, except for being so hairy, he looks very child-like: honestly amazed by what she thinks of as normal human emotions.

"Well, because surely it's too painful, for one thing."

"Why would it be?"

"To see someone you've loved, however badly, marry some-body else? It seems like such a final cutting off of the past. An end to history." Although hardly as cutting as a train bearing down. Which Jack had the grace not to point out. "What I mean is, being invited—doesn't it feel like a last slap in the face? If it were me, I expect I'd have heard it as Edgar's last 'hah.'"

"You'd have been jealous?"

"I guess. Insulted he'd decided somebody else was better than me. More lovable. Desirable. I'd be hurt more than jealous, exactly."

"Yes." He nodded. "I see. Perhaps the difference, partly, is time. My time with Sylvia's long gone, and there's no longer much for either of us to regret. Now I just wish her well and," he grinned, "she wishes me to come to her wedding, for what-ever reasons she may have. It might be her 'hah' as well, but I don't think so, and if it were it'd be no concern of mine. Five, ten years down the road, you might not have minded watching your husband be married. Anyway, I have my own impure thoughts: I'm by no means a failure, you see, and I have a public substance of sorts, if no money at all. So I think, in fact, I'll do well, stacked up against the new husband. Not that she'll regret my loss, but I do expect to add a bohemian glamour to the occasion." He was smiling, self-mocking of course.

Gwen, too. "I see what you mean. I must have been picturing Edgar marrying someone more exciting than myself. Whereas I might have been by far the more interesting one."

"I have no doubt whatever you would have been."

Jack is good for her in a number of ways, not least this blunt admiration, this faith that she is interesting and worth-while. She—what is the word?—she basks in it. Feels, too, how unfamiliar it is.

His ex-wife's wedding is a big chunk of the continent away, across the rest of the prairies and through the mountains, all the way to the ocean. "I left lots of room for the journey, since I wanted to hitchhike and camp, see the country again properly. I didn't dream of this luxury, though. And I include in that your own excellent self. I'm very glad you were kind enough to share your journey. This," and he gestured around them, "is nothing at all how I thought I'd be travelling. With that wretched tent and my poor clothes rolled up in the sleeping bag."

"I never intended to be uncomfortable or deprived," she told him. "I only wanted to move."

"It's soothing, is it not? A comfort, the road's rhythm."

Maybe. Howling babies can be calmed, she has read, by a ride in a car. Perhaps that's the sort of thing he meant.

"What will you wear to the wedding?" Because, frankly, she'd seen nothing appropriate among his belongings, no tuxedo, not even a suit, and everything he did have was crumpled.

"I've no idea yet. Thought there'd be no point carrying fine clothes on the road, so I'll just wait till I arrive and find out what kind of wedding it's to be. I'll be in some difficulty if it's formal, or in a church. But it may only be in a backyard. In which case I might just press a pair of shorts, what do you think?"

"I think the new husband might feel defeated by your legs alone, and in kindness to him, you should cover yourself. Do you know much about him?"

"Very little. Except my kids say he's a good man. And Sylvia'd not marry for any reason but affection, especially now the kids are grown and she's not struggling for money." He looked briefly sad. "It was money, or the terrible lack of it, that mainly did us in, I think. Which I understand is often enough the case."

Not for Gwen and Edgar. Money wasn't their trouble, even in the early days when they did have to take care. Neither was reckless or frivolous; at any rate not till the end, when Edgar went mad with his car and Gwen subsequently flung cash at this motorhome.

But she knows many marriages do run aground over money: too little, too much, different purposes for it. "Want to tell me?" She's been hesitant about that sort of question; not for fear of intruding, more of learning small and ordinary things about Jack. Because it must be the details, the pickiness and forgetfulness of the day-to-day, that corrupt. Still, she smiled at him warmly, inviting his confidence; and see? That's exactly the sort of small smile that easily becomes habitual, turning false, although it's true enough at the moment, and leading to terrible misapprehensions.

"It's an awfully ordinary tale, I'm afraid," he warned, as if he also knew the dangers of becoming small. Abruptly though, he, too, smiled. "I'd find that depressing enough, even if nothing else about it was. It was my impression as a lad that the lives of poets were by definition unique and dramatic, so it was quite deflating to find myself in the midst of so ordinary an event."

"I know what you mean." Sort of. In reverse. She'd been astonished to find herself in the midst of events that struck her as extraordinary.

Jack leaned forward, ran a finger down her jaw, across her chin. For some reason the gesture reminded her momentarily of David. "You know a great many things, I think, my dear Gwen." He, too, must make large assumptions, see broad outlines. He leaned back again.

"I married, you see, very young, just twenty, Sylvia twenty-one. A nice lass from my university, a student of English literature like myself. She had it in mind to be a teacher, as many did—it seemed the likeliest possibility, if not an exciting one. I called myself a poet even then, and the pursuit of poetry was my intention, although it's clear to me now what an arrogance that was, since I'd barely begun and knew nothing, really, at all. But my hair was long and wild, my clothes untidy, and here was this sweet, lithe girl who thought my ambitions remarkable, who adored me and loved my words, she said. Well, you can see the seeds of failure right there, can't you?"

Gwen frowned slightly; she couldn't see, really.

"Me, I was a happy captive of her tenderness. This may sound cruel now, but I think, looking back, that she was rather like my hair and my clothes: part of the vision of myself. That she was slender, with hair that fell to her waist and large eyes and the narrow sort of delicate hands, with fingers that taper and look as if they should lift nothing more difficult than a flower, or for that matter a volume of poetry—she looked *right* to me, a poet's partner. As perhaps I looked right to her. In any event, youth is naturally not very far-sighted or wise, and lust and hope are a powerful force, and so, in short, we married."

Jack shook his head. "And we did all right. In fact it's never been clear to me when we began not to be all right. Sylvia taught and I wrote my poetry, and began to be published now and again. We had our son, then our daughter. We looked around and thought, this country is going downhill, and by that we meant not only for teachers and poets. I think when its power in the world got overtaken and lost, the country turned on its own people, became like the town I grew up in, cruel, often, and mean. Anyway, it felt to young people like us as if there was far too much past and not enough future. Some of our friends were long since gone by the time we left.

"And so here we came. We'd been married eight or ten years then, the time when you're into the hard slog of a marriage. Sylvia was tired, although not entirely yet of me, and never of the children. We must have thought there'd be fresh possibility in a new place. As in fact there was.

"She got work, and I wrote and did a bit of editing and published here and there myself. Now and then Sylvia'd point out we had no savings, had the expenses of growing children and lived almost entirely on her wage, but I thought that's what she'd expected. And so she had, I believe. Only, her feelings about it changed, and I can see that a poet may be romantic enough in youth, and poverty can be borne, but when you're coming up to middle age and still scrounging for the day's meat and milk, she'd perhaps be discouraged. Although I was there for the children, she had no complaints in that regard and nor did I." His eyes turned soft and sad. "It's them nearly killed me, not Sylvia herself.

"But I can't say she didn't warn me. Unlike your Edgar. She'd tell me I might consider getting work like herself, could no doubt teach even in a university, the art of writing poetry, perhaps—but imagine, Gwen! I thought sure that'd be the death of me. I'd say, 'You knew how it'd be when we married.' I guess," and his grin was wry, "I must've thought time stopped on the wedding day: that the rules set then would be forever in place. Not very smart, would you say?"

Not very; Gwen nodded.

"But I learned fast the day she packed up herself and the kiddies and took herself off to live with a man I hadn't dreamed existed, a fellow she worked with, another teacher she'd grown fond of while I was so busy writing my fine words and paying insufficient attention. My surprise was probably something like yours, although the conversation was different. Your Edgar at least didn't leave you for someone else. Sylvia said the man loved her, paid attention to her, would care for our kiddies and made a good living, to boot. She said, 'I'm sorry. I know what I promised, but I didn't take growing up into account'. And I must say, that hurt.

"It hurt more, the children. They were eight and ten by then, and we were close and still are, but they'd known some things and not told me. They'd known they were moving to live with this man—they knew the fellow existed, for heaven's sake, which was a good deal more than I did—and they'd kept the secret for Sylvia. I was a while recovering from that, let me tell you.

"But you know, Sylvia was right, things can change and not be ruined entirely. My kids and I learned to keep close and I've been around when they've needed me, and I've been to their big occasions, their graduations and weddings, and I was there, or at least at the hospital, when my grandson was born, and now here I am headed to Sylvia's wedding, which is in its way another moment of family history." He shrugged. "It's only some of the things that come along in a life. And it made me wiser, and it made Sylvia happier, and the children are already wiser and happier than either of us. So you see," he held out his hands, palms upturned, "progress is made, and it turned out not tragically, for any of us."

"Still." Gwen remained dubious. "Going to the actual wedding—and why are they marrying now? After all this time?"

"Oh, she's not marrying the fellow she left with. They lasted a few years, but this is someone else entirely. I admit, I might not have gone so easily to the wedding if it was Sylvia and Jeremy's. I never did like the man. Well, you could say we got off to a bad start, him walking off with my children, not to mention my wife. Difficult to see him as the good fellow he no doubt was. But no, Sylvia left him too, just, she told me, because he wore on her nerves after a time, not because he did any bad thing like fail, as I did, to support a family. I admit to some pleasure from that, when she told me.

"I hope this husband's a good man, and I even hope he never wears on her nerves. She's quite a nice woman, Sylvia, maybe not as nice as when we married, but a good deal nicer than the day she left me. So I do wish her the best. And I'm flattered and pleased to be asked to the wedding."

"You sound fond of her." Would Gwen have become fond of Edgar? Could she, at some point, have said of him, "He's quite a nice man"? It sounded a gentle, kind outlook, a pleasing, graceful conclusion. Although it seems she would have had to get to know him first.

"Oh fond, yes. Although it's not altogether flattering to know someone's become a better and happier person for not being around me."

Did Edgar not predict something like that, somewhat desperately and unconvincingly she'd thought at the time? "You'll be able to find out who you want to be. What you care for and want to do." And has she not indeed gone rather ardently after what she cares for and wants? If just for the moment?

"Mainly," Jack went on, voice tender in the dusk, "I have affection for the people we were. A sense of the sweetness of my own lost self as well as hers. It's a little like remembering someone who's died." His voice hardened abruptly. "My children, however, do not fall gently into the past. I would kill for them. Or die for them." And so, it sounded, he would.

Imagine a passion that never falters and never recedes. Imagine that. Her most enormous and most thwarted longing: exactly that.

"Gwen?" he asked. "You're not crying?"

No, not quite. She didn't feel well, though. In fact she felt slightly ill. "Do you see them often?"

"Twice a year, perhaps, these days, but then it's for days at a time. Sometimes a month, although it won't be for so long this time, I'll have to be home in a couple of weeks." His home, as it happens, is a third-floor apartment in an old house in a city two hours from Gwen's. A city she and Edgar visited once or twice a year for the theatre, a convention, a weekend away. Just away. And they took that for adventure!

She used to wonder who lived in those houses like the one Jack described. She had thought perhaps students, the poor. Jack has admitted to poverty. Or rather, acknowledged his poverty, with no sign of embarrassment. "You do not," he said, "grow rich from a poem," and she could see that would have to be true.

She wished she also had a passionate longing for something so important it would be worth deprivation, even suffering. Children; there was that.

Jack said, "My goodness, you have a mobile face. Your expressions change moment to moment. I should be a photographer, not a poet, to have any hopes of capturing you on the page."

"Do you?"

"Have such hopes? Oh yes, I do. I will."

She will have to keep an eye out for his name in the future. Keep up on her reading.

What will he find to write about her? What words will he use? Their time together is very brief and requires no judgment; which may be why she's still lying awake under him, so as not to miss any of it.

The time they have had, though, has been very well occupied. Today they went skinny-dipping in a cold little lake. He is a travelling companion who says, "I wonder where that road goes, want to try it?" so that they have wandered several times into dead ends and minor wildernesses. Gwen has learned to turn her home around in some very tight quarters, or hold her breath while Jack does.

This afternoon they'd ambled off the main highway along a road that was not, to be honest, of much appeal, until Jack pointed off to their left, towards a patch of blue. They looked at each other. "Want to?" he asked.

Well, sure.

"I'm forty-two years old," she told him as they shivered, rubbing each other's skin, in the frigid water, "and I have never done anything like this before."

"Like what?" He laughed. "Like this?" One great arm went around her back, his other huge hand lifted her butt and set her down, laughing too, and struggling for balance, onto his cock. Her eyes went wide. Heat and cold collided in conflicting, contrasting sensations focussed precisely in a single place. "My God," she said.

Was this what Edgar was talking about?

Jack raised and lowered her with his large hands and strong arms, raised and lowered her, watching her eyes until his own went blurry and gauzy, and her legs wrapped themselves hard around his hips. "How did we do that?" she asked when they'd fallen apart.

"We fit. We balance. Also," and he grinned, "my feet are touching the bottom."

And Edgar wouldn't even stop the car so she could pee! She laughed aloud, and so did Jack; not for the same reason, of course.

"Tell me," she asked when they were dried and dressed and standing tightly side by side in the narrow kitchen, "what won't you do? Does anything scare you?" They were making ham-and-mustard sandwiches, both of them famished, especially Jack. He's a big man, and besides, feels to her as if he moves inside a field of his own energy. Throwing off heat, he must consume a great deal also.

He looked surprised. "Oh my dear, there's a thousand things I'm afraid of."

Edgar would never have admitted such a thing; although too, she couldn't recall ever actually asking him. "Like what?"

"Swimming, for one. I'm not happy in water. Comes of learning too late, I expect—you North Americans must learn soon after you're born, you're like porpoises, but I was in my thirties and the water's not at all a natural place to be."

"But you were swimming today. And it was your idea."

"Did you consider that swimming?" Those eyebrows went up again. "I thought it nothing to do with churning my way over a distance of water, nothing at all. It was the vision of your lovely white breasts, grand enough to keep us both afloat, that's what I wanted, nothing to do with a swim. For that matter you frighten me yourself, although no doubt I shouldn't say so, since it's my impression women go off men who admit to such things. Do you think less of me, now I've confessed?"

This was one of those odd conversations that are part play-ful and quite serious.

"Well, I suppose if you were afraid of me beating you up, I'd think you lacked any sense of reality, and that might, yes, put me off. But what could possibly make you nervous about me?"

"You underestimate yourself, my dear Gwen. You're like, oh, these boxy things you keep your food in," waving his hand over her plastic containers of lettuce, meat, leftover sliced tomatoes and onions. "See? Everything's sealed up safe and mysterious, and you can't get to it without doing that popping business with the lid, but then inside you find things that are good and nutritious, cool and fresh. You, now, you have a sim-ilar power of containment, a bit risky, it feels, to invade, but delicious inside."

Flattering. Also an exalted and perhaps romantic view of a woman who might just have spent twenty years with her lid on too tightly.

"But why go near a lake if you don't care to swim? Or near me, either?"

"Well you, for one, are irresistible." He fell silent briefly. She could see him considering something. "Let's take our picnic outside, shall we? And I'll tell you a story about me and fear, if you'd like." He enjoys, it seems, telling stories.

Settled on lawn chairs, plates in their laps, two glasses and a bottle of wine on the small, round folding table between them, he took a deep breath. "You'd not know to see me now, but until

I was fourteen or so, I was a little boy, short, small-shouldered, no chest to speak of whatever." He was right, it was hard to imagine. There's room within his bulk now for three small boys like that.

"And it was a rough place, our town in England's north, relying mainly on a few small, dirty industries, even then going out of date, always seeming about to collapse. Which they've since done. Even the owners weren't so rich any more, although there was a time they had been, and they still seemed so to us. Otherwise men were out of work regularly, the women struggling, and plenty of violence between the two. I see now it happens everywhere, that people who can't control anything else will turn on each other; from a distance it's a simple matter to see reasons and patterns.

"My own mum and dad were all right, he was a school-master and had work, but the despair and anger, those were all around, including of course at the school. When things are falling apart and there's little hope for better in their own lives, children turn rough, you know, Gwen. Their hearts grow tough skins, and they cause damage, not so much because they're bad but because they're trying to fling their grief onto somebody else, they don't care who, or how. They just need rid of it. That's what I think now, at any rate.

"It's an odd age, fourteen, for a boy. For girls too, no doubt, but for a small boy it can be a terrible turmoil. My dad being teacher, we had food and a roof, but we were looked on as soft, you see, had it too easy. Some people'd see us as thriving, to all intents and purposes, while they went down, and I was punished for that.

"I tried ducking through yards, and down alleys, and even went long, long ways around, but I could never get to school and back home without blood, or some part of me broken or bent. The yobs always got me. I guess I was irresistible to them in my way. My mother was in an awful state, complaining to my father and the parents and anyone else, but these were terrible boys in bad times, with far worse troubles than one small lad being picked on.

"'Walk him to school and back yourself,' she'd tell my father, 'they won't harm him before you,' but he would not. There were still Saturdays and Sundays, he'd point out, and I couldn't stay safe inside every moment. He couldn't always be there, and if he was not, I'd only end up being hurt worse. That's what he said, anyway." Jack paused. "He was—a complicated man, my father. Perhaps a bit of a bully himself. I suppose I was becoming more and more one of those cowering sorts of people it's tempting to kick just because they're cowering, which is a very annoying thing. It's possible he felt some of that, too.

"A few times, my mum kept me home against my dad's wishes, and a few weekends I wouldn't poke my nose past the front door, but my dad wouldn't let that go on. 'Get out there, boy,' he'd say. 'You can't sit in, it's not healthy.' As if it was healthy for me outside. But he was used to being schoolmaster, facing lads down whatever their size or desires. He didn't care that if you didn't have the power of the school and his position, and if you were little and his son, you'd no face to face anyone down with.

"It seemed this went on forever, but I know it didn't; only, a few weeks is forever in the life of a boy. But are you familiar at all, Gwen, with that sudden notion something's finished? It will not go on, because it cannot?"

She was, yes.

"I was astonished one morning to make it the entire way to school, and it was almost a mile, you know, without damage or threat. By then, of course, it didn't make a great deal of difference. I was such a rabbit, twitching at every shadow and sound, I'd beaten myself into a state anyway, by the time I arrived. But nothing was actually broken or bleeding. All I thought was, I'd not make it home at the end of the day, then. I'd never get both ways unscathed.

"Oh Gwen, you'll be thinking so ill of me, that pathetic, frightened creature—am I spoiling myself for you?"

She could see what he meant: that it could happen that, instead of Jack, she would picture the timorous, skulking child he described, and feel contempt, or pity. Something one shouldn't feel towards another adult, anyway. But, "No," she said, speaking slowly, weighing it out in front of him where he could see it. "I'm looking at the man that boy built out of himself, and waiting to hear how he did it."

He leaned forward, took her hands, then released them and returned to the pictures inside his own head. That's what happens, isn't it: that the one telling a story is seeing it, while listeners can only take the words and form their own pictures, which might be entirely wrong? Gwen didn't know if the streets the young Jack had hurried along were paved or dirt, wide or narrow, dense with housing or open to vacant lots and parks. She didn't know if the school was squat or sprawling, and had no idea what his parents looked like, or what sort of home and household they lived in.

In her mind, the streets were wide and roughly paved, lined mainly with narrow, attached, close-to-the-road houses with tiny front yards, little fences and window boxes. There'd be some scrappy, scrubby open spaces, a pub or two, some shops, the odd alleyway that would feel particularly menacing to a small boy. His mother would be small, too, and fretful; Gwen gave her wringing hands. His father would also not be large, but perhaps had a beard and stern eyes: portrait of a patriarch.

She didn't suppose it mattered hugely whether all those details were precisely correct.

"I thought I'd died and gone to heaven when I got to the end of the day, through two sport periods and lunch, without drawing the attention of the bully boys. But of course I didn't ever feel safe till I was tucked up in my own home, preferably in my own room.

"So out the front door I scooted, looking left and right and getting ready to go like the clappers. And I saw the bunch of them off at the side of the school, in their leather jackets and shit-kicker boots, looking at something along the side that I couldn't see. I thought, 'What luck,' and headed off at a clip, and then, I don't know, I just stopped. I don't know if I caught a stray word or heard a sound or had a feeling, but for some reason I turned around and went back. Every step, I thought, 'You're a fool, Jack. What are you doing? It's not too late, turn and run, what the hell are you up to?'

"I don't know if you've ever had the feeling, Gwen, of being two different people wanting two quite different things, but seeing yourself doing one of them, willy-nilly." Again, she nodded. "Not that I wanted to make a spectacle of myself, I only wanted to see, not draw attention, so I crept up, crept up behind them and off to one side, trying to stay out of the line of their vision. But when I saw what they were looking at, what they were doing, something went off in my head. An explosion in the brain.

"They had a dog, you see—oh, this is disgusting, I'm sorry— but there was a big dog belonged to one of the pupils, used to hang around the schoolyard sometimes of an afternoon."

He paused. "They were torturing it?" Gwen asked.

"I don't know if you'd call it torture or not, from the point of view of the dog. What they'd done was capture this poor fat pasty lass, stripped off her clothes, and two of them were holding her while a couple of others were trying to get the dog to mount her."

"Oh Jesus."

"Now you realize, I've no idea if they could have succeeded, but at the time, that didn't seem the point. And the girl—I don't know how long they'd been there, but more than long enough for her to be beyond crying, I think. She was just twisting and flopping a bit under their hands, her poor flesh rippling and wobbling, and making a pathetic small sound, something between a wail and a moan—I've not since heard anything like it."

"Where were the teachers? Where was your father?"

Jack shrugged. "Inside. And out the front. This was a blank wall at the side, you see, and just a narrow sort of space between the school and a wire fence separating it from a building lot. Not an alley, exactly, more a passage, with mainly an assortment of rubble, broken glass and bits of bricks and candy wrappers.

"At any rate, when this thing burst in my head, whatever that was, I let out a shriek and *hurled* myself at them, all fists and boots and a voice like I'd never heard before from myself, as if it changed from a boy's to a man's in that one moment, the way you hear of hair turning white overnight from a shock. There was commotion all around, but all I saw were parts of bodies I could hit or kick or bite, anything I could reach I was trying to hurt, and my own voice coming from a long way off and wholly unfamiliar. It must have made quite the scene. Certainly it got the necessary attention."

Again he paused. "Then what?" she asked cautiously.

"Well. Once we all got pulled apart and the girl was covered up and taken away and the boy whose dog it was led him off home, my father expelled those lads on the spot, and called in the police. They all wound up in court and finally, down the road a while, in jail.

"I never saw my father so angry. White and shaking, as out of control in his way as I'd been in mine. But he hadn't been *there*, you see. He praised me later, told me how brave I'd been, but I knew it wasn't courage, it was that bomb going off in my head, and it wasn't all on behalf of that girl, either. Afterwards I was never afraid again of pissing him off, because he hadn't been there. And I wasn't a bit worried by bullies because I thought I could count on the thing in my head; they'd never beat me while I carried about a weapon like that inside of me.

"And if I wasn't afraid of my father, and I wasn't afraid of the yobs, it came to seem that I needn't fret about any fear whatsoever. So I'm still afraid of many, many things—including you, my dear Gwen, and of splashing about in strange lakes—but I've no fear of being afraid. Do you see? It's not that I often go seeking it out, but I don't back away for being afraid of a thing."

He grinned. "Anyway, shortly after that adolescent epiphany, I began my growth to the size you see now, so that was a help in itself. The sad thing about yobs is that they're very likely ill-nourished, and have little in the way of true muscle. For their strength they mainly rely on the group, and on a menacing look."

David came to mind: would Jack see him, looking weedy and ill-nourished, as a yob? That was how she herself first saw him, at the bar, a couple of hours before her view altered.

"What happened to the girl?"

Jack shrugged. "She didn't come back, she got sent else-where for her schooling. You'd never recover from a thing like that, though, would you, wherever you went?" Gwen shook her head; she could not imagine such an event wouldn't over-whelm in large and small ways all that girl's years.

"And the dog was another sad thing. No one wanted to know it after that, except of course the boy who owned it, so when it turned up back at the school it got chased away, and no one threw sticks for it any more. It must have wondered, in its small doggy-brain, what it had done wrong. Because of course it did nothing wrong whatever, it was only a tool of torment in the hands of those lads. I could see that myself, but even so, I couldn't bring myself to touch that dog again, nor even look it in the eyes." Jack shivered. "At least it'll be dead now. Not the girl, I suppose, she was a couple of years younger than me, but the dog'll be out of its misery." He sighed.

"But however dreadful that day was for the dog, and for the lass, it was the one that saved me, and isn't that a terrible thing? It sounds cruel, I know, and unfeeling to the girl, but believe me I don't forget the grotesque thing they did, or her fear. And it's not that I never saw blood again myself, or got bones broken one way and another. But what I mean is, it seems to me that once you've endured certain pains, and learned they're endurable, there's a whole new aspect to life. You come to a moment, or a number of moments, when you win your way through something and everything looks different. *Is* different."

"I know," she said quietly.

"I know you do. That's why I told you."

Because their time together is short, their stories are compressed into accounts of vital moments: the highest and lowest. Their conversations have to be like poems, or the way she supposes poems to be: brief lines, coded, each word containing far more than itself.

Making love is another code. He's far into sleep now, and has turned slightly away from her. She touches his hair, greying but full, even bushy. She tries to memorize the sensation of this hair, and this skull, under her hand; memory is also a code.

Love in whatever form is never simple, is it? It may be clear, and passionately attached, and to her surprise perfectly temporary, but never, it seems to her, uncomplicated. In a few days, this man in Gwen's arms will be with his children. And grandchild! That must be the clearest, purest variety of love.

It suddenly occurs to Gwen, so startling that her eyes fly open, that her own lost babies remained just that, babies; except for the odd occasion, like Edgar's funeral, when they appeared all grown up beside her, comforting presences propping her up. But who might John or Sarah have been at four, at seven, at twelve, at sixteen?

Her visions of them seem to have been as stunted as their seeped-out existences. She sees she failed in more ways than one at giving them life.

Who might they really have been, with their individual virtues and flaws and temperaments? What would they have inherited from parents who, even to themselves, turned out to be ciphers? What sort of example would she have been to a Sarah or John? What of Edgar?

If there had been a Sarah, a John, they would have been loved, at any rate. Edgar, also, would have loved them. And if she and Edgar had had that variation of love in their lives, they would each have become different people themselves, and different, too, with each other.

So much lost and unknown and unknowable. It's ridiculous, the way tears spring up without warning. Here she is with a big warm man in her arms, tears running onto his unconscious shoulder—if he woke, what would she tell him? That she is mourning lost children, non-existent parts of her life? This is a man, from what she can tell, who celebrates what is, doesn't grieve long for what is not. Like Edgar, he might well say, "Get on with things, Gwen. Enjoy and use the blessings you have."

And they would be right, Jack and Edgar.

Oh dear, she hopes she isn't going to start hearing Jack in her head as well: a bass duet exhorting her to swallow her sorrows, march forward. Upwards and onwards. She really could not bear the din and racket of that.

How silent this countryside is. Often at night it is not silent at all, there are calls and rustlings, tree frogs, running water; but tonight the darkness is perfectly still. Waiting, perhaps; holding its breath.

She sleeps finally, and wakens to light and the smell of bacon. Jack turns from the stove towards her, smiling widely, happy as he generally seems to be with the day's prospects. He doesn't have what she would call joy, exactly. That's too serene. What he seems to have is a huge capacity for hope, anticipation for whatever the moment may lead to. Contagious pleasures. She smiles back, although again, she doesn't feel entirely well.

"Hungry? Ready for coffee and breakfast?"

Neither of those, actually. The bacon smell is a bit overpowering. "I don't think so. Nothing, thanks."

He frowns. "Are you ill?"

"Slightly queasy is all. Nothing to worry about." Still, she's glad he's here. She hadn't thought, taking off, of being sick on her own, on the road. Not that there's much he can do. But if she needed help, he would give it. He is a presence. Soon, this will not be the case. Perhaps that's what makes her shivery. This won't do. She can't afford to be lonely, and certainly doesn't want to get scared. She has already spent far too many years vaguely, unreasonably, depending.

He comes to sit beside her on the narrow bed, stroking her hair. She tries to remember what she ate yesterday that he did not, ticking off meals in her memory.

She wonders what his ex-wife looks like. She wonders who, back home, he touches with these adept and clever fingers, whose body his thick, blunt penis enters, who hears, and makes, the sounds of pleasure in his bed.

Is it odd that the many passionate privacies she assumes he must have are exciting to her? That these speculations, these pictures, arouse her?

It may only be fever. Anyway, she needs to go to the bathroom. "You ought to eat something," he says. "Settle your stomach."

"Boiled egg on dry toast? That might do."

She can see, though, that his concerned, thoughtful eyes are not wholly on her. A corner of them is also aimed at another location and a different part of his life that must not be too much delayed.

For herself, it's still hard to imagine what she is heading towards, besides more prairie, then foothills, mountains and finally sea. Mere geography. Or whether there's a point in thinking about a particular destination at all.

They are driving now through the main broad prairie expanse, an infinity, an eternity of gold-green-white-blue that makes her head spin and her eyes water with its brightness. Jack, driving, hums softly; Gwen closes her eyes now and then against rushing scenery. She is alert to his details: the voice that sounds as if it has travelled a great, deep distance inside him; the grizzle of prickly grey hairs on his face, on his arms; the grey depths, too, of his clear, observing eyes.

His toes are broad, stumpy, his fingers and hands sure of themselves. Deft. His concerns are both vast and particular. His heart is large, his compassions broad. What are his unhappier, less fortunate aspects?

It is probably a good thing there won't be time to find out. It is perhaps the speed of the journey between the Gwen who not so long ago assumed a mainly agreeable, foreseeable existence and the Gwen who has no notion what will happen that is causing this dizziness. Brave Edgar, after all, who kicked her off, booted her into this new life, and incidentally into those quick, thick, capable arms, which lift and embrace her, and are now at work at the wheel.

seven

It's beyond David what use he'll ever get out of knowing how to make the kind of weird shit he's shaking up at the moment. Stuff that's fluffy and pink and gets topped off with tiny umbrellas and cherries, or things that turn blue or green when they're mixed. Shit never dreamed of, or desired, in Gully's.

On the other hand, it happens to be something he's good at: a dash of this, a jigger of that, sort of like a chemistry class except with nothing very explosive. He can *remember* drinks, it turns out. Also he's finally in a class where he's not the only one who knows that he's smart. Students less skilled look up to him. This is so unaccustomed that he's almost sorry the course, which consumes three hours every afternoon, only lasts two weeks, the prize a diploma at the end of it all.

If real school had been like this, a lot of things would be different; but David began his education at what Fink last week called "a slight disadvantage, socially."

He meant that David had been a little boy accustomed to living in corners: at Gully's, and even upstairs in the little apartment with his mum and his dad. They were friendly, benevolent corners, though. Even when no notice was taken, equally no harm to him was ever intended. On his first day of school, he already had an education in what adults did— some adults, sometimes.

But he knew almost nothing about other kids. He didn't know how loud they yelled, how fast they ran, how swift they were to grab toys or take offence. His mother, who walked him to school the first day, also seemed uneasy. She, too, watched for a while, perched on a tiny chair against the wall of the bright, tempestuous classroom. And then she left: patted his arm, squeezed his shoulder, said, "You be a good, big boy now, and have a good time," and just left.

It seems to him he never got out of the corners. Schoolyards and schoolrooms, however he kept himself tucked to one side, struck him as actively hostile and, if not necessarily dangerous, certainly without guarantees he'd be safe. He watched—for years he watched, eyes alert to the secret ways the others must have, the ones who flowed like smooth rivers around each other. There were rocky places here and there, quarrels and altered alliances were perfectly visible, but some people knew how to manoeuvre, they shifted, they took on new stances.

He could see what they did, but he couldn't tell how. He didn't know how people his own age went along, got along. He guesses he never did learn.

He didn't get invited to play, or to parties unless everyone in a class was to be asked. He also wasn't especially tormented. Mainly he supposes he just wasn't noticed. At least he must have been good at invisibility, at least he had that skill.

But he wasn't stupid, any more than he is now. He knows the information he observed and absorbed was stored smartly, if not very usefully. Even so, teachers' eyes, too, must have passed right over him, and his exams and his essays got only cursory notice, while other students' papers might be returned with long notes running down margins, as if they'd done something important.

He imagines teachers struggling to remember which kid he was when it came time for report cards. And he remembers in particular Ms. Cross, in fifth grade, who was nothing like her name, but pretty and dark-haired, with big round glasses and what seemed to him smiling, kind eyes, and, always, bright dresses, as if it were part of her job not only to pass information to pupils but to make them feel cheered.

He remembers that sometimes, walking by his desk, she put her hand on his shoulder in a way that felt sort of like a caress. He remembers she smelled sweet, like a flower. The report card he took home from her at the end of the year said, "David completes his work well and competently, but is very withdrawn and contributes little to the class. His social skills require considerable attention and development."

He remembers those exact words, and how exposed he felt, and also betrayed, by a woman he had trusted, for no good reason it seemed. His mother looked worried and asked, "What does she mean? Are you not getting along well? Are you unhappy at school?"

"No, it's fine," he told her. "I don't know what she means. Maybe she's got me mixed up with somebody else."

Was it truly like that, or does he exaggerate, or is he just retroactively feeling bad for himself? "Don't," Fink warned, "take any progress here in this office as an opportunity for self-pity."

Actually, David thinks that it was all maybe more sad than bad. And that maybe now he'd do better.

As he is doing, because look at him!

Because he's older? Or because here, he knows what he's doing? Or because a few months ago someone finally looked at him with desire? Anyway, here he is behind a fake classroom bar, wielding a shaker with the flair of a magician, confident in the results and of the admiration, for this single small achievement, of the rest of the group.

It's not a large group: a retraining program, people who took wrong turns in the first place and wound up in dead ends, who are now groping their ways along a new route, hoping for better. This is a route David knows better than they do, although not to the extent of having any history with fuzzy pink drinks, or green ones or blue ones. Anyway, in how many places do people actually order this kind of thing? A martini, okay; a Manhattan, maybe; even in a pinch a Black Russian. But pink things with paper umbrellas?

On his night shifts, he describes these drinks to Gully's patrons, who hold their noses, or pretend to puke, and laugh and slap the tables.

Well, most things learned in school likely turn out to be laughably useless. The main thing is that in this one, he's an A student, top of the class. He even feels very slightly boisterous with success. He owes, he guesses, Keith Miller for this.

Keith Miller really bugged him about it, even phoned him a month ago at Gully's to say, "I checked, there's still an opening in the next program, and if bartending's for sure what you want to do, you might as well get properly qualified. A diploma in anything's always a leg up."

Who knew there were diplomas for bartending? "It's not like it'd come in handy here at Gully's," David argued.

"But is that where you'll always be? You've got a lot of years ahead, and nobody knows what can happen." David felt that chill again: his feet on the precipice.

Sometimes there are good surprises, though. Gwen was one, at least until she betrayed him by driving away. And now this is okay. It's like what Fink said a few weeks ago: "It seems to me, David, that with the exception of your peccadilloes, your crimes, which you seem to have been unrealistically optimistic about, you have a tendency to look on the dark side. You think of the worst that can happen, instead of the best. Does that ring true to you?"

Yes, probably. "But the worst *does* happen. People die. They go away. And I mean, I've been to *jail*." Was this another black hole in Fink's imagination?

"That's true. But you might also want to consider that some unhappy events may come about largely because you expect them to. In some ways, you may even invite them because you expect them. I'm just suggesting that if you anticipated pleasure, that's what you might more often get. Could you consider that, do you think?"

Probably not. But David nodded.

"All right, think of something you're dreading."

At the time, this course.

"Now think of a happy outcome for it."

Who would have dreamed how well he'd take to words like grenadine, how easily to substances like Angostura bitters? "The diploma, I guess." Who would have imagined how cool it is, standing up here pouring bright liquors into a glass, handing it to Joe Myers, the teacher, watching him sip, watching him nod. Knowing nine other people are watching the same thing, some maybe with envy but also admiring.

He wishes Gwen could see him like this.

He's driven by her place a couple of times since she left, but it's so clearly not hers any more, a mere house, repainted and ripped up, and with a tricycle on the little porch where he used to stand in the darkness observing.

Or maybe he doesn't wish Gwen could see him. "Why ever," she would wonder, "is a law student taking a bartender's course?" He sometimes forgets all that she never knew about him.

Edgar, now, Gwen's husband—he observes silently, from David's bedside table, what goes on in David's life; his photograph is a witness to the things David never told Gwen and barely confides to Fink, never mind to Keith Miller, and certainly not to his father, who has his own life, his own concerns.

And, it must be said, his own recent pleasures. David has never had this unease about his father before; another reason it's been good, coming here, getting away for a while every day.

Look at Tina, looking at David. What's that in her eyes, invitation? Tina loses marks for chewing gum while she mixes her sample drinks. She's trying to "work up" from serving food at what she says is "a dive, a greasy spoon." Everybody had to tell their histories and hopes the first day; David too. He told a kind of truth: "I want to upgrade my qualifications for the job I already do." He didn't mention that his father owns the bar where he works, or that it's mainly a draft joint, or many, many other things.

Tina's okay, but the way she's looking at him is maybe just kind of vacant. What if David put his ice-chilled hands into his pants and waved his dick in her direction? Would her glance get keen, would her jaw fall open, her gum topple off the end of her tongue? Would she look at him in a perfectly definable way, in that case?

She doesn't have the moves, though, and isn't all that appealing. She's scrawny in her tight T-shirts, and the way she pulls her blonde hair back into a ponytail makes her nose look too sharp.

Scrawny, sharp-featured—she could be David's sister, or cousin.

There are three women in the class. That's quite a few, almost a third. Even at Gully's, David's mother mainly served, and only worked behind the bar in emergencies. It seems a tough, kind of inappropriate desire. These women are, what? Bold, maybe. He can imagine how any of them would react if they met, say, on the street, and he tried in his hopeless way to get their attention. What a scene! He shivers, and it has nothing to do with chilled hands.

It's not that he's unused to bold women, lots of Gully's customers are not exactly shy, and have not exactly had reclusive lives. But they are different, old (but wasn't Gwen?) and in a different relationship to him, sort of honorary aunts. These women here are his equals. That he can meet their eyes at all is an achievement. He tries now to catch Tina's eye. He even winks. Winks! What possessed him? But that wakes her up. She's looking startled now.

"Excellent, David," Joe Myers says. "You might want to think about putting a sharper angle on your elbows when you're mixing, though. A bit more of a flourish. And smile, hold the smile."

David never considered before how much showmanship can be involved. It sure isn't at Gully's, where bartending is a matter of moving a lot of beer fast around the room, keeping a lid on emotions that threaten the general peace and, of course, listening. They spent two whole three-hour classes with Joe Myers play-acting different sorts of situations, to see how the students would handle them. David was best at that, too: at firmly steering hostile Joe out the door, pacifying obnoxious Joe, quieting maudlin Joe. These abilities come so naturally to him, having grown up at Gully's, that until now he didn't even know they were abilities.

But evidently there are places where patrons want more, where bartending's like stepping up on a stage to perform an act that's fairly complex.

Will he retain this new knowledge, these skills, back at Gully's, where they're no use whatever? Like learning a language and then never using it, will this fall out of his head, then his life?

"Just try to enjoy," Fink might say, "don't rethink everything so much."

Would Fink say any such thing? It seems unlikely counsel from a shrink, even one trying to get his patient to look on the bright side.

The class is having a graduation ceremony in a couple of days, just themselves and whoever they invite. David is slightly embarrassed to be looking forward to this, but he's never graduated from anything before. Also his dad said, "I'd be pleased to come, son. I'm real proud of you." His father looks lighter these days, for his own reasons but also because of David's successes. "You've come a long way the past few months." His father attributes this to Fink and Keith Miller, and why wouldn't he?

"Any promising gals?" His dad's next hope, no doubt, although not something he raises much. David's mother rarely did, either, although dying, she did say, "I know you'll find the right woman when the time comes. I'm so sorry I won't know her, but I know you'll choose well. You'll have lovely children, David. I wish so much I could have seen my grandchildren." At the time, although he understood it was a very sad moment, and also a kind of blessing from her, David couldn't connect with the pictures she was trying to draw: the right woman, children. Unfathomable.

Since Gwen, a woman who would look and could see him, the idea of a right woman does actually hover at the edges of his vision. The idea, at least. The possibility. But children, no. They're beyond him. He supposes that, too, may change, but what would have to happen? Far too much, far beyond his reach, not to mention his desires.

"Yeah," he told his dad, "the girls are okay. Nobody special. Anyhow, there isn't much time for anything but work. It's really a tough course. Well, I mean, not tough, exactly, but there's a lot to cover."

David spends odd hours, and moments, memorizing recipes. The main textbook isn't big, but it has instructions for about a hundred drinks, and a picture of each one, so everybody knows what something's supposed to turn out like. Also a description of the taste, although that's never as clear as a picture—what exactly does "light, but with an edge of tartness" mean? How does he gauge something like that, from just words?

Joe Myers says, "Depends where you get a job, how useful this is. But whatever kind of bar, this is basic knowledge. Even if you don't use all of it, you need to understand how ingredients work together, because it's not just *making* drinks, it's *knowing* them. It's the expertise and confidence, that's the foundation you want." They believe what he tells them because, when he isn't giving this course three times a year, he runs the bar of one of the big hotels, which means he's in charge of other, lesser bartenders, and he also sometimes pitches in for a friend's catering company when it's doing a private, special party. So if anybody knows what's important for a bartender to know, it's Joe Meyers. "It's why I emphasize style as well as content," he says. "The way you make a drink being as important as what you put in it."

Behind Gully's bar at nights, David practises the tilt of the head, the deft, angular movements of arms Joe recommends. Sometimes, exaggerating, he makes the regulars laugh.

It's like his life is in a whole bunch of separate places: here for another couple of days, at Gully's, in Fink's office and in Keith Miller's for a little while longer and always, forever, inside his own head. And all those places are busy and challenging. David feels as if he suddenly has a very active life.

Not full, though. Full isn't the same thing as active.

But something's sure different, because when today's class wraps up, Greg says to him, "We're going for a beer, Dave, want to come?" Lean Greg and plump Andy hang out together and are taking the course, they said the first day, because they hope to open a small bar and grill of their own, although meanwhile Greg's saving what he can from some low-level government job, while Andy does landscaping and lives with his folks. Nobody here graduated high school. That way, they're all like David. They maybe had a tough time there too.

"I can't, sorry. I have to work. Tomorrow, maybe? It's my day off."

Not everything's different. That was too quick. Having been practically forced by Keith Miller into this course and then having it turn out this way, and taking into account Fink's advice, David wonders now how often he's said a too-quick, nearly automatic kind of "no" to other things that might have gone well. Something Fink might suggest he should "work on"? He could have said yes to Greg, could have called his dad and said, "A couple of guys want me to go for a drink, is it okay if I'm late?" and his dad wouldn't have said no. He'd have been pleased. Relieved, unless he had his own urgent plans.

It's amazing David managed to say yes to Gwen. Except she moved fast, and didn't give him a whole lot of choice once the event started rolling. If she'd asked while they were still at Gully's, "Would you care to join me in bed?" he would surely have panicked.

Greg shakes his head. "No can do tomorrow. The next day, though, after graduation, we're all getting together, right?"

So David will hand the diploma to his dad and send him off, back to Gully's, and go drinking with his classmates. "Yeah, great," he says. And so it is, or may be. His hopes are cautious, but at least they are hopes.

He had hopes starting high school, too: to be a new, unknown person in a new, unknown place. The opportunity of his lifetime to that point—he was very keyed up.

At Gully's, people must have wished him well, and also perhaps had their own memories of hope, because the night before he began high school one of the regulars, a retired barber named Sam, a nice guy who long ago had pressed quarters into David's small palms for no reason at all except generosity and maybe, sometimes, a whole lot to drink, said, "Come on, kid, let's start you off right."

So a chair was set in the middle of the floor, a bar towel draped around David's neck, an extension cord found for Sam's trimmer. A considered gift; a considerate one. "It's been a while," he said. "Styles've changed. But I see boys, I know how you fellows want to look these days, although myself, I don't always like it. Here we go then," and the clippers started up at the back.

It took some time, trimming and scissoring. People watched, quiet with respect for Sam's effort and craft. When he finished, David couldn't quite assess the result. He looked unfamiliar to himself, but that wasn't necessarily bad. And he could see similarities to cuts he, too, saw on the street.

That night, he couldn't sleep for wondering who he would be, if he slept, when he woke up.

What faith in magic he must have had. What trust in miracles.

"Just relax," his mother said from the top of the stairs as he left that first day, "you'll do fine." From which he saw that she knew he had not, for the most part, done fine once down those stairs. She spoke as if it was simple, doing fine. Walking towards the school, heart pumping fast with longing and dread, his feet did a shuffling pause when he saw ahead the scary spectacle of people already with people to talk to. But could he not, this time, with his will for a new life, walk up to one of those laughing, shouting, shoulder-punching groups, move right in, make some smart comment, or an incisive one, or a friendly but not too friendly one? Why would they necessarily stare at him coolly, or ignore him, or walk off by themselves?

There are moments of such failure, they still make his stomach cramp and cringe; incidents so vivid they're like stamps on his life: humiliation, withering, fatal ineptness. So small and brief, probably nobody else even remembers them; worse, maybe nobody else even thought they counted for much at the time. "Don't exaggerate, David," his father used to say impatiently, in the days when David was little, concocting stories, maybe embellishing events as a child might, in his attempts to interpret them. Maybe he continued to exaggerate, but effects were true. What he became in the aftermath of certain events, that is true.

The whole school was called to first-day assembly. Hundreds and hundreds of kids, lined up by class but breaking quickly into the anarchy of friendships: pairs and groups. The auditorium was huge, rows of terraced seats semi-circling a stage on which adults—principal, teachers—were gathering, also in knots of pairs and groups. A guy behind him poked his shoulder. "Hey pal, cool hair you got there."

In what tone of voice was that spoken? David heard derision. He had already turned, fists up, shocking even himself, or especially himself, and snarled, "Fuck off, asshole," before he even thought about it.

"Hey." The guy turned his palms towards David. "Back off." And then turned away, towards the rest of the line, said, "Do you believe this guy?" and that was that. David was marked and ruined; or if not, felt marked and ruined. He supposes now, nearly a decade later, that he was not so important, and no one paid so much attention. And was it not possible the guy really did admire his hair? Or David's boldness, his courage in wearing it in that long-topped, buzzed-back-and-sides style?

Defeated in any case, if only by himself, David failed to recover. Three years later he left school for the last time; until now.

Leaving today's class, Tina stops him in the hall. "Were you winking at me?" She sounds—not unhappy.

"I guess. Yeah." Up close, her eyes are narrow and small, like the rest of her. She moves so that her upper arm touches his, pushes into his, a sort of languorous nudge.

"You're really good. I really admire how you remember everything and do it so well. Sometimes I'm just hopeless, I think I've memorized a drink and then I start making it and I get all confused trying to smile and make my arms move right and remember everything that's supposed to go in it, and it never comes out the way it's supposed to. How do you do it?"

David blushes. "Well, you know, I already work in a bar. But I guess it's hard for a while." There's a long pause. "You do okay, though."

"Good enough to pass, I guess, but not like you." Another long pause. "So. You working today?"

"Yeah. I should get going, I'm late."

"But you're going for drinks with everybody Friday, right?"

"For sure. And anyway," he begins moving away, "see you tomorrow."

Could he be clumsier? What's the matter with him, how much plainer could she have been? Doesn't matter whether she's pretty or moves right or any of that, she was interested, and he had another of those stupid, foot-shuffling moments. Shit!

Maybe he can prepare himself to do better on Friday. He doesn't seem to do well when things take him by surprise. Except with Gwen, of course; he did okay with that surprise. He isn't hopeless. His shoulders straighten, knowing that he isn't hopeless.

At Gully's, where the late-afternoon rush is under way when he gets in, his father, behind the bar, is whistling. This is part of his recent, general lightening, which has to do with David, sure, but also with Beryl. Another surprise, not a totally happy one.

Beryl is his father's new friend. Well, not so new, she's been around a few weeks and anyway is in her late fifties. She doesn't spend much time in Gully's, which David thinks is because she and the place don't suit each other: Gully's is shabby, dark, weathered as its customers but also as sturdy as they are, and Beryl is trim, slim-ankled, blue-eyed, silvery-haired, barely wrinkled, feminine in an unfamiliar way, smiley, humble, and also like steel.

David remembers thinking of his father someday taking up with a woman who would become David's stepmother, with all the unpleasant Hansel-and-Gretel implications of that, but again he must not have believed this truly could happen.

And maybe it won't. Beryl and his father first got to know each other at a meeting of property owners alert to possible development plans for this part of town; his father was there because this might be important to Gully's, Beryl because she owned two houses inherited from a dead husband, although she lived elsewhere herself, in an apartment.

Now she often appears in Gully's doorway but vanishes upstairs, into the home part, to wait for David's dad to break free. Or she and David's dad slip away together for a few hours, out to movies, other meetings, other bars, better than Gully's. David imagines his father won't, in the long run, take kindly to her not hanging around Gully's itself much. For the time being, though, it's very strange to hear his father whistling, or to see Beryl and his father touching randomly, tenderly, often. He doesn't remember his mother and father touching each other that way. He wasn't wrong that they loved each other, but if this is love with his father and Beryl, it must be a somewhat different sort: more determined, more conscious. More aware of paying attention, and also of losing no time.

Maybe it's age. Maybe it's losses they've already had.

Beryl speaks kindly to David, and respectfully in a way, as if she understands his prior claim, but she focusses on his father. She has been widowed twice, which, David joked once, ought to make his dad nervous, but his father glanced at him sharply and David hasn't been careless about Beryl since. She has a son and a daughter, both grown and living at the far ends of the country.

His father will have told her about David, if only in that kind of necessary recounting of major events. They have a lot of years to catch up on, and David's privacy would not enter into it. Beryl would tell his father, comfortingly, "It wasn't your fault. Sometimes young people just go through strange, frightening phases, that's all. He'll be fine. Look how well he's doing now. I can see you've done your best."

"Poor boy," he imagines his father saying. "He's had a difficult time. And he was very fond of his mother, that was hard for him, although the trouble started before she died. So I don't know." He might have said, "Maybe it was growing up in a bar, maybe it was the wrong kind of people around. And he was never very successful at having friends. It may be he was embarrassed to have people here. Or if he'd had brothers and sisters— so many things make a difference, it's hard to tell exactly where things have gone wrong."

Beryl, who can have no investment or real interest in David, would say, "But you did everything you could, it must be good to know you stood by him, no matter what. And Gully's is a fine business, nothing for anyone to be embarrassed about."

Beryl has never indicated by so much as a flicker that she is aware of David's history. She has never flinched, or drawn back, and he has never caught her glancing at him with unease. She has only been kind to him. "You're a good-looking young man," she said just last week, facing him upstairs in the kitchen, putting her hands on his shoulders, regarding him gravely. "You have very fine eyes. I know you'll meet someone and be happy." Without actually meaning to, he jerked away. But who did she think she was, hoping anything for him, looking at him as a woman might, assessing him and pronouncing her judgment?

They aren't much used to talk, David and his father, but his dad makes occasional efforts. Last Sunday morning, he and David were getting breakfast upstairs, moving around each other as adeptly and unconsciously as they do down in the bar, when his father asked, hesitantly, anxiously, "Do you like Beryl?"

"Sure. Why wouldn't I?" He wouldn't hurt his father for the world.

"Well, I can see you might be a bit upset, her suddenly around here so much. You might think I'm forgetting the past, but I'm not, and I want you to know that for sure. Your mother, she's always a part of my life, always will be. Only, you can't stop when other things stop, you have to keep going and make the best of it. I don't guess you've found it so easy, Beryl turning up the way she has, but it says nothing at all about your mother and me, except your mother's not here any more and I don't want to be alone for the rest of my life."

He wouldn't have to be, he could have David. But of course that's not what he meant. "As long as you're happy. I'm happy with whatever you want." And he is, really, he must be. His dad deserves every bit of love from Beryl and loyalty from David they can each drum up.

So when his dad now asks, "Okay if Beryl and I take off for a while, Dave? Do you mind taking over?" David naturally nods.

Actually it's kind of nice sometimes, feels interesting, looking around Gully's when he's left on his own, imagining how it might be if he were really in charge, if this were really his place. If he took over, someday, from his father, and went on and on with these people who are comforting and familiar to him even if it's their first time; and if he knew nothing more needed to change, that he was king of his very own castle and could not be dislodged.

Imagining this, he feels expansive. Feeling expansive, he becomes generous. "A round on the house," he calls out, and is immediately the centre of a rush, outstretched hands holding glasses, like starving children on TV lined up jostling for food. David's hands, drenched with beery foam, fly back and forth over the bar, from hands to taps back to hands. What will his dad, who does this on only the rarest, most special occasions, say when he hears?

"Thanks kid," people say happily, turning away. Also, "You're a good boy." No wonder: by the time they're done, his generosity has cost Gully's, his dad, quite a few bucks.

David's father, and his mother, worked hard and long hours here to keep the place going. They washed glasses by hand, in steaming water, late into the night when he was a kid, and in the mornings scrubbed floors, tables, walls before opening. For a long time, David's mum made, all by herself, hot lunches to sell alongside the first brews of the day. They were careful with every dime and dollar because they had to be.

His parents' tired hands, their weary feet, dragging up the stairs. The smells of the two of them tucking him in: yeasty, smoky, damp. Their exhausted, soft voices in the next room. When David got sick, his mother rustling, touching, comforting, but also hurrying downstairs to help out, rushing back to feed him juices or soup and to touch his forehead with a hand soft as flannelette. They smiled and laughed downstairs, but upstairs their faces fell loose, hard to read, resting, maybe.

He is wasteful, thoughtless, ungrateful. The damage he's caused, the grief he's brought, the tears shed on his behalf—oh. Those good people. He could weep, right here, right now, too late, for their struggles.

He could also—this must really be terrible—go out into the street and jerk off in front of the first passerby. There is something about shame that makes him want to do something truly shameful. Something about it that, it seems, he finds arousing.

He is a bad person in bad trouble. He sees the cheerful faces, hears the laughter of a lot of people with free drinks, and can see no connection at this moment between himself and anything as innocent and human as Gully's.

Look at these people who call him "a kid" and "a boy," what does that mean for someone who turns twenty-four very soon? Something wrong, something recognizably pathetic. At last he sees, truly and terribly—how could he have been so senseless and selfish and blind?—what so many people, cops, lawyers, judges, cons, his dad, Fink, Keith Miller, have tried to tell him: he has fucked up, very badly.

No wonder women scream and get angry.

They *used* to scream. They *got* angry. Nothing awful has happened for quite a while now. He is not a virgin. He will have a diploma. He has acquaintances with whom he'll be going for a drink Friday. He is not entirely without prospects.

And on Friday his dad will be proud. His mother maybe would have been, too, although he thinks she had higher hopes. Maybe it's mean, but he has not invited Beryl. David's graduation is a family occasion.

Here they come now, his dad and Beryl, back from doing whatever they've been doing, wherever they've been. They weren't gone very long. They stand for a few moments inside the door, heads tipped together, talking earnestly. David sees Beryl touch his father's shoulder finally, smile and, turning towards the stairs, wave lightly at David. His dad comes to the bar, puts a hand on David's shoulder. "Doing okay, son?"

"Yeah. Except I did something stupid." He needs to confess— that must be good, right? "I gave a round on the house. Didn't think first. Sorry, the totals aren't going to be so hot tonight."

There's only the tiniest pause before his father says, "Oh hell, they'll be fine. We don't do enough of that anyway. That something you learned in your course? Make people friendly, bring them back?"

What a nice man, a good father. How could David, raised by his mother and this man, have gone so badly off track? On the other hand, in another mood his father could have been annoyed, if not angry. Maybe Beryl's influence: a kindly one. "A lot of things you've learned in that course I've never heard of, I bet."

"A lot of things hardly anybody's heard of and not too many'd want to."

David's father laughs and slaps his shoulder, accepting the joke. David looks at his father's hands: the veins on their backs are purple and prominent, the skin is loose and kind of foldy. His dad is only sixty-two, his hands should not look so old. How much of this is David's fault?

When Beryl looks at his dad, what does she see? Someone handsome and appealing, or only someone sturdy to rest against? She can probably still make out his features. David can't, really. He sees the whole figure that constitutes his dad, now and then catching details as well; like those hands. Which join David behind the bar, making everything manageable again.

When closing time comes and the last customer leaves, it's just the two of them downstairs, as it often is: stacking chairs on the tables, wiping the bar, packing glasses into the dish-washer that has made life so much easier and different from the early years. Tonight, his dad hauls himself up on a barstool—Gwen's barstool—and pats the one next to it. "Got time to talk, son? A few minutes?"

Uh-oh. In the evening's last hour, has he worked up an anger over lost, free beer? "Sure," David says warily. His father's eyes are wandering, he's uncomfortable, uncertain, reluctant. Whatever it is, it can't be good.

"You know Beryl."

What? "Well, yeah."

"She and I had a talk while we were out tonight. Actually it's why we went out, to discuss some things. You know I care about her, right?"

"Yeah." Something bad is coming, something that should make time stop right here, no further words, no further any-thing.

"And how I've told you it has nothing to do with your mother, or not caring about her, just that life has to go on?"

"Yeah." So all that about never forgetting was really about softening David up.

"Okay." Deep breath. "So. What we were deciding tonight was whether Beryl should move in here. Upstairs. She's been thinking about moving out of her apartment anyway, the building's going downhill and she wants to get out, so this'd be a good time to come here. See how it goes. Put some of her things in storage for a while, till we get sorted out a bit, and figure out more about how we go along together. That'd be our idea. But it's your home too, and if you wanted to bring in somebody to live, you'd talk it over with me, so I should do that with you. Only right. If you're dead set against it, okay, we'll understand. It's how we see things for ourselves, but you need a say."

Beryl upstairs. Her clothing in closets, her underwear in the drawers, her flowery scent, that perfume she wears, in the air, her robe tossed over a chair, like his mother used to do. Her thises-and-thats dotting the place, even if her furniture goes into storage. Storage! They've gone so far as to talk about that sort of detail.

Look at his dad's face: anxious and old. David can't remember his father not looking this way; besides the familiarity that comes of seeing him every day, David was a late arrival in his parents' lives, so his dad has always looked old to him, even when he actually wasn't.

David's being given a choice here, and that's kind and also right, as his father says, but of course it's not really a choice. If he said no, what? On what grounds could he do that, and what would his father's face tell him? David has grieved and disappointed his father before, but he has never said, "No, of course I'd like you to be happy, but I can't bear what would make you happy. So no."

"I think," David says instead, in as true a tone as he can manage, "you should do what you want to. It's nice of you to ask me, but all I got to say is, Beryl's fine, and if it's what you want, it's okay with me."

This lie—is it strange?—hurts, but it also makes him feel virtuous. He has done something good, his sins and shortcomings feel slightly redeemed.

"You sure?" David sees how tense his father must have been by how relieved he now looks, the way his face relaxes, his eyes and mouth softening. "You don't want a while to think it over? Beryl's a nice woman, as you say, but if she moves in there'll be changes, naturally. Another person's bound to make a difference."

No kidding. "I know. That's okay." How closely, and clearly, is his father regarding David's tone and expression? Does he discern any true feelings, or does he see what he wants to see?

The latter, evidently. "Thanks son. I was pretty sure that's what you'd say, and I'm glad I was right. Beryl and me, we're not getting any younger. I like the idea of her being here, so we can spend as much time together as we can." David's lucky father. Lucky Beryl. To have each other and, it seems, with such natural ease: go to a meeting, run into a stranger, spend a little time and all of a sudden be a couple living together. If old people can do that, what prevents David? Some knowledge, some appeal, maybe even some chemical?

"How do you know?" he blurts, and realizes his father won't have a clue what he means. "How do you just meet somebody and then things fall into place and you decide it's what you want?" And, maybe more to the point, how does the same thing happen, in return, in Beryl's head and heart? How does this become reciprocal?

His dad looks at him curiously, but then, it was a pretty big question, covering a lot of unclear ground, with plenty of room for incomprehension or misunderstanding. Also, they're more used to actions that demonstrate their affections, like the smooth ways they work together, than using words. It must have been hard, taken a lot of gearing up, for his dad to put the extremely personal subject of Beryl into actual words.

"It doesn't," his dad begins slowly, "happen all that often, that's for sure. When I met your mother we were young, and I remember thinking, 'There she is, that's the one,' but I couldn't have told you why at the time. I can't tell you now, either, but it's probably different when you're younger anyway, or maybe that kind of thing only happens once. When I met Beryl, I just thought she was an attractive person, well-spoken, and that seemed enough reason to see if she wanted to spend some time with me, but it wasn't an instinct, like it was with your mother. With Beryl it's more slow and steady. Getting to know each other. In a lot of ways your mother and I did it the other way around, we got to know each other after we, I don't know, fell in love, I guess. Anyway, however it happens it doesn't come along very often, and when it does it's maybe just luck. Right place, right time. And I guess maybe you have to be looking for it. Ready. I know there's probably lots of nice women I didn't notice because it wasn't on my mind to. They didn't register."

"So when you met Beryl, you were ready?"

"I guess. I don't want you to think I was looking, but I must have known it was time. I was getting pretty lonely, you know. After your mother, I wasn't lonely for a long time outside of missing her, but it was building up."

The word "lonely," so naked and truthful and trusting, hangs in the air between them. His father's been lonely—of course he must have been, a man entirely accustomed to a companion, a helper, a wife—how could David not have known that? The two of them, he and his father, rattling around here together, both lonely; because hearing the word, David also absorbs it as the truth of his own condition, although he wouldn't have before, he couldn't have borne its hollow sound. And it is hollow, it continues to echo.

Would this be a moment to say, "Me, too, it feels like I've always been lonely, and I don't know how to stop being that way"?

No. His dad can say the word because it's over for him. For David it's still a true word, chronic, like one of those muscle-wasting diseases that leave people crippled. He couldn't possibly speak it himself. Tears already come to his eyes. His father reaches out, touches his arm. "Of course it's a risk. I don't know what'll happen with me and Beryl, it may not work out, but that's partly what her moving in is for, to see." His father has mistaken David's expression. He must have thought it some kind of concern for himself. Also, what does he mean, "to see"? What else might he have in mind?

David slips off the barstool, free of his father's touch. "Sure it'll work out," he says as heartily as he can. "It'll be great for you. I'm glad you've found somebody."

And still his father hears what he needs to, sighs, and also descends from his stool, Gwen's stool. "You will too, son, when the time comes, and when it does, I hope it's like the feeling I had for your mother when we were as young as you. I guess we should head upstairs. Beryl's there. She wanted to know what you thought, and now we can tell her. It's late. She might stay over, I guess. Might as well."

Up the stairs they go, David following his father with the feeling that, instead, he is plunging down and down. A bar-tending diploma, his own small triumph—what is that, against another involuntary upheaval, another shift at the hands of others? Even when those are loving hands, as his father's are.

Some signal that is silent passes between his father and Beryl when they enter the living room. She smiles so brightly and, it seems, truthfully, that David's heart wavers. He has done a good thing, he has made happiness possible. "Thank you," Beryl says, taking both his hands. "It's very generous of you to share your home with me. I hope you'll help me settle in, let me know what your customs are. I don't want to disrupt things, and I certainly don't want to annoy you."

She sounds too meek. She is not a mouse-like person. David's eyes narrow; but no doubt she intends to sound reassuring, to make him feel comfortable and safe. That, too, is nice.

It's not as if it would be better if he disliked her.

What does she ordinarily do with her days? If her days are spent here, what will she do with them while his father's downstairs and David is either there, or at Fink's office, or Keith Miller's, or out wandering, or driving? Can he trust her to stay out of his room, for instance? Not to scrutinize any books he has lying around, or go through his bureau, or pick up the photograph of Edgar Stone on his bedside table and wonder just who that might be? What will she say, or worse, think, of the time he spends alone reading, or thinking, or watching TV in his room, all those spare hours—will she decide he is too strange and off-course? He knows that's how it could look, from the outside. He doesn't have many secrets, but he does cherish his privacies.

"Big moment for Beryl on Friday," his father says in the jovial tone he usually keeps downstairs in Gully's. "She's going to handle the bar for a few hours by herself, while I go to your graduation. So tomorrow we'll be training her." He smiles at them both. "Should make everyone happy. It's a while since we've had a woman down there."

A long, awkward silence; they must each be reminded that the last woman who worked Gully's bar was his wife, David's mother. How can Beryl do this, move into another woman's place as if she could erase years, a whole family history? "I know," she says quietly, "I'm not replacing your mother, David. And I hope you know I would never want such a thing."

He nods, because there's nothing to say to that, except maybe "How did you know what I was thinking?" Either she's very smart, or he's very transparent.

His dad looks restless. Maybe he's uncomfortable, the three of them together tonight. Maybe he's eager to push off with Beryl; their first night here together, if not, it now seems likely, their first night anywhere. David looks again at his father's hands, and at Beryl, and feels creepy. Like a voyeur, or someone left out, or an unwelcome guest. All those things.

He pretends a yawn. "I think I'm off, then. It's been a long day." He cannot, cannot, touch Beryl: kiss her cheek, or offer a good-night embrace; and so he leaves the living room awkwardly, as if he's also leaving behind an incomplete sentence, an up-in-the-air act, along with Beryl and his dad.

From behind his closed door, he can hear their quiet voices in the living room. Beryl's is higher and not as husky as his mother's, but it's still strange to hear conversation out there. From his bed, he hears Beryl and his dad taking turns in the bathroom, and his father's door opening, closing.

What will they do in there? What are they doing right this second? Is it something David will ever do again himself?

It's the wrong way around, his father having pleasures David has barely experienced. It's David who should be touching skin, while his father settles into dignified, celibate age.

Silent, smug Edgar offers no comfort, no advice. David could hurl the photograph against the wall, except he mustn't disturb them, couldn't bear to expose his despair, either. He knows it's stupid, or means something, that exposing himself on the street wasn't as shaming as it would be to display his unhappiness through broken glass.

He would like one goddamn thing to be clear; just one thing. Or rather, he'd like so many things not to be clear all at the same time. He's not large enough for so much. Stuff inside swells and bubbles and pushes to escape through his pores, his toes, the tip of his scalp. It's uncontainable. But it has to be contained.

Is his dad touching Beryl's breasts, sliding his lips around her nipples, the way David did with Gwen's? Is he asking her desires, or does he already know them?

Cotton sheets, the cool glass of a photograph, that's what touches David's skin. He tries touching himself, but that's not where his desire lies, and he pulls away. His desire seems to lie at the moment not with strangers on the street, nor with

Gwen exactly, although she located it for him, gave it a name and a picture and a sensation, but with someone unknown, untouchable, maybe out there, maybe not.

Whatever his father and Beryl are doing, they're doing it too quietly to be overheard. It's very, very quiet in the middle of the night, in David's bed.

eight

When Edgar was driving, not only did Gwen not get to stop for a pee, or a wayside orgasm, they also never pulled over for hitchhikers. Edgar was death on hitchhikers, apparently in fear one of them would be death on him.

"You never know," he would say, speeding past a backpacked man, or a weary young couple, he and Gwen both avoiding their eyes, and each other's. "You simply can't tell," he'd insist, as if Gwen were arguing. "They can't tell either. Only an idiot does that any more." He meant that for all the backpacked man or weary young couple could know, he and Gwen were out roaming for prey, hunting the innocent, aiming to force the unwitting into grotesque acts and torturous deaths.

Well, yes. There was, merely looking at people, no knowing. So no, Gwen would never pick someone up on her own. Obviously there were awful acts on both sides of the wheel, the most smiling, bland-looking person might well be concealing the most dreadful desires, she had to agree. Look, as it turns out, at Edgar! Never mind total strangers.

Jack, she learns midway through the prairies, has quite a different perspective. He is actually halting for a couple of hitchhikers! Without even asking! In the hot desert of grain, in the midst of miles and miles of flat shimmering gold and brilliant blue sky, he has pulled over for a pair of boys with their thumbs out. Now they are running to the door, pulling it open. What is he thinking?

They both wear packs, and low-slung jeans. One has an elaborate tattoo she can't quite decipher on his forearm, and they both have small golden earrings. What are they doing out here in the middle of nowhere? Although perhaps it isn't nowhere to them. "Don't!" Edgar's voice warns urgently in her head—and he so rarely talks back. "They might have knives, and evil intentions. Or be running away."

How annoying, Edgar reaching into her head, still trying to take charge. "Get the hell out," she thinks. "You have no business."

She herself picked up Jack, didn't she? No doubt she wouldn't have if she'd spotted him at the side of the road instead of cursing the weather and helping her out in a drenched campground, but she can't now see what difference that makes. Picking him up was taking a chance, and look how it's worked out: no bad thing, only very good things; except for that decision he just made without asking. If they had a future, she would have to speak up. But they don't.

Funny. With Edgar, she often enough failed to speak up because she assumed they did have a future, and in the scheme of things its harmony outweighed more trivial matters. She wouldn't make that mistake again. She frowns at Jack; a gesture.

"Oh God," says the first kid in the door. "Thanks. I thought we were going to die out there, we been standing forever. We didn't know it would be so hard, hitching." Thanks to people like Edgar, and Gwen.

"Sorry," says the second. "Our stuff's kind of dirty." Indeed, slapping themselves and their packs, dust does fly up into the light. Gwen frowns again briefly. Some changes come quickly, some very slowly, it seems.

Did she do that to Edgar? When he came home from work, or indoors from gardening, he right away slipped off his shoes. Was that some ancient demand of hers? It might very well have been. She turns in her seat, smiles back at the boys. "Just dump your stuff on the table. Don't worry." They smile back, and she thinks, they're just boys; only young, rather sweet-looking, surely harmless.

"Thanks, ma'am."

They are Jason and Tony. They shake Jack's hand and hers. They have unlined, open faces. They look to Gwen like babies, up close. They are sixteen and seventeen, buddies from school in a town north and east of this place on the road, and set out yesterday for a town in the mountains and a huge three-day concert. They're still excited, but slightly discouraged by hardship, which they're grateful to Jack and Gwen for relieving.

"I've noticed a number of hitchers," Jack says over his shoulder. "Is it the concert accounts for that?"

Gwen sees them shrug. "Guess so. Probably." Their feet in huge adolescent sneakers go up on the sofabed upholstery, and they slump, bodies curving into immediate indolence. Gwen wonders if she would have been a nagging sort of mother. She hopes not. She always assumed her relations with Sarah, or John, would be wonderfully benign, gentle, understanding, optimistic.

How would she have decided to let Sarah or John set out on foot, looking for lifts with strangers, to a concert far from home, at sixteen and seventeen? At any age? What's wrong with these kids' parents, don't they care, don't they love them?

Their packs are similar to Jack's: sturdy, efficient, durable and unaesthetic. Gwen used to have a six-piece set of matching luggage in a floral tapestry design, with wheels on the two largest cases. Not much used, really, over the years. Certainly the whole set at once was never called for. She and Edgar didn't travel so far or so lavishly that she needed to take along that much in the way of possessions.

She has kept only half the set: the largest case, the smallest and the shoulder bag, all now empty and tucked one inside the other on a shelf in the cupboard over where the boys lounge. Edgar, of course, leaving home, packed his rich calfskin set full of clothing and toiletries and other possessions and took it with him. She gave it away, when the time came.

The boys do not appear to be armed, nor do they demonstrate, so far, malicious intentions. All they may be is disobedient, Jason, at any rate. "You're gonna be in so much trouble," Tony is saying.

"They might not find out," Jason shrugs.

"My folks'll tell them when my sister rats you out." Tony catches Gwen's eye and raises his voice. "All our parents are away at some farm conference. Jason wasn't supposed to come with me."

"So they find out—what can they do?"

"Ground you forever, I bet. Look around, pal"—Tony leans to punch Jason's shoulder—"this'll be your whole life: wheat." They're laughing, though, as if anything beyond getting where they're going doesn't matter, isn't real. This may be youth, or it may also have something to do with the scratching of a match and the smell of smoke of a certain sweet kind. Gwen breathes in deeply. She hasn't smelled that for years. Jack sniffs the air too, glances at her, grins.

"How about you guys?" Jason asks. A polite boy, if a scruffy and disobedient one. "Where you going?"

"Myself," says Jack over his shoulder, "I'm off to the coast to see my ex-wife get married. My friend here's running away from home and isn't sure where she'll land up."

The boys look surprised—adults should not be, surely, so random? Then Tony's thin features break into a smile. "You want to come with us?" he asks Gwen. "If you're running away anyhow?" Clearly they regard this as absurd, and so it is. If Tony had thought for a moment she might agree, he wouldn't have spoken.

"Thanks, but I imagine I've been to my last big rock concert." Which was also her first. With—who else?—Edgar. This was before they married, and should have taught her something more useful than recognizing marijuana when she smells it. She hopes the boys don't set something on fire.

Now Jack's slowing for three girls up ahead. "Safety in numbers," he says in a low voice, "and they'll want to impress each other." Not, Gwen hopes, with a small adolescent crime spree; but he has at least perceived her unspoken concerns and taken them into account, and so is nearly redeemed.

The girls, like the boys, all wear jeans, but with big floppy hats and tight tank tops and loose shirts over breasts of various proportions. Each of them also has two rings in one earlobe, three rings in the other and a nose ring. It looks like something they all did together, to match. Girlfriends. The kind of thing girlfriends do, in this case to startling effect, at least to Gwen.

Climbing in they pause, briefly assessing, sniffing the air literally and, it seems, metaphorically. Reasonably enough they are nervous, no doubt as aware of danger as Gwen. "This is Jack, and I'm Gwen. Back there's Tony and Jason. They're headed to a concert, you too?"

"Yeah. I'm Janice. This is Tracy," jerking a thumb over her shoulder. "Back there's Sarah."

Gwen's heart leaps up. Her eyes widen. She almost falls out of her seat, leaning to lay eyes on the girl.

Janice and Tracy are thin, narrow, tight-skinned. Sarah is more fully fleshed, rosier, browner, broader-hipped and broader-lipped. Her dark hair is bundled by a tie at the back. Her eyes, dark too, meet Gwen's in a way that is puzzling. They become, slowly, almost hostile; as if Gwen has accused her of something unjust. Why would that be?

Perhaps a peculiar light in Gwen's eyes has caused her to be wary.

"Thanks for picking us up." This is Tracy, whose voice is high-pitched and whose features are peaky. She strikes Gwen as the least appealing, the one most likely not to have a good time at the concert. Her anxiety shows. Janice, however, is introducing herself, and Tracy and Sarah, to the boys, and Sarah tosses her pack on the table with an easy thump, rummages briefly in her purse and tells them, "I got a stash, too." Where do they get it, away out here?

For goodness sake, this is farm country, they probably grow it themselves.

When they take off their hats, Gwen sees the spikiness of Janice's and Tracy's hair; a contrast to the lushness of Sarah's. Is Sarah a kind of rebel, then, holding her own against fashion? That's the kind of daughter Gwen would have liked: someone who didn't starve herself, someone who knew her own beauty. "She could have been ours, Edgar." But that's too melancholy a thought; too eerie, also. She must not get confused, or stupid. Perhaps it's the dope in the air.

"You smoke?" Jack asks.

Not for a long time. Presumably (although there is little she can presume about Edgar), he didn't consider it something a lawyer should do. The last time she had a toke might even have been at that weekend concert she and Edgar went to before they were married, camping with thousands of others on a remote, ruined farm. Neither Flo nor Gwen's father kicked up any fuss about her and Edgar taking off for the faraway concert together. "Be careful," said her father, while Flo, typically, advised, "Have fun."

Gwen remembers baking in sunshine, lining up forever for bathrooms and showers. She remembers being barely aware, after a few hours, of the music blasting tinnily from a distant stage. She remembers people dancing anyway, and herself pulling Edgar into a dance of their own, eyes closed, in her bare feet. She remembers public acts of affection—people even screwing more or less out in the open. She remembers placing Edgar's hands on her breasts (and has a flashing recollection of performing the same act with David) and Edgar (unlike David) pulling away, although he seemed happy enough later, in darkness, under cover of canvas, to reach for her.

He was, perhaps, simply shy. At the time, somewhat stoned, she said to him, "What a tight-ass you are," making him angry.

She remembers him complaining by the second day about the heat, the food, the line-ups, the crowding and the noise—what on earth did he expect! "Well, nobody's comfortable, are they?" she argued. "It's not about comfort, is it? It's about having fun."

Whatever happened to that brief, bold, Flo-ish Gwen?

Smoking up made Edgar sleepy. It made her loose-limbed and passionate. She is reminded, glancing behind her, of the joys of young bodies, and thinks again, as actually she seldom does, of David.

These boys, Jason and Tony, half a decade or so younger than him, more than three decades younger than Jack, have much growing to do: legs lengthening, chests filling out, shoulders broadening—but what is she thinking? She should keep her eyes on Jack, or the highway. Sternly, steadily, watching the road roll under the wheels, though, becomes in a short time hypnotic, unsettling. She burps, and almost throws up, swallows sourness.

Something's still wrong.

By the time the concert was over and she and Edgar were driving home, he cross and aggrieved, she sunburned and headachy, they were not speaking. She shouldn't have called him a tight-ass; he shouldn't have been such a complainer. But sharp moments recede, she supposes, or are overcome by softer ones, and hope. They must have more or less forgotten those three days, and married anyway, looking ahead to adventures they might have in common instead of the kind that pointed up differences.

Her stomach gives another warning lurch. "Quick, pull over, please." Jack takes one look, slows, wheels onto gravel and stops hard. She tears open the door, down the steps, and heaves at the side of the road.

These are violent spasms that send her to her knees and leave her trembling. Scary and strange: she hardly ever gets sick. Even so, her first, ridiculous thought when, finally, she stops retching, is that she wishes Jack hadn't seen this. Her second is that she's being closely observed not just by him but by five young, worried faces. And that it's Tracy, not Sarah or even one of the others, who with Jack takes her arm. Tracy has a small hand, but it's as firm and encouraging as Jack's. Gwen looks at these faces and sees both worry and a tinge of irritation. She is middle-aged—old, to them—and her sickness is holding them up.

She looks especially at Sarah, and sees a forehead wrinkled with what could be concern, if it weren't for two lines that look like impatience at the sides of her mouth.

Children turn away; they abandon. In her rosy supposings, Gwen never much thought of that.

Nothing she has assumed or imagined may have ever been true.

She's afraid she might faint. Light-headed, she gropes her way past the kids to the bed, lies down, closing her eyes, ignoring their debris and possessions. Does she not own this space? Is it not her bed, for her to lie down on?

She is shaking with something like anger. One of them puts something warm over her, a jacket, a blanket, although it's a hot day and she shouldn't be cold.

She shouldn't be angry, either, but it seems that she is.

And it seems to be a fast-moving, expansive rage, taking over as thoroughly as the nausea, rolling up in strange, hot, high waves. The fury begins with these kids cluttering up her rolling home, takes in Jack for inviting them, grows to the motorhome itself, cramped and moving, constantly moving, flashes across miles to her former beige home, innocently maintained and sustained for so many years, absorbs cool Sarah, the passionately desired child who would have abandoned her, and lands finally on—Edgar.

Twenty years! Not a new thought, but one burning now at a ferocious, excruciating new level of rage.

Half a life with a man keeping his secrets, building his garden, stealing his bits of money, fucking his women, walking out her door with a few airy words. Dying on her, with mysteries all intact. She could kill him. If he were here, she would. If he touched her, his flesh would shrivel. This is rage with a disgusting, acrid smell, like hair burning, or skin; rage with a corona of brilliant white light. If she opened her eyes, they would bubble and boil.

One tiny part of her mind, off to one side, speaks up quietly: "This is too much. Excessive. Be careful of indulging yourself."

Careful! Gwen, who was careful for so long—how dare any voice, even her own, recommend taking care? Where did care get her? Twenty years of vapour; one of those invisible, undetectable gases that kill. Of course it explodes, of course it destroys. Naturally caution and care get blown up with everything else.

Is this how madness begins? Or ends? Will she die from it?

It does not seem endurable. She is very, very frightened.

And fear turns her icy, freezing and shaking, making her bones hurt. There are voices, tones of voices, the weight on her heavier, hands, cloth holding her down. She is going under, burning and freezing. Going under is an anaesthetic; like lies? Is that what Edgar thought he was doing with his lies: protecting? She hurts too much to think, or feel, or care. No more.

So for a time, there is no more.

She lies quite still when she wakens. Something feels broken, as real as an arm or a leg, but she can't locate exactly where the fracture is. Just as she would feel unbalanced, off-centre, with a broken arm or a leg, though, she is now aslant, overturned.

People unfamiliar with her, which is everyone now, will not know this. There is a kind of freedom in unfamiliarity.

The small, tucked-away voice insists, only a fever, only a chill, nothing as dramatic as you make it out to be. You exaggerate, you overstate.

The voice may be Edgar's, or her version of his. At any rate, it lies. It diminishes. She is aslant and overturned. She's also still very cold, but sleep has filed down some of the hot spikes of rage.

Edgar was wrong about hitchhikers, and just as wrong, more often than she dreamed, about many other matters. Most likely he didn't know any better, was inaccurate not only with her but with himself, and how was either of them to realize that? Where should the blame lie?

Perhaps nowhere; or everywhere. Perhaps blame is just no longer relevant.

"I want a home, Gwen," he told her at the start. Having grown up following a corporate father transferred here, transferred there every couple of years, naturally he wanted a place to feel settled, from which he could successfully, serenely, radiate outward. At the time, did Gwen not enjoy the picture of herself as the hub of that particular wheel? Was it not tender, protective in her mind's eye?

Perilously maternal.

"My father," said Edgar, "did what he was supposed to do, I guess. He was the way he thought he was expected to be. So he was always pretty much in charge." Gwen heard that as grudging, almost a complaint, but must have heard wrong because Edgar, too, took on decisions. Like much else, the two of them rather fell into this, not his fault, since she fell into it too. With what? Relief? It's hard to be responsible; tempting to let responsibility lapse. And how easily it happens: one decision at a time, one opinion, one act—who notices? So how could she place Edgar at the centre of her rage without herself beside him, like the cardboard couple on a wedding cake?

"Poor Edgar, were you exhausted? Were you just too tired finally to climb out of that car?"

Opening her eyes, she sees herself in these girls, although of course without the nose rings, and Edgar, too, in the boys, although without the boldness—he would not have made himself at home in a strange place so readily. He was polite, and would never have lit a joint without asking permission. Also, had he lit one, he would have shared it. Gwen reaches out from under the mound of coats and blankets they've piled onto her. "May I?" she asks, intercepting a pass from Tony to Janice.

They jump. "Oh, hey!" says Tony. "You're awake. You okay? Geez, you really scared us." Gwen's outstretched hand remains steady. "Oh. Right. Sorry." He gives her the joint. Gwen sucks in deep. It's supposed to be good for nausea; or is that only with cancer? She's barely passed it on to Janice before she is sleeping again.

When she comes out from the blackness next time, remote, beautiful Sarah is perched on the bed at her feet, leaning forward. The others are jammed together on the smaller seat across the narrow aisle, also leaning forward. The light is dim, and there's a gentle slapping of cards and a subdued voice whispers, "Gin." It's very smoky and warm, and Gwen reaches up to discard some of her coverings. How wrecked are these kids? They should at least open more windows. She wants to say that, but slips back under to the sound of Edgar saying, "You're lucky. You just got lucky." Beneath her, the tires hum on the highway, solid and comforting.

They're still humming when she wakens again, this time into darkness. She can make out the forms of three kids, Janice, Tracy and Tony, she thinks, asleep across from her, leaned against each other, young, garish rag dolls. How is it that darkness feels so much quieter than light? Even when it's not silent, night feels muffling, swaddling the road and this rolling, shifting space. Stretching, her feet encounter something thick and soft, and she remembers, "Oh, yes, Sarah," but when she raises her head, the person she sees turns out to be Jack, slumped at the end of the bed.

He comes awake instantly, regards her sharply, worried; and suddenly she's worried, too, because if he's here, who is driving? Someone is, they're still moving. Jesus, is that Sarah up there? Jason in the passenger seat? She sits up, too fast.

"You okay?" Jack puts a hand on her knee. "Any better?" He follows her eyes. "It's all right, they've both got their licences, and I showed them how everything works. Jason already took a turn and did fine. Anyway, the road's so flat and straight it'd be difficult for a blind man to go amiss." All right. But still. A bubble rises again in Gwen's throat, because has he not been frivolous once more with her well-being, her possessions? His exuberant energy is not an unmixed blessing, it seems.

"What time is it? How long was I out?"

"Middle of the night. You've given us quite a fright, you know. We stopped a few times for one thing and another, and you've not stirred. We couldn't seem to get you warm, either, you were shivering up a storm, but to the touch you were hot. Here, let me feel your forehead." He places his large, skilful hand on her, like a faith-healer, and nods. "Yes, better, I think. We could have pulled over but we didn't know if we should be getting you to a hospital, and anyway the young people are keen to get where they're going, so taking turns seemed the best answer. They're pleased with themselves, Sarah and Jason. Being trusted. It'll be a happy part of their journey. They make me think of my own at that age."

Oh yes. Jack's children, who exist in his immediate future. He, too, must be keen to get where he's going.

Gwen has lost ten, twelve hours, sunk in the darkness of a state, whatever it was, more than sleep.

She needs to pee really soon.

Sitting up, then standing, both her head and her body feel nearly balanced, if not quite sturdy. "Lie down, Jack, get some sleep. I'm going to the bathroom, then I'll see how they're doing up there."

"You're really all right then?"

"Much better. I'm fine." Fine is overstating, but yes, she surely feels better: back to a mere thrumming of anger, no longer in that furnace of rage; and not especially frightened, either, only normally, humanly anxious.

There is also that mysterious and unquantifiable distance she has travelled in recent hours. That makes a difference, although not quite a definable one. There is everything before that blazing, frozen, black journey, and everything that will now come after it, and all that's clear to her about time and history at the moment is that division.

Jack stretches into the warm space where she has been lying. "Thank you. It's true the muscles were starting to seize up and," he smiles, "I'm not sure the mind wasn't doing the same." Then his eyes close and he's gone. What would she have done without him, left on her own? She regards him with great gratitude and tenderness. She is very pleased to have met up with him. Very likely she'll miss him, which adds poignancy to watching him sleep.

In the tiny washroom, she spends a few moments scrutinizing her own face. It's puffy, but that might only be from so many unconscious hours. Her mouth, though, looks more drawn-down; not petulant, exactly, but saddened. Her eyes almost glitter: a remnant symptom of fever?

Her skin is slick and clammy. While she has the bathroom to herself, she dampens a washcloth and takes a few moments to get herself clean. Poor Jack, lying in her sweaty bedding. She wouldn't want him to be sick for his ex-wife's wedding, or for seeing his children, his grandson. Not that rage itself is contagious; just, perhaps, its symptoms and residues.

Time to be responsible, an adult, time to make her way to the front, past an army of legs of the sleeping. In the dim dashboard lighting, she sees something easy in the postures of Jason and Sarah, relaxed in how they're slightly turned towards each other even with Sarah's eyes on the highway and both hands firm on the wheel. "Hi," Gwen says softly, stooping between them. "How you guys doing? Where are we?"

"Hi!" They look up, surprised—to see her, in particular, or at any intrusion into their private communion? Jason unfolds a map, brings a long, skinny, young finger down on an empty space. "Right about here. Just getting into the foothills. How're you feeling?"

"A lot better, thanks." But how did they get so far? She has missed many, many miles, a large portion of one aspect of her journey.

"Sarah and me, we don't think we should likely drive once we get into the mountains. Too tricky." Hairpin curves, Gwen remembers. Steep drops, grinding climbs.

She shakes her head, partly to clear it. "It's okay, I can take over. Jack's gone to sleep, and maybe there's space for one of you to crash back there too. I'm sorry, you both must be tired." Of responsibility, if nothing else, these two kids who were only looking for a free, wild weekend, an adventure—by now maybe being on the road has been sufficient adventure. Maybe they'd like to go home.

"I slept a few hours ago," Sarah says. "I'm not tired. You go, Jason, I'm okay here."

Yes, Gwen thinks, you go, Jason. Aloud she asks, "Are you sure, Sarah?" How warm the name still feels on her tongue. "Will you be comfortable enough in the passenger seat?" She would like to say "Sarah" again, but that would hardly sound natural.

They stop and switch places, Jason heading reluctantly to the back, Sarah propping her feet on the dash, Gwen settling in behind the wheel. "Look at the stars!" In the black velvet darkness they really are an immense, astonishing, glittering spectacle. How lucky Gwen is, not to have missed this.

"Yeah, awesome," says Sarah. Well, perhaps she's accustomed to it. Or perhaps that really is enthusiasm, as she expresses it, who knows? Not Gwen, who missed not only miles of prairie but any stories these kids might have confided. They seem fairly unscarred, except by themselves, but obviously neither disaster nor joy has much to do with the amount of time spent on this earth. Critical events might well have occurred in any of the rustling, muttering lives back there. Jason might, for all Gwen knows, be beaten by a father, assaulted by a brother, be a figure of ridicule in a schoolyard. Tony or Janice might be gay, hoping to survive till they can move to a city, and Tracy might be ill, or triumphantly recovered from illness. Sarah might be a prom queen, or a scholar, or in love for the first and best time.

Gwen is biased, and also still sentimental: she gives Sarah the happiest, easiest prospects.

One of the boys is snoring back there, a far flimsier sound than Jack makes. Someone else giggles. Gwen stares ahead into darkness, white line flying by under the wheels, and feels the road rise, then drop. Glancing sideways she sees Sarah, too, wide-eyed and focussed forward, into the night. It's like a spell, a trance, driving on and on through the black unknown.

"Tell me about where you come from, Sarah," Gwen says softly. She means, really, who Sarah is, but that would sound intrusive, and also unanswerable.

"A little place. You wouldn't know it. Pretty much built around elevators. Grain elevators, you know?" As if she is explaining to someone from a foreign culture; which she is, at least when it comes to grain elevators.

"Are you planning to stay there?"

"Me? No way! It's a dump. Nothing happens." Sarah sighs. "Except when too much's happening. So I'm going to university as quick as I can get there, and after that if I go back more than for Christmas it'll be too fucking often."

"You sound angry." Gwen keeps her tone carefully bland, although she is startled. Her Sarah would not have been angry, her Sarah would have had a full, happy heart, the natural outcome of being desired.

Sarah shrugs. "Yeah, well, it sucks. There's nobody cool besides maybe us, I mean me and Janice and Tracy, we're like as cool as it gets, and there's a shitty old movie theatre and a couple of grocery stores and about a hundred hardware stores. And bars. We got bars, and a pool hall—I mean, shit!" She sighs. "I feel like right now we should keep driving forever and I'd never go back."

"There is that sense about it, isn't there?" Gwen agrees. "A highway like this, at night. But your family, wouldn't you miss them? Won't you, when you really do leave?"

"No." Sarah's voice is flat as a slap. Gwen's Sarah—she would leave home, Gwen understands that now, but not gratefully, not with bitter relief. "My parents are nuts. Fucking freaks. Hey, Jason said Jack said you're running away from home, but that sounded too weird, is it true?"

Fair enough: a confidence to get a confidence, trust for a trust. "Actually I sold my house, so if I wanted to go back, I'd have no place to go back to. My husband left me, and then he was killed by a train, so I sold everything, bought this thing and took off. I suppose I'll land up somewhere, but I just wanted to be moving for a while, going someplace, although I have no particular place in mind. It's not very long ago all that happened, so I don't know, really, if I'm just getting started. Or not."

Sarah is gazing at her, Gwen has her attention now. Good. "Oh man, that is so cool. You must be brave."

An attractive thought; but, "I don't think so. Desperate, maybe, for one thing and another, but not brave. It's more what seemed necessary. Although I don't suppose it would look necessary to anyone else."

"Aren't you kind of ..." Sarah's voice trails off.

"Old for this?"

"Well, yeah."

"I certainly am. But that only means I can't afford waste. I mean time, not money. Experience. Although you're young and I bet you feel much the same."

"I can't wait to get away, that's for sure."

"From what? Besides being bored in a small place."

There's a long silence before Sarah speaks again, her voice, already low, now also hard again. "Can you tell I'm part native?"

"Well no. It never occurred to me one way or another, why?" That would account for skin that's deeper-toned than her friends', though, and her very dark hair. "Is that a problem?"

"Yeah, well, it's a problem for my parents. My real parents, their house burned down when I was a baby, somebody got me out but they were killed. My father was native and my mother was white, they weren't married but they had me, and I guess then nobody on either side wanted to take me. So I get put up for adoption and along comes this couple looking for a kid they can raise for God. Not that they could've told anybody that, they must have faked it or else I don't think they could have got a kid. I hope."

"For God? I don't understand what you mean."

"I mean they're this weird kind of Christian, and they made a pledge to God to take in an unsaved heathen baby—that's how they put it, not me—and raise it and save it. Guess who won that lottery?"

Gwen's foot lifts off the accelerator and she turns in her seat towards Sarah. "Are you sure? Not for love?"

"Yeah, love. Sort of. But not for me. I'm, like, their project that's supposed to get them into heaven. Or it would if I wasn't turning out so bad and fucking up their plans. It makes them pretty crazy." She grins. "Like, I left a note on the fridge saying where I was taking off to, so right about now I figure they're praying and hoping their salvation isn't already right in the toilet." Beneath the satisfaction, Gwen thinks she can also hear fear.

"What are they likely to do when you get back?"

Sarah shrugs. "Nothing much. Pray. Tell me I'm evil. Say I'm a wicked mistake, born so low even they couldn't save me."

"My God."

"Yeah. Well. Fuck them. I know what I'm doing. I'm not like Janice, I don't take shit out on myself, I take it out on them."

"Janice?"

"Yeah. She carves herself. Didn't you see her arms? Geez, hard to miss." Unless, like Gwen, you've slept through the opportunity.

"What do you mean, carves?" Gwen feels slow-witted, as if she's doggedly asking stupid questions with obvious answers.

"Cuts. Not pretty pictures, I mean she takes razors to herself. Man," Sarah shakes her head, "I'd never do that. When I go, which is, like, another six months, I'm taking her with me. Tracy, too, if she wants, but there's nothing very fucked up about her, so she might not want to leave so bad. Janice isn't real school-smart, so she'll get a job, but I'll go to university and get me a degree or two, and then, watch out."

"What?"

"First I'm gonna track down my real mother's family, and my real father's family, and I'm going to kick shit out of them all for nobody wanting me. And then I'm going to get those bastards who adopted me."

This is not a young woman whose bad side Gwen would care to be on. "How will you do that?"

"Nothing against the law, I don't mean that, but, like, I could be a land claims lawyer, and maybe stake a claim for the whole fucking town? Or only their house, I don't care. Or their church. Or get famous and write about them. Some public kind of shit like that."

This sounds vague and even fantastic. An adolescent dream of revenge. On the other hand, looking at Sarah's jaw, Gwen would not be surprised to hear of her again. Maybe they really ought to keep driving. Maybe she should keep Sarah, even Janice, possibly Tracy, Jason and Tony with her. In the darkness, this doesn't seem entirely unreasonable.

And what does she think she would do with them? Protect, nurture and cure these nearly grown humans, who must already be far more experienced at sorting one future from another, one emotion and one decision from another, than she will likely ever be? Gwen almost laughs aloud. "Isn't it strange," she says, thinking of Flo, "how much even people we can't stand can control us? For instance, I didn't mean to, but I think I made some really poor choices because I didn't think much of my mother." Obviously, it could have been much, much worse. Sarah would have been relieved to have had a zesty mother like Flo.

"Yeah?" Sarah isn't interested in Gwen, or other perspectives; and why should she be? She has a full plate of her own. "Anyhow," she stretches, then curls into the seat, "that's the deal. That's the plan. I think I'll crash for a while now." Exhausted by thoughts of vengeance? No doubt that gets tiring.

It's long ago now, and far away, but Gwen can't recall thoughts of revenge crossing her mind when Edgar left. There was suffering, yes, shock and grief and bewilderment, and anger, of course, although it looks in retrospect fairly mild compared with what swept over her a few hours ago. But she didn't for a moment contemplate slashing his tires, or trashing his apartment, or his office, or even screaming at him in public. "Are you in any pain yet, Edgar? Did David distress you, or Jack? Did my red rage upset you, or is the worst thing that I can't find it in me to really grieve for someone I couldn't have known? In your place, that's what would hurt me most, I think: insufficient, inadequate grief."

Sarah is already breathing as if she's deeply asleep. She must be accustomed to her heavy heart, if it doesn't disturb her rest.

She is beautiful, and vivid, but otherwise, she doesn't resemble Gwen's Sarah. It's tragic how children can be wasted on the most dreadfully wrong people. In this sort of dark silence, though, many things can break the heart.

Including loneliness. With melancholy, soft, sleeping sounds all around her, Gwen is suddenly aware of herself as utterly, completely alone. Isolated, solitary, unique as a unicorn. What will she do? What is to become of Gwen all alone? She feels like putting her head down on the wheel and weeping and weeping.

This may still be the remains of illness, though; how else to account for these swinging emotions, rage, terror, now sorrow, hurling her first one way, then another?

Nevertheless. Whatever their cause, these are tears.

When the road dips slightly, in a contrary response her heart begins lifting. Now a sunrise is beginning: a remarkable, golden-red glory rising over looming, ominous mountains. The scenery itself contains too many sensations; the scenery itself perhaps makes her sick.

Jack rises, too, comes stretching and yawning to join her. She is no longer alone, and it is no longer dark. Of course she'd be lonely sometimes. No doubt she'll be afraid often enough, and uncertain to the point of tears. That doesn't seem unlikely, or unmanageable, in the light.

"How long you been driving?"

"A couple of hours. Since we started getting into the hills."

"Sarah do okay?"

"She was fine. But tired." They both look at Sarah, asleep and relaxed in the seat beside Gwen. They sound like parents.

"How about you? Think you should check in at a hospital, next place that's big enough to have one?" He touches her hair; she is immensely grateful for this tenderness. That he is here.

"I'd rather wait till we're through the mountains. I'm better now, all that sleep really helped."

"That was more than sleep. I'm very glad you're back among us."

"Sleeping your life away," Flo used to say, shaking her awake for school. Is this what she meant? Evidently Gwen missed an incalculable portion of her time with Edgar, and has now missed precious, diminishing time with Jack; although with the kids along, they couldn't have embraced very fervently anyway. Is this, too, how parents feel?

Jack rouses Sarah, and sends her stumbling off to bed. "My turn at the wheel again, I think." Gwen pulls over so Jack can whiz at the roadside and they can switch places. It's going to be an uphill day: grinding into the mountains, even up into the clouds, and then of course steeply down. Gwen is happy to be a passenger again; the prospects are dizzying.

Although having to drive might keep her mind off her body. Thinking about sickness, she begins feeling sick again, and several times has to clamp her teeth and lips tightly shut. She must not throw up, she must not. But late in the morning she does, gesturing to Jack to pull over, racing out the door, vomiting this time not precisely at the side of the road, but down into space. She wonders what's at the bottom of that chasm; she hopes nothing living, at least. It is interesting to see vomit raining downwards in separate particles, individual unpleasant particularities.

"I think," Jack says, "you must see a doctor very soon."

"I will. When we get where we're going." She does not want to be stuck someplace in the mountains on her own, and everyone else has places they need to get to. Anyway, the mountains themselves may be making her sicker. They're spectacular, but also overwhelming, and too, there's an airiness at this altitude that makes her light-headed again.

She hasn't fallen back into darkness, and she's not in a rage, so at least she's certainly better. "I'd rather not drive, though. It might not be safe. Do you mind?"

And so they spend much of the day creeping around perilous curves, encountering universes of heights and depths, near and distant snowed peaks, slopes embroidered and quilted with pines, sharp drops and deep valleys. A blue lake below sparkles with abrupt and dazzling brilliance in a sudden clearing away of clouds. "Oh!" Gwen cries, clamping a palm over her mouth.

"Fuck," says Jason behind her. "Oh, man, look at that."

Up, up they travel and, naturally, down, down. Even Jack tenses now and then, she can tell from his jaw, and his arms. How, if she wanted to, could she ever go back through this on her own, steering herself through the curves, drops, narrow climbs, the panoramas that turn into leaping, plunging, roller-coastering kaleidoscopes?

They pull over for a stretch and a rest. Muscles are cramping and the kids aren't speaking much even to each other. Gwen tries to catch Sarah's eye, but the girl avoids her. She feels, perhaps, she has said too much and, with no saviour in Gwen, to no purpose. Even surrounded by monstrous beauty, it's easy for spirits to sink like stones; like the rock falls the road signs keep warning of.

Huge, straining trucks rumble past their lay-by, and cars filled with travellers. Are those people irritable with each other, disheartened and trapped in the midst of their journeys? Are they stunned silent by their own frailty in this hard, ancient terrain?

Rolling again, Jack calls back to the kids, "We're on the last stretch for you folk. You'll soon be where you intended to be, and I think in good time as well." A cheer goes up. What would they have done if Jack hadn't stopped? What might have happened to them?

And, of course, how will they get home? And when they get there, what will happen? Trouble for Sarah, and Jason, and maybe Janice as well—who knows about the others?

Now Gwen can feel a kind of geographic dwindling, a general descent that isn't constant, but steady. The five young people are gathering themselves together behind her, a leaping up and bustling, sorting of possessions, a buzz of electric, renewed anticipation. Their lives, she sees; nothing to do with her. But defiant, determined, vengeful Sarah—Gwen turns to watch them all, but especially her.

The little town they've been aiming for, set in a crater surrounded by peaks, looks overwhelmed by youth, many of them much odder in appearance than Gwen and Jack's crew, who pile out pell-mell, eager. But they do pause to say thanks. "You're going to see a doctor, right?" Tracy asks, frowning slightly.

"Very soon."

Sarah says, "Thanks for letting me drive. It was kind of scary, but it really felt good."

It had nothing to do with Gwen, but, "I know what you mean. Good luck, Sarah, with everything." Sarah makes a brief, brushing-aside, waving motion and is gone. Well, after all, what are good wishes to her? They must be about as welcome, or as useful, as prayers.

Gwen watches them walk away, sticking together, still a single group, no longer the pair of boys, trio of girls Jack picked up. While she was on her own unconscious, dark journey, they had other events entirely going on among themselves; not unlike Edgar conducting his unseen life right alongside hers. Will they stay together, or split off with new acquaintances, lightly shifting attentions?

Sarah and Jason are walking close together; the hours of driving, Gwen supposes.

What sort of mother would Gwen have been, after all?

Better than Sarah's. Imagine!

She and Jack, alone again finally, spend their last night together in another small, quiet campground. They make dinner, and love, as they did before they were interrupted by kids, and are more gentle with each other than they were any previous night, or day. Again Gwen lies awake, hearing Jack breathe, watching the dark sky out the window, feeling the last of the mountains around them, feeling still slightly hemmed in. She is, perhaps, simply a true city woman, unsuited to both emptiness and huge overpowering presence, or for that matter to nature itself.

How precious Jack is. How precious last moments are. If, that is, they are kind, passionate, truthful last moments; which they are for her and Jack, were in a quite different way with David, but were certainly not between her and Edgar.

There's no telling how future last moments will unfold; except their quality does seem to be improving.

Touching Jack's hair, committing its texture to memory, keeping time to the pace of his breathing, alert to the length and breadth and heft of his body against hers, she cannot bring either David or Edgar clearly to mind. She understands why that would be with David, but Edgar—not to recall how his hair felt under her fingers, or how his body shaped itself when he slept, or what parts of it, in what ways, she felt against hers—what sort of failure of memory is that?

The prairies are past, the kids are gone, the mountains nearly overcome. She and Jack part tomorrow, and this entire upending journey, with its distance, geography, geology, conversations, touchings, revelations, departures, rage, fear, illness and loneliness, is all forever unknown to Edgar, and eternally remote from him; and finally, it seems, now, tonight, so is she.

nine

Going, going, gone: this is the day David's world ends, with a whimper and the bang of an auctioneer's hammer.

He's glad his hands are busy, because otherwise who knows what they'd get up to? Outside it's sunny and warm, the kind of blissful early-spring day when women will be out in their sundresses and shorts, swinging their hips and tossing their hair, perhaps making that mysterious gesture he still hasn't defined but which used to be irresistible to his fingers, his dick. It's a really long time since that's happened, all the long months since Gwen, but today he feels very shaky: vulnerable to temptation, dangerously open to whim or desire.

So it's a good thing that instead of being out in the sunshine, testing himself (or proving himself), he's behind the bar in the dim confines of Gully's, wrapping glasses and packing them into boxes. The tables and chairs, the one stained-glass window, the ancient juke box, the pool table, the microwave, the bar itself—everything goes tonight. And tomorrow David's father, like Gwen, drives away from this life into another.

His father says he hopes David is excited, anticipating new prospects, pleasures and challenges out of all this upheaval. David knows his father's hopes are genuine, but also thinks they are more his own, for himself, than for David. And that they are too enthusiastic. Probably what he really hopes for David is more basic: that he survives, and stays out of trouble.

David wants his father's mind to be easy. He wants his father to drive off with a light, trusting heart, the only good going-away present David can give. And so, having graduated from Dr. Fink and Keith Miller, he has only Cecile to tell his fear to, and for that he does not have the courage. He hasn't known her long. She doesn't know him well yet, and he thinks maybe she shouldn't.

There's Edgar, too, but his picture is attached to David's attachment to Gwen, and although she naturally remains a large figure in his mind, she has grown irretrievably wispier, her skin, her smell, her voice no longer always recallable. That's sad in itself, but it also means the connection to her husband's experiences is not as clear as it used to be.

Fink might not be out of the question, of course. "If you ever feel yourself slipping, or just want to talk," Fink said on their last night together, his arm around David's shoulder, walking David for the last time to the door, "call me. There's no reason we can't meet again if you need to. You've done very well, David. You don't ever want to jeopardize that."

That was almost a proud moment: he had done "very well." But with that tickle of doubt that he could necessarily continue to do so.

Anyway, Fink thought he, not Gwen, had healed David. He thought he, not David, had triumphed.

Today, triumph seems too strong a word, and too permanent.

It would be nice in a way if Cecile were here, standing beside him right now, helping with the wrapping of glasses and keeping his attention off other, more dangerous matters, but he won't see her till tomorrow. For one thing, she's not a person who belongs in Gully's. For another, she couldn't know what today means.

He should pay attention to the packing; one thing at a time. Think how many lips each of these glasses has touched, how many small plots, celebrations and sorrows it's been part of.

Besides himself, it's the customers David is sorriest for. If he feels uprooted, dislodged, the regulars must feel something similar. They, too, found a place for themselves here day after day, and night after night. Inside Gully's they made friends and enemies, feuded, fought and embraced, kicked back with both laughter and rage. One time a skinny stranger who made trouble for one of the women and was thrown out by David's father, with help from a couple of customers, returned with a .22 and shot through the front window, but that was a rare and startling event that involved the police and had nothing to do, really, with the regulars. There's bullshit, for sure, flying around, but David sees it as mainly a clean kind of bullshit. The place has been like a dim and slightly grimy living room; David doesn't think it feels that way to him only because it actually is his living room.

How can his father just leave? He's spent a lifetime in this huge room, with those people, with David and his mother upstairs in that intimate family space—how can he drive away from his whole history?

Gwen did. Maybe other people do, too. Maybe almost everybody but David knows how to leave things behind.

David's father is whistling again, up on a ladder unscrewing one of the big green-shaded lights that'll be sold tonight. It's Beryl, of course, at the root of all this. He is whistling "It's a Long Way to Tipperary," although that's an old war song and David's father has no connection to any war.

"You'll do fine, son," he's been telling David since the day Gully's went up for sale. "And I want you to come see us, often as you want. We'll take the boat out, go fishing, shoot the shit." Painting a whole different picture of fatherhood, sonhood, the two of them sitting out on a lake, alone under the sun; as if they weren't already together working the bar, knowing what needs doing without even words. David thinks they know each other as well as they're ever likely to, and this will not change with a couple of fishing rods and a boat.

Beryl has fallen happily in with his father's dreams as if she has no life of her own to abandon. Is that not strange? But David would have done the same, if he'd been asked. It would be an odd way and place to live, but it would also be safe. Maybe that's how Beryl thinks of it, too, who knows? Won't she miss her friends, though, and the things she likes doing?

To David's surprise, she's gone out quite a lot since she moved in: off to dinners, movies, bowling and bridge, with or without David's dad. She has not stuck around much to observe David's lack of event, and on the days and evenings they have been in the same place at the same time, they've moved cautiously around each other, not getting too close. Their mutual interest is in David's father, of course, and in not giving him grief. All in all it's been less disruptive than David expected, not as grim and strange as he feared.

But what pictures does she have of living with his father in a cabin that isn't even finished yet: endless mornings, afternoons, evenings and nights, just the two of them—what will they do? How do they plan to occupy themselves? "Of course we'll often come back," Beryl has said. "There will certainly be things we'll want to do that we won't be able to, way up there." She means north; where they're headed, where as far as David can tell there are trees, water, wildlife and emptiness.

His father says, "I'm glad all that business from before is over with. And now look—you can do anything. So it's all turned out for the best." Like a benediction, he also said at one point, "Your mother would have been so pleased with how you've turned yourself around." David didn't say what came to mind: that he doubted she'd have been happy with how his father's turned himself around.

Did she ever dream, while she was dying, that in a matter of a very few years her devoted husband would be merely shifting his plans from her to someone else? Perhaps, though, she and David's father discussed that very thing. Not Beryl precisely, since no one knew then she existed, but a Beryl kind of person. For all David knows, his mother said something like, "I hope you find happiness after I'm gone. Don't feel you should stay alone. You're a man who should have someone."

His father would have said, "No, no, I could never do such a thing, you've always been the only woman for me." He might have thought that was true, but it has turned out not to be.

Dying, David's mother became more remote, more judicious, less intensely connected. David can see that she might, detaching herself, have encouraged his father in ways that would make death less onerous for her, less responsible. But would she, in her heart, have meant it?

Who knows what she and his father whispered to each other in the night, upstairs here, and then near the end in the hospital, as she grew more gaunt and translucent, his father more exhausted and prematurely bereaved?

The glasses David is rolling in paper and packing in boxes will be bought mainly by owners of other bars; a few, perhaps, by sentimental customers. In a little while it'll be standing room only here, with even the chairs and tables for sale, and David and his father will be draining the taps into glasses people are to bring from their own kitchens, and for the last time they will be back-slapping and speaking, as best they can, in hearty, hopeful voices. Tomorrow the last of the packing will be finished upstairs, his father and Beryl sorting the remnants, and the movers will come, and Gully's will be vacant, finally. So many years and then—it's all over.

So much for David's vision of living his life here until he died on his feet, drawing a final draft.

It's been kind of like camping out in the high-rise one-bedroom David moved into a month ago, with his father's help, after the "Sold" sign went up at Gully's and his choices were so suddenly narrowed. The rooms still have big empty spaces, but tomorrow, on their way north, the movers will pause to deliver some essentials and keepsakes: a couple of lamps, his mother's favourite chair, one of the tables and four chairs from the bar, some pictures and cutlery, pots and pans. Then it may begin to feel safe, like a home, an effect the new stuff he's been buying hasn't provided; not even with the company and help of Cecile.

"I'm sorry, son," his father'd said. "But times have changed. There's no way a place like Gully's can last much longer. We won't get another chance like this, to get out at a good price, with something to spare."

With the "something to spare," he is helping with the rent on David's new place for a while, and with its furnishings. "Are you sure?" he asked when David chose the apartment, which is on the fifth floor of a plain, featureless high-rise. "It's a pretty big change from what you've been used to."

"Why not?" David shrugged. As far as he could see, if he wasn't at Gully's, it didn't much matter where he was, and this was at least inoffensive. Or offensive only in being so unremarkable. He still finds it strange, though, after a month, to have to walk through a lobby whose spare furnishings are chained to the floor, and to rise in an elevator and walk down a hallway to get to his own place. He can still be wakened by unaccustomed footsteps overhead, and repelled by stale cooking smells in the corridor. He assumes people get used to these things.

With this fresh start, David gave his old narrow bed to the Salvation Army and bought himself a cherrywood queen-sized, with matching bedside tables and no history as yet. He wonders if somewhere his old bed is disturbing the sleep of a youth who, at first, might have been delighted to have it but is now confused by the distress rising out of it.

Cecile helped him choose a sofa and chair for the living room. The salesperson called it a practical, durable material, but Cecile's point of view is that its dark-of-night blue shade with faint moss-green threadings is the important thing. "So peaceful, Daveed, so serene. Very good." Cecile calls him "Daveed," charmingly, because she is French. In fact she is foreign to him in a number of ways, not least because in the thirteen days since they met, she's continued to show an affectionate interest in him for no special reason he can see.

This is another miracle, like Gwen only different. He's very scared that, as with Gwen, it will end with a vanishing.

Cecile is also good at finding the small touches to make the apartment his as well as, he is aware, in some ways hers: little ceramic boxes, grass baskets, a brass-like container of tall, silvery silk flowers, and for over the sofa a painting, well, a print, of something that looks faintly like a field of pastel flowers around a pastel lake, but isn't plainly or exactly flowers around a lake. "I enjoy most the very simple," Cecile says. "Not so much patterns. All my life, with my mother's work, there is to me too much pattern."

Her mother is a fabric designer, her father a man of high, undefined business. The three of them arrived nearly a year ago from a city south of Paris, which Cecile has pointed out on a map—imagine, to come from so far away and land in this place and time, what's that but a miracle?

David has not met her parents.

Cecile gave him two small crystal candleholders, each with a delicate yellow candle. They have eaten a few times, cross-legged, on the floor of David's apartment, the overhead light turned off, only the candles burning between them. It looks romantic.

David can't tell what she sees in him, but he doesn't want her to see him at Gully's.

Everything here is organized. Beryl mainly, but his father as well, have planned every detail with a sharp eye on efficiency. Beryl, who is the only one of them with much moving experience, has already expressed her views on sentiment: "The best thing is to walk out fast and final. Otherwise you can sit around getting sadder and sadder, but it doesn't make any difference and finally you have to leave anyway." It's the sort of thing she must know, having buried two husbands and promptly moved on.

Is that what women are like? Gwen, too, did not linger. If they are truly so unsentimental, why was David supposed to feel bad about some of them screaming or crying? How upset could they really have been, with their hearts so cold?

His mother wasn't like that, though; she proved the possibility of tenderness. Except, if his father had died, what would his mother have done?

Sold Gully's. Moved on.

But maybe she would have continued to shelter David, one way and another. Instead, he's had to find not only a new place to live but a new place to work, this job full-time, with a real salary (plus tips), instead of what, mainly, has felt like a kind of allowance.

The job, which he got thanks to his bartending diploma, and from graduating top of the class, and with the help of Joe Myers, is in a sprawling dark bar in the basement of a big chain hotel. Of course they don't call it the basement. It's called The Downstairs, its signs composed in calligraphied neon.

Gully's regulars regard this as quite a step up for him. They do not expect to see him again, and he supposes they probably won't. It's a little painful, actually, that they don't seem to mind. Of course they've adapted, a lot of them, to far more difficult losses than having to find a new place to drink or saying good-bye to a kid who grew up at their tables and knees. What they seem to think is, good for him, he's moving up in the world, to a better place than they would be welcome in. They admire his father, too: for leaving, for his cabin and plans, and for Beryl. They seem by and large happy for the lucky choices of others.

The difference for David is that none of this is his choice, only the outcome for him of other people's decisions. He is flung out of here by his father's plans, flung into his new job and apartment by necessity.

"How you doing, son?" His father, passing behind David on his way to the basement where there are still memories and debris to be sorted, the precious from the junk, a little of the former, a lot of the latter, briefly puts an arm around David's shoulder. How much does he know? "You getting along okay here?"

There are different ways of asking questions; this one seeks a happy answer. "Fine, Dad." David smiles brightly. His father does not want to hear about desolation, and why should he? He must be hoping with all his heart that David is on the right track, his own labours complete, no more surprise calls from police, no more legal bills, court appearances. No more trouble, just a leisured, tranquil retirement in a place he loves, with a woman he evidently feels something for.

How long before he gets restless for voices and lights, how long till he's fed up with fish and rustic pursuits?

Even if he came back, his desire to go in the first place makes too many things too clear to be undone.

"I'm almost finished the glasses. What's next?"

"Help me carry a few things up from the basement? Most of it can get wrecked along with the building, but there's some stuff we should keep. I forgot your mother stored things there wasn't room for upstairs. Her mother's good dishes—your mother never wanted to use them, so they've been in the basement for years. The pattern's all flowery, not something a fellow would use, but they shouldn't be thrown out. I thought you might have them."

"You don't want them?"

His father looks uncomfortable. "I don't think it'd be right. With Beryl. She has her own things. Anyway, the dishes belonged in your mother's family."

Does neither his father nor Beryl consider that besides David, whom they're also getting rid of, David's father himself is the biggest possible memento of David's mother? They seem to have no qualms about that. Does Beryl never think, touching his father's body, about the other places it has more momentously and for much longer been? If his mother's dishes are inappropriate, how about her husband?

Does his father, touching Beryl, not find it strange and unfamiliar? At least does he never think his hands do not belong there?

David knows his own desires are unreasonable. As Fink said at their last meeting, "It's not easy to stand responsibly on your own." At the time, that seemed more a platitude than an instruction or message. Today it has a real, sharp clarity. Today David does not feel remotely up to the discouraging tasks of adulthood. Other twenty-four-year-olds, finding parents oppressive, rules and small rooms restrictive, desires and longings curtailed unnecessarily, are not reluctant, or scared. "Now," they cry, "at last, it's all up to me." But what do they do then about loneliness? How do they feel about fear? What do they think when they start toppling backwards and there are no hands behind, able to catch or support them?

Fink also reminded him, "Try to think always of what you can look forward to. One happy thing to anticipate."

Cecile. She'll drop into The Downstairs tomorrow, as she has taken to doing, just before closing time, when his shift ends.

Cecile is so little, so appealing, so dark-haired and graceful—what does she see in him? What did she see two weeks ago when she and three friends pelted into The Downstairs, halting just inside the doorway, looking around, orienting themselves to its dimness, checking it out? It was Cecile who caught David's eye behind the bar, raised her eyebrows—a question about safety, comfort, seeking his judgment—and when he nodded and smiled slightly, so did she.

It helps that she's foreign. She doesn't necessarily know what to expect, and is also unguarded, whether because she is French or because she is Cecile, he can't tell. When he took their drink orders, she reached out her hand to shake his, an odd gesture. Her hand, like the rest of her, was tiny but very firm. She wore rings on almost all of her fingers, and several glittering, dancing earrings. Her body, even walking through The Downstairs, moved like a dancer's, stepping lightly and high, aware of itself but in a practised, unconscious way.

As it turns out she is a student of dance, "although I am not very good, I think," she has told him. "Never good enough to be someone important, and also not tall, and so it will not be my career, only something I love." When she speaks like that, she looks with her large brown eyes directly into David's large brown eyes, solemn, confiding, truthful. His eyes don't always meet hers.

She regards him with such frankness and openness, as if she assumes his in return, that she can't possibly perceive darker aspects. If she did, something in her gaze would cloud over. As it is, his shadows, he feels, could burn away under that warm directness, and when that happens, when his shadows are gone and he knows his intentions are as clear as her gaze, that's when he will be able to hold far more than her hand.

At least he knows his body will work full-heartedly, even skilfully, when the time comes. So thank God for Gwen. Even so—she was so old! And lithe Cecile is young, her twenty-two years exactly right for a man turned twenty-four.

Cecile, too, has had a lover. Only one? When she says, "You are a man who is, I think, very special," how widely is she comparing?

She abandoned that lover in France. As she tells it, she did so with startling ease, although perhaps she hasn't gone into details of anguish in case they upset David. The boy's—well, man's—parents were Algerian, she said, his father a labourer, "not a family my parents could approve of, they could not even speak of similar matters." She meant, David assumed, they had nothing in common. "And the religion is different, and the habits, what they know about, everything. My friend, my parents say he is rough, not suitable, so they say I am not permitted to stay behind in case something foolish should happen. And so, here I am." She spoke placidly, as if it didn't especially matter. "But I see they are right. I am happy here now. There, I would not very long have been happy. I understand this, now that I do not see him, and even then maybe I know, also. It was that he knew different ways, it made more an excitement feeling than was true. Do you understand?"

David tries to imagine how that man might feel, left behind. Angry, bewildered, or is he like Cecile, considering it all for the best? Also David wonders if Cecile wonders how that man feels. And if her parents will look at David with the same eyes with which they viewed her "rough" boyfriend with his labouring Algerian parents. What does he have to say to rich, elegant, foreign people with whom he, too, will have nothing in common? Surely, they will know: not his specific shameful secrets, he doesn't mean that, but his clothes won't be right, his movements, his manners, his habits of speech. They won't be wrong, exactly, will just sound a minor key with people like them.

"You will like to meet them," Cecile has insisted, "they enjoy to have a good time, good food, laughing, we can all go together to dinner, yes? Or to their apartment? It is very nice, very high up, large," and she spread wide her narrow, beautiful arms.

"We will do this when they are together at the same time, and restful." David gathers that is not often the case, with her father flying here and there, her mother occupied with her designs, perhaps with an element of avoiding each other, as well. "They are, what would you say, lively, the two of them, but not often together. They enjoy to do different activities. My father, he likes the money, the business, you know? And to fly everywhere to hotels and meetings and to smoke cigars and to meet many women, I think. My mother, she likes pretty things, to make them and see them, so she works and goes to theatre and dance and buys nice clothes and," Cecile broke into the smile that David thinks of as, well, French, "she smokes cigarettes and meets many men."

This sounded very strange to David. "But they are still young," Cecile explained, as if he were missing the point. "When they will be old they will have many enjoyable things to tell each other, that they have done. Unless," she frowned briefly, "one of them should fall in love. But so far they only enjoy." She seemed to mean they enjoy other people; people not each other.

"It sounds confusing to me," David ventured. "Not happy."

"Oh, happy, what is that? They are to me—suited, yes. And they have much respect. They," and she threw her thin arms up slightly, "they belong with each other, you see?"

Not really; but what did David know? Only his own benevolently connected father and mother, and at that, Beryl demonstrates the flexibility and unexpected turns of emotion of which his father, at least, can be capable. And there was Gwen, who took David, for God's sake, to her bed on the day of her husband's funeral—what could be more variously complex than that? He guesses he just doesn't understand very much. But he's trying.

It's heavy work hauling the two boxes filled with his grandmother's, then his mother's, inherited china up from Gully's basement. What he finds, opening them on the bar, is a riot of pink and mauve flowers on plates and cups so thin they're like his mother's skin, near the end. There's even a gravy boat, and three sizes of plates, along with saucers, cups, bowls, a teapot, a tiny cream pitcher, a sugar bowl. But it's beautiful—why did his mother put it away in the basement? Why did his father not consider it suitable for David—not masculine? What's the difference, when it's so beautiful?

Although he can see that he, too, will hardly use these things. They're too fragile for anything more than the lightest, most delicate foods and occasions.

He can't recall his mother speaking much of her mother. And she put her inheritance, her mother's dishes, in the basement. He never noticed any of that. Well, all children are self-centred. All adolescents needn't be, however, and surely twenty-four-year-olds shouldn't be. This may be part of what Keith Miller meant when, more bluntly than Fink, he instructed David to "just grow up."

He might run into Keith Miller at The Downstairs, it seems a likely place, slightly musty with well-dressed desire, for a guy like him. It's a place where discretion is appreciated, a darkened, below-ground haven for trysts, of politics, business or love, that might not be wholly comfortable in the light. The sort of place where David would not feel at ease as a customer, although it's okay being a bartender, with a particular function to perform.

At their final appointment, Keith Miller snapped David's file shut and said, "I gotta tell you, Dave, it looks like you're doing okay. Looks to me like you've broken a real bad habit—because you know, I kind of think that's mainly what it's about, just not doing something for so long you stop thinking of doing it—and what you had was a big bad habit, a lot worse than picking your nose in public, or scratching your ass, but the same kind of deal when it comes to learning not to do it any more. Am I right?"

David shrugged. Like Fink, Keith Miller didn't know about Gwen.

"And," Keith Miller went on, "the bartending course was great. That we were able to pin down something you want to do and take action. You did real well."

As with Fink, David was slightly ashamed of his own pride: that in some way, which he ought to resent, it mattered what Keith Miller thought of him. "Yeah, well, it wasn't so hard."

"Not the bartending, maybe, not with all your experience. But doing it. Sticking it out and," Keith Miller suddenly grinned, "not sticking other things out. I think those are both achievements."

There he was again, taking important things lightly, cracking jokes about terrible troubles. How could David not want to hit him? But he could also see Keith Miller no longer intended malice, this last reference to David's problems more light than sharp, more a potentially shared amusement than a threat.

"Thanks," said David. "Yeah, I think so, too."

"I don't have that many good endings," said Keith Miller. "So I'm pleased about yours." That was the most personal thing he said to David in their year of monthly meetings: that he didn't have many good endings. And counted David as one. David felt a little sorry for Keith Miller, and for all the other people who more frequently, perhaps daily, have to face small and large bad endings.

That was before Gully's was sold, of course. But also before Cecile. It's hard sometimes, sorting good and bad endings.

He can hear his father, upstairs now, shifting more stuff around. It's an echoey, strange sort of sound. Already Gully's is unfamiliar, with its heaped tables and chairs, its dangling-wired gaps in the ceiling, its labelled boxes, bared walls. While David's been packing, it's been disappearing on him. Like Beryl being upstairs instead of his mother, a fundamental change alters the view. As with Gwen, he cannot always recall easily his mother and father sitting opposite each other over their breakfasts. He can't hear their voices together any more.

He can still hear strange women yelling, though, and see the fear, shock or anger on their faces. There is something satisfying about that, on this helpless day, that causes his dick to stir restlessly.

He could do that. He could take an hour and go for a walk in the sunshine. He could watch carefully for the elusive signal, wait for it, act on it. He could give himself one more outing. This may be how an alcoholic feels: just one more treat. What harm could it do, how much difference could it make? He deserves some recompense, a reward, doesn't he? For being so good, for so long? He could walk right now across this barren floor and out that door, into the light and air.

And what? The phone here would ring and his father would answer, his face collapsing, his heart despairing. He would slump, and rub his forehead with the weariness of it all; he would straighten, and phone the lawyer. He would explain to Beryl that all their plans are off.

David could ruin his father's hopes with a few steps, a few movements. An unhappy sort of power, but a power nonetheless. Just as it seems to David that his father's power is unhappy, but complete.

And wouldn't that be great to know: that he'd wrecked everything? Would he, sitting in jail, feel warmed by knowing his father also was being thoroughly punished? Too fucking stupid.

Fink and Keith Miller would be pleased he's finally considering consequences. Now, too, somebody walking around out there will get through her day without the drama of encountering David. Although there's always a chance today's the day he would have met one who would have smiled in a friendly way and invited him into her life.

He'd be destroyed with Cecile, of course. And he's already in her life, although not very far. Is that not enough? She is not yet the woman with whom he sits side by side after work, their feet up on a coffee table, watching TV and discussing their days, and their desires. They do not yet go off to bed together, to make love and then rise in the morning to share the bathroom and the kitchen, him shaving and her making coffee, her showering and him pouring cereal into their two matching bowls. None of that, not yet.

This is the kind of life even his father has again, with Beryl.

Beryl is moving most of her stored possessions north to the cabin: crystal, good silverware, an old walnut dining-room suite whose elegance will surely be out of place. Maybe Gwen, having cast off her own previous life and possessions, has also moved in with someone. Would he resemble Edgar, whose photograph is now propped on the bureau in David's new bedroom, or David? In all the weeks David kept watch, no man kept her company. A good thing. It would have been too hard to see her placing someone else's hands on her breasts, drawing someone else down to the carpeting with her.

Gwen wanted David. An attractive, unlikely woman took to him without hesitation and set out to enjoy him. And Cecile likes him. "You are so nice," she tells him. "So kind to me, and handsome," although he doesn't know what she means by any of that.

Photographs of Beryl's family, including small snaps of her dead husbands, appeared on shelves and tables upstairs when she moved in—not everything went into storage. Her husbands don't much resemble each other, or David's father, but then, they're all different ages, so for instance the husband who died when she was young remains forever lean, dark, clear-eyed. Her children are products of her longer second marriage, to a man eternally middle-aged, prosperous-looking and slightly thickened, with streaks of silvering hair. Her son manages a home-supply store franchise out west, is on his own second marriage and has three kids, two from his first and one so far from his second. Her daughter is a lawyer out east and has one child, also a girl.

Beryl speaks of them all with pride. Later this year, when the weather up north gets more difficult, she and David's father plan to spend a few weeks visiting each of them, and then David's father will be part of their families, too. They will remain mostly strangers to David, no doubt, even if they travel this way to visit. His father will take on new aspects that will be unfamiliar to David. He will have instant grandchildren, and expanded loyalties and affections.

All this. All this. Too much, very fast.

"Your new brother and sister," Beryl told David, identifying the photographs as she made space for them upstairs. "And your nieces and nephews." Not very likely; and not when they know more about him. Which, he supposes, is another sort of consequence Fink and Keith Miller meant: that an unfortunate action has unforeseen ripples down the road that put unexpected crimps in a life. What sensible parents would encourage their children to frolic with a new uncle with David's history?

And how, and what, can he ever tell Cecile? He can imagine her sweet features turning horrified, her little body moving away, distaste in each precise movement. At what point would he be able to make her see he had no ill intentions, no wish to cause harm, was merely overcome by impulses he no longer contains? That with Gwen's help, and Cecile's own existence and presence, those formerly irresistible desires have entirely vanished?

Except it seems they have not, quite.

He has only known her two weeks; it's too soon for either to confide an entire life story.

"Time, son," his father says from the foot of the stairs.

So it is.

The glasses are packed, the microwave boxed, the tables and chairs now ring the perimeter of the room, stacked high on each other. The floor is bare and enormous, the lights, taken down, line one side of the bar. The old jukebox is in the corner where it's always been, since whoever buys it can unplug and haul it from there, and meanwhile people will want music tonight. The pool table, too, hasn't been moved, although all the balls and cues have been wrapped and laid across the green felt in boxes and rows.

This is it, then. Gully's, bleak and barren, is now only its history.

His father is shaking his head, looking bleak also. "Feels strange, doesn't it? A lot of memories here, a lot of our lives." To his distress, David sees tears glinting; he doesn't want his father to cry, he truly doesn't want him to feel bad. Tentatively, he puts an arm around his father's shoulders. They are not men who touch.

His father has shrunk. He is shorter than David. His hair is mostly grey, and some of it's even gone white. He is no longer the barrelly figure David has never resembled. He is old, for the moment at least.

But now he straightens. His body fills out and he grows taller, shoulders rising beneath David's arm. "Still," he says, "life goes on, doesn't it? And there's always good things ahead, as well as behind. For us both, you know."

"I know. You're going to have a great time."

"I just hope," his father frowns slightly, "Beryl knows what she's getting into. She's never lived in the country. Although neither have I, and I'm sure as anything. We used to dream of this day, your mother and me: packing up, selling off, moving up there. We used to talk for hours, making our plans. This day has been years in the making."

Was it truly his mother's dream? She wouldn't exactly have lied, but might just have fallen into his father's visions. For lack of her own, or because she thought he deserved it. "Is it really what Mum wanted?"

His father looks surprised. "Oh yes. 'I can't wait,' she used to say. 'Imagine waking up every morning to the sound of loons, and lazing around doing whatever pops into our heads.' She went on about it sometimes, when she was tired, or before she knew how sick she was. When she found out, I remember her saying, 'Now I'll never get to the cabin.' Broke my heart. Because it was true, and I couldn't lie to her that it wasn't. Still," he brightens, "she'd had the idea all those years. It helped her through the rough spots, thinking about something good at the end of the day."

What rough spots? Was she often unhappy even before she was sick?

His father is turning the sign on the battered front door so that Gully's is now, for the last time, officially open. Trucks pull into the parking lot, their drivers keen-eyed men here to buy and cart away Gully's interior. And here are the regulars drifting in to stand uncomfortably in poses to which they're not accustomed, unable to slump, to slouch, to slumber at tables. Several have remembered to bring their own glasses, but for those who have not, David unwraps a few, undoing a tiny portion of what he spent his day doing.

"Cheers, lad," they say, lifting their final beers. And, "We'll miss the place," and, "Off to the good life then, are you?"

The auction itself is oddly subdued: more intent than the boisterous affair David expected, the auctioneer businesslike, not one of those yodellers. David had anticipated a sharp, electrifying event that would slice into his skin and cause pain.

Instead it seems he is seeing and hearing from a distance, remote. These people, known and unknown, are actors to him, in a poor play finally winding down. None of it's real: not the money changing hands, or the furnishings going out the door, or the strangely muted talk or quiet laughter. Not the twenty-four years of his life here, or the ones he expected. How can that be?

Beryl is standing at the bottom of the stairs leading up to the apartment, almost out of sight. She is watching him, not unkindly. He smiles at her carefully. What is she thinking? That soon he won't be in her daily life? That he will not be a trouble to his father again, and his father will have a peaceful retirement in her arms, far away?

Or, perhaps, that this is the packing up and ending of a life she knows nothing about. That years and years of another family's days have been conducted here, and her own attachment comes late, and only to one of its members. And maybe that this is sad, or a triumph.

Or perhaps, like David, she is panicked by what she is committed to: a life entirely strange to her, living with a nice man but nevertheless one she hasn't known all that long, in an unfamiliar, almost primitive place. Oh, she may be as frightened as David. Impulsively he joins her, lightly touches her arm. "It'll be fine."

She looks startled, and slightly confused, but smiles. "I know. We're all doing what's for the best, although it's going to be a big change, and I can't quite imagine what it'll be like. And this," she gestures to the big, dark, increasingly hollow room, "I know it's been your father's life. It's meant so much to him. And you. I think it's going to be harder for him than he knows, I think he's going to miss it, you, more than he realizes yet. You'll miss him, too?" She is looking up, right into David's eyes; his best feature.

"Yeah. A lot of things, I don't know how they'll be." This is intimate, for them, but maybe it's only possible—and such a little revelation, a tiny doubt—because after tonight they will hardly ever see each other.

Beryl puts a thin, manicured hand on his forearm; he looks down at its slim fingers, this hand which touches his father equally gently and far more fondly. "You're a good young man, and you will do well." She says this firmly, as if it's both an assessment and a command.

"You know?" he dares to ask.

"About your troubles?" Two lines appear between her eyes. "A little. I'm sure it was a difficult time for all of you; I mean, with your mother so ill. Cancer's a terrible thing, has all sorts of effects on people besides the illness itself. When my second husband died of it, it was hard in different ways for all of us." By "us" she means her real family, the people in her photographs. One person can have many lives, in many different circumstances and places. Like fields, all fenced off from one another, but with gates here and there.

Having passed through a gate, it's not possible to go back. David knows this now, but it's still hard.

"David! Dave?" He's left the old man alone out there, trying to keep up. He offers Beryl a half-smile, a nod, and heads back to work.

"Sorry, Dad. I was talking to Beryl."

"You were? That's good." He looks touchingly pleased. "Can you run a couple of pitchers around? On the house, we're just about done."

The people left are the hardest-core regulars, swaying slightly and, with the booze, the oddness of having to stand for a long time and, perhaps, the realization that this is truly an ending, looking sentimental, bereft. As David tops up glasses, a raggedy version of "For He's a Jolly Good Fellow" begins, directed towards David's father, who turns to these last of his customers. "Hip, hip, hooray!" someone pipes from a corner. "To Gully's," and glasses are lifted. "To good times and Gully's." A few people cry, "Speech!" and finally David's father steps forward.

"My dear old friends," he begins, and David feels tears leap into his own eyes. "I've spent all my adult years with you people down here and my family upstairs, so it's very hard, saying goodbye. We all have to move on now, but speaking for myself, I thank you for being part of my life, and letting me and my family be part of yours." He stops suddenly, turns away, a hand over his eyes. David can see his shoulders trembling. Raising one of his pitchers, David calls into the silence, "To my dad!"

The end of the night, with people shaking his father's hand, some embracing him, reminds David of his mother's funeral, when likewise people lined up solemnly to shake hands and embrace. This, too, is a kind of ritual for a necessary ending, and a kind of comfort. It puts his dad in a funny mood, though.

"Finally," his father says when the last person wanders reluctantly out, pausing in the doorway to look sadly back. "The first night ever we don't have to clean up. We don't have to do one goddamn thing." He sounds nearly angry; and why not? David is nearly angry himself.

But when his father looks at David—what does he see?—his tone turns gentle. "Come upstairs, son. Say goodbye to the place."

Up here, too, just about everything has been packed, the floors piled with labelled boxes, only a few necessities left out for his father's and Beryl's last hours here. There is nothing of David's life remaining, or his mother's: just, as his father said, more truly than he likely intended, the place itself to say goodbye to.

David touches a pale yellow wall, places his hand on a white window sill, both last painted long ago by his mother. Unshaded lamps throw harsh light on unfamiliar boxed shapes. He looks out over the familiar nighttime street and feels—nothing. Or, he feels a sort of faint, light-headed sorrow that there is nothing to feel.

He shakes hands with Beryl, touches her shoulder. But his father has tears in his eyes again, and his lips are trembling—well, what did he expect? Still. This time David puts both arms around his father, and feels his father's around him. David can't think of a single important thing to say at this point.

How did Gwen feel, driving away? How about Edgar, leaving home for the last time?

If this is what leave-taking is like, it must be more wrenching for those left behind; and here, no one is left behind. So. It really is over.

Walking slowly the five blocks to his apartment, David pictures his father and Beryl kicking off their shoes in the living room. Beryl will have much less to think about than his father, but she, too, must be saying goodbye to something; just not something in that room. After a while they will head into their bedroom, undress wearily, hold each other while they talk in low tones; the way David used to be able to hear his father and his mother talking. At the door to his own apartment, turning the key, he thinks for, really, the first time, "This is where I live now." Looking around, he sees that, even with the familiar furnishings arriving tomorrow, he won't last long here. His father was right, this isn't for him.

There are elegant old houses that have been broken into cosy, well-worn and slightly shabby apartments. Cecile might enjoy helping him look.

It's interesting, and unusual, having an idea of something he'd like; keeps him awake for a while.

He wakens in full daylight to a sharp drilling that has him out of bed and halfway across the room before he understands it's the intercom. The movers already? He doesn't get visitors.

"Are you awake, Daveed? It is only me, may I come up?"

What's Cecile doing here? How fast can he get dressed, brush his hair, get sleep washed away? Tidy up, make the bed, what time is it? She has never dropped in on him before, he didn't expect to see her till tonight; and tomorrow night, when he's off duty again, they planned on a movie. At theatres, Cecile holds his hand in the darkness and jostles him with her elbow and sometimes puts her head on his shoulder, and afterwards she likes to go for a drink or a coffee and discuss what they've seen.

He's disoriented, confused by surprise, although probably happy surprise.

By now the movers will be at Gully's. Should he feel something about that? Instead, he finds himself thinking ahead again, to his own next place.

He's buttoning his shirt when Cecile knocks. "Daveed!" she cries, and touches his cheek, "I have wakened you! I am sorry. I thought you might be sad, from leaving your home, so I bring us a breakfast, see? Croissants, and three little jams, and strong coffees, so you will be happy anyway, yes?"

He is standing in the doorway, staring at her. Imagine! She thought of him. She thought he might be sad and did something to cheer him. How does he deserve this care from this graceful young woman, now whirling past him, who spends hours each day with young men who are as graceful as she?

He wants to live up to whoever she sees.

When they walk through to the kitchen, he finds his steps matching hers, which are long for someone so little—part of being a dancer? He likes being absorbed into her rhythm, and maybe her grace.

Gwen must be about Cecile's parents' age. Kind of embarrassing now, but still something spectacular, and better than being a virgin.

David's old desire to create enlarging stories is apparently gone, at least when it comes to Cecile. Instead he finds himself, with her, wanting to shrink the truth, make it, for the most part, as small as he can. Nothing big, nothing outrageous. If she were to leave him—a couple of weeks ago he didn't dream she existed, but already, he cannot contemplate what terrible thing might happen to him if she were to leave.

"Your father?" she is asking as she sets out breakfast, "is he very sad? I would wish to have met him before, but soon we could go to visit him and his friend, yes?"

She speaks of future events. "You bet." Meeting parents is what serious people do, isn't it? And his father would be delighted if David showed up with this buoyant young woman, would see Cecile as not only charming herself, but as another kind of diploma for David. Might he let something slip, though? David would have to warn him of how much Cecile doesn't know.

Neither Cecile nor his father knows about Gwen: nothing of how they encountered each other, or the small mole on her right thigh, or the quality of light on her skin, dim in the bar, golden warm in the bed, or how she told him to lock the door on his way out in the dark, or how, later, he watched. Cecile wouldn't like that, would consider his watching peculiar, even dangerous-sounding, or mad. It would be hard to make her understand that he meant no harm with that, either; was looking only for possible life-saving messages.

Cecile's body is not as fleshy as Gwen's. She is lithe and athletic, which will feel quite different, when the time comes.

She might also have high expectations, which Gwen did not seem to have, as far as he noticed. Gwen, the new widow, would have had other things on her mind than his skills, although his skills, he still thinks, were fine all things considered. She seemed as happily surprised as he was by how the day turned out. With Cecile, circumstances will obviously be different, and she will also have different experiences setting different standards for him. An Algerian! Well, a Frenchman of Algerian origin—what tricks of pleasure might such a man know?

David stares at Cecile, as he sometimes does, wishing to see into her memories and desires. He could, right now, bring her towards him, draw her across the room, through the doorway to his bed, draw her down, draw himself down upon her body.

She would not, he thinks, object.

There are times for events: wrong times and irrefutable, irresistible times. He knows some things about the irresistible ones. He is waiting for the irrefutable.

Meanwhile he does take her shoulders, turns her towards him, wraps his arms around her so that her lips touch his throat and his cheek rests on the top of her dark head. "Daveed," she says. When the time comes, he will be so sure and so purified that making love will be an act of redemption.

As, he sees suddenly, he must have been, in some different way, Gwen's act of redemption.

These are beautiful, circular, sacred gifts.

Cecile steps back, smiles gloriously up at him. She is not someone who stays solemn for long. "You are hungry now? You must eat and be strong for the furniture coming, your new things, which we will arrange."

She is quite forceful. She takes for granted her place in his life, and his in hers. This feels, somewhat to his surprise, consoling.

A year, six months ago, could he have imagined today? Himself today?

A year ago he was unzipping himself and startling strangers. Six months ago he was watching Gwen drive away. Even yesterday, he was prepared to grieve not only a lost past but an indefinable future. And today—isn't time strange and wonderful—today, for the moment, his hopes have no bounds.

t e n

ello, Benny.

Benny, hello.

Will it wear off, this compulsion to keep Benny at hand, in view? For now, he's so entrancingly new, and the two of them are so irrevocably attached, it's impossible not to find him compelling. Gwen might have assumed in the past that she knew some people, like Edgar, for sure, but now the difference is obvious.

She might also have thought she'd learned all she needed to, with Jack in particular, about the pleasures of male flesh, but there, too, she was wrong. Benny's flesh is sleek as sealskin, tender and juicy as veal, oh, she could eat him right up.

She loves watching him sleep, and for the most part adores his wakefulness, too. It's completely a miracle when his fingers touch hers, or when she nuzzles into his shoulders, his belly, his chest.

When he's sleeping, he resembles no one she knows: the perfect stranger. When he's awake she sees his eyes are much like David's: vast, deep and brown. She could fall right into all they seem to know. Or, when he gets a particular wrinkled, crumpled expression, he looks just about how he'll probably look when he's a very old man. Imagine! At different times, he will be Benny, Ben, even Benjamin. In that way he is more fortunate than someone named, inflexibly, Gwen.

Moments like this, leaning forward in her chair in a darkened room, watching him sleep, are like being in a canoe in the middle of a very calm lake: too peaceful to lift even a paddle. Her desire right now is simply not to disrupt, not to have ripples; to coast.

Such moments don't last long. She is also so tired even her scalp hurts, even her hair is exhausted. She is weary right into her bones. The trouble is, she's so thrilled, too, that she can scarcely sleep, even when Benny does. Drifting off, the word "Benny" comes into her mind, neon-bright, and she's awake again.

A few times in the past couple of weeks, though, she has fallen into sleep so deep she wakens terrified at what she has missed: something fatal, or dangerous, that requires a catapult to his side.

Could she really sleep through a quiet disaster?

For the first time in her life, she has found herself thinking, "I'm too old for this"; for both the unexpected strain and the joy. Dr. Ogilvie warned, "It's going to be tough, you'll have to take good care of yourself," and she would if she could, but she doesn't have a lot of control, and Benny's demands are quite strict.

Her interests are narrow: getting Benny and herself through each day. That means, among other things, that she hasn't vacuumed, and can't recall when she might last have dusted, and the bathtub has a minor ring of grime.

If she ever gets around again to cleaning it, their ground-floor duplex should suit them far into the foreseeable future; although, except when it comes to Benny, Gwen has mainly lost her sense of foreseeable futures. It has two bedrooms and a great deal of light, and the backyard is bounded by both vaulting shrubbery and a tottery wooden fence. Perhaps they'll fix the fence and get a dog: a golden Lab, or a spaniel with eyes as large and brown as Benny's. Or David's.

She doesn't want to think about David. She doesn't know what to do about him.

She doesn't suppose, really, she'll do anything at all. It's whether she ought to or not that prickles sometimes, not so much whether she will.

Would Benny like a dog? Some other kind of pet? He will have his own opinions, and it will be interesting, taking them into account.

The duplex is outrageously expensive, but everything seems to be, out here on the balmy, favoured coast. Once she and Jack finally got through the mountains and said their goodbyes, a lot of decisions, including finding a home, became abruptly, unexpectedly urgent. But she's content here; more than content.

Edgar would have loved its plush, west-coast yard, where the garden, without effort on her part, seems more to explode than to grow. Sometimes a flower has even struck her as so wildly voluptuous it might be some sort of alien growth. When she moved in early last fall the yard was still a jungle: rampant, overgrown, monstrous. Now in early spring, it's showing signs of fearsome renewal.

Perhaps, though, Edgar would have been discouraged by the lack of challenge involved, the too-easy flourishing of greenery here. This garden is also much smaller than his, but it suits Gwen, who has no intention of doing much work on it except maybe for cutting it back. She hopes it will suit Benny, too.

"Oh boy," she says, looking down at him sleeping. "Oh boy."

The expression is entirely literal. He is her boy.

Often in recent months she has found herself thinking of Flo: of Flo more than four decades ago, growing huge and unwieldy, Flo running her hands over her belly contemplating what might be growing inside; and perhaps Gwen's father resting his head and hands on Flo's stomach, feeling the internal rhythms.

An experience David, of course, missed.

Benny is Gwen's. He has David's eyes, but nothing else that she can see. Except, naturally, a penis, but that hardly constitutes "taking after" his father.

"Father" is not the right word. There is no word for David.

What did Flo think, how did she feel, looking down at Gwen for the first time? Raising Gwen to her breasts, and her shoulder, and turning her tenderly into her crib? Gwen thought, "Benny," a name she had never contemplated before she finally saw his plump, purply face, first in a sharp, tortured wail, then lapsing into a kind of bewildered innocence. Obviously he was no Sarah, but it was evident he was no John, either. "Benny" came into her mind and got lodged there.

She has no idea what David's last name was. Is. Surely not Gully. Anyway, David has his own life, his own girlfriend, his own prospects, his own future. He's young and doesn't need Benny as well. Very likely he would not be even slightly grateful to hear about Benny.

Still, there is something wrong about this; on the other hand, as is often the case, there is also no obvious right.

She cannot see going back, ever. For one thing, how could she return through those mountains, never mind track her way across that prairie infinity? Well, of course there are planes. But the expanse of land that lies on the other side of the mountains is now a separate universe, a distant life, a history as remote as the Conquests or the Inquisition.

She now prefers to regard things this way: she purged herself, into ditches and crevasses, of all sorts of sicknesses, purifying herself in order to make way for Benny. She is Gwen at, now, forty-three, and she is as much an infant as he is: just beginning on a new, unformed, unenvisioned, unknowable, untried, untested future.

She exaggerates, romanticizes, indulges herself; an easy habit to fall into. She has experience, many useful experiences, and considerable defensive and some offensive knowledge. She has Benny. She is no fool. She's come this far.

The trouble in that remote other existence of hers was mainly, she thinks, that she made too many assumptions. Took too much for granted; and what's unusual about that? What else do most people do? People have expectations, for the most part sturdy but fairly modest ones, and hope not to have unhappy surprises. That's all. That's supposed to be a life, and why not? At that, it still takes some courage to get out of bed in the morning, counting on dependable patterns but knowing there's always a chance that instead, some upheaval will erupt that will change things forever. But people get out of bed anyway.

And their reward? Minor lives, mainly. They're left at a loss for miracles, or even an expectation of miracles. As she and Edgar were at a definite loss.

Edgar may have headed off in that very search: for a miracle. But it's Gwen who wound up with one.

Edgar would have adored Benny. Except for the David eyes, he would have loved this fat-bellied infant whose fingers spread across his rosy mouth as he sleeps, curled hair damp on his forehead, the tiny blanket with red and blue clown figures drawn up to his roly-poly shoulders.

Those shoulders nearly killed her, but then he slipped and wriggled free, into the universe between her legs, and into the world in her arms.

Whereupon she looked down and said, "Benny," out of nowhere.

He seems, in his two weeks so far in the world, a generally happy baby. When he screams, though, his little fists wave help-lessly, his spine stretches and arches, his face screws up like an apple doll's. Gwen wonders how familiar he may already be with the concept of thwarted desire. So far she has not had to thwart his desires, which are obvious, straightforward and simple, for more than a moment; but that day will come.

Not only her interests but her own desires have narrowed to him, and have since the moment she learned he might exist. With that knowledge Jack slipped, just a day after they'd said goodbye in a waterfront bookstore, into history, and so did lust, and so did flesh, except for her own flesh, and now Benny's.

Jack's words are on a shelf in Gwen's bedroom: his farewell gift, as promised, two collections of his poetry. "I want," he said, "to give you something. Besides, I mean, my gratitude for your existence and for this unexpectedly grand journey. I will be eternally grateful for that storm, I want you to know."

The bookstore where he took them had shelves to the ceiling and one of those rolling wooden ladders hooked to a curving rail at the top. Jack, hands on hips, looked up, up, before finally climbing high and descending with two volumes. How slim they were! She was amazed at how powerfully he apparently felt about something so small; although now she has a better idea how consuming something small really can be.

Inside the cover of one, called simply *Wounds*, he wrote, "For Gwen, giver of lifts to the traveller and love to the sorry of heart." Inside the other, called *Singing Praise*, he wrote, "To Gwen, a singular voice of the road, the highway, the trail—and the lake."

On the back cover of *Singing Praise* was a photograph of a man she would not have recognized: the young Jack, black-haired, intensely solemn; a man who must have been married at the time, his children still little, a man with, however many stories he told her, a life she could never catch up with. A stranger, in fact.

"Thank you," she said. "I'm sorry. I have nothing for you."

"Memories." He tapped his head. "Your gifts will always be here." He touched the top of her head, as if she were a child, and leaned down to kiss her lightly: the last sensation between them. "Now, you promise me you'll have this illness of yours looked into?"

"I promise."

"And if I leave you here, you'll be all right, you'll take care of yourself?"

She nodded. "I'll be fine. Thanks for the books. And the inscriptions. And everything." They smiled the sort of smile she liked but slightly mistrusted: as if kind, fond and fully comprehended words were being spoken. And then his sturdy, strong body, bearing its backpack, was vanishing out the door. On the sidewalk he shaded his eyes, looked back, waved, and Gwen lifted her hand in return.

She's taken her best shot at reading his poems, several times. She'd supposed, from the very physical nature of her knowledge of him, and maybe also just because they met in wilderness, that his poetry would be somewhat landscapey, like the kind of woods-lake-sky pictures some people frame for over their sofas, although not, of course, so predictable. It turns out, though, that his poems do not move in straight lines. She's tried reading them aloud, and they sound in different places like music, but they also leap about and don't make straightforward sense. They seem mainly to concern themselves with muscles and factories, bones, flesh and labour. Men's labour, not the sort Gwen would recognize anyway; nor, for that matter, would men like Edgar. Sometimes they sound like anthems to furnaces and mines and the loading and unloading of ships. She read a couple to Bob from upstairs one night he and Cathy were visiting. What he said was that they didn't seem like poems to him, because they struck him as true. Funny man, Bob.

If Jack ever does write about their time together, Gwen wonders if it will strike her as true. It doesn't much matter, she supposes. Those are Jack's dreams made real in words. Edgar had his dreams, unknown to her, too; and David must surely have his; and now Gwen is enthralled by her own. Is this Benny entrancement anything like how Jack feels with his poems? Did Edgar ever come close, bent over his blueprints and plants?

By now Jack will be long back in his eastern-city apartment, writing and drinking, courting and seducing, his ex-wife's wedding safely behind him, another farewell to his children well in the past—do unfamiliar pleasure points on his various surfaces ever tickle a remembrance of Gwen? How does he shift from one circumstance to another, is he a man who steps over a threshold and closes the door firmly behind him, or does he carry traces along from one room to the next?

How easily her body went flying in his hands. That was a remarkable discovery, but now her body flies in other directions which are far more remarkable.

And David will be pouring drafts for sad customers, swiping at tables with the cloth from his back pocket, leaning over his law texts; while Edgar, of course, remains safely and solidly right where Gwen left him.

Not a soul from that other world knows where she is, or how she is, or cares particularly. If she died right now, the police, for instance, would find no one to notify.

If she died right now, what would happen to Benny? What a terrible thought. She recalls Sarah, hurtled by a fatal house fire into the arms of virtuous, unloving, ruinous parents.

One big responsibility, surely, of becoming a parent is finding a safe haven for a child if suddenly one stops being a parent, or anything else, but Gwen has failed so far to make friends here, besides Cathy and Bob. She has been too intent on herself, and now on Benny. For any number of reasons, this is unwise; he will need playmates, she will need grown-up companions. These are the sorts of necessities that drift away during a long marriage, and she hasn't had time since, really, or energy, to do more than cope with the moment. "I must have supposed you were my friend, Edgar," she says; so many false eggs in that marital basket.

She rarely speaks with Edgar any more, but today is special, an anniversary of sorts: ten months exactly, give or take a few time zones, since he died. "It's not so long ago, is it, you were sitting on those tracks in your little red car—have you recovered from that, are you over it yet? Is eternity a pure attention, the way I can sit here watching Benny, breathing right along with him? Is it like gardening, rooting your hands into the soil, touching flowers and leaves? Or is eternity more like a permanent past?"

She can't get over how Benny smells, the sweetness of skin barely arrived in the world, and a faint sourness that, she imagines, has to do with his first absorptions of the world's impurities. She leans over him and inhales. The impurities will multiply, but will not always be discernible. Complications between them are bound to arise, but oh, not yet.

Sweetness was also in the air of the hotel room where she stayed her first night in this city, but it was the kind of adult scent that soaks into the skin, doesn't emerge from it. There were little jars of oils nestling in a basket on the bathroom counter, along with tiny, cunning bars of soap. For a few moments she just stood inside the door, grateful to be somewhere steady, not moving.

And grateful, also, to be alone. Silence—she didn't realize she'd been craving an absence of voices; even Jack's.

From the high, broad window, she gazed far down onto slivers of highways and roads, past ribbons of green onto an expanse of dark ocean pitted mistily by the odd little island and a very large one. Miles of tiny lights clustered themselves into shopping areas, office towers and apartment buildings, then were strung like festive bulbs through homes and subdivisions, before diminishing and receding into the distance.

Each light signified a human being. Of those humans, she imagined, many must have been going about lives not dissimilar to hers and Edgar's. Some people would be studying, others cleaning, many slumped in living rooms watching television, waiting for the evening to pass. Some would be engaged in lively conversation, some in lively dispute. Some would be listening to music at concerts or in bars or at home, and some would already be reading in bed at that early hour. In other beds, people would be taking pleasure, or dismay, in each other's bodies, and some would be in pain, from illness or cruelty. In some beds, babies were at that moment being born, and in others lives were ending. Some people were singing, while others were weeping. Some people's hearts were filling with love right at that very moment, while others emptied themselves of love.

Gwen stood over it all, in her silent, scented hotel room.

Now other people are looking down from their hotel rooms, and some of the lights they see are her own.

Edgar didn't like being so high. When they travelled together, he insisted on rooms close to the ground. In hotel rooms with Edgar, early on, she bounced around naked, even posing boldly in front of bright windows before cascading into bed with him, the two of them excited by an anonymity that, it seemed, included even each other.

How long ago was that? Years and years. Before everything.

Perhaps it was distance from the ground, or being in a room that didn't move, but that first night she had driving dreams and slept badly. In one, she steered along an endless flat high-way, through infinite darkness, but then in the distance a set of headlights emerged, headed her way, huge headlights, a truck's. They rushed towards each other, the transport roaring directly down on her, unswerving and dark, while she struggled but was helpless to steer off the road. She wakened gasping as the motorhome began tipping onto the verge of the highway, the truck skinning past with a black rushing of wind.

In the other dream, she was driving a track in the moun-tains, not even a road, with a cliff on one side and a great drop-ping off on the other. The terror was knowing she had to manoeuvre forever along this unchanging trail that would never improve or get worse, and for eternity every morsel of concentration would have to be on never, never falling, and if she relaxed for even a moment, she would fall. She woke in a sweat. And she woke really quite ill.

Sometimes it's hard not to reach out and wake Benny, just for the delight of his company; but of course she'd regret that. He tends to be cranky, with a real infant querulousness, when he first emerges from sleep.

In her hotel room, sick, alone, in the reality of daylight very scared, very far from the ground, missing Jack's care or even Tracy's concern, Gwen admits she was sort of panicked when she called the front desk. What did she expect, a resident doctor, a physician on call? What turned up were two white-outfitted fellows carting a stretcher and a third guy with a hotel logo on his jacket. How embarrassing! "I'm not *that* sick," she said, although maybe she was. "I didn't call for an ambulance, exactly."

The stretcher-bearers were oddly mismatched, one a good foot taller than the other. Poor planning, surely—wouldn't a patient balanced between them hover on a treacherous angle? "I think since we're here, we should get you checked out anyway," said the shorter, stockier one, but at least they didn't insist she lie on the stretcher. And actually the fast, dodging ride through red lights and around traffic was kind of fun.

At the hospital, though, among the broken-limbed, the accidentally cut, a screaming red-faced child without evident marks of injury, and all their various companions, Gwen grew sober and fearful again. A purple-faced man was wheeled fast, chest heaving and apparently under attack, past her, past the other patients, past even the nurses. This large waiting room was the front line in one of life's battles between hope and doom. Gwen felt herself flush and turn hot with possibilities.

At least Edgar went fast, was healthy right to the last moment, and even then got to die, she assumed, while he was still bright with fresh, heartening prospects. Whereas in this suffering space, she could feel intimations of a long-term dread heading her way; something internal gone bad.

Cancer, of course: the decayer, the destroyer, the hurtling-celled sour candy. That, in one form or another, was what grew stealthily, hidden behind organs and skin, quietly gnawing until finally a delicate, barely perceptible symptom, or for that matter an abrupt wrenching pain, made itself known.

Did Gwen want to know? If she knew, what would she do?

She was too young! But people died at forty-two, they died much younger, and of diseases, not always accidents, like Edgar. Oh, not fair, not fair! She began to shiver, prospects forming on her skin like frost. Was the unfairness of it Edgar's last foolish thought as he watched the train bearing down? Gwen clasped her stomach, heard herself moan.

The tiny, dark-haired, brisk, white-coated woman who finally called her name and then led her through double doors, along a broad corridor and into a small, white-and-steel examining room, slapped Gwen's new thin file down on a cabinet. "Right then, I'm Dr. Sullivan. You've been nauseous? What else?"

"Light-headed. Dizzy. Hot and cold."

"Pain?"

"Not really. Except for throwing up, that hurts."

"How long?"

Gwen liked this crisp shorthand, and also this crisp woman. "A week or two, anyway. I thought it might stop once I got through the mountains, stopped driving, but this morning it turned out it hadn't."

"So," Dr. Sullivan flashed a quick, white smile, "by now I bet you're thinking the worst. Something really nasty, right?"

"That," Gwen admitted, "or it's nothing and I'm being ridiculous. I hardly ever get sick, so for all I know it's just flu."

"Then let's get down to the business of finding out, shall we?"

This involved a brief medical history—measles, mumps, dimmed rooms, Flo bustling; years later the miscarriages. "That's a shame. Then after three you didn't try any more?" Dr. Sullivan said this not as if it had been the abandonment of a powerful purpose, but a perfectly understandable outcome.

"It was—too hard." Gwen's own words brought her nearly to tears.

"And you're on your own?" So Gwen told her about Edgar: his departure, his death.

"How terrible." Well, yes.

Dr. Sullivan probed here, tap-tapped fingertips there, pressed on various spots. "Feel anything? Any pain?" When she stepped back, she was frowning a little. "How long since you had an internal?"

"A couple of years, why?" Gwen knew why: cervical cancer, uterine cancer, some falling apart of fallopian tubes.

"Because I'd like to do one now." She was already putting on gloves, and getting out the shiny, cold, steel utensils. Here it came. How strange, this inflexible, impersonal, internal chill, its angular reachings; such a contrast to the fleshy heat of a man. Men, Gwen reminded herself. No longer just Edgar.

"How long," asked Dr. Sullivan, leaning back finally and stripping off the gloves, "how long, did you say, since your husband was killed?"

"Just over three months. Nearly six since he left." It seemed a much shorter time and also much longer. Had he left her an unpleasant bequest? Some horrid contagion from one of his secrets?

"And when was your last period?"

Had there even been one since the funeral? Gwen was so busy her last weeks in the house—who paid attention, when so much was happening? Shock does strange things, and whatever else he may have been, Edgar came as a shock at the end. "I haven't a clue. Why? What have you found?"

And here it came: "Well. In the circumstances this is strange, but it looks like you're pregnant."

Gwen's mouth fell open, her eyes rolled wide, she almost passed out there on the table. The words floated over her head, dangled above her, a nursery mobile turning and dancing and playing a high, tender tune.

Over Benny's crib, a mobile of farm animals plays "Old MacDonald Had a Farm" when she sets it going. The purple cow, the red horse, the yellow goat, the green pig go around and around. He seems to enjoy it, although of course he's too little to see it properly.

"When did you last have intercourse?"

An easier, earthier question, that one. "Two days ago."

Dr. Sullivan's surprise wasn't quite hidden before she nodded judiciously, said, "I see." Gwen doubted it.

"How pregnant?"

"Roughly three months, I'd say. We still need to make absolutely sure, but it definitely feels like the case. Does that help?"

It certainly did: for the first time, she'd made the three-month hurdle. Gwen's smile at Dr. Sullivan was radiant, her surge of hope almost violent. As she had done three times before in her life, she stared down at that bubble of belly flesh. Behind the skin was not something ghastly or fatal, but her gravest desire; right in there, centimetres from her fingers, almost touchable, nearly visible. Possibly real.

Three months. Oh Christ. David.

Did he, halfway across the country, feel a tickling of something large occurring that had to do with him?

Or would not have to do with him.

She recalled her first view of him as she stood in the dim doorway to Gully's, and his shy, stork-like stance in her beige living room, and the narrow aspect of his ribs and hipbones in her bed, and his beautiful eyes locked on hers. She heard his young voice inquiring about her preferences and desires.

This preference and desire, though—far larger than he could have intended, or than she, for that matter, would have dreamed.

Hello, Benny. Now and then he stirs, and a tiny bubbly sound escapes from his lips, but he settles back into sleep.

Getting dressed in the examining room, she did manage to pass out at Dr. Sullivan's feet, fortunately missing all the room's sharp corners and metallic edges. Then, of course, Dr. Sullivan insisted on admitting her. "Might be blood pressure. Or the news—I bet it took your breath away. But I think we'd better check out some things." A flash of fear then, that this wild, joyful gift could still be taken away.

Gwen spent three days lying, entirely up in the air, lighter than helium, on a narrow hard hospital bed, periodically being prodded and examined, wheeled here and there for this test and that. "What can you tell?" she kept asking. "Is it all right?" Aside from fear, it felt all right; nothing like other occasions, nothing sharp about it, nothing flowing out.

"Everything seems fine," nurses and doctors and technicians kept saying. "Just bear with us a little while longer."

Another woman, very pregnant, bulged hugely beneath the sheets of the room's other bed. She was hooked to a large bedside contraption and seemed to be in a constant deep sleep. Gwen kept herself turned away, wanted nothing to do with whatever troubles were silently occurring, wished for no contact at all with misfortune. She kept touching her own belly—someone in there, imagine!

A fellow in his fifties, more or less Jack's age but less vigorous, more weary, announced himself as an obstetrician. Dr. Ogilvie. It took a while to get fond of him, but she did grow grateful over the months for his firmness of voice and hands, his confidence that he knew what he was doing, and that she was safe. They only got off to an unhappy start because he wanted to know not only her own medical history but the father's. David's.

"I know almost nothing about him, except he's a law student and works in his family's bar. He's young, and looked healthy enough and obviously," and Gwen smiled because she couldn't help these surges of tremendous, persistent happiness, "he's potent. His mother died of cancer, although I don't know what kind, but his father looked pretty strong. Beyond that, I can't tell you a thing."

Dr. Ogilvie frowned. "You should try to find out. A first child, after so long. Your history."

Later they became much better acquainted, both of them alert to her body and its delicate contents. Well, it's hard to have many secrets from someone who peers deep into interiors. There he crouched, again and again, between Gwen's legs, hunched like a miner working a dodgy coal seam—of course she talked about Edgar, and David, even Jack, and mainly herself, why not?

On Gwen's second day her roommate was wheeled out, still asleep and attached to various tubes, and did not return. "A Caesarean," the night nurse explained later. "We waited as long as we could to give the baby his very best chance, and," she smiled, "it turned out fine. The mother's had a tough time, but she'll be all right too, that'll just take a while longer." It was nice the nurse cared. Gwen took that as a good sign.

There were many good signs. Gwen hoped her joy's electric, jolting qualities would be a source of pleasure, not disruption, to her child. Happiness kept sneaking up on her, rolling through her body, making it quiver and flush. Surely, though, the child would know that this pleasure was tied like a rope, like a cord, to its well-being; surely it could only be encouraged, made stronger?

On her third day, she was evicted. Dr. Ogilvie entered her room rubbing his hands, saying, "Right then, we've done our bit, your blood pressure's stabilized and now you can get on with your life. I gather you have some arrangements to make, and I'll want to see you fairly often, but you're right as rain now. I doubt you'll even feel sick for very much longer, if at all. So off you go."

So off she went. Back to the hotel, by taxi. Thank goodness for all Edgar's money; which now has two to support. "What do you think, Edgar?" she asks. "Is this not amazing? All of it? How things turn out?"

She sold the motorhome without a twinge or backward glance. She found this place to live. She ordered furniture and a household's worth of goods, from sheets and towels to dishes and trash cans, from catalogues and stores. She was fiery, for a while, with the strength and energy of hope: because she was making a home, not a mere place for herself, or for herself and a husband to settle into, but a home. For Benny, looking back at his childhood, this will be the place containing his most powerful, forming, altering memories.

It's all lively colours: an ocean-blue sofa with red and yellow throw cushions, a bright-yellow-painted kitchen that captures sunlight through the back window and door, a deep maroon bedroom for her, a wallpapered one with ducks and geese, cardinals, blue jays and canaries, for Benny. A tapestry footstool for the wooden rocking chair in the living room: a gift from her to the two of them.

She was very busy for a while; and then for a few months mainly sat, sometimes outside on mild days when it wasn't raining, turning her face up into the sun, warming her belly like a snake, otherwise indoors on the sofa, napping or reading or staring at nothing. Her mind was curiously empty. Most of the time she couldn't even carry on a coherent conversation with Edgar. Sometimes Cathy from upstairs came down and sat with her, reading aloud from magazines about babies or celebrities.

Cathy has been very enthusiastic. She and Bob look like people who'd be perfectly at home drinking, say, at Gully's, and in fact that's how Gwen met them, the night she moved in, when they knocked on her door to ask her along for a drink. "I'd love to," she said. "But I can't drink for a few months. Till the baby comes."

That was her first public announcement. She wanted to say the words over and over. Cathy's pink face went fuzzy as a stuffed toy with sentiment. "Oh, isn't that lovely." Bob's pinker face stayed pretty much that of a man looking forward, not necessarily impatiently, but keenly, to a night at a bar. But he, too, smiled. "Hey, congratulations, that's great."

Cathy came downstairs on her own the day after, carrying a small but flourishing potted ficus, healthy plant-green against her purple-and-brown-striped dress, with which she wore fluffy purple slippers. "I thought," she said in the warm, gravelly voice of a sixty-year-old smoker who drinks, or a drinker who smokes, "you might want some greenery to make you feel at home."

Greenery! For Gwen! She had to smile.

One thing Gwen especially appreciates about Cathy is that she neither pries nor makes judgments. If Gwen struck her as old for first-time motherhood, and alone in the world, and apparently interested in doing little except staggering off on short walks twice a day, sometimes to the diner down the street with Cathy or on her own small errands, Cathy never gave the slightest sign she might privately think things ought to be different.

She likes, in fact, to say, "You're okay by me," not just to Gwen but to people in stores, or to the servers down at the coffee shop, as if "You're okay by me" is an actual motto to live by.

"A person pretty much just does what they have to," she also likes to say. She has a voluptuous way of shrugging, a massive raising and lowering of shoulders, that suggests she could account in this way for everyone from serial murderers to blessed blunderers like Gwen.

Bob is Cathy's third husband, "except to tell you the truth, we're not actually married. He's a good old boy and I like having him around, and that's enough for me any more." Her first husband died young, a roofer who tumbled a three-storey distance still with, Cathy said, "a shingle and his hammer in his hands." The second "was an awful mistake. After Jim died, I still wanted bad to be with somebody so I got hitched up with Terry. Stupidest thing I ever did, which as soon as I figured that out, I dumped him. Whole thing start to finish took about fifteen minutes."

"What was wrong with him?"

Cathy's shoulders rose and fell in her large shrug. "A couple days after the wedding, he told me to do something, get him a beer or a sandwich or something, what I mean is, he told me, didn't ask, first time ever, and you know what that means. So I said, 'Ask right or do it yourself,' because you know, things like that should be plain from the start, and he actually hauled his arm back. If I hadn't grabbed his wrist and held on, he'd have laid right into me. We were just staring at each other, and I don't know what he saw, but I sure didn't like what I was seeing. So I kneed him in the nuts to give me long enough to grab a few things and get out."

Gwen was somewhat gape-mouthed—to act so fast and firmly—she could imagine herself going on believing, or hoping to believe, absorbing dozens of blows before she got off her ass. It seemed to have taken forever for her to catch on to anything, and even then she practically had to be hit over the head.

Naturally, Gwen told Cathy all about Edgar—how often and for how long would this be her most interesting story about herself?

No longer, not any more.

"Holy shit," Cathy laughed, "you sure get your own back. A guy screws you around and next thing he's gone off the face of the earth? Wish I could have done something like that. Seeing a big old train come down on him would have done Terry the world of good."

Bob is easygoing, relaxed, happy enough with his arm around Cathy and a beer in his hand. He spent forty years in a car factory "hoisting goddamn doors into place. The heaviest thing I'm ever going to lift in my life again is a full glass of beer." Not quite true; he is happy also, and tender, about cradling Benny. Bob is a man with a soft, rough heart and no kids of his own.

Gwen is aware that in her earlier life she was never so attached to even the friendliest, warmest of neighbours, not even to Beth-Ann, as she is to Cathy and Bob. She is also aware that's a change in herself, not other people.

It was Cathy and Bob who took her to the hospital when she called upstairs to them, and who brought her and Benny home. Cathy even offered to be in on the delivery, but Gwen said no. She wanted to be as alone as she was permitted to be. Or rather, she had the strange and disruptive idea that if anyone were to be with her, she'd have liked it to be Flo.

Flo would have been an exuberant grandmother. She'd have been thrilled and indulgent. A playmate.

If Gwen is too old to begin motherhood, she must also, she thinks, be very old to be wanting her mother. But there it is: times in recent months she has cried, silently or very loudly, "I want my mother!" Moments of sagging, or frailty, or fear, or, in the delivery room, the most astounding, grievous pain.

Flo went through that for Gwen? Flo must have loved her, then; no one should go through that agony for anything but love. Gwen must have confused love and tenderness, and in the absence of one, assumed the absence of the other. "I'm sorry, Flo," she whispers now. "I didn't know."

There'll be no such confusion for Benny. Gwen already tells him again and again, even though he can't possibly know the words, that she loves him.

Could Flo have done that? Before Gwen understood words? Why did Gwen take Flo, with her big voice, her grand gestures, her bright clothes and her vast, unyielding energy, as such a poor example? Why would Gwen set out to shrink herself, so that she could settle for twenty years without her heart's desire? Which was not only a Sarah, a John, or Benny for that matter, but something else also, less definable, but huge.

There are a great many things Gwen would like to talk over with Flo, two grown women sitting over cups of tea, or wine, discussing matters of common interest: love, full breasts and sore nipples, blood, men, pain of various sorts, losses and gains, keeping a firm eye, and grip, on true aims. Flo was good at those; at least that's now Gwen's view. As with Edgar, she sees, although doesn't quite accept, that she never really will know.

If she can't have her mother, she's damn lucky for Cathy and Bob. Even Benny screeching every few hours, which is apparently unavoidable however fast Gwen is on her feet, with her breast, doesn't seem to annoy them. "Oh," Cathy says comfortably, "we hear him, of course, but it's not as if we have to get up in the morning for anything. I'm up in the night often enough myself any more, and so's Bob, we don't sleep through. We're just happy he has a good set of lungs. And everything else." Gwen's happy also for that. With everything that can go wrong under even excellent circumstances, who wouldn't worry? Dr. Ogilvie said that fretting, if it had any effect at all, could only be harmful. But just try to control it!

Benny could have had terrible troubles, but it seems he does not.

A fat little arm flings itself outside the blanket, and a tiny sigh seeps into the air. What do babies dream of? She wouldn't think he has enough images in his head yet to make much of a dream.

When he's awake, Cathy likes to nibble his toes; Bob nuzzles into his belly. Gwen does both those things, but likes best Benny's fingers curling around one of hers: the innocence of the gesture, the trust, although he doesn't need to have any idea yet what trust and innocence are.

What kind of boy will he be? What sort of man?

Better than Edgar, at any rate.

When Grace looked down at the infant Edgar, it must have been with eyes much like Gwen's: hopeful, faithful, determined, ferociously loyal. She would not have imagined, could not have dreamed of him turning into a liar, a cheat or a coward. Or for that matter of him ending under the screaming wheels of a train. Gwen shivers; not her first touch of dread.

Infants are, as they say, just cherubs, simply lambs—round creatures with appealing, wondrous eyes. Soon, though, Benny will have experiences that will begin to show up in those eyes. His body will lengthen, stretch and harden as he becomes a boy, a youth, a man. Gwen expects he will be tall, more like David than her, with long legs, but his features are, so far, more like hers, and small rather than narrow.

But more than appearances change over time.

Whatever Edgar became, Grace would have adored him. Whatever Benny becomes, Gwen cannot imagine she won't adore him. She hopes he's a kind boy. A truthful one. At least his father was frank enough: an impulsive, excellent lay and he was off. Also he seemed thoughtful. Kind. Someone who paid close attention. These are not likely inherited qualities, though; no genes for kindness as there are for eyes and bones.

How unhappy will Benny be about not having a father? What should she tell him about David? What will Benny think of her, that she doesn't even know his father's last name, the most basic sort of information a kid would expect his mother to have?

She can imagine a furious curiosity arising. She can imagine David, robust and middle-aged, a prosperous lawyer (or one committed to the downtrodden, as he suggested), surrounded by a group of merry children and a wife as dedicated as he is, answering the telephone or the door one day years down the road to encounter this grown-up surprise.

It's hardly ever impossible to find someone if the seeker's determined enough, and she would like Benny to be a determined sort of person.

There are no unflawed upbringings. If Gwen has much to make up for—a shortage of fathers, for one—Benny will have equivalently more of her attention. Instead of the occasional meal out with Edgar, the odd office party or street barbecue, those occasions for couples, she will throw parties for neighbourhood children. She will take Benny to kids' movies and concerts and plays. She will push him on swings and balance him on teeter-totters. She will keep watch while he approaches other children, and as they approach him. She will read to him, and later will listen to him read to her. She will often have her arms around him. She will listen to silly jokes, and they will laugh and laugh.

She will watch, terrified, as he goes off on his own. She will teach him to ride a bicycle. She will read his report cards with pride or concern. She will sometimes have to speak sharply to him. There will be occasions when he speaks sharply to her.

Before any of that starts to happen, she could really use some sleep. She could almost nod off sitting here, but he'll be waking up soon. Now and then his legs rustle and shift, and he groans. At two weeks, what does his consciousness feel like when he returns to it? Is it as fuzzy as his vision, and still mainly a matter of warm, safe sensation?

She wishes she hadn't thrown out so many photographs. The few she still has are very old, scenes with her father and Flo, and from only the early days with Edgar. She can see her hands dropping picture after picture, whole handfuls of shiny, coloured images, into a green garbage bag with the rest of the trash. A whole posed, smiling history gone. She must have been awfully angry. She must have thought she would not want to see Edgar again.

As it turns out, however, she wouldn't mind another look at that face, those eyes, that mouth, their expressions, to see what might be discerned at this distance. One picture in particular is a mystery. She has her own framed photograph, which sat for years on her bedside table, but can't find the matching one of Edgar. She's almost sure she didn't throw it out. All she remembers is turning it face down on his bedside table after he left. She couldn't bear him in the room, but also couldn't quite put him away. Now she can't find him at all.

She would, after all, like to have more possessions, for herself and for Benny, that have stories to tell. If he doesn't have a father, he should at least have some kind of history.

What might he want to hear about Gwen?

She can tell about Flo and her gritty liveliness, about her father and his calm, absent-minded affection. About picnics with them, holidays, Sunday afternoon swimming trips to the lake. Not much that's disruptive. She will want to create happy impressions of grandparents who would have purely delighted in him.

It's too bad he won't have grandparents. It's not only David who will be absent, but David's father, as well. The one time she briefly saw David's father, though, in Gully's following Edgar's funeral, he looked disapproving of David's intention to drive her home. Unlikely he'd be pleased about the result.

She could tell Benny about Edgar's fingers touching hers at the end of the aisle, Edgar's eyes, and hers, filled with hope and sentiment. Visions of sunrises and sunsets, thunderstorms watched together, lightning rippling out of Edgar's fingertips, his tongue, all of his skin, making love in the early days. His pale eyes looking down at her, up at her.

Perhaps not that.

Where does desire go?

Edgar's, it seems, turned towards various secrets and a passion for plants. What were those thrusting, graceful irises and lupins, those extravagant, ground-hugging hostas, but desire displaced? And then in the end, he had only ugly things to say, he left out all the beauty.

No wonder she behaved badly at his funeral.

Behaving badly at the funeral led to David. Who led to Benny.

The difference a moment can make: one small event, or the absence of one small event. The day early on when she was losing a Sarah, a John, and Edgar didn't go home. Ten months ago, when he failed to get off the tracks—moments like those, changing lives utterly.

An impulse with David.

Some moments can't be redeemed, but look at Benny—at least if they can't be redeemed, they can certainly be transformed.

His eyelids are fluttering, and he's beginning to frown, tiny lines forming between his eyes. In a moment, those eyes will open slowly, slowly, gummy from sleep, and briefly he will look slightly resentful, then puzzled, and then his mouth will open to howl. But even as his eyes are opening, she is already reaching for him.

Her back hurts, her thighs feel stretched, her breasts weep with exhaustion. Her arms are soft with middle age and love. He's sweet as honey, sleek as sealskin, tender and juicy as veal. She has to be careful they don't eat each other right up. Benny, groping and demanding, finds her breast, very close to her heart.

Every day he changes, and something new happens—an extraordinary way, surely, to be in the world. His soft spot pulses in time with his mouth. So does hers. Good endings make good beginnings, and maybe vice versa as well. She hopes that's something Edgar might know by now, too. Because look what she owes him! She is more grateful than he could have predicted, intended or dreamed, and she does, after all, wish him well in return.